Living with a Writer

Also by Dale Salwak

KINGSLEY AMIS: A REFERENCE GUIDE
JOHN BRAINE AND JOHN WAIN: A REFERENCE GUIDE
JOHN WAIN
A. J. CRONIN: A REFERENCE GUIDE
LITERARY VOICES: INTERVIEWS WITH BRITAIN'S 'ANGRY YOUNG MEN'
A. J. CRONIN
THE LIFE AND WORK OF BARBARA PYM (editor)
CARL SANDBURG: A REFERENCE GUIDE
PHILIP LARKIN: THE MAN AND HIS WORK (editor)
KINGSLEY AMIS: IN LIFE AND LETTERS (editor)
BARBARA PYM: A REFERENCE GUIDE
MYSTERY VOICES: INTERVIEWS WITH BRITISH CRIME WRITERS
KINGSLEY AMIS, MODERN NOVELIST
ANNE TYLER AS NOVELIST (editor)
THE WONDERS OF SOLITUDE
THE WORDS OF CHRIST
THE WISDOM OF JUDAISM
THE LITERARY BIOGRAPHY: PROBLEMS AND SOLUTIONS (editor)
THE POWER OF PRAYER
A PASSION FOR BOOKS (editor)

LIVING WITH A WRITER

Edited by

DALE SALWAK

Professor of English
Citrus College
California

Chapter 1 © Malcolm Bradbury Estate 1988
Selection, editorial matter, Preface and Conclusion © Dale Salwak 2004
Individual chapters (in order) © Ann Thwaite;
Paul Theroux; Edmund Morris; Michael Holroyd; Margaret Drabble; William Golding Ltd and Judy Carver; John Halperin; George Howe Colt; John Updike; David Updike; Catherine Aird; Brian Aldiss; Kathleen Symons; Frances H. Bachelder; James J. Berg; John Bayley; Felix Licensing BV and Nadine Gordimer 2004 and by permission of Russell & Volkening as agents for the author; Amanda Craig; Anne Bernays and Justin Kaplan; Jeffrey Meyers; Mary Ann Caws; Laurel Young; Betty Fussell; Rob Rollison; Hershel Parker 2004
Softcover reprint of the hardcover 1st edition 2004 978-1-4039-0476-8
All rights reserved. No reproduction, copy or transmission of this publication may be made without written permission.

No paragraph of this publication may be reproduced, copied or transmitted save with written permission or in accordance with the provisions of the Copyright, Designs and Patents Act 1988, or under the terms of any licence permitting limited copying issued by the Copyright Licensing Agency, 90 Tottenham Court Road, London W1T 4LP.

Any person who does any unauthorised act in relation to this publication may be liable to criminal prosecution and civil claims for damages.

The authors have asserted their rights to be identified
as the authors of this work in accordance with the Copyright,
Designs and Patents Act 1988.

First published 2004 by
PALGRAVE MACMILLAN
Houndmills, Basingstoke, Hampshire RG21 6XS and
175 Fifth Avenue, New York, N.Y. 10010
Companies and representatives throughout the world

PALGRAVE MACMILLAN is the global academic imprint of the Palgrave Macmillan division of St. Martin's Press, LLC and of Palgrave Macmillan Ltd. Macmillan® is a registered trademark in the United States, United Kingdom and other countries. Palgrave is a registered trademark in the European Union and other countries.

This book is printed on paper suitable for recycling and made from fully managed and sustained forest sources.

A catalogue record for this book is available from the British Library.

Library of Congress Cataloging-in-Publication Data
Living with a writer / edited by Dale Salwak.
    p. cm.
    Includes bibliographical references and index.
    1. Authors, English—20th century—Family relationships. 2. Authors, American—20th century—Family relationships. 3. Authors, Commonwealth—20th century—Family relationships. 4. Authors' spouses—Commonwealth countries—Biography. 5. Authors' spouses—Great Britain—Biography. 6. Authors' spouses—United States—Biography. I. Salwak, Dale.
PR107.L58 2004
820.9'0091—dc22
[B]
                                            2004045622

10 9 8 7 6 5 4 3 2 1
13 12 11 10 09 08 07 06 05 04
ISBN 978-1-349-72225-9   ISBN 978-1-137-07998-5 (eBook)
DOI 10.1007/978-1-137-07998-5
Transferred to Digital Printing in 2009

For writers, their relations and friends

Contents

Preface	x
Acknowledgements	xiii
Notes on the Contributors	xiv

Part I The Pleasures

1	The Spouse in the House Malcolm Bradbury	3
2	Living with Writers Ann Thwaite	13
3	Lady Naipaul Paul Theroux	25
4	Lady of Letters: Living with Sylvia Jukes Morris Edmund Morris	27
5	Yesterday's News Michael Holroyd	37
6	The Open Door Margaret Drabble	40
7	Harbour and Voyage: The Marriage of Ann and Bill Golding Judy Carver	44
8	C. P. Snow and Pamela Hansford Johnson at Home John Halperin	56
9	Hong Kong Time George Howe Colt	65

10	Writers as Progenitors and Offspring John Updike	77
11	My Grandmother's Only Son David Updike	80
12	I am Two Fools – Or Home Alone Catherine Aird	85
13	Margaret Brian W. Aldiss	92
14	Living with Julian Kathleen Symons	99
15	When Writing Entered My Mind Frances H. Bachelder	107
16	Pen and Ink: The Life and Work of Christopher Isherwood and Don Bachardy James J. Berg	114

Part II The Problems

17	Forget She (or He) Is a Writer, and All May Be Well John Bayley	131
18	Getting Along with Myself Nadine Gordimer	134
19	The Pantomime Horse Amanda Craig	137
20	Can This Collaboration Be Saved? Anne Bernays and Justin Kaplan	142
21	Maugham's Marriage Jeffrey Meyers	146
22	Being Two of Us Mary Ann Caws	163
23	The Mystery of the Vanishing Wife Laurel Young	176
24	Room for One Betty Fussell	184

25	Peter Levi: A Corresponding Friendship *Rob Rollison*	189
26	Damned by Dollars: *Moby-Dick* and the Price of Genius *Hershel Parker*	202
	Conclusion: A Perilous Art *Dale Salwak*	223
Index		230

Preface

'They wrote in the morning, they walked in the afternoon, they read in the evening.' Quentin Bell's description of the happy and productive life that Leonard and Virginia Woolf lived at Hogarth House in Surrey strikes many of us as ideal for the serious writer. 'Despite madness, suicide, infidelities, resentments and betrayals', said one commentator, 'in some important ways these people had their priorities straight.'

It may be said of many authors that they refined their relationship at home into a work of art. In Donald Hall's marriage to the late Jane Kenyon, for example, 'loving to work' became their nature: although the poets did not speak all morning, 'her presence in her own study', working on as he worked, meant everything to him, enabling him to concentrate on his own writing. Had he married someone who preferred society and conversation, Hall admits, he would have wasted his time at parties. Solitude won out over company because their personal and professional relationship thrived on it.

But life with a writer can be troubling, too, especially when one partner is spending so many working hours wandering far off in a fictional landscape and the other is not. Estelle Faulkner never adjusted to her husband's moods and closed-mouthed ways. 'Without open communication between them', writes Stephen B. Oates, 'they both drank too much: Faulkner when he wasn't writing, Estelle when he was.'

And in her last years, Emma Lavinia Gifford, the first wife of Thomas Hardy, lived and died in two miserable attic rooms as her husband wrote *Tess of the d'Urbervilles*, *Jude the Obscure* and other fine works in the study directly beneath. 'He treated her with a cruel lack of understanding,' says John Fowles. 'You stand there and still feel the pain, their separate isolation, in those tiny upper rooms.'

The idea for a volume of essays on the subject of life with a writer had been percolating in my mind since 1985, when I read an interview with Fowles in which the questioner asked: '[Elizabeth] plays a very important role in your life as wife and critic, doesn't she?' To which Fowles responded, 'A writer's wife is vital. Always, without exception ... I wish someone would study novelists' wives – or husbands now.'

With that challenge in mind, three years ago I invited twenty-seven people whose lives were intertwined in some way with authors to reflect upon the following questions: What does it mean to live with a writer? What makes the arrangement work, or not work, and why? How does life at home contribute to the creative process? What is the cost of a masterpiece or a caring relationship? In one way or another I suspect that most writers have asked these questions – though not necessarily of someone who might be able to answer with such insight and candor.

Thus prompted, the contributors take us on journeys that are full of startling turns – oftentimes humorous, many times saddening, but always fascinating as they reveal some of the pleasures and problems of living with a writer or, in two instances, with themselves as writers. As the title implies, I cast my net wide to include not only novelists but also poets, biographers, scholars, editors and collaborators. I provided the focus and theme for the book, made suggestions for possible approaches, but left it to each contributor to decide on a direction. Husbands and wives, other relatives and friends – all have a say about the sometimes volatile, sometimes magical chemistry that drives and shapes the creative process.

The collection may seem eclectic, even somewhat random – certainly it does not aspire to be comprehensive. What the essays do have in common is a glimpse behind private doors into very private worlds. Twenty-one are entirely original; most of the others the authors have revised, some heavily, to fit the book's theme and focus.

As always, my task as editor has been much eased by my parents, Dr Stanley and Frances H. Salwak, by my wife, Patricia, and by my colleagues, Dr Reginald D. Clarke and Dr Laura Nagy. Above all, of course, are my contributors, for whom I only provide a forum. This book is truly theirs, and I am very grateful for their eloquent essays. I hope that readers everywhere will experience what I have felt throughout the project from inception to completion: pure pleasure.

Dale Salwak

Acknowledgements

Grateful acknowledgement is made to the following for permission to reprint previously published materials:

Anne Bernays, Justin Kaplan and the editor for 'Can This Collaboration Be Saved?', *New York Times Book Review*, 5 January 1997: 31.

Curtis Brown on behalf of the Malcolm Bradbury Estate for 'The Spouse in the House', excerpted from *Unsent Letters: Irreverent Notes from a Literary Life* (1988).

Margaret Drabble, Michael Holroyd and the editor for 'The Open Door' and 'Yesterday's News' (with revisions), *Threepenny Review*, XXII (2001): 18–19.

Paul Theroux and Houghton Mifflin for 'Lady Naipaul', excerpted from *Sir Vidia's Shadow: A Friendship Across Five Continents* (1988).

John Updike and Alfred A. Knopf, a division of Random House Inc. for 'Writers as Progenitors and Offspring', excerpted from *Odd Jobs* (1981).

Every effort has been made to trace all copyright-holders, but if any have been inadvertently overlooked the publishers will be pleased to make the necessary arrangement at the first opportunity.

Notes on the Contributors

Catherine Aird is the author of nineteen detective novels, the latest of which is *Amendment of Life* (2002), and two collections of stories, *Injury Time* (1994) and *Chapter and Hearse* (2003). She has edited a number of parish histories and has produced both a *son et lumière* and a video on local subjects. She is a past chairman of the Crime Writers' Association.

Brian W. Aldiss has had to rejig his life since the death of his wife Margaret in 1997. His titles since then reflect something of the upheaval: *When the Feast is Finished* (1999), the story of his wife's life and death, being balanced by an utopia, *White Mars* (1999), written in collaboration with Roger Penrose; and *Super-State* (2002), a grim vision of Europe forty years on, being balanced by *The Cretan Teat* (2002), a rumbustious comedy. Aldiss is now working on an opera, *Oedipus on Mars*. His short story, 'Supertoys Last All Summer Long' (2001), is the subject of the Kubrick/Spielberg movie, *A.I.* His website is at brianaldiss.com.

Frances H. Bachelder, pianist and teacher for over forty years, studied at the University of Massachusetts and Purdue University. She now resides in San Diego, California, and while continuing her career as pianist also writes poetry and non-fiction. She is the author of essays on Barbara Pym, Anne Tyler, books, music and the power of prayer, as well as *Mary Roberts Rinehart: Mistress of Mystery* (1993) and her first novel, *The Iron Gate* (2001) – to which she is now completing a sequel.

John Bayley, husband of the late Iris Murdoch, has written two highly acclaimed memoirs about his wife and her battle with Alzheimer's disease: *Iris: a Memoir* (1999) and *Iris and Her Friends*

(2000). He is also Warton Professor of English Emeritus at Oxford University and acclaimed author of the novels The Red Hat (1998), The Queer Captain (1995), Alive (1994), and George's Lair (1994). His most recent work is Widower's House: a Study in Bereavement, or How Margot and Mella Forced Me to Flee My Home (2001).

James J. Berg holds a PhD in English Literature from the University of Minnesota. He is the co-editor, with Chris Freeman, of The Isherwood Century (2000) and Conversations with Christopher Isherwood (2001). He is associate director of the Center for Teaching and Learning in the Minnesota State Colleges and Universities System. He lives in Minneapolis with his partner, Gary Schiff.

Anne Bernays lives in Cambridge and Truro, Massachusetts and is the author of Professor Romeo (1989), Growing Up Rich (1975), and six other novels as well as What If?: Exercises for Fiction Writers (1990, with Pamela Painter). She is a graduate of Barnard College and teaches at the Nieman Foundation for Journalism at Harvard. With her husband, Justin Kaplan, she wrote The Language of Names (1997) and a memoir, Back Then: Two Lives in 1950s New York (2002).

Malcolm Bradbury (1932–2000) was born in Sheffield, grew up in Nottingham, and studied at the University of Leicester, Queen Mary College London, at Manchester and in the United States. He taught at Hull University, Birmingham University, and the University of East Anglia where he became professor of American studies and where he remained for the rest of his life. He was a prolific writer as an academic critic, novelist and humorist, and for television, and is also remembered for founding in 1970, along with Angus Wilson, the creative writing program at East Anglia. In 1959 he married Elizabeth Salt who was, throughout his life, the greatest single source of happiness and support to him, and by whom he had two sons. He was appointed CBE in 1991, for services to literature, and was knighted in 2000.

Judy Carver, younger child of William Golding and his wife Ann, was born in Marlborough, Wiltshire in 1945. She grew up near Salisbury, did a first degree in English Literature at the University of Sussex and a research degree at Oxford. After her marriage to Terrell Carver, an American fellow student at Oxford, she worked in publishing. Since giving up paid work to raise her three sons, she has studied French, done a master's in Information Technology, and published a novel. Since 1993 she has managed her father's literary estate, and is currently preparing selections from his journals for publication.

Mary Ann Caws is Distinguished Professor of English, French and Comparative Literature at the Graduate School of the City University of New York, and the past president of the Modern Language Association, the American Comparative Literature Association, the Academy of Literary Studies, and the Association for the Study of Dada and Surrealism. She is a translator, and has written widely on art and literature, most recently Women of Bloomsbury (1990), The Surrealist Look: an Erotics of Encounter (1997), Picasso's Weeping Woman: the Life and Art of Dora Maar (2000), Virginia Woolf: Illustrated Life (2001), Marcel Proust (2003), and edited Manifesto! (2002), Surrealist Painters and Poets (2002), Mallarmé in Prose (2002), Vita Sackville-West: Selected Writings (2002), and the Yale Anthology of 20th Century French Poetry (2004).

George Howe Colt, a former staff writer at Life magazine, is the author of The Enigma of Suicide (1991) and The Big House: a Century in the Life of an American Summer Home (2003). His wife, Anne Fadiman, is the former editor of The American Scholar and the author of The Spirit Catches You and You Fall Down (1997) and Ex Libris (1998). They live with their two children in rural western Massachusetts.

Amanda Craig was born in South Africa in 1959, and grew up in London and Rome. Educated at Bedales School, she won an Exhibition to read English at Clare College, Cambridge (1979–81). She worked for the J. Walter Thompson advertising agency before becoming an award-winning journalist. She is currently on contract to the Sunday Times as a columnist and feature writer, and reviews for The Times and the New Statesman. She also reviews children's fiction for the Independent on Sunday, and is currently completing her first children's novel, The Witch-King. In 2003 she published her fifth novel, Love in Idleness – a romantic comedy set in Tuscany and based on A Midsummer Night's Dream.

Margaret Drabble was born in Sheffield in 1939 and educated at York and Cambridge. Her first novel, A Summer Bird-Cage, was published in 1963. Since then she has published fifteen novels, most recently *The Seven Sisters* (2002). Among her non-fiction works are biographies of Arnold Bennett (1974) and Angus Wilson (1995), and she edited the fifth and sixth editions of *The Oxford Companion to English Literature* (1985, 2000). Margaret Drabble has three children by her first marriage, and is married to the biographer Michael Holroyd. They live in London and Somerset.

Betty Fussell is the author of ten books, including a biography of silent-film comedienne Mabel Normand (1982) and several works about American food and its history. Her most recent work is a memoir recounting her marriage to writer Paul Fussell, titled *My Kitchen Wars* (1999). Adapted to the stage as a one-woman play, it has been performed in Hollywood and New York. Her current work-in-progress is a history of American beefsteak.

Nadine Gordimer was born in South Africa and has lived there all her life, with frequent travels in many parts of the world, the most recent being Cuba. She has written thirteen novels, ten short-story collections including the latest, *Loot*, published in 2003, and three collections of non-fiction. She has received numerous literary awards, culminating in the Nobel Prize. She is an Honorary Member of the American Academy of Arts and Sciences, the American Academy of Arts and Sciences, a Fellow of the Royal Society of Literature, England, vice-president of PEN International, and a Goodwill Ambassador of UNDP. She is a Commandeur de l'Ordre des Arts et des Lettres, France, and has received the Order of the Southern Cross conferred by President Nelson Mandela.

John Halperin's books include *Trollope and Politics* (1977), *Gissing: a Life in Books* (1982), *The Life of Jane Austen* (1984), *Novelists in Their Youth* (1990), and *Eminent Georgians* (1995). A Fellow of the Royal Society of Literature and twice a Guggenheim Fellow, he is Centennial Professor of English at Vanderbilt University.

Michael Holroyd is one of the most influential of modern biographers. Among his books are biographies of the painter Augustus John (1974–75, 2 vols) and the Bloomsbury Group biographer Lytton Strachey (1967–68, 2 vols, filmed under the title *Carrington*), as well as the landmark biography of Bernard Shaw (1988–91, 3 vols). He has also written a family memoir, *Basil Street Blues* (1999), and his most recent book is a selection of essays, lectures and reviews about biography and autobiography called *Works on Paper* (2002). He is a past president of English PEN, past chairman of the Society of Authors, and president of the Royal Society of Literature. He is married to the novelist Margaret Drabble.

Justin Kaplan lives in Cambridge and Truro, Massachusetts and is the author of the Pulitzer-Prize winning *Mr. Clemens and Mark Twain* (1966), as well as biographies of Walt Whitman (1980) and Lincoln Steffens (1974). He is general editor of the 16th and 17th editions of *Bartlett's Familiar Quotations* (1992, 2002) and collaborated with his wife, Anne Bernays, on *The Language of Names* (1997) and a memoir, *Back Then: Two Lives in 1950s New York* (2002).

Jeffrey Meyers, a Fellow of the Royal Society of Literature, has published forty-three books and been translated into ten languages. He has written biographies of Katherine Mansfield, Wyndham Lewis, Ernest Hemingway, Robert Lowell and his circle, D. H. Lawrence, Joseph Conrad, Edgar Allan Poe, Scott Fitzgerald, Edmund Wilson, Robert Frost, Humphrey Bogart, Gary Cooper, George Orwell, Errol and Sean Flynn, and Somerset Maugham. He lives in Berkeley, California.

Edmund Morris was born and educated in Kenya, and emigrated to the United States in 1968. He wrote *The Rise of Theodore Roosevelt*, which won the Pulitzer Prize and American Book Award in 1980. In 1985, he was appointed President Ronald Reagan's biographer. Fourteen years later, he published *Dutch: a Memoir of Ronald Reagan*. The book's stylistic innovations caused an international stir. In 2001, he produced *Theodore Rex*, the central volume of a projected trilogy on the life of Theodore Roosevelt. It won the Los Angeles Times Book Prize for biography. Mr Morris is a member of the Modern Library Editorial Board, and in 2003 was a writer in residence at the University of Chicago. He lives in New York and Connecticut.

Hershel Parker has been associate general editor since 1965 of the Northwestern-Newberry edition of the writings of Herman Melville, and general editor since 2001. His awards include a

Guggenheim Fellowship, a USC Creative Scholarship and Research Award, and a Research Fellowship from the University of Delaware. His publications include 200 articles, editions and anthologies, as well as *Flawed Texts and Verbal Icons* (1984), *Reading 'Billy Budd'* (1990), *Herman Melville: a Biography, 1819–51* (1996) and *Herman Melville: a Biography, 1851–91* (2002, the first volume a Pulitzer finalist and the Association of American Publishers winner, the second the AAP winner). He lives in Morro Bay, California.

Rob Rollison was born in Adelaide, South Australia, in 1943. He attended a Jesuit school, and graduated with an Honours degree in History from the University of Adelaide in 1968. He taught History and English in a high school for three years. From 1971, he lectured in Modern European History at the University of South Australia, specializing in the rise and fall of Russian and German dictatorships. He also taught modern Chinese political history. In 1996 he took early retirement from the university and is currently researching and writing on modern poets and their politics.

Dale Salwak is Professor of English at Southern California's Citrus College and a recipient of a National Endowment for the Humanities grant as well as Purdue University's Distinguished Alumni Award. He was educated at Purdue University (BA) and then the University of Southern California (MA, PhD) under a National Defense Education Act competitive fellowship programme. His publications include *The Literary Biography: Problems and Solutions* (1996), *The Wonders of Solitude* (1995, 1998), *A Passion for Books* (1999) and studies of Kingsley Amis, John Braine, A. J. Cronin, Philip Larkin, Barbara Pym, Carl Sandburg, Anne Tyler and John Wain. He is now completing a memoir on more than thirty years of teaching.

Kathleen Symons was married to Julian Symons (1912–94) for fifty-three years – a time when Symons distinguished himself as crime novelist, editor, historian, biographer, critic and poet. His literary career began in 1937 when he founded *Twentieth Century Verse*, and in 1944, after being discharged from the army, he started working as an advertising copywriter in London. Symons went on to write more than twenty-five detective and crime novels beginning with *The Immaterial Murder Case* (1945) and continuing through *A Sort of Virtue*, which was published posthumously in 1996. In 1975 he became a member of the Royal Society of Literature. In 1977 he was made a Grand Master of the Swedish Academy of Detection. He was given the Grand Master Award from the Mystery Writers of America in 1982, and in 1990 he was awarded the Cartier Diamond Dagger by the CWA for a lifetime achievement in the crime genre. He was chairman of the CWA and president of the Detection Club.

Paul Theroux published his first novel, *Waldo*, in 1967. His subsequent novels include *The Family Arsenal* (1976), *Picture Palace* (1978), *The Mosquito Coast* (1982), *O-Zone* (1986), *My Secret History* (1989), *Millroy the Magician* (1994), *My Other Life* (1996), and, most recently, *Kowloon Tong* (1997). His highly acclaimed travel books include *The Great Railway Bazaar* (1975), *The Old Patagonian Express* (1979), *Riding the Iron Rooster* (1988), *The Happy Isles of Oceania* (1992), and *Dark Star Safari* (2003). *Saint Jack* (1973), *The Mosquito Coast* (1982) and *Half Moon Street* (1984) have been made into successful films. His *Sir Vidia's Shadow: a Friendship Across Five Continents*, was published in 1988. He lives in Hawaii and on Cape Cod.

Ann Thwaite published many children's books before writing her first biography: *Waiting for the Party*, the life of Frances Hodgson Burnett (1974). *Edmund Gosse* (1984) and *A. A. Milne* (1990) both won prizes and were published on both sides of the Atlantic. She is an Oxford D. Litt. and a Fellow of the Royal Society of Literature. Her two most recent biographies, *Emily Tennyson, the Poet's Wife* (1996) and *Glimpses of the Wonderful: the Life of Philip Henry Gosse* (2002), have been published in the United Kingdom but not yet in the USA. She has used some material from *Emily Tennyson* in the present essay. She and her husband, the poet Anthony Thwaite, live in Norfolk, England, interrupted from time to time by ten grandchildren.

David Updike is an Associate Professor of English at Roxbury Community College, Boston. He has written one collection of short stories, *Out of the March* (1988), and six children's books, and is currently working on a collection of essays. He lives in Cambridge, Massachusetts with his wife, Wambui, and his son Wesley.

John Updike was born in Shillington, Pennsylvania, and attended Harvard College and the Ruskin School of Drawing and Fine Art in Oxford, England. From 1955 to 1957 he was a staff member of *The New Yorker*; since 1957 he has lived in Massachusetts. He is the father of four children and the author of many books, including twenty novels and five collections of criticism. His novels *Rabbit Is Rich* (1981) and *Rabbit at Rest* (1990) both won the Pulitzer Prize for Fiction and the National Book Critics Circle Award.

Laurel Young received her BA from Berry College and her MA from Vanderbilt University – where she is currently completing her PhD in literature. Her dissertation, entitled '(Re)Inventing a Genre: Legacy in Women's Golden Age Detective Fiction', includes a chapter on Agatha Christie. She has presented papers on British Modernist fiction and the Gothic and detective genres. She has also taught popular fiction to undergraduates at Vanderbilt.

Part I

The Pleasures

1

The Spouse in the House

Malcolm Bradbury

Now and again I get a letter in my mail which is a perfect pleasure to answer, and one of these arrived just the other day. There is no need to explain its subject. That should be perfectly clear from the reply I have been drafting, and will probably send — if, that is, my wife approves it:

Dear Miss (?) X,
Many thanks for your letter, which I read with very great interest — not something that I say about all the letters I get these days. Many of these come from people who want to become writers — a very humane and worthy desire, of course, but one which now seems to be reaching epidemic proportions, and I fear we shall all soon be crushed under a mountain of paper unless something is done about it. There are times when I wake in the blackness of the night and think that what we need is not more books but fewer of them. I have even turned towards the view that the reason wicked publishers reject so many manuscripts is that they are right. Of course I do try in all cases to be as helpful as possible, but quite often my heart is not completely in it. In any event there is no shortage of handbooks and creative writing courses to help with the matter. You will see now why I am grateful for your enquiry, which is quite different — and on a topic about which there are, as far as I know,

no handbooks or courses at all. For you do not ask me how to become a writer, but how to become a Writer's *Wife* – a much more interesting question.

Your letter does not tell me which sex you subscribe to, though really that does not matter. For, of course, Writers' Wives, like writers themselves, can be of either sex, though admittedly in the folklore it is almost always women who are famous in the role – with the possible exception of George Henry Lewes, the literary wife of Marian Evans, also known as George Eliot, to confuse matters further. Nor do you explain whether this is simply a general, speculative enquiry about your career intentions, or whether you have a specific example of authorship already firmly caught in your sights. Again, though, that does not really matter. The important thing about your letter is its wise, clear-headed assumption that marriage to a writer is like no other known form of matrimony, that writers themselves are a breed of person quite unlike any other, and that the whole project therefore requires intensive forethought and research. In that you are absolutely right, and you will go far – though whether you are wise to is another affair entirely.

The fact is that, in the hard commercial and bureaucratic world of today, there are few writers who would survive for very long without the support and activities of a really first-class Writer's Wife. May I offer you my own case as an example. I am, like quite a lot of writers, though not all, quite a sensitive sort of person, and therefore not greatly at home in reality – one reason, doubtless, why I became a writer in the first place. After rising of a morning, I spend most of my days and much of my nights bent across a typewriter, locked in a universe of literary fantasy. Most of what I know of real life comes to me from very old newspapers, or odd remarks dropped incautiously by the people who bring me my food and then collect the soiled plates afterwards. I go out rarely, my wife having warned me that the risk of infectious disease in our neighbourhood is absurdly high. The telephone makes me jump, and as for that complex world of tax accountancy, VAT registration and royalties that bedevils writing and keeps so many nice young men in Porsches and riverside apartments in Dockland, I really want no truck with it at all.

Happily I am partnered in my enterprise by my really first-class Writer's Wife, who looks after reality for me while I am absent from it, which I am most of the time. Superbly combining, as she does, the roles of sexual companion, confidante, literary agent, solicitor, accountant, libel lawyer and doorstep bouncer, and somehow managing to run several other careers of her own as well, she turns me from a person writing into an actual writer. Thus the mountains of manuscript I produce during my long and industrious days are always carefully collected, wrapped into bundles, and sent off to persons unknown, who quite frequently then ensure their publication. Changes of clothes are quite often provided, and I am fed on most days with a reasonable frequency. Ashen-faced accountants occasionally pass through the house, and she has somehow talked them into letting me have pocket-money of ten pounds a week, which enables me to send out quite frequently for tobacco and the occasional box of chocolates. She is in short the ideal Writer's Wife, a paragon of the kind. Not surprisingly, other writers are constantly attempting to poach her from me, or otherwise seeking a share of her services. Very fortunately, she confesses herself of the opinion that to manage one writer in a lifetime is quite enough, if not far too much, for any human being, and I quite see what she means.

All this, I think, confirms my point that literary marriage is a very specialised form of matrimony, and certainly not something to be entered into lightly. I am afraid, though, that the whole area has been bedeviled by many false impressions, largely fostered by the press, various sycophantic biographers and Hollywood movies, in which writers are depicted as charming, witty people who but rarely sit down to a typewriter, and usually keep on chatting even when they do so. That is really not the way of it. It is often assumed that because writers are sometimes, though not always, sensitive, intelligent and creative people they will therefore make attractive and exciting partners. A few moments' thought should shatter that notion. Remember, it takes a person of distinctive psychological traits – obsessive, narcissistic, egotistical, self-excoriating – to become a writer in the first place. If that person is successful, other qualities will be needed as well – probably including jealous combativeness, paranoia, and profound self-love. Nor is life in the presence of literary creativity the load of fun it may sometimes appear. There can be much pleasure gained from watching a potter pot a pot, or a painter paint a painting. But writing is an activity that goes on largely within an inaccessible location, the writer's own head. The results are then transferred onto paper and duly published as a book, which can be read by anyone. I think you should ask yourself the question whether you really want to marry a writer, or are looking for the address of a really good bookshop.

But if you are determined, and you strike me as the determined type, I can indeed give advice on the care and management of this peculiar breed of person we call writers. I have studied the species quite intensively, and know a good deal about their maintenance, social customs, mating habits, diet, and so on. Briefly, writers, as you might expect, spend a good deal of their time writing. This is especially true when the roof has to be fixed, when there are children to be fetched from school, and such like. Strictly speaking, for their work they need no more than a pencil and piece of paper, but in the age of the word processor and advanced office equipment their desires have increased alarmingly; this needs watching carefully. They require, I find, light, airy rooms, a fairly warm temperature (that of Corfu does very nicely), and supplies of food and, especially, drink; personally I recommend a constant flow of coffee for creative stimulation without intoxication. An ideal diet is a light midday snack, which can be served over the word processor, so not greatly interrupting production; then perhaps a heavier meal in the evening, when the odd guest may be introduced to the house, preferably a publisher with another contract.

Of course different kinds of writer do have different needs. Novelists need to work longish office hours, or they will soon turn into short-story writers. Poets, on the other hand, unless they are writing Miltonic epics, usually work best in short, sharp bursts, and have decadent needs for inspiration, which usually they find in low public houses; on the whole this tendency should be discouraged. There are, in my view, two distinctive kinds of writer, the failures and the successes. The failures, not surprisingly, are in a permanent state of depression, believing themselves despised, neglected and rejected by publishers, the world, and probably you as well. The successes, on the other hand, are quite different. They live in a permanent state of depression, believing themselves despised, neglected and rejected by much the same parties, but also by the judges of the Nobel Prize, the compilers of the New Year Honours List, and above all by posterity – which of course does neglect them, not even having managed to arrive yet. Two other classes of writer can also be distinguished. There are those who work best early in the morning and grow lethargic later in the day, and those who work the other way round. It is very important to discover what pattern suits yours best, because the really fundamental thing about writers is to keep them writing.

It is when writers stop writing that all your troubles will start, so it is crucial to keep a careful eye on this. Briefly, writers stop writing for two reasons. One is when, like drains, they become 'blocked'. As with drains, it is of the utmost important to get them unblocked at once, or the whole house will soon no longer be fit to live in. Always keep by the telephone the numbers of their literary plumbers who specialize in this kind of thing; they can be anything from an agent to a psychiatrist. Even more worrying is the other kind of stoppage, which occurs when a writer suddenly decides he or she needs to 'start living', or 'gain experience'. This, I am afraid, can lead to anything – a trip up the Amazon, a British Council lecture tour abroad, an orgy in the brothels of Cairo, the start of a spectacular affair, anything, indeed, that can later be explained to journalists, magistrates or the tax inspector as 'gathering material'. Fortunately the symptoms are easy to spot, since they almost always occur between books. Good Writers' Wives, needless to say, know exactly how to deal with such lapses. They know it is necessary to take writers for walks from time to time, so that they can 'see life', and even be allowed a reasonable number of parties, to 'keep in touch'. I would particularly recommend ladling the writer suddenly onto a plane for a surprise summer holiday, so that afterwards they can say they have had a 'rest from writing', something all writers claim they need constantly, though why I do not know.

As I am sure all this makes very plain, a literary marriage is not something to be entered into with many illusions. I am afraid, however, that many abound, particularly among young literary groupies, who have the notion that they can become the writer's 'best critic', or 'fellow writer', or, even worse, 'muse'. Let us be clear about this. Most writers do not like critics, and the last thing they wish to do is share a bed with one. Nor do writers like other writers, and certainly not someone who wishes to work in the same field. When two writers do choose, as they sometimes do, to live together, it should always be quite clear who gets which material, and for how long. This simple but golden rule was unfortunately overlooked by Scott and Zelda Fitzgerald, with very unfortunate results. When Scott started *Tender Is the Night*, Zelda apparently started in jealousy her own novel, *Save Me the Waltz*, about something they did indeed share in common, their own lives. He took seven years, and she took six weeks. Unfortunately the competition was not a success; Zelda ended up in a mental home, and Scott in Hollywood, much the same sort of thing. There is no reason why a Writer's Wife should not be another writer, but I would recommend a rather different genre.

As for the question of being the Writer's Muse, this should be avoided at all costs. Many young Writers' Wives cherish the hope of having a poem addressed to them, or being put into a novel. Experienced Writers' Wives – and I checked this at a party I was allowed to go to just the other day – are terrified by the very thought. The truth is, of course, that there is no escaping the dilemma, since readers will always assume that characters of the opposite sex in any piece of writing will either be representations of the Writer's Spouse, or else a much desired alternative. There was a time when writers were able to escape all this by claiming that all their characters were purely imaginary, and they wrote notes to that effect in the front of their books. Alas, since Sigmund Freud came on the scene, notebook at the ready, all alibis are off. In fact the problem of Spouse Representation is possibly the biggest crisis in literary marriage, many of which have foundered because the Writer's Wife became jealous of one of the partner's characters, or even worse, fantasies. Once a suspicion starts in these matters, there is no stopping. Depict a drab, monogamous marriage in a novel, and this becomes a depiction of one's own; depict rhapsodic couplings and adventurous fornications, and this becomes evidenced of having it off with someone else, or wanting to. This is why writers frequently set novels on other planets, but it does not help. A truly jealous wife can become suspicious of anything, even rabbits.

In these matters I can warmly recommend the elusive strategies pursued by my own Writer's Wife, whose habit it is to insist to all and sundry that she has never read a single word of my novels, would never dream of discussing or criticizing their composition, always delivers them to the publishers with averted eyes in a tightly sealed envelope, and therefore has no notion whatsoever whether she or for that matter anyone else has been depicted therein, though she is quite certain she has not been. Just who it is who moves silently through my study of an evening, shifting papers, correcting typing errors, and leaving notes to indicate when a character's eyes change suddenly from blue to brown without good reason, therefore remains a total mystery to me. So, too, does the content of those long, mysterious and late-night telephone calls that occur between my wife and Mary Lodge – a fellow literary wife who has also never read her husband's novels, and is equally certain she is not in them – after one or other of our books has just come out. However it would appear that some notes are being compared, since there is now talk in that quarter of something called a Union of Concerned Writers' Wives, the aims and policy of which are not yet fully clear – though you will know very well whom to address if you wish to receive a leaflet.

You will see from all this that my field of research has extended, for reasons I do not care to go into here, not just to writers but to Writers' Wives. I can fully confirm that they are indeed a formidable breed on their own account, as anyone who has ever met a phalanx of them, perhaps, say, at the Booker Prize dinner, will know, and probably to their cost. My findings show that there are as many kinds of Writer's Wife as there are of writer – indeed more, probably, since many writers I know have been sufficiently fond of the species to have had more than one of them. However they do fall into a distinctive number of types. There is, for example, the Deferential Wife, who possesses a wonderful respect for her partner's genius, nourishing and respecting it; feeding it with esteem and hot coffee, always busily answering the telephone and preparing the syllabub. They are widely to be found, and they appear perfection; alas, like perfection, they often do not last long. For as their spouse's fame and ego grow, they soon appear not to respect fully the *profundity* of the genius, the *depth* of the talent, the *transcendental meaning* of the work. Good as they are, they are frequently displaced, as often as not by someone with an MA in Literary Theory and a more advanced critical vocabulary.

Deferential Wives can be contrasted with their opposite, the Utterly Contemptuous Wives, who appear to be destined for some other and quite different activity, like success on the stage or marriage to the aristocracy. 'Oh, God, if only they knew', they say, as their spouse brings out a new book, and they stand there at the signing, watching him surrounded by literary groupies. 'They think he's so clever and artistic. If they only knew he never gets up before midday. If they only knew the book was completely rewritten by the editor. If they could only hear him trying to explain snooker...' The odd thing is that the Utterly Contemptuous Wives often manage to last a good deal longer than the Deferential Wives, and often it is not their spouses but they themselves who finally grow totally bored, and marry someone else altogether whom they can despise even more.

Far more impressive, in my eyes, are another class, the Sexy Wives — those literary companions who, male or female, have a sexual splendour so palpable it seems like inspiration incarnate. Often they are so obviously stimulating that it seems that they are art and style itself, and writer and spouse go about together, two beautiful people, in a kind of glowing wonder, splashing each other with champagne, transforming parties, giving each other necklaces and wristwatches, and living in a narcissistic self-fascination so great it often becomes part of the art itself. This is what happened to Scott and Zelda Fitzgerald, two beautiful stylists who became the fashionable figures for their age. Unfortunately style does have a way of being evanescent, and it is often not long before the Sexy Wives are replaced, by even Sexier, and certainly younger, equivalents. Nonetheless there is much to be said for them, and they are greatly to be preferred to their opposite, the Genteel Wives.

The Genteel Wives are, I fear, to literature roughly what dedicated teetotalism is to a really good party. Like the Yuppies of Greenwich, their main aim in life is gentrification, and the chief role they perform in their spouse's work is to bowdlerize it. They were perhaps more common in the nineteenth century than this one, though many examples of the species persist. There was, for instance,

Mrs Nathaniel Hawthorne, who used to read Nat's manuscripts and remove from them anything that looked too much like a gratifying fantasy. There was also Mrs Samuel Langhorne Clemens, who married Mark Twain, the naughty boy of the Mississippi, and tried, like Aunt Sally, to 'sivilize' him. The fact of the matter is that all art is filled with erotic secrets, and happily most of these have passed on to posterity more or less intact, the Genteel Wives being too genteel to notice them all. It seems fairly certain that Genteel Wives should not marry writers, and probably not anyone else for that matter.

The truth is that there are many, many kinds of literary marriage. But, literature indeed being filled with erotic secrets, the marriages frequently have a great deal to do with the kind of literature an author produces. This is one reason why writers of the more experimental type often try several, changing their styles along with their spouses, while other writers claim they can write only when they are between wives. In this matter Ernest Hemingway was a fascinating example, marrying four times at different points in his career. A careful study of his understandably posthumous novel *The Garden of Eden* may explain why, since it largely concerns a Writer's Wife who wishes to be a man and turn her spouse into a woman, thereby discouraging his talent. Like Fitzgerald, Hemingway clearly saw a complex relation between matrimony and art. His early and possibly happiest marriage ended quickly in disaster, perhaps because his first wife lost a briefcase of his manuscripts, one of those solecisms better avoided in any creative ménage. Two later marriages pushed him into big-game hunting, deep-sea fishing, and fighting in wars. Finally, at the height of his fame he married his fourth wife, Mary, whom he wooed by shooting up the toilet at the Savoy Hotel. Thereafter followed physical deterioration, increasing depression, and finally suicide. Mary Hemingway, as she confessed herself, was not always entirely happy with her Papa, but she did survive him. Thus she became the final apotheosis of the Writer's Wife, which is the Writer's Widow.

Of course, my dear Miss (?) X, this may not now be the first thing in your mind as you contemplate your marital and literary future, but it is worth a thought or two. After all, the Writer's Widow is one who attains the apparently unattainable prize of literary marriage, which is the Last Word. Now one becomes the final arbiter, the one who sifts and sorts, shapes and changes, burns and selects, scraps the diaries and sorts out the letters, authorizes the publications and the disposition of the manuscripts, and generally determines how one's spouse is to be seen, which is, of course, in the light of your own great part in the author's achievements. The Writer's Widow is the one who knows the secret intentions, the unexpressed desires, and takes every advantage of that fact – until, of course, the triumph is over, for Widowhood itself is transient, and the last word is not quite the last. For now comes the moment that was always intended, and the writer, if posthumously, contracts the most destined marriage of all – with the Literary Biographer, for whom, in the end, all the doings were really done, the writing written, the life so carefully lived.

Well, there, Miss (?) X, that is all I can tell you, and from this point onward you are out there on your own. All I can now do is to wish you all good fortune in the arduous career you are on the brink of choosing, and hope that all your doings become publishable. You seem to me to have the shrewdness and sense to do it right, so it is very possible that we shall meet one of these days, perhaps at some literary brunch or prize day or other. If so, do please get in touch; I should love to hear, in confidence, how it has all worked out. Perhaps, though, you should be just a little cautious about how you approach me. The fact of the matter is, I rather think I shall have my wife with me.

Yours, etc.

2

Living with Writers

Ann Thwaite

This title in the plural has a sort of resonance. I realise it reminds me of a recent BBC TV series 'Walking with Dinosaurs', and perhaps my kind of writers *are* dinosaurs in the figurative sense. The dictionary spells it out like this: 'fig. Something that has not adapted to changing circumstances, a clumsy survival from earlier times.' And here I am, a survivor at seventy, writing this with a pen, in a house not only devoid of e-mail or DVD, but even of a word-processor.

I've always lived with writers. My earliest memories are of returning from New Zealand aboard ship in 1934, after ten months away from England – a round voyage of 25,000 miles. (Do I *really* remember or is it just that from my earliest years I saw photographs and heard tales of shipboard life and Pitcairn Islanders?) Going home to London, my father, A. J. Harrop, typed away at a book published the following year by Allen and Unwin under the title *Touring in New Zealand*. It was, his preface tells us, 'purely a private enterprise', presumably funded by the publisher's advance, but also, certainly, having the encouragement of the New Zealand government, who then had no spectacular scenes in *Lord of the Rings* to lure visitors to that beautiful country. My father travelled – some of the time with us children and always with his wife – 8,000 miles round the two islands, the book making it possible for them to see again their native land, after many years abroad, and for us to meet grandparents, aunts, uncles, cousins for the first time in our short lives.

This is one of the joys of the writer's life – being able to do the things you want to do, paying for them by writing about them. I was told my father earned the cost of his honeymoon in the South of France by writing an English language brochure on Nice for the local tourist board. When he wanted to travel in 1945 (taking in Hollywood and a signed photograph of Deanna Durbin for me on the way), to collect my brother and myself from our wartime exile in New Zealand, he not only persuaded his newspaper to fund the trip, but also published afterwards his eighth book, *New Zealand after Five Wars*, again writing a lot of it on the long sea voyage.

The year after that, when I was thirteen, he got me a commission to write a short story, which eventually appeared in the *Empire Youth Annual* for 1948: 'Meet you at the station' by Ann Barbara Harrop – the cumbersome name I was known by in those far off days. There is nothing in the book to announce my own youth, indeed there are no biographical notes of any kind, nothing to excuse the banality of the plot: stolen Maori treasures, with the thieves foiled by clever children. The story is redeemed only by some rather remarkable wood engravings by a friend of my father, a distinguished New Zealand artist, F. H. Coventry – very different from the normal illustrations in children's annuals.

The publisher, after sending me a small cheque, apparently failed to send me a copy of the book. My 1948 diary records that I first saw my story in print (my first published work outside the school magazine) in the local bookshop in north London. My mother then sent to the publisher for some copies and I was naively pleased to record that we could buy each book for ten shillings – five shillings less than the price in the shops.

Just as in those days a baker might hope to pass on his trade to his son or a dressmaker to her daughter, so my father made it likely that I would be a writer, following that non-gender-specific craft. It was not just that I was quite good at writing; my parents showed me that it was a possible way of life. My mother, arriving in London to marry my father (ten years after they had first met as school children in Hokitika), found she could go to as many theatres as she wanted by writing about them for the New Zealand papers.

The next year, 1927, they started their own paper in London, the New Zealand News, which still continues with its main purpose – to keep New Zealanders on the other side of the world in touch with what is going on 12,000 miles away. But it could also cover other things. There was a book you wanted to read: review it. There was a hotel you wanted to visit: give the place a free mention. My mother, interested in clothes, could go to fashion shows and write about them afterwards. I grew up accustomed to galley proofs, review copies and the necessity of a study, a room of one's own.

In 1948 my mother was asked to write a book about New Zealand for children, to be one of a long-running series, published both in England and America, called The Young Traveller in... whatever country it was. Years later, in 1955, down from Oxford and about to go out to Japan with my new husband, Anthony Thwaite – also, of course, a writer – I discovered that Japan had not been one of the thirty countries already covered in the Young Traveller series. That was lucky. I wrote and asked the publisher if I could do it. 'Write a couple of chapters after you've been there for six months and, if we like them, we'll give you a contract.' So I did and they gave me one. My first book, The Young Traveller in Japan – the story of a fictional family in real places – was published early in 1958, when I was twenty-five.

Since then I have never stopped writing and living with another writer. I've just checked in Who's Who and find Anthony lists around twenty titles (poems, criticism, travel), apart from the books he has edited – most notably Philip Larkin's poems and letters – and all the multitudinous related tasks expected of a man of letters: judging competitions, reviewing, sitting on committees and so on.

Over the nearly fifty years we have lived together there has usually been at least one book in progress in the house and often more than one. But we try to avoid having deadlines that coincide. And we have closed the back staircase (its steps becoming extra bookshelves), so that there is no quick way between our two studies – mine on the ground floor, his above it – and we are saved from the temptation of interrupting each other by the long walk.

When I started work on my first biography, *Waiting for the Party*, the life of Frances Hodgson Burnett, Anthony was not a freelance. He had a full-time job as Literary Editor of the *New Statesman* in London. We had four children, the youngest just beginning school. Looking back, I don't know how I did it. I do remember how complicated it was, organising the weekly envelopes of dinner money and a hundred other things, when we farmed out the children with different friends, the youngest with her grandmother. This was for my first research trip to America in 1970, when Anthony was both representing the *New Statesman* – meeting all sorts of interesting people – and giving a poetry reading tour of assorted universities. This was at the time of the widespread protests over Nixon sending the troops into Cambodia and the shooting of the Kent State students – an extraordinary time for the first of many visits to libraries all over the States. I remember Anthony taking part in a protest march down Fifth Avenue as I worked in the New York Public Library.

In the last twenty years, with the children grown, when I have been writing a biography (rather than reading and researching for one) my husband has always taken on most of the regular domestic tasks. He has shopped, got lunch, prepared the vegetables for the evening meal and so on – leaving me free to spend most of the time writing. I find the only way to keep the narrative thrust is to write nearly all the time and each one of my five long biographies has been written in six or seven months, after the years of research and the months of soaking myself in my material and getting ready for the terrible moment of actually writing the first important sentence.

My father wrote one biography: *The Amazing Career of Edward Gibbon Wakefield* (1928). It is rather short, only 213 pages. He justified its length like this: 'the present work is intended to be a memorial to Wakefield, and, to be an effective memorial, a book should be widely read. To be widely read in these days it must be reasonably cheap. To be reasonably cheap it follows that it must not be very long.' His daughter never learnt that logical lesson. Nor did my father live long enough to read any of my long biographies, though I had published a handful of children's books before he died.

My books are long because, with people's lives, I work on the principle that anything I find interesting should go in. If it doesn't, it may be lost forever. This is particularly true when reading the unpublished papers of the sort of people I choose to write about. When will anyone read again the hundreds of letters Edmund Gosse wrote to his wife whenever they were apart, the almost indecipherable copy books of Philip Henry Gosse's copious correspondence with collectors all over the world or the masses of letters in Emily Tennyson's very difficult handwriting, written to her sons when they were away at school?

All my biographies are about writers and I've lived with these writers for almost half my life. Frances Hodgson Burnett, the two Gosses, father and son, and A. A. Milne were all prolific writers. I've just counted the titles in the bibliographies at the back of my biographies and the four of them published more than two hundred books altogether. Emily Tennyson never published a book under her own name, but she was responsible for very large numbers of letters and journal entries, and she wrote a good deal of the great two-volume memoir of Alfred Tennyson, published under the authorship of their son, Hallam.

Reading about Emily Tennyson's life, all writers must wish they had such a one in their own lives. She is a model writer's wife. For years the public image of her (from Edmund Gosse, from Thomas Hardy, from Virginia Woolf's irreverent farce *Freshwater*) was of a pale woman, helpless on a sofa, somewhere on the edge of Tennyson's life. But it turned out that she was in fact intensely involved in everything that concerned him. For most of their married life she was Tennyson's devoted amanuensis and helpmeet.

I described my interest in her, when I was working on some Tennyson material at the University of Rochester, to a young black lifeguard at my hotel, where I was relaxing in the pool after a day's work at the library. She found Emily Tennyson's job totally understandable. 'Oh, I see,' she said, 'She was the poet's manager.' For many nineteenth-century women running a household was their only commitment. For Emily, it was subsidiary. Her grandson, Charles, would describe her as Tennyson's 'secretary and business manager'. She would herself use the word *secretary*. Emily always valued 'work' above 'society', not just for herself, but for other women. (And for men too, of course, with the example of those idle Tennyson brothers often in her mind.)

For the next twenty years Emily was often 'overworked with business'. She paid the bills and subscriptions, kept the accounts, and dealt with the entire money side of the marriage most of the time. She found tenants for the various houses they came to own (letting even Farringford itself so they could afford 'the necessary change'); she organised and supervised builders during the extensive additions that would be made in the years to come. She became deeply involved with the Farringford farm when they took it over in 1861. Emily would often consult Alfred – about the rent they should ask for the chalkpit, for instance – but he would say: 'I must leave it in thy hands to manage.' They were very capable hands; Tennyson would one day say that his wife was 'so clever in many things – could do almost anything'. Tennyson knew how lucky he was, however little Edward Lear thought he showed it.

At one point in 1856, when Tennyson was away, Emily reported herself 'binding manuscripts for A and weeding his potatoes' and 'busy planning a new dairy'. Another time he was away she put 'his books in the new shelves' and he was surprised to find them done on his return. There survive a number of catalogues, or library lists, in Emily's hand, different attempts over the years to keep track of where the books were.

When a sudden thaw once brought floods of water through the roof, Emily said to Hallam, 'I am glad Papa is not here to be vexed by it.' She was always protecting him from bother of one sort and another. 'It is fortunate,' she wrote in 1856 to Thomas Woolner, 'I have been able to burn some insulting lies apparently from a newspaper sent anonymously to Alfred, and so spare him the sight of them.' She would pounce on abusive letters, but some of them got through. Tennyson would groan through his beard about libellous letters, addressed '"Miss Alfred, the Poet Laureatess" and worse things than that.' Emily herself had the sustaining belief that one must expect bother in this world, that it was good for her 'in some way or the other' – as an idle, self-indulgent life would not have been. Reading once about the painter 'poor Turner', she reflected: 'How one wishes one might have done something to soothe his spirit and make his life happy.' That was what she sought to do for Tennyson.

Emily would scheme to spare Tennyson the sight of guests who might bore or annoy him – though very few did, provided he was allowed to read to them. 'I must try and stop his return,' she says at one point when the Jesses are visiting, knowing his brother-in-law's 'chatter would drive him wild'. She would largely take over the burden of his family, not allowing the visits of his strange siblings and their mates to alter his routines. Unmarried Matilda lived with them for years on end.

Emily checked the linen, dealt with beggars, tried, with little success, to keep Alfred clean and tidy. She ordered fish direct from Grimsby (having discovered the Isle of Wight fishmonger procured Grimsby fish via a London wholesaler), and Parian marble from Corfu for Woolner's bust of Tennyson, the chippings to be made into marbles for the boys. She kept the wine cellar stocked and checked it regularly. There are many lists in her hand surviving. They consumed a vast amount, though Henry James's later report that Tennyson 'got through a whole bottle of port at a sitting without incommodity' was not always true. In 1863, he would be advised to give it up and Emily had the job of exchanging a quantity for Amontillado, which can hardly have been what the doctor intended.

Emily even sometimes ordered Tennyson's tobacco, much as she encouraged him in his frequent attempts to give up smoking. 'We make a bonfire of leaves and burn the box with all the pipes in it, he having put the last bit of tobacco into his study fire,' Emily wrote on 12 December 1855. 'Cardboard resolves,' his brother Frederick called them.

'I am writing in the greatest hurry in the midst of a thousand things,' Emily told Edward Lear. 'My brain is nearly riven. Proof sheets all around me.' Correcting proofs was part of the real work, which included talking over ideas for poems with Alfred, listening to the poems as they were written, discussing them with him

(Which line did she prefer? This one or that?), giving the encouragement Tennyson always so badly needed, copying the poems out for the printer, checking the proofs with him. 'It is a labour of love, dearest, and my privilege,' she told him. She would even check over some foreign translations of Tennyson's poems. 'A rather hopeless task', however, she said of one French version of one of the Idylls.

Tennyson disliked writing out his poems. Some poems disappeared entirely because, formed as they were in his head, he never got round to writing them out. 'Many and many a line has gone away on the north wind.' Even more, Tennyson hated making further copies of his poems once he had written them down. Emily spent a great deal of time writing things out for him. On one occasion, she wrote just the first words of every line – as a precaution in case the master copy of 'Enoch Arden' went astray. Tennyson obviously knew his own poem well enough to reconstruct it if necessary from those single words.

Letter writing Emily saw also as a labour of love, something she could do for him. She was a natural writer, if not an elegant one, with her pen running on, just as if she were speaking. But she often found the answering of letters tedious and it was extremely time-consuming. 'Reading, I grieve to say, is nearly impossible. My time is so occupied by the letters that must be written today.' Reading, she told Woolner, 'is so much better for you.' Lear would chide her for spending so much time 'answering fooly people's persecuting pain-provoking pages', but she felt it her duty to try to make sure Tennyson escaped criticism.

The work would become more difficult for her to fit in once she started teaching the boys. She taught them herself, with some help from Alfred, until Hallam was eight and Lionel nearly seven. When they were small, she would sometimes write with the children in the room and confess the fact in letters to their father, or to Edward Lear, Benjamin Jowett or Thomas Woolner, all of whom were as devoted to the boys as Emily could wish. 'Very darling chaps indeed', Lear called them. 'I heard little feet pattering which caused this disconnected sentence,' she wrote to Alfred. Her sentences were quite often a little disconnected, but she got through a dozen letters a day, sometimes more. She told Lear,

'You know I have generally a hundred letters to write in ten minutes.' Only occasionally did she falter in her task of placating her correspondents, who often felt cheated at being deprived of a letter from their favourite poet or even their dearest friend. Edward FitzGerald and many others had to accept it was either a case of hearing from Emily, or not hearing at all. Before Tennyson's marriage they had generally not heard at all.

Even Alfred's brother Frederick, who would later make the only really derogatory remarks about Emily that anyone ever made, was full of admiration for what Emily was taking on. He wrote to Mary Brotherton, who had asked for an example of Alfred's writing for a devoted admirer: 'I have some difficulty in hunting up an autograph of Alfred's – as he never writes to anyone – making over the whole of his correspondence to his unfortunate wife, who really is the best creature in the world and submits without a murmur.' Alfred was not alone in hating to write letters, Frederick said: 'Our family, with the exception of myself, are so little addicted to correspondence that the gravest vicissitudes, short of death itself, might occur without finding an historian.'

It was in the 1850s that Alfred made his much reported statement that 'I would any day as soon kill a pig as write a letter.' He *did*, of course, write letters and not only his regular bulletins to Emily when he was away. Walt Whitman said of one letter that it was 'better than a poem'. But he was constantly exasperated by the 'plague' of the penny post, by the avalanche, the small mountain of mail that arrived for him every day. 'I am buried most mornings under a monticule of letters; I and my wife do our best to get them answered. We do our best but cannot get through them all,' he wrote to someone who had complained of not having had an acknowledgment.

Frederick Tennyson's statement that Alfred left everything to his wife was inaccurate. Emily and Alfred often tackled the mountain together. Some of the letters were actually written together, with contributions from each of them. Others written by Alfred have brief additions from Emily, sometimes across the top or even on the envelope – a warmer word of welcome, a kinder word of criticism, a gentler refusal. Many of the letters are completely Emily's, though dealing with his affairs. Others are entirely in her hand, but signed by Alfred and perhaps dictated by him – though probably not. He could generally rely on her to say what he wanted said. There is even one of this sort to a close friend, John Simeon. There also survive both drafts and copies of Alfred's letters in Emily's hand – including ones to the Queen and to Gladstone. This suggests that Emily was not just making a copy for their files, so that they knew what had been said, but that the letters themselves were often joint productions.

Then there are some third-person notes in Emily's hand: anthology permissions, refusals of invitations, 'Mr Alfred Tennyson begs to enclose an order for 5/9 ...'. In these cases, a recipient unfamiliar with Alfred's own handwriting might well suppose he had written the note himself. Indeed Martin Tupper once wrote: 'As Tennyson autographs – so-called – are usually in his wife's handwriting, this holograph is worth keeping.' George Routledge told an enquirer after an autograph that he had no specimen of Tennyson's writing: 'His correspondence with us is generally managed by his wife...'.

Emily believed that her work for Tennyson was as important as any work could be. Some feminists may not like it when we 'structure our view of women through their relation to male achievers', but it is often both realistic and inevitable that we should do so, considering the history of so many women.

I used as an epigraph to *Emily Tennyson: the Poet's Wife* a quotation from George Eliot's *Middlemarch*: 'Many who knew her thought it a pity that so substantive and rare a creature should have been absorbed into the life of another, and be only known in a certain circle as a wife and mother. But no-one stated exactly what else that was in her power she ought rather to have done.' Nowadays, with nearly everyone, male and female, too busy with their own lives, finding lots that is in their power to do, it is rare for male writers to have the sort of support that Alfred Tennyson was able to rely on. And rarer still for women writers to have the sort of support my husband has been able to give me, because of the nature of his own work and his understanding, as a fellow writer, of my needs.

Poetry is at the opposite end of the scale from biography and Anthony Thwaite is, above all, a poet. There have been many times, over the years, when I have delayed a meal or a conversation because I realised Anthony needed a little more of the solitude all poets need when working on a poem. It is natural that I should think it might have been better for him if I had been in the Emily Tennyson class – and had not had my own books to write. I remember just a few times when I have actively helped to make a poem 'happen' – sending the poet off for the day, for instance, in the middle of a family holiday. Emily Tennyson sometimes left notes around with prose ideas for poems, but I know that does not work and that if I ever do say 'that would make a good poem', it is more likely to hinder than help the process.

Poems are elusive, mysterious things and rarely come when called, unlike biographies, which need a great deal of sheer hard work, years of application and only a little art and imagination. I accept that, for all our contemporary concern with biography, the art of the biographer cannot justifiably be elevated to that of the writer who creates a work of literature out of his own imagination. There is no question that 'Dover Beach' and *Persuasion* exist on a totally different plane from any life of Matthew Arnold or Jane Austen. But of course I would much rather write a really good biography than the mediocre poem or novel I might otherwise produce, addicted as I am to writing. It is fortunate that both Anthony and I are equally committed to the problems and pleasures of living with writers.

Together, Apart

Too much together, or too much apart:
This is one problem of the human heart.

Thirty-five years of sharing day by day
With so much shared there is no need to say

So many things: we know instinctively
The common words of our proximity.

Not here, you're missed; now here, I need to get away,
To make some portion separate in the day.

And not belonging here, I feel content
When brooding on the portion that is spent.

Where everything is strange, and yet is known,
I sit under the trees and am alone,

Until there is an emptiness all round,
Missing your voice, the sweet habitual sound

Of our own language. I walk back to our room
Through the great park's descending evening gloom,

And find you there, after these hours apart,
Not having solved this question of the heart.

Nara, Japan: 1989
Anthony Thwaite

3

Lady Naipaul

Paul Theroux

In the many books that V. S. Naipaul has published, Pat Naipaul is mentioned only once, and obliquely (the prologue to *An Area of Darkness*, where she is referred to as 'my companion'). But her intelligence, her encouragement, her love and her discernment are behind every book that Naipaul has written.

'She is my heart,' he told me once. She was also that most valued person in any writer's life, the first reader.

In Uganda, thirty years ago, in what I considered to be highly unusual circumstances, I met Pat Naipaul and was immediately impressed. The Naipauls had been given a house in the grounds of Makerere University in Kampala, and Vidia was asked by the Building Department how he wished his name to read on the sign. He said he did not want his name on any sign. He was told he had to have something. He said, 'All right then, letter it "TEAS".'

As he told me the story, Pat burst out in appreciative isn't-he-awful? laughter. And then – this is the unusual part – Vidia continued to do what I had interrupted. He was reading to Pat from the last chapter of *The Mimic Men*, a novel he was just finishing.

I felt privileged to be a part of this intimate ritual. He read about two pages – a marvellous account of a bitter-sweet celebratory dinner shared by the guests in a hotel in south London. Brilliant, I was thinking, when the reading was over.

'Patsy?' Vidia said, inquiring because she had said nothing in response. Pat was thinking hard.

Finally she said, 'I'm not sure about all those tears.'

She was tough-minded and she was tender. For more than forty years, in spite of delicate health and in latter years serious illness, she remained a devoted companion. It is a better description than wife. (In *The Mimic Men*, the narrator says that wife is 'an awful word'.) The Naipauls made a practice of not reminiscing, at least in front of me, but I knew from casual remarks that in those early years they had to put up with the serious inconvenience of a small and uncertain income and no capital; Vidia used to laugh about the only job he had ever held as a salaried employee lasting just six weeks. Pat laughed too, but she had worked for a number of years as a history mistress at a girls' school.

While she was still in her thirties, she resigned from her teaching post to spend more time with Vidia, which she did as a householder in Muswell Hill, in Stockwell, and in Wiltshire; as a traveler in India, in Africa, in Trinidad, and America. She helped in the research for *The Loss of El Dorado*, and she became involved in the complex issue that Vidia described in *The Killings in Trinidad*.

As the first reader, highly intelligent, strong-willed and profoundly moral, Pat played an active part in Vidia's work. She understood that a writer needs a loyal opposition as much as praise. She enjoyed intellectual combat and used to say, when Vidia and I were engaged on a topic, 'I love to see you two sparring'. She always said it in a maternal way, and it touched me.

I loved her for her sweetness and her unselfishness, for the way she prized great writing and fine weather and kind people. She had no time for their opposites. ('Life's too short,' she said.)

I see her always as I first knew her, in the garden of the Kaptagat Arms in up-country Kenya, where Vidia took refuge from our political troubles in Uganda, to finish his novel. Pat sat smiling, reading in the sunshine, sometimes writing, and always alert to – just beyond the hedge of purple and pink bougainvilleas – the sound of typing.

4

Lady of Letters:
Living with Sylvia Jukes Morris

Edmund Morris

From the moment I first walked into her rented room in a townhouse in Marylebone, London, I knew I was in the presence of a lady of letters. And – unusual for that breed – a woman of elegance, too. The books on her Sheraton-style shelves, or between brass ends on her polished side table, were not only lovingly arranged, but manifestly read. I remember in particular a two-volume set of Boswell's *Life of Johnson*, bound in red padded leather, the page blocks gilt-edged and divided with silk ribbon markers. Newly arrived in England from Africa, I had never before seen this greatest of biographies. It sits still in her library, one floor below me as I write.

Elsewhere, I noticed Dorothy L. Sayers' translation of Dante, Shakespearean commentaries by Jan Kott and Caroline Spurgeon, W. H. Auden's *Poets of the English Language*, essays by Mary McCarthy and Gore Vidal, and – on the night stand by her bed – Henry James' *The Ambassadors*, with some scribbled notes protruding.

'I teach,' she said, by way of explanation.

'At London University?' A friend had told me she'd won a distinction in history during her student days there.

She shook her head, the dark-brown glossy bob swinging and falling. Colonial though I was, I somehow recognized that cut as more Mayfair than Marylebone.

'Acland Burghley School', she said. 'Near Highgate.'

'You don't look like a teacher,' I said, eyeing her trim black skirt and American-style pumps. Harold Wilson's Britain was then at the nadir of its dour unstylishness.

'I haven't been one for a while. A couple of years ago I went to live in New York. But now I'm back at Acland, as temporary head of the English department.'

'New York. That's where I want to be.'

'Me too! I'm regretting this move already. It feels so ... regressive.'

During the courtship that followed, climaxing in our marriage fourteen months later, I never ceased to assure her that we would someday settle in New York – possibly even (why not dream?) rent that plush pad on Central Park South, where by firelight Rossano Brazzi made love to Candice Bergen, in a movie we'd seen at the Leicester Square Odeon....

Rather more confidently, I predicted that by then Sylvia would be a published author. 'You're so interested in literature, and in literary lives. Biography is the career for you.'

On the strength of a lucid analysis of the structure of *The Ambassadors*, which she delivered over dinner at Beoty's one night (her hands undulating in the candlelight, as spontaneously as they do today on the lecture platform), I suggested she write a life of Henry James. She remarked that Leon Edel, at four volumes and counting, seemed to have cornered that particular market.

'Well, how about George Eliot?'

The bob shook and fell again. 'No, the only biographical thing I've ever done was the story of that hat.'

She glanced at the rack by the restaurant door, where hung a silver fox busby she'd bought at Bonwit Teller. 'A sort of whimsical account of the places it's been and the things it's seen. Not for publication – just an assignment in a writing class I attended once. When we read out our pieces, everybody said mine was the best!'

'There you are, you see,' I said, triumphant.

*

I must correct any possible impression, arising out of the above references to fashion and coiffure, that I had married a young woman of means. On the contrary, Sylvia has always had to earn every nickel. Her elegance is made possible only by the most austere economies. This frugality is reflected in the way she writes: spare lines, subdued colors, and now and then a discreet flash, as of half-hidden jewelry.

Never once in those early days – indeed, not until long after I had made good on my promise to emigrate with her to New York – did I think of becoming a biographer myself. She was so much more culturally sophisticated than I, so quick and unerring in her textual inferences, that I left literature to her, and dreamed only of earning *beaucoup* bucks as the chief copywriter of some Madison Avenue 'hat shop'. This would enable me to keep her in fur hats as she penned a series of lapidary lives for Knopf, perhaps, or Harvard University Press. . . .

Realities of the advertising business kept postponing this fantasy. My limited ability to write 'selling' copy for Good Seasons Salad Dressing made me an unlikely candidate for promotion at Ogilvy & Mather, Inc. Our combined income floated only a notch or two above the hardship index for Manhattan. (Sylvia, unqualified to teach in the United States, was then working as a travel counselor for the British Tourist Authority.)

Suddenly at thirty, after penning a failed campaign for Diaperene Peri-Anal Creme, I found myself on the street. For the next year or so – *ironis ironarium!* – my scholarly wife supported *me* as I hacked at whatever freelance jobs came my way – record liners, wine articles, insurance brochures, travel pieces. Meanwhile her literary half-life went on. Bored by her job, intellectually starved, she would buy books on the way home from the office and read them two, three, four at a time, until our studio apartment began to look like a library cubicle.

Her break, creatively speaking, came in 1971, when I needed help writing some audiocassette scripts for a European tour packager. She resigned from the BTA, not without trepidation ('What will we do for money, once this assignment's over?'), but took instant satisfaction in the work. I did the segments on military history and wine; she wrote cultural sketches and introductions to regional cuisine.

Next, a friend who worked at Reader's Digest Books assigned us to produce, at seventeen cents a word, a series of chapters for a history of exploration entitled *Great Adventures That Changed Our World*. The assignment was open-ended, in that we could write as many chapters as we liked, within a two-year delivery schedule. Intoxicated by the prospect of unlimited pages to fill, while the great slot machine in Pleasantville showered us with shining pennies ('What about punctuation marks?' I asked her, '—shouldn't we charge for those too?'), we congratulated ourselves on becoming, at least for the moment, full-time professional writers.

Thirty years later, we are scribbling still, with five books published and three more big ones on the way.

*

We have never collaborated. We are simply too different in temperament, sensibility, working methods, and attraction to particular subjects. At the beginning of our history of exploration, we followed the example of the fifteenth-century monarchs of Spain and Portugal, and divided the world between us. Sylvia sailed west with Columbus while I discovered the East Indies with Vasco da Gama. Later, she accompanied Burke and Wills across Australia, and William Beebe into the depths of the Atlantic ocean, while I brought Stanley and Livingstone together at Ujiji, and walked on the moon with Neil Armstrong.

As this list of names indicates, we both (and here we *are* similar) took a biographical approach to history. We built our narratives around the personalities – often as not, the antisocial neuroses – of the great explorers. Sylvia was intrigued, for example, by Florence Baker's determination to transform herself from a young Victorian wife into one of the first discoverers of the source of the Nile. I became obsessed by Prince Henry the Navigator, who 'navigated' only in his imagination. In the course of our research, a more radical difference between us became evident: Sylvia is equally interested in men and women, and can write about either at length, whereas to me, *das Ewig-weibliche* has always been an enigma.

Her biographical ambidexterity (were I to die tomorrow, she could complete my life of Theodore Roosevelt) makes her wiser than me in analyzing the relations between the sexes. I tend to adopt, or at least empathize with, the masculine viewpoint of my subject, whereas she, being a woman, is aware that no man is an island – that he can be fully understood only in so far as he relates to the other half of the human race. I stand on the promontory. Sylvia inhabits the main.

After completing her half of *Great Adventures*, she became fixated not only with F. Scott Fitzgerald, Napoleon, D. H. Lawrence, and both Richard Burtons (the Sir and the star), but also with Sonya Tolstoy, George Eliot, Wallis Warfield Simpson, Virginia Woolf, and a whole harem of Bloomsbury bluestockings. However, she had no literary designs on any of them. Neither she nor I yet believed that we could swing a solo book contract. Our names did not appear on the title page of *Great Adventures* ('Against company policy', the editor breezily explained), so we remained unknown in publishing circles. The flow of cents from Pleasantville ceased. As the recession of the mid-1970s worsened, the freelance assignments that paid our rent became fewer and fewer. Then, as always happens in New York when you are truly desperate, the phone rang.

*

A speculative script I had written on Theodore Roosevelt's Western days had been 'optioned' by a film producer. This did not guarantee that *The Dude From New York*, as I called it, would ever preem at Radio City, but it did mean enough money to keep our landlord happy for another year or so. On the strength of this success, I acquired a literary agent. (Amazing how quickly you can sign one up, when there's a check in the mail.) A remark from the agent changed our lives. 'Since you've done all this research on Teddy Roosevelt', she said, 'why don't you write a short popular biography of him?'

The next thing I knew, I had a contract for $7,500, one-quarter payable in advance. Forgetting all about the screenplay, I found myself willy-nilly becoming a studious, driven biographer. I had become what I used to think my wife should be. The work was so absorbing I did not stop to ask myself, 'What about *her*?'

*

She soon began to ask the same question – not in regard to herself, but to someone named Edith Kermit Carow. That young woman was already looming, in the early stages of my manuscript, as Theodore Roosevelt's first love – only to be supplanted by Alice Lee, the Boston beauty he married fresh out of Harvard. Both of us knew, vaguely, that Edith would get her man in the end, after Alice's tragic death. But Sylvia's curiosity as to how their romance rekindled became so intense that she moved ahead of me, and began to research the story herself.

Day after day, she accompanied me to the Theodore Roosevelt Birthplace in Manhattan, where I had access to a dusty heap of old family papers, and buried herself in those pertaining to Edith. Her research ranged beyond mine, to the years when the Roosevelts were the first family in the land, entertaining the likes of Henry Adams, Henry James, and Augustus Saint-Gaudens. Meanwhile, I was discovering that the 'short popular biography' my agent envisaged was going to be long, serious, and only the first installment of a trilogy.

With my encouragement, Sylvia made a proposal to Coward, McCann & Geoghegan. 'I feel very strongly that there is sufficient material for a truly absorbing book on Edith Kermit Roosevelt,' she wrote. 'She was a quietly powerful woman of great charm and ability; she was also an amazingly complex personality, with a fine mind and an aura of mystery that lends itself to a probing study.'

The proposal went on to sketch the story of a New York girl born in the age of Abraham Lincoln, who became one of the most brilliant hostesses in White House history, and who long outlived her husband, dying in the age of Harry Truman. Like Sylvia, Edith was passionately literary. There was an unconscious self-identification, I thought, in this paragraph of the proposal:

> According to one family chronicler, Edith 'needed books as she needed air'. Consequently a good part of every day was set aside to read history, philosophy and poetry. Her friends considered Edith an expert on Shakespeare, and even Theodore, one of the best-read men of his day, conceded that her views on literature were sounder than his own. 'She is not only cultured but scholarly,' he said proudly.

Here were words that I could echo – indeed have done, many times over the years.

Not then, and never since, have either of us felt competitive about our respective projects. I could perhaps have taken Sylvia's proposal to imply that *The Rise of Theodore Roosevelt* (though still less than a quarter written) was not uxorial enough, and needed to be supplemented. Instead, I had a pleased feeling that she meant to place my very male biography within the larger context of a female biography, a *vas insigne devotionis* benignly enclosing Theodore's life and Edith's, and those of their six children.

The publisher signed. The agent endorsed. One year after me, Sylvia had her own contract and her own calling.

She has pursued it to this day. *Edith Kermit Roosevelt: Portrait of A First Lady* was published to wide acclaim in 1980. R. W. B. Lewis, in a front-page review in the *Washington Post*, called it 'an endlessly engrossing book, at once of historical and of human importance'. The *Christian Science Monitor* remarked, 'This biography represents craftsmanship of the highest order.' Reissued as a Vintage paperback in 1987, it has recently been published again by Modern Library, and is accepted as definitive.

In the interim, after fifteen years of prodigious labor, she produced *Rage For Fame: the Ascent of Clare Boothe Luce* (Random House, 1997). Gore Vidal, in the *New Yorker*, hailed it as 'a model biography...of the kind that only a real writer can write'. And now, having shepherded me through my last two presidential biographies, *Dutch: a Memoir of Ronald Reagan* and *Theodore Rex*, Sylvia is absorbed in the second volume of her life of Mrs Luce – working title, *Price of Fame*.

We are therefore separately qualified to write essays for this volume. Were space available, it might be amusing to construct a sort of Alexandria Quartet: She as seen by Him, He as seen by Her, She as She imagines He sees Her, He as He hopes She sees Him. Here, at any rate, is the first perspective:

*

I live with a perpetual clipping machine, a female Edward Scissorhands who cannot open a newspaper or magazine without reaching for the shears she always keeps near her – on the breakfast table, in the sitting room, in her library, at her desk, beside her bed, in her purse when she travels. (Current airline security regulations have severely cramped this habit.) Mostly, the columns she clips are biographical in nature – obituaries, interviews, profiles. But on some days her slashing frenzy is such that when I ask for today's *New York Times*, I get little more than the masthead and, with luck, the lingerie ads.

She files these clips according to a system only slightly less abstruse than the Heisenberg Principle. Years later, however, she will quickly exhume a yellowing filament of newsprint in reference to some point she needs to corroborate. It was just such a filament, containing a 1975 interview with Clare Boothe Luce, that flowered out two decades later into *Rage for Fame*.

Oddly enough, for a woman who so ruthlessly treats periodicals, Sylvia cannot bear to see a mark in the margin of any printed book. That white space, that snowscape over which words float like prophet birds, must never be defiled. Not so long ago, in a secondhand bookstore, I came across a copy of *Edith Kermit Roosevelt*, which some reader had respectfully annotated. I bought it for her amusement. But after glancing at a page or two, she put it down with a pained expression, and has not taken it up again. Respectful or not, that stranger had trespassed.

When writing, she wields a fat Pelikan fountain pen on the backs of old xeroxes, faxes, fliers, and press releases – anything that is blank and 8½ inches by 11. This satisfies her double desire to save trees and sow words. She sits for hours, motionless except for the moving pen, deaf to outside sounds, even to loud conversation in her vicinity. Every now and again I will force her to get up and walk around, lest she write herself into a spasm. Fortunately she is limber from regular exercise – indeed, less desk-damaged than I am.

She writes in the rounded 'Marion Richardson' style taught to so many English grammar-school girls of her generation, using a chisel nib that gives a semi-calligraphic curve to her *g*s and *y*s and an incisive sweep to her crossed *t*s. Unlike me, she tends to through-compose whole sections, sometimes whole chapters without stopping, her hand racing after the speed of her thoughts. Before she rewrites, which she does over and over, pruning and refining, it is imperatively necessary for her to read me her day's work. I confess I find this something of a trial, because unfinished prose always makes me dizzy, and hearing it, rather than seeing it on the page, increases the vertigo. But exposition *viva voce* is part of her creative process; without it, she cannot proceed to the next silent stage. And so, draft by draft, reading by reading, the thing eventually gets done to her satisfaction. Only then will she sit at the computer and render her manuscript into type – the first printout, of course, prompting yet more revisions.

Final text is final text, but as the house archivist, I'm most inclined to preserve her handwritten sheets, since their interlineations and heavy load of patches and coagulated white-out give such tactile evidence of the struggle every word cost her. I feel particularly tender toward a late page describing Edith Roosevelt's death, which bears evidence, in the form of a couple of teary blotches, that the biographer had finally lost her objectivity. And who can blame her, given the poignancy of the paragraph?

> With the signing of her will Edith, in effect, severed her formal attachment to life. The four seasons of 1947 found her largely bedridden, as did the spring and summer of 1948, the last she was to encounter. As the leaves began to fall in September and the days shortened, the final weakness stole upon her....

Sylvia's perfectionism extends right through every stage of her book's production. As passionate about design as she is about prose, she harried her editor so obsessively over the sizing, screening, and placement of *Rage for Fame*'s illustrations (which cost her eight thousand dollars) that he ordered the compositor to show her the final film of the book before it went to press – an unheard-of concession to an author's judgment.

Next, she fought with her publisher in a determined effort to make the cover design simpler and more stylish. 'Why all these clashing typefaces?' she asked. 'And the gold curlicues? Keep it just plain black and silver.' He threatened to drop her from his spring list. She went on fighting; he capitulated. The result was a book so beautiful that it is displayed to this day in the production department at Random House, as an example of what a good biography should look like.

*

She says that after *Price of Fame* she will retire and go back to what she was doing when I met her, and still loves best: reading, reading, and more reading. For the next few years, though, her life will continue to consist of writing, writing, and more writing. Pleased though I am to see her absorbed in her newspapers over breakfast, and her stack of three or four books after dinner, it still fills me with content to hear the steady scratch of her pen all day, and see the well-cut bob, still dark, still glossy, swing and fall as she reaches for another sheet of paper: the age-old, eager gesture of so many scribes with something to say.

5

Yesterday's News

Michael Holroyd

Over the first twenty years of my life, I had the benefit of observing both the unhappy marriage of my grandparents, who remained miserably chained in wedlock all their adult lives, and the unhappy marriage of my parents who, having quite quickly divorced, were free to make several more unhappy marriages. Which was the better course?

Conventional wisdom has it that mothers and fathers should stay joylessly together for the sake of their children. Mine didn't – which is why I lived largely with my grandparents. I have no doubt that the instability of my background (I was provided at various moments with Hungarian, French, and English step-parents to add to my Swedish mother and Anglo-Irish father) gave me the advantages of a slow start and low self-esteem. Driving a car, publishing a book, marrying – all seemed as unlikely for me as captaining the English cricket team.

I didn't drive a car or publish my *Lytton Strachey* until I was in my mid-thirties; and I didn't marry till my late forties. But deferred pleasures, especially when unexpected, are all the keener (I am still waiting for the call to captain England at cricket and plan to enjoy every second of it).

My marriage to Margaret Drabble in 1982 was reckoned to be highly unusual. After all, was I not a happy-go-lucky bachelor? Hadn't

Margaret sworn never to remarry following the divorce from her first husband, the distinguished actor Clive Swift? And, most surprising of all, did we not apparently continue living in separate London houses? This was certainly how our marriage was presented in the newspapers – though had we not married, the same newspapers would happily have reported that we were 'living together'. In fact, we had a fine precedent in Mary Wollstonecraft and William Godwin, who, after their marriage, lived as near neighbors.

Of course I went into training for the marriage: taking a honeymoon in Hollywood with Margaret before the actual ceremony, briefing Beryl Bainbridge as our best man, and studying Hugh Kingsmill's famous panorama of marriage *Made on Earth* (1937). From all this I emerged as a radical. Legal proposals to make divorce more difficult are popular in England these days. But I agree with Milton, who objected to the 'discord of nature' involved in keeping an 'ill-yoking couple' together; and I liked the Shavian notion of limiting the marriage contract (easily obtainable at the drugstore) to one year, with a joint option to renew it every twelve months. Such bold ideas strike me as good-natured and sensible.

But though I am a radical theorist, the fact is that Margaret and I were not conducting a brave experiment so much as exercising romantic common sense. I notice how envious other couples were of our arrangement. Except for at weekends, there was little room for me all day in Margaret's house along with her children, a secretary, and the commodious *Oxford Companion to English Literature*, while my own apartment was amply filled with Bernard Shaw, about whom I was then writing.

Then, when the *Oxford Companion* and GBS eventually moved off, we began living together at the same house in London – and lost our notoriety. We also have a house now in Somerset (where Margaret finds it easier to write her novels) and chase each other from town to country and back – occasionally, too, taking holidays from each other. But we are no longer newsworthy. Thank God.

Any hopes I may have had that Margaret would take on the burden of writing my biographies, in addition to her novels, have proved false. Though we share much, the secret part of ourselves remains our writing. Everyone knows those promising authors and intimidating scholars who, developing into brilliant non-stop speakers, waste their talent in the air. Margaret and I are almost always silent about what we are writing. What we can sometimes do is lift the other's morale. When we instinctively become aware that one of us needs a reinvigorating rest from work, the other can take the initiative and supply it. Otherwise we must not trespass. There have been occasions when I indirectly introduced some theme that I was exploring and see if Margaret's response sets me off in a new direction, though she may not have known that this involved my work. And there was an occasion when I was able to show her a legal document that may have been useful for one of her event-plots. But that is the limit. We never read each other's print-outs and typescripts.

We live together, and living with us are many fiction and non-fiction characters. They are not confined to our studies (which are themselves separated by two floors), but though they may roam the rooms freely they do not haunt us both.

6

The Open Door

Margaret Drabble

There is much in my early novels about marriage. I got married in June 1960, three weeks after my twenty-first birthday, and just after taking my Cambridge Finals. I married my first love. Then I sat down to write my first novel, *A Summer Bird-Cage*, while expecting my first baby. So the subject of marriage was much in my mind as I began my career in fiction.

The success of this novel depended largely upon its title, which I stole from John Webster's *The White Devil*. The quotation goes thus: "'Tis just like a summer bird-cage in a garden: the birds that are without, despair to get in, and the birds that are within despair and are in a consumption for fear they shall never get out.' All these years, I have been thinking that the subject of this quotation was marriage, but I now discover that I have remembered it quite wrongly. I have just looked it up, and I find that the subject is not marriage at all, but something much more louche. In fact, I'm not sure if I now really understand what the speaker in the play means, though I was sure that I did then. But that is irrelevant. I co-opted the image for my own purposes, and it has served well.

I was one of the last of the Early Marriage Generation. It is hard to believe now that so many of us married so innocently, so young. We should have known better. In those days, women still married to get away from their mothers, because a career was not considered a good enough reason for leaving home. Careers were not taken seriously, whereas a marriage, however implausible, had to be respected.

My parents would probably have been surprised by the immense and probably irreversible changes in attitudes to marriage that we now take for granted, though my father, as a lawyer, was always a keen advocate of the right to divorce. He saw two of his three daughters through divorce and remarriage, but did not live long enough to know that five of his great-grandchildren would be born, most respectably, out of wedlock. I do not think this would have worried either of my parents in the slightest. My mother's sister, aged ninety-two, and less progressive in her ideas than my mother was, accepts the situation without any sign of concern. She has come to think it normal. As it is.

Why, I wonder, didn't things change earlier? Why did the traditional form of marriage retain its stranglehold for so long, and find itself so little lamented when it weakened its grip? My parents would not have contemplated divorce for themselves, even though in principle they approved of it, as they approved of all legislation that improved the social conditions of women. I dimly remember divorce as a painful process best forgotten, and would like to think that it is easier and less painful now. Marriage, I now think, should not be an expectation or an obligation. It is a rare condition, to be handled with care and quit when necessary. It does not suit everybody. The mere threat of it drives some people mad, as Thomas Hardy often pointed out – Sue Bridehead in *Jude the Obscure* was one of my earlier heroines. Marriage is for exceptional people. My second husband, Michael, is exceptional and eccentric. He invents things as he goes along. This is very liberating.

The extended family, one of the by-products of the decline of conventional marriage, is a great gain. Family parties are much more exciting now than they used to be, for they usually include a miscellaneous array of cousins legal and illegal, legitimate and illegitimate, and stepchildren and step-siblings from complicated liaisons the precise origins of which have been long forgotten. I didn't foresee any of this when I started to write in 1960. Like the family, marriage isn't what it was. It's much less constraining, much less deadly, much more inventive. The summer bird-cage has an open door, and the birds fly in and out as they will.

Marriage, for writers married to other writers, poses particular challenges. It has been noted that it seems easier to stay married to a writer who works in a different genre, thus avoiding the problem of competition or the fear of imitation. Couples composed of biographers and novelists or biographers and playwrights seem to get along well, at least in Britain, and Michael and I work well together (or rather apart) in the same manner as Richard Holmes and Rose Tremain, Michael Frayn and Claire Tomalin, Antonia Fraser and Harold Pinter. I think biographers tend to be less moody and difficult to live with than novelists and playwrights, and more sympathetic to the moods of others. Biographers are willing to find a detached biographical explanation for the deep sighs, the days of blank listlessness or bad temper, the forgotten items on the shopping list, the sudden accesses of meaningless euphoria. They are accustomed to looking at context and subtext. I know that when I am working on a novel, part of my mind is taken up with people who are not present at all in the flesh, and with scenes that are only half realised. I think Michael senses these ghostly presences and vistas, and can probably guess at them from questions I randomly ask, or books I unexpectedly pounce upon.

A biographer's hidden life should in theory be less random, more closely attached to a recognizable topic, but I am not sure if this really pertains. Some of the byways of biography are deeply mysterious, and some of its discoveries are shocking. Michael and I are both uncertain explorers, never sure of what we will find, and we tend to keep our separate journeys and disappointments far away from one another. There is one aspect of the literary life, however, about which we have identical and strong feelings. We are both subject to fits of intense panic and terror when we think we have mislaid a vital document — a letter, a draft of an idea, a page of typescript. A missing book drives us into a frenzy of search and anxiety. As both our houses (four hours' drive apart) are full of every conceivable form of printed matter, bound, unbound, and most of it disastrously uncatalogued, we spend a great deal of time in panic and terror. But each understands the despair of the other. Sometimes, triumphantly, we find some item of which the other has abandoned hope. It was Michael who found my annotated copy of *The Prelude*, which had eluded me for years.

It is a very good thing that neither of us is better organised than the other. It would be alarming to be married to somebody who always knew where everything was. We may approach our work differently, and we use different technologies, but at least we share our sense of chaos. We understand that a writer's life is essentially untidy. We shall never be able to organise those tables covered with paper, those bulging drawers, those tottering piles of manuscripts, those letters filed under the bed. They are the literary life, and it takes another writer to tolerate them and live with them.

7

Harbour and Voyage: The Marriage of Ann and Bill Golding

Judy Carver

They entertained each other, first and foremost. They talked. They would sit in the kitchen having cups of instant coffee. In the old days, they used to smoke. They would gesture, the cigarette at the end of the flourish. And their conversation was always a brilliant, real activity, an involvement, like a journey that was full of new experience – for both. They gave each other their thoughts. They also poked fun at each other, gently for the most part. I have a postcard from Egypt written to me by my father in 1976: 'Ann has just described my conversation as consisting of something old, something new, something borrowed, something blue.'

They shared passions: stained glass (Chartres was the place they first holidayed together, in the summer of 1939, before their marriage); language; gardening; conversation. They made room for each other's passions and did their best to share them: music, for my father; politics, for my mother; clothes, for my mother (she was so talented at these that it transcended frivolity – my father preferred old, soft clothes with holes); chess, for my father (my mother never played much, but they did the chess problems together); mathematics, for my mother. It was a family 'given' that my father was hopeless at mathematics. This was quite untrue; rather I think he had usually been uncooperative or even intransigent – one of their favourite words – in the face of it, much as he had been with Latin. So my mother taught him trigonometry during the war, and he passed his officer's exam. Above all, my father was fascinated by the sea, and my mother accompanied and helped him in a series of adventures which would have daunted many. 'Only Bill', she once declared, 'could get us out of the things that only Bill could get us into.' My father used to say that she had the great quality of looking beautiful when dirty. Later, however, he acknowledged in his journal – perhaps rather naively, 'I begin to believe that I was more lucky than I thought, in Ann's willingness to rough it. I haven't met any other woman who would have put up with... the *incredible* primitiveness.'

Politics – her passion – was complex for them. They met in the late 1930s. How could they not be interested in politics? But where he was interested, she was certain and passionate. In the earlier 'thirties she had gone to a Mosleyite meeting with a bundle of leftwing leaflets. Eyeing the bulging muscles of the patrolling blackshirts, she prudently sat on the papers and then took them home. She told this story as an example of cowardice: I am still staggered at her courage in taking the leaflets at all. My father, however, claimed never to have done anything brave except by accident. He told us how he had slipped out of a huge pre-war demonstration in Trafalgar Square by showing his briefcase to a policeman – the policeman let him through without a word. In later life he became very fidgety about the whole matter, hated political certainty, distrusted political analysis, and had discussions with my mother that sometimes ended in silent disagreement. When my generation in our turn felt political argument was natural, we could not understand my father's distaste. My husband, a political theorist, eventually became irritated. 'Well,' he asked, 'why on earth did you become involved in the Left Book Club?' My father replied, 'Because I wanted to sleep with the Pasionaria of the South East.'

In June 1938 my father finished his Oxford teaching diploma, and in September took a job at Maidstone in Kent, in the local boys' grammar school. He got the position on the strength of his musical qualifications. The school needed a new teacher, part of whose job would be formally to supervise its first pupil ever to do music at

Higher School Certificate (the equivalent of A Level). There were many expert musicians on the staff, but they were valuable elsewhere in the school and could not be spared for this new activity. When my father was not supervising his talented pupil, he ran a chamber choir, taught English, directed plays and took sports lessons. The pupil's name was Michael Tillett, later Director of Music at Rugby School, and he was a very accomplished musician already. He remembers my father as quite jolly, very friendly and full of energy. He also remembers that he and his fellow pupils were aware that this new member of staff had published a book of poems. In my father's short time at the school (he left in April 1940) he seems to have done much: music, sport, drama and politics. The last three of these activities were likely to bring him into contact with my mother's family.

My maternal grandfather, Ernest William Brookfield, had a grocery shop in Maidstone, rather a posh one, or as they might have said then, 'superior'. The business flourished under his care, and his large household – he and his wife, ten children, a nanny and parlour maid – all lived in a roomy old house on the outskirts of the town. My mother and her three younger sisters had gone to the girls' grammar school. In 1938 one brother was still at the boys' school and the youngest had yet to go there. Many of the teachers were friends of the family. The splendid sequence of ten clever, good-looking children had made the Brookfields a local phenomenon. Mrs Brookfield was welcoming, and the house a pleasant meeting place. My mother, a beauty, with blue eyes, black hair, and lovely features, led a very busy and social life. She worked at Reed's paper mill near Maidstone as an analytical chemist. She had already finished one engagement – she told me she gave him up with some sadness, came home and ate a particularly substantial tea. By 1938 she was engaged again, though not – her family felt – very seriously. She had lovely clothes, went out to dances, acted, organised a local hockey team. And she was passionately involved in politics.

In 1930s England it was normal, even patriotic, to be leftwing, and many young people were communist. Fascism was the great object of fear and ruled supreme little more than 100 miles from the English coast. It was not a distant or theoretical threat. Nevertheless, for most of the 'thirties, life was good for the Brookfield children.

Their father was indulgent and prosperous enough to be so comfortably. They wanted for nothing, except perhaps time. However, one by one the elder children left school and began their adult lives, leaving the younger ones with almost too much space at home. Family life became less carefree, and the sense of political crisis also deepened. Ernest Brookfield, demonstrative, affectionate, sweet-natured, died of cancer in the summer of 1938, and his suffering and decline had by then darkened their lives for many months. Prosperity began to die away too, and the benign presence of Ernest Brookfield proved to have done more than keep the family in comfort: his death began a time of great difficulty. Grieving over him was hardly begun before the third son, Norman, fourteen months younger than my mother, was reported missing in Spain. Soon all hope was relinquished for him too. He had volunteered as a member of the International Brigade, and died in the bloody struggle for the River Ebro. So my grandfather and my uncle Norman, both very dear to my mother and her family, were lost within a few months. My grandmother was a brave woman and had survived a very harsh childhood, but this left a mixed legacy in that she organised rather than nurtured, and though she loved her children she did not easily show it once they were beyond babyhood.

In September 1938 my mother was twenty-six, my father twenty-seven, both of them attractive, perhaps slightly self-centred people, both engaged to others. Soon, in this smallish town in the south-east of England, they knew of each other, had seen each other. (When my mother – I should think, in the 1970s – said she had definitely noticed my father before they had met, he blushed.) They finally met during that autumn, or possibly just in the new year of 1939, at a meeting in London of the Left Book Club. It was a *coup de foudre*. They found themselves later that evening, walking up the Strand together, talking excitedly in rapid French. From that moment on they were a couple, a partnership, each more important to the other than anyone else in the world. Other ties, with siblings, parents, friends, receded for both.

My mother had the easier task of breaking her engagement by letter, since her fiancé was in Malaya. But my father was more enmeshed. The break was an ugly one and angered his parents. He felt his fiancée's misery, his parents' disappointment and displeasure, and the resultant guilt – combined with awareness in himself of what he would later call original sin – recurred in thought and in terrible dreams at least as late as the 1970s. Nevertheless, he also had a contradictory feeling, of a right to freedom, to love. There was great happiness. Something of this, and its inevitable ruthlessness, is reflected in the meeting of Sammy and Taffy in *Free Fall*. And the description of Taffy might pass for one of my mother: 'She was dark and vivid. She had the kind of face that always looks made-up, even in the bath – such black eyebrows, such a big, red mouth. She was the prettiest girl I ever saw....'

They married on 30 September 1939, as soon as Reed's Paper Mill acknowledged the exigency of war by allowing married women to keep their jobs. In April 1940 they left Maidstone. My father had been offered a job at Bishop Wordsworth School, Salisbury, where he had done his teaching practice. This took the new couple – my mother three months pregnant – out of the ambit of her family, and much nearer to the Goldings and their house in Marlborough. We as children were far more affected by our paternal grandparents. The family in Kent were at a distance.

My father's war was varied. He went into the Royal Navy in December 1940 and spent a year as a rating before becoming an officer. Then he was seconded to a weapons research establishment, and he and my mother and brother moved to Beaconsfield. He left the research establishment a year later, requesting a return to active service, and at that point my mother and brother moved in with my father's parents at 29 The Green, Marlborough, while he returned to sea.

The Goldings, Alec and Mildred, had initially felt doubtful about my mother after the painful break-up with my father's fiancée. However, there was a rapprochement, partly because my brother was a frail little boy and my mother needed support. In any case, my grandparents were happier being generous than harbouring grievances, and were from then on unstinting in offering support. Decades after Alec's death, my father said to my mother that it had been one of the pleasures of his life that she and Alec liked each other so much.

She enjoyed herself in Marlborough. Because of the Blitz, London schools had been evacuated to country schools to share their premises. The City of London School moved in with Marlborough College, and some of their staff, attractive Londoners many of whom were socialist, became lifelong friends of my parents. My mother joined the Society for Cultural Relations which tried to create links with the Soviet Union, who were of course our allies at that point. An old friend told my parents years later that my mother's good looks were a puzzle to some in this group: they concluded that she must be a right-wing spy. But this theory did not last long, and my mother, despite having a small child, and missing her husband at sea, led a busy and interesting life.

She also brought interest and colour to my grandparents' lives. Mildred Golding, a quiet, shy, rather invisible woman, soberly dressed in things she had had for years, was persuaded by my mother to have some new clothes for herself, and in colours too – claret, turquoise, primrose. The memory of this achievement gave my mother satisfaction in later years, and it was not a superficial one. Her parents-in-law were soon very attached to her, and looked after my brother with such affection that this was one of the happiest periods in his life. My father's adopted sister Eileen (younger than him by nine years, and by birth his first cousin) was mostly away during the war, except for holidays, and the house had seemed empty. Now, it became livelier. Alec made toys, and played with David and read to him. At the same time he, as a devout socialist, found a political ally in his daughter-in-law. It was she, not my father, who said to me how good it was that Alec saw a Labour government in power before his death.

My parents were reluctant to talk of the war, but there are photographs, one in particular showing the young couple in the garden at 29 The Green. He is in a lieutenant's uniform, she is wearing a fur coat and thick stockings. He looks grim, she looks fragile. His rank, the winter clothes, the state of the garden, their expressions, all make me think this was before his departure for Walcheren and Operation Infatuate, in November 1944. After it, he was reported missing, and the operation itself resulted in heavy casualties. But he had survived, against the odds, though many of his closest friends died. It was an episode which he recalled with particular horror, amid all the horrors of that time.

In the early years after the war, both were ambitious and active. They were an attractive pair. They both wrote to the BBC, suggesting projects. My mother read her account of 'Life in a large family' on the radio; my father sent various works, initially without success. Both acted with amateur companies in Salisbury. My mother had real talent as an actress, and my father directed as well. So far, their efforts were at least similar. But my father kept stubbornly at the task of writing, whereas my mother, trying it and finding little success, gave up. There are two shortish novels (unpublished and likely to remain so) written by my father between 1945 and 1952, the year he started Lord of the Flies. There are also poems, published and unpublished, two accounts of holidays in our first boat Seahorse, and part of a diary, as well as other writings probably stemming from this period. My father taught full-time, ran several after-school clubs, commanded the school Combined Cadet Force, converted a boat, pursued his acting and directing activities, and played in the school orchestra. Meanwhile, somehow they found time to raise their children: David, born in 1940, Judy, born in 1945. Of course I remember time with my parents, bicycling out to pick blackberries, listening to the radio, going to plays, singing, reading and above all sailing. But both my brother and I also remember that they were much pre-occupied with themselves and each other.

My mother was a central figure in play after play: Hermione in The Winter's Tale, Inez in Sartre's Huis Clos, Olivia in Twelfth Night, Elvira in Coward's Blithe Spirit, Catherine de Troyes in John Whiting's Marching Song. She was striking, intelligent, had a clear voice, and a good sense of timing. Her range was wide. She also sat on committees; she made many friends. She dressed smartly on very little money. When, in the mid-1950s, she felt she had spent too much money getting an old fur coat re-furbished, she went out and got herself a job at a small private school for young boys, where she showed an unmistakable talent for teaching arithmetic (I can vouch for this personally, having seen it in action more recently with my own sons).

While she went out acting, discussing, lobbying, my father stayed in and wrote. When I was about seventeen, he told me that he had at this period conjured up an unsparing view of himself as an undistinguished teacher, a dull stay-at-home who wrote unsuccessfully, even ridiculously, while his wife went out every night. He told me that after a while he even considered that it might be better for everyone if death were to remove him, an extraordinary conclusion for someone happily married, with two small children. He reported this to me as an exercise in objectivity, and indeed he was recommending such an exercise to me.

Four decades after that puzzling conversation, I have wondered if the post-war period was for him, at least, partly one of real depression, masked by incessant activity. He had started marriage in a state of exhilaration, putting his guilt to one side, rather like a rash bargain in a fairy story, until a time when he might have more leisure to consider it. Then came the war, with its allotted tasks and disciplines, its dangers, hopes and, eventually, reliefs. Then again, during and after 1945, came the full realisation of the story of that war. As he says in his essay 'Fable', 'I had discovered what one man could do to another.'

So he wrote Lord of the Flies knowing just how cruel human beings could be, and acknowledging that he could be cruel, too. This was no doubt a harsh experience as well as a starting point of great intensity. He could not have written the books he did without some interior experience of the evils and terrors that they explore. Nor do I believe for a moment that all his sense of such things came from the war. I think he had the courage to face the rooted potential for evil in himself, saw that he, too, was 'suffering from the terrible disease of being human'. However, I believe that he would not necessarily have completed that task so well, or fulfilled that opportunity so marvellously, without my mother.

What did she do? She encouraged him. She let him write. Crucially, she didn't make it difficult for him to spend time writing. She made a life for herself. More than that, with her he felt safe to acknowledge his own, potentially disastrous, humanity. In a modern phrase, her love was unconditional. And I believe she also helped to feed his imaginative life. That life was evident in him when they met – even his pupils at school could see it. She cannot have expected it to vanish or wither. They were both intensely competitive people, but she nevertheless helped him achieve. There is significant evidence of her contributory role in his writing. She was always his first critic, the first person to whom he read what he had written, and he trusted her judgment in all its aspects, rightly I believe. But she helped in other ways. She pointed things out to him: the strange punk in *Darkness Visible* was one result of this process, and there are many examples in the journal. More, her perception, her social ease and social talents, and her experience and understanding as a woman, provided him with vicarious life. They talked together with ease. It may be that he had never talked so intimately to a woman before. And he did not waste this resource. He tells us that he talked to her about *Lord of the Flies* and its successors. Concerning the inception of *Lord of the Flies*, he credits her with recognising that he had a first-rate idea, and should turn it into a book without delay. She was the dedicatee of *The Inheritors*, his own favourite among his novels, believed by many to be his best. Their copy contains his inscription acknowledging her collaboration.

I believe my mother brought another very specific quality to their life together, one that was crucial to his achieving a personal voice in his writing. She was a brave woman, physically and morally. The best example I know of this is her saying in Prague, during a visit shortly after the Velvet Revolution, that she hoped they would not throw away the good with the bad. No doubt her hosts were well mannered, but she felt their deep hostility and scorn. She had, I believe, expected it – it least partly. And they may have had all the right on their side. But she said it anyway, and it was still brave of her.

In a marriage of half a century there must be great change. During those five decades, their lives were gradually transformed, and not just by money. In the 'forties and 'fifties the four of us sailed round the coast in ramshackle old boats and came to no harm in those sparsely populated waters, although almost every landing point bore remnants or ruins from the war. In 1967 we were sailing an expensive well-equipped yacht – we had made good – and yet the English Channel was so crowded by then that we were run down and the boat sank. In my early childhood, when my father's parents wished to 'phone us, twenty-seven miles away, they went to a neighbour's house and 'phoned our neighbour. It was an event, usually an emergency. A fridge was exotic then, a car a luxury. People mended socks and even stockings; they didn't just go out and buy some more.

There were differences of background between my parents. My father grew up in austere circumstances with parents who exemplified dedication, virtue, intellect, honesty and thrift. The Brookfields, not as austere, were nevertheless people of similar standards. But the great tribe of Brookfield children were used to having fun together, playing, putting on plays, going out to dances, meeting people. It is true that at Christmas all the Golding descendants packed into 29 The Green, the old, uneven and cold house at Marlborough, with its wavy and gabled roof, ancient cellars and small, square garden next to the graveyard. But the Golding family were not really gregarious. Certainly they did not entertain. Nor were they given to comfort. Nothing in the house had changed much since 1911 when my grandparents moved there, except that after the war electric light had been extended to the upstairs, and the old, leaky kitchen roof had been lowered. My grandfather built a radio in the 1920s, but his motives, apart from a passionate curiosity, were those of a passionate educator. Years later, when my father was filling in his first entry for *Who's Who*, he wanted to write 'Attended Marlborough Grammar School and Brasenose College Oxford. Educated by the BBC.' My mother dissuaded him, and to my knowledge this well-deserved tribute has been unpublished till now. The house, beloved by us all except my father, was teetotal and full of the unmistakable scent of thrift. The few expensive objects (elegant brass fire tools; some silver, some glassware, and a flamboyant china washstand set) were gifts from that January day in 1906 when my grandparents married in Truro Cathedral. The Goldings played music, but on instruments – you might hear a string quartet in the drawing room as you walked along the lane outside. The Brookfields had a gramophone, probably more than one, and they danced impromptu in the downstairs rooms.

Naturally my parents' partnership constrained as well as liberated. Each made sacrifices, large and small. In the early 1960s my mother gave up her teaching job, which she loved, in order to be at home with my father when he became a full-time writer. About fifteen years later my father relinquished with grief a friendship which my mother felt threatened her. Their marriage contained other sadnesses, as may be imagined.

Time, moreover, brought a change of balance in their relationship. To begin with, my mother was the admired, successful one – my father lucky to win her, and by his own judgment – not, I think, hers – rather a dull figure by comparison. By the 1960s, my father was famous and successful, and my mother growing older. She had merged her life and her ambition with his, and she had relinquished her own occupation. His increasing status, while it had a comic side for them both, sometimes produced an asymmetry which angered her.

She was always attractive and striking, and moreover she was witty, producing a number of aphorisms which seem to have wandered into others' works. She said early on, for example, that every great novel needs an element of boredom in it. But she was an adjunct to him, during their later years, in the eyes of strangers. They met a couple on holiday in 1979, and when (in my father's absence) the husband learnt who his new acquaintance was, he apparently said how lucky my mother was to marry a man like that. His wife and my mother, still relative strangers, replied in unison: 'Nonsense'.

My father became a quarry – for journalists, zealous readers, academics. My mother, while partly enjoying her role as gatekeeper, would often have to stand by while my father bravely suffered more flattery than was good for him. She found it irritating but also believed it could not help him, and did her best, not always in private, to provide him with his own personal reality principle.

In his late fifties and sixties, he had a bleak time as a writer. Following *The Pyramid*, published in 1967, he found he could not achieve another novel. It is because of that period of blankness that we have his journal. He began it in 1971, initially as a dream journal, with the aim of encouraging his imagination to work again – as it did. In the journal his relationship with my mother is clearly a foundation of his work as well as his life. They are shown as companions and friends, as well as lovers, and they jointly treat his writing as the primary task. It was my mother who said to him in the early 1970s that he would have to choose between literary journalism (tempting for many reasons) and being a novelist. She added that she personally believed he was a novelist. She demanded he take himself seriously, do justice to himself. And once more she provided him with courage.

During that bleak time, he writes in his journal on their thirty-third wedding anniversary: 'It might be a good thing to record in an unbritish way here, how much I love her, and how much she has done for me, from bed to books. For I would never have been as happy in the one with someone else, nor have written the others with someone else – or indeed, written anything.'

On that terrible morning when I took her hands, sat her down, and told her he was dead, she stared at me, lost. Then she replied, 'But I've got so much to say to him.'

8

C. P. Snow and Pamela Hansford Johnson at Home

John Halperin

I first met Charles Percy Snow in the summer of 1977, when he was seventy-one (he was born in October 1905). He had published his excellent study *Trollope* two years earlier, and perhaps for that reason chose to review my book *Trollope and Politics* (1977) in his regular *Financial Times* column. Tim Farmiloe, my editor at Macmillan, introduced us; Snow's publisher was also Macmillan, but his editor was Alan Maclean, the brother of the late British spy Donald Maclean. I was duly summoned to Eaton Terrace, where Snow (he was by then a baron, but I will forbear from referring to him here as Lord Snow), his wife the novelist and critic (excellent monograph on Thomas Wolfe) Pamela Hansford Johnson, and I talked books. Like some of his characters in the *Strangers and Brothers* novels (1940–70), Snow and his wife tossed back the better part of a bottle of whiskey in the course of an hour or two. I was invited again. During that summer I read the entire *Strangers and Brothers* series (eleven novels) and became convinced that it ranked, in the mass, among the best work in twentieth-century British fiction. The characters, many of whom move from novel to novel, are utterly believable; and if you like realistic novels of politics, as

I do – politics both public, as in *Corridors of Power*, and out of sight, as in *The Masters* – Snow is your man. (Thus we both loved Trollope.) *The Masters*, in my opinion, is one of the greatest novels ever written, and certainly the greatest of all academic novels; as Pamela said to me once, 'It is a perfect novel.' It continues to astonish me that while Snow's novels are read everywhere in Europe, not a single one of them was in print in the US in 2003. Nor has the thirteen-part BBC television dramatization of *Strangers and Brothers* ever been shown on American television.

I had an idea, back in 1977, of writing a biography of Snow, an idea he encouraged, promising his family's cooperation and access to all of his private papers. After his death on 1 July 1980 I discovered that he had not arranged any access for me to people or papers; and his family was the reverse of cooperative. These formidable obstacles were among the reasons I abandoned the plan; another was the fact that by this time I had begun a life of the late Victorian novelist George Gissing, a complicated book that took some years to complete. The Snow project fell by the wayside.

But I didn't know any of this in March 1978 when we agreed to conduct a series of ongoing interviews; between then and 13 June 1980, just eighteen days before Snow's death, we filled eleven ninety-minute cassettes with questions and answers designed to tell me what I thought I wanted to know about his life and its many connections to his novels. Much of the information in this essay comes from those interviews of a quarter-century ago.

At least half of them were conducted in the cluttered study Snow occupied on the fourth and topmost storey of his home in Eaton Terrace – a fascinating sunlit room bulging with manuscripts, proofs, correspondence, and various mementos, including a photograph of the mathematician G. H. Hardy. The tapes, sixteen and a half hours altogether, are in the Huntington Library in San Marino, California, where they await Snow's future biographers. There, also, is the tape-recording of a long conversation I had with Pamela Hansford Johnson on 22 February 1980, sixteen months before her own death in June 1981 at age sixty-nine. The 'he saids' and 'she saids' in this essay are taken from these recorded conversations between March 1978 and June 1980.

They met in July 1941 at Stewart's of Piccadilly, 'a very nice place to have tea', Snow told me. On that site now is the Australian airline Qantas. Pamela had reviewed the first of the *Strangers and Brothers* novels, now titled *George Passant* (originally called *Strangers and Brothers* and published in 1940), in the *Liverpool Post*. She described it as the most original, the most personality-laden of any novel she had read in many years. Apart from a rave by Desmond MacCarthy in the *Sunday Times*, hers was one of the few encouraging reviews Snow received for this overture to the great series. Perhaps because of this, the next novel in the group, *Time of Hope*, did not appear until 1949. Snow wrote to Pamela and suggested they meet. He was at the time a physics don at Cambridge and a civil servant, and not yet famous. She was a well-published novelist in 1941 (though only twenty-eight) and better known. Pamela was married to another man, had a son, and lived in the country to avoid the bombing.

Anyway, they had lunch at Stewart's. 'I thought how clever he was – and how shabby,' Pamela told me. She and Charles discussed *Le rouge et le noir* at that first meeting. She didn't like it; he did. They could meet only sporadically throughout the war. She then lived in Staines, in Middlesex; he commuted between Cambridge and London.

His civil-service job at the time was to recruit for the Ministry of Labour people who could be taught how to use radar, which was new then; a scientific background was what he was looking for. Later he was asked by the government to find out, any way he could, how much progress the Germans were making on an atomic bomb. He was required to send men, mostly Norwegian scientists who had escaped the Nazis and immigrated to London, back into their native country and scout out and report on the Germans' heavy-water factory there. Many of them did not return. He had been picked to run this British nuclear intelligence unit largely because he was one of the first Englishman to predict the eventual building of the atomic bomb – he had done it in the September 1939 issue of *Discovery*, to be exact. The agents he recruited were usually taken by submarine up the northern coast of Norway and dropped there. Snow's job was to evaluate the information they sent or brought back. It became clear by the end of 1942 or early 1943, he told me, that the Germans were nowhere near to producing an atomic bomb – primarily because they had expelled or executed so many of their scientists, many of them Jews. In any case, most spying is done by gentlemen wearing spectacles sitting down at a desk, Snow was fond of saying.

After Pamela divorced her first husband, she and Charles Snow were married in July 1950, nine years after they met for that lunch in Piccadilly. As a matter of fact, they were married twice: first in a civil ceremony at the Registry Office in Paddington, then in a Church of England ceremony at Charles' Cambridge college, Christ's, in the chapel there.

They lived first in Hyde Park Crescent, then in a house in Clare, in Suffolk, after that at 199 Cromwell Road in South Kensington, and lastly in Eaton Terrace, Mayfair. Here Snow died at seventy-four as the result of bleeding from a perforated ulcer. During their thirty years of marriage, Pamela continued to write novels. *The Last Resort*, *The Unspeakable Skipton*, *An Impossible Marriage*, and *The Humbler Creation* are among her best-known titles. Charles finished the *Strangers and Brothers* series and kept on writing, both fiction and non-fiction. In case there is any question – there shouldn't be – 'he is Lewis Eliot, there's no doubt about that', Pamela told me in 1980, referring to the chief protagonist of the *Strangers and Brothers* saga.

What was it like for two working novelists to live in the same house? Did they read each other's work? Did they edit each other? How well did it go?

The obvious conclusion is that it went very well. Both continued to be productive and each helped the other on many occasions. They did read each other's new work as it was being produced, usually in blocks of between 15,000 and 30,000 words. And they were brutally honest with one another. 'Once upon a time we both used to take it rather badly and sulk a little bit', Pamela told me, 'but that soon wore out, and we took each other's advice, and on the whole it was good advice.' She gave Snow the title for *The Affair*, suggesting that the novel deliberately invoke the memory of the Dreyfus case. She also named, superbly, *The Conscience of the Rich*. He gave her the titles for *The Last Resort* and *An Impossible Marriage*. They often worked in the same room at different desks. It was the rule, Pamela told me, 'to be very quiet, and we don't interrupt each other in the middle of the work.' They wrote in longhand

and always in the morning. 'And we don't work in the evening,' Pamela said. 'We've always agreed not to, because we thought we'd have no marriage if we did that.' They didn't go out much in the evening. During the eleven years they lived in South Kensington they never got to know any of their neighbors. The only neighbors they saw in Eaton Terrace were those who brought books in to be signed — especially Snow's last novel *A Coat of Varnish* (1979), a bestselling whodunit set in his Mayfair neighborhood. As I was talking to Pamela there one afternoon, Charles was in another room editing her current (and last) novel, *A Bonfire* (1981), published just a few months before she died. She told me he was probably taking out all the adjectives.

Pamela's first husband was very nearly the Welsh poet Dylan Thomas. He proposed to her when he was nineteen and she was twenty-one, in 1933. 'It was plain that we should marry,' Pamela told me. They were together for three years. They had actually put up the banns in the Chelsea Registry Office, but then had second thoughts. Dylan Thomas, according to Pamela Hansford Johnson, was a man who tended to keep his friends separate from one another, almost never introducing them to each other. 'He kept me in a separate compartment', Pamela said, 'and I got rather tired of that. And then he started to live the wildly bohemian life in Chelsea, which I didn't fall in with, and so we drifted — very painfully.' She told me that he began by pretending to drink too much to impress his friends and later wound up acting out the role he was playing. 'He was a very alluring young man, and he had this beautiful voice, and wonderful eyes,' Pamela said. 'And he was wonderfully verbal... I think everybody who met him at that time fell for him.' As she said, they drifted apart. She encountered him only once after the war, 'and then I didn't recognise him, he'd got so fat.' She didn't see him again before his death in 1953.

Men were attracted to her. When she was eighteen it was Leopold Stokowski, who was then in his late forties. That happened during the summer of 1930.

Pamela was not impressed by contemporary British novelists other than Charles Snow. 'I think it's rather a dim period,' she said in 1980. She was even less impressed by F. R. Leavis, who in *The Significance of C. P. Snow* attacked Charles for his famous essay on 'The

Two Cultures', a plea that scientists and humanists try harder to understand each other's disciplines. As a physicist who wrote novels, Snow was one of the few men of his day who knew both science and literature. Pamela's view of Leavis was unequivocal. His critical perspective, she said, was 'against everything I feel, and I don't like the ideas behind it'. She especially objected to Leavis' canonical declarations – 'singling out a certain amount of literature that is to be accepted, and a certain amount that is not accepted'. And of course (as Pamela did not say) Leavis was always changing his mind about what should be in and what should be out (Dickens' novels, for example). Snow was upset by Leavis' onslaught but decided not to reply immediately, and didn't for many years. 'It was an attack by a man who should have known better,' Pamela said.

I liked her immensely. She was a tiny woman who sometimes reminded me, in the way she moved, of a panther: she was strong, lithe, resourceful, graceful, and beautiful. She must have been a remarkable woman when Dylan Thomas first saw her. Like her husband, Pamela enjoyed a drink and a cigarette. She was a good listener; her talk was sharp but sometimes sparse after the stroke she suffered some years before I met her. She was a warm, loving person with whom one felt instantly at home – though she was also a woman I felt I wouldn't have wanted to cross. A few things Charles said to me in confidence made it clear that he wished to avoid her displeasure, though in ordinary social intercourse she always took the supporting role. It was clear to me that she loved her husband passionately and perhaps possessively. She wanted him to be first and made sure that he was and that he perceived it to be so.

C. P. Snow was from Leicester, the setting of the early *Strangers and Brothers* novels. He was the son of a leather-cutter in a shoe factory there. By dint of scholarships, he got himself to Christ's College, Cambridge, where he became a physicist. Though he published a number of other books, his reputation today rests on the eleven *Strangers and Brothers* novels. For the record these are: *George Passant* (originally *Strangers and Brothers*), *Time of Hope*, *The Conscience of the Rich*, *The Light and the Dark*, *The Masters*, *The New Men* (required reading for all freshmen at Bowdoin College in 1959 – I was one of them), *Homecomings*, *The Affair*, *Corridors of Power*, *The Sleep of Reason*, and *Last Things*.

The Masters and *The Affair* were successfully dramatized on the London stage in the sixties. Taken together, these novels cover more than fifty years of British history. Their relevance lies not only in the chronicle they give of a distinguished man's life at the center of academic and political power (for Lewis Eliot *is* C. P. Snow, as we know), but also in the cultural and intellectual history they provide of a large chunk of the twentieth century in Britain. Many of the problems, issues, and quandaries Lewis Eliot faces are those of the sentient modern man.

A superb novel of 1934, *The Search* (revised and reprinted in 1958), shows Snow deciding to devote his primary energies to literature instead of science. He could have been a good scientist, he told me, perhaps a very good one, but never a great one. After completing the *Strangers and Brothers*, he produced two novels in the seventies in addition to *A Coat of Varnish* – *The Malcontents* and *In Their Wisdom*, both first-rate political novels, one of the left and the other of the right. The present obscurity of these later novels seems to me undeserved. There were also an early and rather unsophisticated whodunit, *Death under Sail*, his first book, and three volumes of non-fiction in addition to *Trollope* – *Variety of Men*, largely about some of the better-known scientists and mathematicians he had known; *Science and Government*; and *The Realists*, which reveals his literary debt to the great French and Russian novelists. Russia was one of his passions; his novels were popular there, and he always seemed to me to have an unduly rosy view of the Soviet Union. I am skeptical, however, of Leavis' charge that Snow was a fellow-traveler of the Communist Party.

Finally, let me try to give the reader some personal impressions of C. P. Snow. I saw him as a man reserved yet friendly, cagey (one of his favorite words) yet often candid, loving a good joke but essentially serious and, in his last years, unmistakably pessimistic. What no words can convey is the physical presence of the man and the eccentricities and idiosyncrasies that made up his personality. We have heard Pamela Hansford Johnson say that when she first met her ambitious future husband in the summer of 1941, she thought: 'How clever he is – and how shabby.' The shabbiness was still quite spectacular in the 1970s, famous though he was by that time. No matter what he wore, C. P. Snow looked as if he'd been left for dead by a bunch of thugs or trampled in Filene's basement. His clothes were good, but put on carelessly. Often he wore dingy yellow thermal underwear that stuck out everywhere; he was wearing it in the House of Lords on the day he took me into the Members' Bar there. Perched on the crown of his hairless head – he had been bald since his thirties – there was usually a shapeless hat. Had he worn a sign saying 'will work for food' no one would have been surprised. At the clubs we met in they knew who he was (they always know in those places) but in restaurants I would see the *maître d'* watch him and remove from his proximity anything shiny and portable. His external appearance was obviously unimportant to Snow and always had been. He knew who he was. When occasion demanded decent dress Pamela made him put it on. In his last years he grew almost entirely impervious to the ordinary accoutrements of life and as a result spent a good deal of his time looking for things he had misplaced. During our interviews he smoked cigarettes incessantly and was continually astonished to hear that I did not have any matches with me; several of our sessions – most notably one in the House of Lords interview room – were devoted in part to searching for matches. I learned to carry some to every meeting.

C. P. Snow was a large man, both tall and wide, yet abstemious when it came to food, in which he seemed to have little interest. He was so bored by what he ate, Pamela told me, that she once considered serving his chicken raw to see if he would notice. He liked to drink and to smoke. In his smooth Oxbridge voice there was no trace of any Midlands accent. Like Lewis Eliot he had come from nowhere, and he worked hard – a long-distance runner afraid to pause long enough for his past to catch up with him. He made money after World War II in Britain's fledgeling electronics industry, and in later years from book royalties, but you'd never know by looking at him that he had a penny. In several of our conversations Snow used the analogy of a prize-fighter (he got it from his son Philip, he told me) to characterize Lewis Eliot's ambition. The hungry fighter, he said, is more likely than the well-fed fighter to be successful: he has more reason to fight. The Lewis Eliot of the *Strangers and Brothers* novels is a hungry man in this sense, and so was the son of the Leicester shoe-factory leather-cutter.

Beneath his apparently placid exterior he was a worrier, a fretter. There was an enormous amount of sheer nervous energy in the man. He drummed his fingers and stamped his feet. His insecurities were accelerated by the cardiac arrest he suffered during a second operation he underwent to repair a detached retina, recounted in *Last Things*. What isn't in the novel is Snow's pride and amusement at having crossed, if only briefly, a barrier few of us find ourselves in a position to describe after the fact. He was always delighted to be asked what it was like to be 'dead', if only for half a minute. 'Do you know what happens in the afterlife?' he once said to Pamela. She told me that he proceeded to answer his own question – triumphantly, since she was a believer and he was not. 'Nothing happens. I've *been* there.'

He's there now, and so is she. Unlike the Thomas Hardys, they lived and died together. I doubt that they're still passing their manuscripts back and forth and excising adjectives, but I'd bet he's still badly dressed.

9

Hong Kong Time

George Howe Colt

Hanging above my desk is a copy of an engraving by William Hogarth, printed in 1736, titled 'The Distressed Poet'. In a dreary, one-room Grub Street garret, a vain-looking fellow wearing slippers, a dressing gown, and a fretful air scratches his bewigged head as he confronts a sheet of paper on the table in front of him. The distressed poet's wife sits nearby, darning his trousers. Other chores await her: clothes drying on a line before the fire; a mop and bucket of suds on the floor; a baby squalling in the corner; the indignant milkmaid, come to collect, waving a bill in the doorway. The firewood has run out and the cupboard is bare, but in this hovel the division of labor is clear: the woman must maintain what passes for hearth and home, while the man of the house awaits the arrival of the muse, who, thus far, has visited only long enough to supply him with the first stanza of a poem called 'Poverty'.

'The Distressed Poet', Hogarth's satirical take on the proliferation of would-be writers in the London of his era, and the penury to which they doomed their families, was given to me by a writer-friend with whom I shared an apartment in New York City during my bachelor days. At the time – financially, if not emotionally – we were distressed poets ourselves, but we were not averse to lampooning our lot. Whenever the phone rang, my roommate would throw a hand to his forehead in mock exasperation and cry, 'Oh, why won't they let us get on with our work?'

I chuckle when I look at the Hogarth print now, but I'm embarrassed to admit that as a teenager, dreaming of becoming a great poet, I had just such a marital arrangement in mind (albeit without the poverty). Having read one too many biographies of poets and not enough poetry itself, I nourished a number of romantic notions about the writer's life, among them the assumption that genius required a support staff. I therefore imagined that – if I were bourgeois enough to marry at all – I would marry someone like the Distressed Poet's wife, a sedulous helpmeet who would sweep the floor, mind the children, and sharpen my pencils while I flirted with the muse. (At sixteen, I believed in the muse the way children believe in the Tooth Fairy.) My wife would also have a career of her own – I knew poetry couldn't support a family – but one that left her enough time to tend the altar of my tortured genius. She would play Mary Hutchinson to my William Wordsworth, Catherine Hogarth to my Charles Dickens, Alice B. Toklas to my Gertrude Stein. I had read what Celeste Albaret had done for Marcel Proust: changed his hot water bottles, prepared his extra-strong coffee, warmed his bed linen, placed his telephone calls, given him footbaths. That was the kind of wife for me. The fact that Celeste Albaret was not Proust's wife but his maid was a technicality I preferred to ignore.

Implicit in my sexist little fantasy was the assumption that I could never marry another writer. My reading made it clear that such a union could end only in alcoholism and madness (the Fitzgeralds), black eyes and hurled martini glasses (McCarthy and Wilson), or separation and suicide (Hughes and Plath). After all, if the Distressed Poet's Wife was a Distressed Poet herself, who would soothe the squalling babies? Who would hang the wash? Who would pay the milkmaid?

*

As the years passed, this distressed poet became a fairly happy journalist, in part because I learned that I didn't really want to be quite so distressed as being a poet seemed to require. In the process, my romantic notions about genius fell by the wayside. After all, one couldn't afford to wait long for the muse with a deadline looming. And I found myself drawn not to those who were content to hang the wash while I wrote, but to those who loved to wrestle words into sentences as much as I did. But I never considered marrying another writer until I met Anne.

Many years ago, during that ticklish early stage of our courtship when each of us was interested in the other but not sure the other felt the same way, I was emboldened to ask Anne out to dinner. She had recently returned from Alaska, where she had researched a magazine article about musk oxen. She frowned. She couldn't see me that night, she said. She had to work. How about the next night? No, she'd be working then, too. The next? No. The next? Sorry, no. I suspected that Anne liked me, so I couldn't fathom her reluctance. When could I see her? In ten days.

Sensing my incredulity – and, perhaps, my bruised ego – Anne explained that she was about to go on Hong Kong Time. Whenever she wrote, she said, she made her environment as interruption-free as possible by working all night and sleeping all day. She saw no friends, made no phone calls, wrote no letters, made no appointments. She ventured outside her apartment only in the most dire emergency (defined, I later learned, as the need to replenish her supply of Häagen-Dazs chocolate ice cream). Depending on the story, her hibernation could last a few days or a few weeks.

Jealous that our budding romance could play second fiddle to a herd of hairy, arctic ungulates, I pled for an earlier audience. 'You have to eat,' I pointed out. 'We could try that sushi place around the corner from your apartment.' Anne looked dubious. 'Or I could bring you Chinese takeout.' She remained doubtful. 'I promise not to stay more than an hour.' She still wasn't convinced. 'If you're worried about breaking your concentration, we don't even have to talk, we'll just chew quietly.'

It was a measure of Anne's devotion to her craft – and of her endearing gullibility – that she thought I was serious. 'Oh', she said, after a moment's reflection, 'I think it would be okay to talk. But only for one hour.' It would be, she confessed, the first time she'd ever let someone other than a roommate into her apartment while she was in her 'writing phase' – a locution that made it sound as if I would be privy to a metamorphosis no less shocking than that of Dr Jekyll into Mr Hyde.

On the momentous evening, however, Anne seemed very much her witty and delightful self as we discussed the defense strategies of musk oxen over wonton soup and roast duck chow fun. Every so often, she cast longing glances in the direction of her bedroom, a development I considered propitious until, an hour after I'd arrived, she ushered me out the front door with a quick kiss. (She explained later that her office was at one end of the bedroom, and that as much as she liked me, she felt she'd better be getting back to her musk oxen.) Nevertheless, the slope would prove slippery. A year later, we moved in together. A year after that, we were married. We recently celebrated our fifteenth anniversary.

*

How can two writers live under the same roof? It is always non-writers who ask; most writers I know are married to other writers. After all, points out Norman Mailer, 'Writers tend to live with writers just as automotive engineers tend to congregate in the same country clubs of the same suburbs around Detroit.' The question is usually asked in a tone that suggests the combination must be as potentially lethal as a pair of Siamese fighting fish sharing an aquarium. The issue has to do not with the boredom that might potentially arise from having identical jobs – after all, one never hears it asked of two accountants or two lawyers or two encyclopedia salesmen – but with the demands of the 'artistic temperament'. People assume that one writer must suck up 90 percent of the creative oxygen in the available air. If there are two writers in the same house, they'll suck up 180 percent – and both will suffocate. The one-writer-per-household myth seems so ingrained that I have come to imagine that one day, inevitably, our house will play host to a High Noon showdown: Anne and I will appear from offices at either end of the hallway, silhouetted in the glow of 200-watt halogen reading lamps. Manuscript pages will swirl around us in the coffee-scented air, the silence broken only by the hum of a distant fax machine. 'This house ain't big enough for the two of us,' one of us growls. 'Isn't', says the other. We reach for our pens. A moment later, when the ink has cleared, one of us is condemned to become a dentist.

In fact, the marriage of two writers is not necessarily any more or less exciting than that of two dentists – as long as the couple is sharing the same time zone. The early years of our married life were perfectly normal, at least until a story came due and Anne went into her writing phase. I learned to recognize the warning signs. Her calendar, usually a palimpsest of editorial meetings, doctors' appointments, and lunches with friends, was suddenly as white as snow, Anne having cleared the decks of all engagements. The refrigerator brimmed with food of a culinary level more rarefied than that of the generic brands with which I usually supplied it. Anne, who used to teach backpacking in Wyoming, stocked up for a writing phase as if she were preparing for a month in the Tetons, but instead of gorp, beef jerky, and freeze-dried stew, she laid in bags of tortellini from the Italian specialty store across the street, cans of Medaglia D'Oro espresso from the Korean grocery, and wedges of Roquefort and Coulommiers from Dean and DeLuca. Her sandbox-sized office was transformed into a shrine whose object of veneration changed every few weeks: shelves crammed with color-coded, cross-referenced, looseleaf notebooks into which she had typed every last shred of research: key quotations from her interviews pinned above her desk; snapshots of story subjects Scotch-taped to every available surface, as magazine photos of pop stars line a teenager's bedroom walls. Anne herself wandered about the apartment in a vague, slightly off-kilter state – staring out the window, rearranging the silverware drawer, rereading old *New Yorkers*, and bracing herself with doses of John McPhee from a folder marked 'Inspirational Writing' – a ritual bit of precompositional thought-settling she compared to a dog circling three times before he lies down. And then one night, like a flight attendant briefing her passengers before takeoff, Anne would announce that she was going on Hong Kong Time.

Hong Kong Time was not achieved overnight. There were intervening time zones to be crossed en route. Anne worked later each night and slept later each day until, about a week in, she was on full Hong Kong Time. I remained on New York Time. Given that Anne's office was no more than twenty pencil-lengths from our bed, living in two different time zones required some adjustment. At 11 p.m., Anne would fill her bucket-sized blue mug with coffee, kiss me goodnight, tiptoe to the other end of the bedroom, and start work. I'd fall asleep to the clickety-clack of her fingers on the keyboard and the dim glow of the computer screen. When I woke, the glow of the computer had dissolved in the dawn light, but the clickety-clack persisted at an even faster pace. After breakfast à deux, I'd kiss Anne goodnight and go to work in my office off the living room. Eight hours later, as the sun went down, Anne woke up, just in time for dinner.

Like the method actor who stays in character offstage, Anne went to great lengths to remain in the world of her story. Other than for meals, she emerged from her office cocoon only to make coffee or import a hunk of Roquefort to her desk. In the morning I'd find, on the kitchen counter, evidence of her wee-hours foraging – a nibbled crust of French bread, a half-empty glass of Martinelli's sparkling cider. Her writing attire never varied: a white terry-cloth bathrobe and a pair of fuzzy brown sheepskin slippers with holes in the toes. I felt as if I were living in a Grimm fairy tale with a beautiful princess who had fallen under a particularly quixotic spell. But just when I began thinking that our ships-in-the-night routine couldn't last much longer, Anne would stumble out of the bedroom, as bleary-eyed as Ray Milland in *The Lost Weekend*, brandishing her finished story. After showering, taxiing uptown, and handing it to her editor, she'd taxi home, climb into bed, and sleep for sixteen hours. Her once-immaculate office had the interrupted look of a crime scene: books splayed face down on every available surface; coffee cups visible here and there in a midden of notebooks and manila folders; a plate encrusted with bolognese sauce atop the printer; piles of paper on the floor so deep they spilled out the door like a drift of snow.

Although Anne made the graveyard shift sound attractive – no phones, no visitors, no desire to do anything but stay glued serenely to her chair – I was never tempted to join her. I am a morning person. I often listen to Bach or the Beatles while I write, and have done some of my best work on the subway. (Perhaps my high tolerance for distraction is genetic. My grandfather wrote a 344-page novel in five months while in traction in a Veterans' Administration hospital, to the accompaniment of sirens blaring, patients screaming, and a round-the-clock parade of nurses feeding him, injecting him, and taking his temperature.) But I knew that other writers had gone to far greater lengths than Anne to limit distractions. Proust, another devotee of Hong Kong Time, had his bedroom lined with cork, his shutters closed, his double-paned windows permanently shut, and his thick blue drapes hermetically sealed. 'He needed that silence to hear only the voices he wanted to hear, the voices that are in his books,' said the long-suffering Celeste Albaret, who kept Hong Kong Time with her beloved master, albeit on the far side of his bedroom door. Thomas Carlyle, to whom the least creak on the stairwell had the effect of a dentist's drill, built a soundproof study with cotton-stuffed window boards on the roof of his London flat; made his wife pay the neighbors to get rid of their rooster (the very thought of which kept him awake nights); and told the servants that whenever a street organ was heard in the vicinity, they must rush outside and hurry it along, lest it disturb the great man's work. Anne once had a colleague who, in search of privacy, retreated to his bathtub, where, in waist-deep hot water, perhaps simulating the soothing conditions of the womb, he wrote on a desk fashioned from an ironing board. In comparison, Anne's *modus scribendi* seemed tolerable enough: she let me open our windows in summer, didn't insist I chase off the neighborhood ice-cream truck, and never hogged our one and only bathroom. She didn't even complain about my snoring.

*

And then our daughter was born. Children create their own time zone, we soon learned — and they couldn't care less about the vagaries of the muse. Anne resumed writing when Susannah was eight months old, but found that every weekend, when she returned to New York Time cold turkey so the family could spend uninterrupted days together, she suffered horrible jet lag. She had a glimmer of hope when she read an article about Neil and Susan Sheehan, writers who had two children yet managed to work all night and sleep all day. (Both Sheehans, I pointed out, were nocturnal animals — and their arrangement must have required massive infusions of childcare.) About the same time, Anne signed a contract to write her first book; the thought of staying on Hong Kong Time for several years gave her pause. Reluctantly, fearfully, she agreed to stay fulltime with us on the day shift.

Motherhood proved to be the mother of invention, not only weaning Anne from her nocturnal schedule but leading her to new literary genres. When three problem pregnancies (two of which ended in miscarriage) forced her to spend months in bed, depriving her of her office nest and her shelves of research, Anne, armed with only a laptop computer, began writing essays. After she returned to her desk, her shrine took on a more domestic look. Photos of story subjects now fought for space among photos of her children; inspirational quotations were squeezed between Susannah's drawings of angels and, a few years later, Henry's crayoned baby rattlesnakes. Although Anne and I made a deal that, in extremis she could revert to her owlish ways for occasional periods of three or four days, she invoked this privilege less and less as the years went by.

*

Anne and I no longer live in an apartment in Manhattan, but in an old farmhouse backed up against a forest in western Massachusetts. We write during the day, mostly oblivious to the Muzak of our children playing, our dachshund barking, and our neighbor's rooster crowing. People imagine a two-writer household to be a small-scale Algonquin round table, sparkling with bon mots and witty repartee, but Anne and I don't see each other much during the day, except at lunch, and even then, we tend to read the paper and grunt a lot. Novelists and poets, I imagine, have it harder. At least journalism gets us out of the house. Periodically, one of us flies off to report a story, returning with notebooks full of new characters and ideas to recharge our otherwise hermetic lives. It is like bringing home an endless series of interesting, albeit invisible, dinner guests who sometimes seem so tangible we might as well set an extra place at the table. Over the years we've hosted Barbra Streisand, Ted Kennedy, Andrew Wyeth, an Inuit activist, and a specialist in monster makeup, not to mention a flock of sandhill cranes, a colony of alligators, and a school of Day-Glo orange nudibranches. No matter how fascinating, however, a dinner guest who stays for several years risks overstaying his, her, or its welcome. And so, for emotional as well as financial reasons, Anne and I have an unwritten rule that only one person in the house can be writing a book at any given time.

Not long ago, Anne met a newspaper columnist who insisted he could never marry another writer because he'd be too scared to show her his work. Anne and I take full advantage of having two writers in the house. We act as each other's clipping service, leaving the New York Times covered with graffitii (AF: FYI. XXOO, GHC). We serve as sounding boards: Listening to Anne talk at lunch, I'll realize that she's trying out a verbal rough draft of her latest essay; knowing that I like to read aloud newly-finished chapters in bed at night, Anne listens attentively long past our bedtime. And whenever one of us is up against a particularly obdurate deadline, the other puts his or her own work on hold and becomes The Distressed Poet's Wife: watching the children, doing the dishes, walking the dog, answering the doorbell, xeroxing, delivering manuscripts to Federal Express, fending off impatient editors.

Each of us also acts as the other's in-house editor, our services varying according to our writing methods. I pour everything into the computer in a language vaguely resembling English, then grope my way toward the heart of the story over ten or twelve drafts. Anne, who never composes the second sentence of an essay until she's got the first just right, needs two drafts at most. When I edit Anne, I find the trees so perfect that I need look only at the forest. I may suggest moving a paragraph or trying a different lead. When Anne edits me, she takes a chainsaw to my wildly overgrown trees, pruning my repetitions, trimming the adjectives and similes until my purple patches have turned handsome shades of red or blue, regrafting my danglers and split infinitives before they can sneak beyond the privacy of our home. (Anne is a gentle arborist. Whenever she cuts a line of which she knows I am particularly fond, she is sure to praise it before she lops it off.) The only writing we don't show each other before publication is our book acknowledgments. (This can backfire. When I presented her with a copy of my first book, Anne thanked me for what I'd said about her, but gently noted that I'd made a grammatical error.)

In our two-person writer's colony, I get much the better of the deal. Anne is a Strunk-and-White-worshipping, one-woman reference library who speaks in syntactically perfect sentences ('syntactically perfect *paragraphs*', says her brother), a perfectionist who holds everything she writes to her high literary standards, be it a letter of recommendation for a student, a book inscription, a bread-and-butter note, or a tag sale poster. (Indeed, Anne's finest work will never be published, having been read only by the housesitters for whom she composed a fourteen-page single-spaced list of instructions.) Just as I keep her love letters, I save story drafts that Anne has edited, so clever and affectionate are her haiku-like annotations. Having grown up in a family of writers, all of whom knew the difference between 'that' and 'which', Anne is congenitally unable to let an error pass. Delivering coffee to my office, she'll glance over my shoulder, steal my pencil, and change a colon to a semi-colon. (My grasp of grammar is less firm, perhaps because I spent my formative years writing poetry; if I misused a word or misplaced a comma, I could always insist I had done it intentionally.) Anne's perfectionism has other benefits: her office is a kind of in-house Staples franchise, stocked with paper, rubber bands, paper clips, Post-Its, White-Out, a calculator, a postal scale, a hole puncher, mailing tubes, boxes of the Pilot Precise Rolling Ball pens she prefers for editing, envelopes of every conceivable size, a tape measure, and even a level (perhaps to gauge if my prose is too flat). Indeed, when she's not in her writing phase, Anne's office is such a marvel of organization that sometimes, when she's out of the house, I visit just to wonder at the soothing clarity of her desk drawers, where, unlike mine, you'll never find a rogue thumbtack infiltrating the pushpins, a blue ballpoint bedding down with a Mongol Number 2 pencil.

Everyone wonders whether we compete with each other, and though we feel a healthy pressure to live up to the other's standards, Anne and I rejoice in each other's successes. (We have to, or the bills won't get paid.) There is one exception. Although we have written double-bylined magazine articles without bloodshed, Anne and I both fancy ourselves masters of the occasional poem, and whenever we collaborate on doggerel for friends' birthdays or anniversaries, we tend to be a bit finicky about the other's contributions: tweaking a rhyme here, insisting a line has one too many iambs there. Writing a WASP rap song with Anne and my mother – another master of the genre – in the car en route to a cousin's wedding proved as politely contentious as a United Nations Security Council debate.

*

I no longer believe, as I did during my years as a Distressed Poet, that writing is a sacred pursuit. But I find it comforting and exhilarating to be married to someone who knows both the joy and the difficulty of putting words together on paper. Anne's former boyfriend, my predecessor, was a lawyer, and though Anne feigned interest when he talked about torts and estoppels – and he seemed all ears when she described the thrill of composing a terrific lead – she always felt that neither of them could fully understand an essential part of the other's self. And as fond as I was of the actress-girlfriend who preceded Anne, the same was true for me. Don't get me wrong. There are times – when Anne is telling me the difference between a restrictive and a non-restrictive clause for the umpteenth time, for example – when I wonder whether I might have been better off if I had married the actress. I'm sure that Anne, too, has moments – probably when she's telling me the difference between a restrictive and a non-restrictive clause for the umpteenth time – that she muses about what it might be like to be married to her lawyer friend. And when money is short, each of us has brief flashes of wishing we'd married a venture capitalist. But at three in the morning – side by side at my computer, thesaurus in hand, tracking down the perfect word (something stronger than 'wonder' but not quite so strong as 'stupefaction') for a story due the next day – being married to a writer seems the best of all possible worlds. How could I live with another writer? they ask. How could I not?

*

These days, we have a third writer in the family. Our fourteen-year-old daughter has written hundreds of poems and stories and admits to having gotten sixty pages into a novel. (Fortunately, in matters of grammar Susannah takes after her mother; she recently corrected her English teacher who, pronouncing the plural of 'haiku', had erroneously added an 's'.) When she was younger, Susannah read aloud each new tale to us; an oak chest in the den is filled with stories she wrote and illustrated between the ages of six and eight. These days, Susannah keeps her work to herself, squirreled away in notebooks marked 'Keep Out' or in remote crevices of her hard drive. But we know she's writing. Late at night, long after her bedtime, as Anne and I head upstairs to bed, passing her room, we see a telltale bar of light under her door, and hear the telltale *ssssh* of pencil on paper as Susannah works her way toward Hong Kong Time.

10

Writers as Progenitors and Offspring

John Updike

As both the son and father of a writer, I feel doubly qualified for this topic. My mother wrote in the front bedroom, beside a window curtained in dotted swiss. With a small child's eyes I see her desk, her little Remington with its elite face, and the brown envelopes that carried her patiently tapped-out manuscripts to New York City and then back to Shillington, Pennsylvania. I smell the fresh paper, the damp ink on the ribbon as it jerkily unfurls from spool to spool, the rubber flecks of eraser buried within the slanted bank of springy keys – an alphabet in the wrong order. We used to travel together to Hintz's stationery store in Reading, and there was beauty and power and opulence in the ceiling-high shelves of fresh reams, of tinted labels and yellow octagonal pencils in numbered degrees of hardness and softness, of tablets and moisteners and even little scales to weigh letters upon. Three cents an ounce it took in those days to send a story to a Manhattan magazine, or to the *Saturday Evening Post* in nearby Philadelphia, and what a wealth of expectation hovered in the air until Mr Miller, our plodding, joking mailman, hurled the return envelope through the front-door letter slot! There was a novel, too, that slept in a ream box that had been emptied of blankness, and, like a strange baby in the house, a difficult papery sibling, the manuscript was now and then roused out of its little rectangular crib and rewritten and freshly swaddled in hope.

My mother's silence, at her desk, was among the mysteries – her faith aroma of mental sweat, of concentration as if in prayer. I knew she was trying to reach beyond the street outside, where cars and people moved toward their local destinies as if underwater, toward a world we couldn't see, where magazines and books came from. That these magazines, with their covers by Norman Rockwell and John Falter, and the books of the world, some of them old and faded like pieces of nature and others shiny new and protected in an extra cellophane wrapper at the drugstore rental library, were written by our kind of people seemed unlikely to me; but now and then she got an encouraging pencilled note scrawled on the rejection slip, and in her fifties, I am happy to say, began to receive acceptances – enough to form her single published book, *Enchantment*.* Though there was much about her enterprise I didn't understand, I liked the smell of it, the silence, the modest equipment required, and the sly postal traffic with a world beyond; at an early age I enlisted in the enterprise myself.

My son David – what did he see? I wrote, when he was small, in a little upstairs room that, like my mother's room a generation before, overlooked a small-town street. The room had a door I could close, and he and his siblings used to scratch at the door, and have quarrels outside it. I moved to an office downtown, a half-mile away, and there they could come visit the confusion of papers, the faded Oriental rug, the bulletin board where jotted ideas and urgent requests slowly curled up and turned yellow, the pervasive stink of too many cigarettes and, after I gave those up, of nickel cigarillos. Dirty windows, without curtains of dotted swiss, overlooked the Ipswich River, and the chief wall decoration was a framed drawing that the great James Thurber had been kind enough to send me from Connecticut when I was a boy in Shillington.

I spent mornings and little more in the office. David and his brother and two sisters were pleasantly aware, I assumed, that I had more free time than most fathers. (Though was I, when with them, entirely with them? A writer's working day is a strange diffuse thing that never really ends, and gives him a double focus much of

---

*Augmented, in November of 1989, by the narrowly posthumous publication of another collection, *The Predator* (Ticknor & Fields).

the time.) My children enjoyed, I imagined, the little mild gusts of fame – the visiting photographer and interviewer, the sudden box of new books in the front hall – that my profession brought into our domestic world. And they said little, tactfully, of the odd versions of themselves and their home that appeared now and then in print. They never spoke to me of being writers themselves. So I was taken unawares when all showed distinct artistic bents and the older son, at an age earlier than his father, became published in the *New Yorker*. At the time I gave his Harvard girlfriend, who herself wrote, and Ann Beattie, who had accepted him into her writing course, more credit than any example I had inadvertently set. The writing enterprise seemed to me self-evidently a desperate one, and though my mother and I – both only children – had been desperate enough to undertake it, I thought my children, raised in a gentler, prospering, gregarious world, would seek out less chancy and more orthodox professions. But I underestimated, it would seem, the appeal of the mise-en-scène, the matrix, that had charmed me – the clean paper, the pregnant silences, the typewriter keyboard with its scrambled alphabet. We are drawn toward our parents' occupations, I have concluded, because we can see the equipment and size up the effort; it is like a suit of clothes we try on for size and then discover ourselves to have bought and to be wearing for good.

11

My Grandmother's Only Son

David Updike

My father, in answer to a question I am often asked, is doing fine, thank you: he lives with his wife in a small pleasant town forty minutes north of Boston, in a large white house overlooking the sea. And yes, he's still writing books, and another is coming out soon; I will tell him you said hello, even though he has no idea who 'you' are, or why you want to greet him. His literary career is going strong, continuing on the high trajectory that began, I must sometimes remind myself, sixty years ago, when he was a small boy in a small Pennsylvania farmhouse, surrounded by four grownups: his parents and his mother's parents, moving around him with a deliberate, animal weight, stirring the thick, Pennsylvania air.

The four are gone now, but he had four children of his own, and we, in turn, have produced seven sons and no girls. Although I have heard him say he's not much of a patriarch, he works hard at being a good grandfather – takes them to movies, goes golfing with my son and me, drops in for tea at my sister's house on the way to the dentist. But you do not write a four or five hundred page book every year by being easily distracted, and I think he would agree that his primary focus in life is his writing, his job is seeing words onto the page, and the pages into books – fifty-something so far, and counting.

Diligent students of his work will know that his mother, Linda Grace Hoyer, was also a writer, and that he grew up amidst the pleasant paraphernalia of literary life: 'With a small child's eye I see her desk, her little Remington with its elite face, and the brown envelopes that carried her patiently tapped-out manuscripts to New York City and then back to Shillington, Pennsylvania.' Not all back, however, for, as an echo to my father's accruing successes, in her fifties she began to publish some of her own stories, in *The New Yorker* and elsewhere, and as a boy, I remember encouraging her in her ambition to gather them and publish them in a collection. Why I was such an adamant champion of the project, or why the opinion of a twelve-year-old boy seemed to matter to her, I am not sure, but the resulting book, *Enchantment*, was published in 1971, and with the money it earned her she bought herself and her husband a new car, a rather sporty, yellow Dodge. A second collection of stories, *The Predator*, was published a month or so after she died, in 1989, at the age of eighty-four. The copy that my father sent me at the time is inscribed '11-22-89', the morning that my son was born. I do not know if he knew at the time, of his third grandson's birth, or that the boy would carry his own father's name, Wesley.

His father, Wesley Russell Updike, was born on 22 February 1900, newly minted with the century. He was a math teacher at Shillington High School, and later at the Twin Valley Regional High School, and is portrayed, in mythological form, in my father's novel, *The Centaur*, which won the National Book Award in 1964. I have heard my father describe this as his favorite of his own novels. 'There's a lot of love in that book,' he said once.

My grandfather appears, as well, in fictional form, as George, the idiosyncratic and sometimes exasperating husband of Ada, in my grandmother's short stories: 'Street Saint, house devil' she was known to describe him – beloved and charismatic in school and in town, restless and subtly fractious at home, often stricken, like me, by a need to get out, among the people, acquaintances and strangers alike. There, he found great virtue and cause for admiration among the unlikeliest of sorts, people who, like him, had a half hour to stop and talk and be told how wonderful – 'wunnerful' – they were. He had a gift for admiration and praise, and I think it was this effulgence of positive energy, as flowing towards his only child, my father, combined with his mother's literary ambitions and the boy's own intelligence, that fertilized the fields of his literary production.

The top shelf of the bookcase in my study is filled with my father's books, and a friend of mine, a poet, once encouraged me to get rid of them, or put them somewhere else, on the grounds that their psychological weight was too much, and was probably inhibiting my own attempts to write. She didn't seem to grasp that, even if I took them off the shelf and hid them in the closet, my father would still be here, with me, in this room, every time I sat down to write a line or two. She also, perhaps, did not notice my grandmother's name and her two collections of stories nearby – as much of an inspiration as the twenty plus volumes of my father's books.

Like my grandfather before me, I have become a teacher, not of high school Mathematics but of English at an urban community college, where most of my students are from far and distant lands: Haiti and Russia, Ethiopia and the Dominican Republic, Nigeria and America. And like my grandfather, I derive most of my sense of usefulness to the world from my interactions with my students and whatever help or encouragement I can give them. I stumbled into writing in my early twenties, but it was not something I had planned for, or even had the dimmest aspirations for; and while I once might have been considered an 'emerging' writer, in recent years have felt more like a 'submerging' one, struggling to publish, and having a few painful tussles with editors. At such moments, in need of help and inspiration, it is more helpful to think of my grandmother, and her persistent efforts in her Pennsylvania farmhouse, in the sleepy hours of the afternoon, between the feeding of the cats and the horse and the birds, after the lawn has been mowed and the drone of the tractor rises and falls in the thick summer air, stealing up to her room and the old manual typewriter there, typing out a few lines of a short story, or the novel, oft re-written and never published, about her hero, Ponce de Leon, and her mysterious love affair with Spain. If I am proud of anything, in my modest literary résumé, it is that my grandmother and father and I are probably the only three generational succession to publish stories in The New Yorker.

My grandmother lived until she was eighty-four, and when I was living in New York, in my twenties, rather ill at ease with myself and wondering what I would do with my life, I used to catch the bus and ride for three hours out to Reading, and then the twenty minutes to the farm; my visits there offered a kind of grounding, or, touchstone, as I tried to figure out what was next expected of me. During one of our conversations she surprised me by saying that it was hard for my father, doing what he does.

'Why?' I asked.

She looked surprised back, with the slightly stricken look of a worried mother, and said, 'Well, because he's rowing his own boat. He's doing it all himself, alone.'

The boat, it occurred to me at the time, was moving along nicely, and the rowing didn't seem too arduous, but I kept my thoughts to myself. He still has to row it every day, the implication was, and it was lonely, and the world is full of people – rivals and critics – who might not be unhappy to see the boat slow down, or bump up onto the shoals and start to take on water.

My grandmother, too, was an only child, and so, with my father and son, form a short lineage of only children. My son is proud of his grandfather, and does not seem to tire of asking me how many books he has written, even though, I believe, he knows the answer. I, too, am proud of him, but when I think of his literary successes, I steer away from the big white house where he now lives, and envision instead a small Pennsylvania farmhouse crouching on the verge between a dark and inhospitable wood and, above the house, fields thick with heat and growing corn. Inside, out of the pall of nature, a small boy is lying on the carpet next to shifting cubes of sunlight, busily drawing, writing, creating on pieces of cardboard his parents had secured for him somewhere in town. Around him, the four grownups move with the slow, languorous rhythms of country living, shifting and communicating in signs and words and ancient codes, while nearby, his grandfather's bare, pale shins are gently rocking. But the boy, rendered shy by psoriasis and asthma, is busy on the floor with his pen, conjuring other worlds, waiting for Sunday to be over and for Monday to begin, so he can climb into the car with his father and drive to school, the ribbon of road finding its way between the fields, and show the world what he's been up to.

12

I Am Two Fools – Or Home Alone

Catherine Aird

The only writer with whom I live is me, myself, alone.
It was not always so. In my mother's lifetime she would read the first two or three chapters of my current manuscript, then write down the name of the character she thought was the villain. This paper she placed in a sealed envelope. When the book was finished this envelope would be solemnly opened by us both – and she was never wrong. Fine words, carefully crafted by me to conceal the murderer among a welter of more suspicious characters, buttered no parsnips with her.

By virtue of still living in what has been the family home since 1946 my father's legacy still exists in such *materia medica* as anatomy textbooks – human anatomy remaining much the same as it always has been – and sundry works on toxicology and forensic medicine and so forth, to say nothing of decades of the counterfoils of death certificates written by him. He had attended many inquests and once given evidence at a murder case. Even more memorably he had been involved in a patient's hostage situation. Our breakfast table was thus the place of the raconteur rather than the autocrat. Here's richness for a crime writer....

But now I live on my own.

There are some natural hazards to this. The current expression 'having one's own space' loses its meaning when all the space is yours. Indeed, precautions have to be taken against the house doubling as an ivory tower. As a matter of policy therefore Persons from Porlock are welcomed with open arms at any time. The other side of that coin is that I shall never now know whether the presence of a Mrs Kipling-type Dragon at the Gate would have improved my meagre output.

Another danger is that the same domesticity, which Carol Shields once described as 'the shaggy beast that eats up fifty percent of our lives', can all too easily be tamed into taking up only 25 per cent of that time. (It is just the first layer of dust that really matters; nobody ever notices subsequent accretions.)

There are positive aspects, of course, to being alone in the house. I have long been convinced that a too-efficient filing system militates against useful material surfacing serendipitously. Living by oneself means that piles of paper can be left lying around and happily hunted through from time to time when who knows what thought-provoking material will come unexpectedly to hand.

And there is nobody to say me nay.

Books, too, can overflow from all the rooms and – joy of joys – work that is left lying around in the evening will be just where you left it in the morning.

So I don't mind living alone.

This does not mean, though, that I am not at the same time also the two fools about whom that splendid cleric, John Donne, wrote. I think his verse:

> I am two fools, I know,
> For loving, and for saying so,
> In whining poetry

could apply to many authors.

Actually very few detective novelists write about loving, save the dark side thereof usually associated with motive (jealousy, mostly; revenge sometimes), because this is not the natural territory of the author (and for that matter, the reader) of the traditional whodunit. Indeed, it is said by some that there are those who chose to write detective fiction just because they are too reticent by nature, unwilling, or even incapable of writing about loving. In this context therefore and solely for my own fell purposes I shall change Donne's 'loving' to 'living'. ('Fell purposes' are second nature to crime writers.)

It is the 'saying so' (and not only in 'whining poetry') that sets the writer apart, even within himself – even perhaps especially within himself. John Donne knew that his two fools were separate and different animals – the lover and the writer.

So did Shakespeare, of course, in what I believe is his only description of his own mind. In *Love's Labour's Lost* Holofernes says:

> 'This is a gift that I have, simple, simple; a foolish extravagant spirit, full of forms, figures, shapes, objects, ideas, apprehensions, motions, revolutions: these are begot in the ventricle of memory, nourished in the womb of *pia mater*, and delivered upon the mellowing of occasion.'
>
> [IV:ii]

Alas, it was brought home to me quite early on in my own career that I would never scale even the lowest of the foothills of a literary Mount Parnassus. It was a pellucid moment of truth that happened some two years before my first book was published. I was – albeit a very young – Chairman of the local Burial Board, which administered a cemetery.

For quite legitimate historic reasons four graves were to be opened and the coffins disinterred for removal to a cemetery elsewhere in the country. Having duly completed the paperwork and appended my signature to the documents, I thought long and hard whether the First and Second Gravediggers would think it embarrassing – or, worse still, unseemly – to have an unknown girl watching an exhumation.

While I knew then that I was a writer of detective fiction, they didn't. I didn't attend and I have regretted not doing so ever since. I know now that a real writer would have risked the men's disapprobation and gone but those were more circumscribed times for young women. To this day my knowledge of the process is limited to Dorothy L. Sayers' descriptions in *Whose Body?* and *The Unpleasantness at the Bellona Club* (and she hadn't witnessed an exhumation either).

I like to think of Donne's dichotomy between the person and the writer as something halfway between a benign bi-polar disorder and the Separation of Powers. Those of us who lack 'the splinter of ice in the heart' can align themselves instead with John van Druten's camera, and be rather like those people who have had a near-death experience. They often recall a sensation of floating somewhat above the grisly scene, watching both their own bodies and the reactions of those involved in the death-bed scenario as from a little distance.

This 'writer's distance' is, I think, a necessary accompaniment to the writer's life and important part of his way of working. By this I mean that way of working that is the compulsive observation of the human condition and the equally compulsive 'saying so' of John Donne. The 'play within the play' has nothing on a writer watching – and marking well – his or her own behaviour in any unusual situation. Happily, it has never – so far, anyway – led to my enlivening a mundane one the better to write about it – but you never know!

Real life – and an intimate knowledge of the same English village for over half a century – has provided all that this crime writer has had in the way of material supplementary to the imagination. (Like rough local wine, I don't travel well.) Hamesucken, abduction and debasing the coinage haven't cropped up here yet but most other sins and crimes have. I have, though, never consciously written about anyone in the community within which I live – another sign, perhaps, that I lack that vital 'splinter of ice' or have let prudence get in the way. (The one exception that proves this rule was an incident so hilarious that it had to be recorded but long after all those concerned were dead.)

The other side of the coin is that I have little idea of how I am perceived by those self-same neighbours. I think that the best comparison is with the tale of the blind men and the elephant. Each man felt a different part of the animal and thus each truthfully described a different creature. I suspect that I am variously thought of – if at all – as the village doctor's daughter, an editor and publisher of local history, a one-time golfer, sometime Chairman of the Parish Council, long-time editor of the parish magazine and so forth but seldom as a writer. If so, this is never mentioned by me and rarely in my hearing. Similarly, I have never consciously included myself in my writings – but, since I am presently working on a murder on a golf course, this may not obtain for long.

By the way, I do not mean that mythological 'way of working' as it is fondly imagined to be by those who do not themselves write: – that the author works steadily every day from nine to five with a break for a light lunch followed by a brisk walk to clear the mind and harvest inspiration for the morrow, and spends the evening revising what has been written in the morning. In my own case none of this is true (especially the light lunch and the brisk walk).

Nearer to the truth could be the heretical statement that I usually write when there isn't anything more interesting or pressing to do (never yet, anyway, having succeeded in being able to sort out the important from the urgent). Even this is not precise enough to cover the working practices of so many – of whom I am one – who cannot settle to pen and paper (or its mechanical equivalent) until every last trivial duty has been performed – what I believe the psychologists call displacement activities.

This is in spite of the fact that I am well aware that it is better to perform undemanding tasks after writing rather than before. This knowledge has not, alas, affected how I actually behave, although I remain convinced that the imagination works better after leaving the desk rather than before coming to it. In any case the brain seems to carry on working better when the hands are engaged in undemanding but necessary work. It cannot be an accident that Archimedes is not the only one to whom inspiration came in the bath.

A similar misconception about a writer's way of working is that real-life dialogue makes for good fiction. I can only say that in such highly-charged dramatic encounters as have been my sad lot in real life, the words spoken by both myself and others have been unbelievably trite – and stilted, to boot. In fiction, the actual has to be discarded in favour of the plausible: that is, what the reader imagines would have been said in the circumstances and it's not the same as what was.

I believe that almost all forms of creativity are cyclical and I have learned to take the long view and accept with equanimity that there will be dog days – and to ride the cycle so to speak on the others. Stuck to my computer are two extracts from the diary of Franz Kafka that I find particularly cheering. That for 1 June 1912 reads: 'Wrote nothing' and that for 2 June 1912: 'Wrote almost nothing'. Equally reassuring is something a composer once wrote about his work: that on Mondays, Wednesdays and Fridays he felt he had done rather badly, and on Tuesdays, Thursdays and Saturdays he felt he hadn't done too badly at all.

I have found, too, that in my own (probably rather feeble) case there is only room for so much creativity at a time and what there is needs to be strictly 'channelled'. (The only winter in which I did not write a book was one devoted to and very satisfied by the working of an intricate tapestry of a coat of arms. I have never taken up the needle again.)

This is something I have to explain to those *faux amis* who suggest flower-arranging, *haute cuisine*, painting, embroidery, jigsaws, and so forth as agreeable ways of passing time suitable to one of my age and station.

What I really enjoy, though, is research and the more arcane the better. I once had a very happy morning visiting all the men's outfitters I could find to ask them whether it was possible to calculate the height of a man from his inside trouser leg measurement. In the way of crime-writing, I had the skeleton in one place and the trousers in another and wished to marry them: this before the days of DNA. Five polite but bemused shop assistants said you couldn't and the sixth gave me the answer I wanted. (Nobody seems to have made the point so far but the advent of DNA, though a boon to jurisprudence, could be unhelpful to we puzzle-setters: on the other hand the removal of the death penalty was thought to herald the end of detective fiction and it didn't.)

I have, though, to discipline myself against over-indulgence in pursuit of any enquiry. Whoever it was who advised authors to 'Write now, research later' couldn't have spoken more truly. Writing is difficult, research is easy and postpones the actual moment of Guy de Maupassant's 'the getting of black on white'.

In my case, a book once begun takes me about nine months to write and this is by no means the only thing it has in common with other, better known, forms of gestation. I also experience a 'quickening' about half way through when the book, like the baby, seems to kick itself alive. In the only instance so far where this did not happen, I finished the book and threw it to the back of the attic. This was twenty years ago and I have not seen it since.

Having reached a certain age I now find it prudent to note down that which I need to remember. This saves much time trying to recall it: then I only have to find the note.

I would like to think — or would I? — that living alone leads to a greater understanding of oneself, but on the whole I suspect not. It does, though, clarify the responsibilities of daily living. They are all yours.

But writing about oneself is heady stuff and carries its own dangers, narcissism being one. Another is the lurking fear of hearing the distant echo of one's friends and family saying 'Her trumpeter's dead, you know'.

Let us be gone before that happens.

13

Margaret

Brian W. Aldiss

I always wrote. I have always written. I wrote irrespective of conditions. I write now. I write on a variety of subjects. Volume 47 of a holograph and illustrated journal is now being compiled in a hard-bound A5 notebook. I also keep a 'Log', which is stored on the computer and in print-out form. The 'Log' details my writing life, and currently amounts to some 215 close-printed pages.

And I write poems.

All these matters are, at least in a sense, amateur, done for enjoyment only, not intended to make money.

The books I write are of a different category, although they are also created to be enjoyed – firstly, enjoyed by me since, if I do not enjoy them, why expect others to do so?

But throughout my life there have been others who assisted me. I mean not the encouragement of my readers, welcome though such encouragement is, but the assistance of my secretaries and my wives.

My first wife would grimly type out my stories on a little Swiss Hermes typewriter. I would have used that same typewriter first of all to write the story, correcting it afterwards in ink. We were poor and could not afford two typewriters. No secretary at that stage!

She also stood by patiently while I wrote my first long novel, *Shouting Down a Cliff*, a contemporary novel with comic intentions. This grew slowly in longhand in two fat hard-bound notebooks. It took me a year and a half, for I had a full-time job. I did not ask my wife to type out the finished novel. I knew it did not function well as a novel. But I also knew that now I was capable of writing a novel. I could do anything.

I never even read my finished novel through. No one has read it. No one has heard the shouting. The notebooks remained closed. They now rest harmlessly in the Aldiss Archive in the Bodleian Library in Oxford. I hear from many potential writers who cling hopefully to their first and only novel, sending it to publisher after publisher, unable to proceed further. In my experience, it is better to throw the first shot away and get on with the second.

Remember: 'Some there may be who have no memorial, who are as if they have never been,' as it says in *Ecclesiastes*. No time to waste!

My second book was *The Brightfount Diaries*, a social comedy first published in 1955. It was a great and modest success, last reprinted in 2001. My first wife was proud of it in its dull pink jacket and gave a copy to her mother to read. That old dragon's one comment was, 'I do not approve of all the swearing.'

It was the sole occasion on which I heard my wife flare up and dare to reproach her mother. 'Is that all you can say about it?' she asked, with great contempt. 'Nothing good?'

We searched the novel later for signs of swearing. There actually is one 'damn' on p. 150 and no less than two 'bloodys' on p. 177.

*

My following novels for some years were science fiction. It was then I stumbled accidentally on a vital principle. If you write a novel set in, say, Wimbledon, it will doubtless sell well in Wimbledon – but may not do as well elsewhere, certainly not abroad. However, if you set a novel on the planet Mars, it can be read anywhere in the world. I soon found myself becoming, if not rich, at least solvent, and famous. I was invited to parties here and there: generally by people more interested in the future than the past.

My wife did not approve greatly of parties. Nor did she like it when, in a fit of glorious imbecility, I threw up my job and became that deliciously, dangerously, independent thing, A REAL WRITER! I was then working at home, writing in a rear bedroom. She did not want me at home all day. And so our rocky marriage fell apart. She kept the house and possessions and the portable typewriter.

A rather savoury taste of doom presided over the fact that just as I was making a little success in life, bam! – I was broke and back where I started, without a home. My early 1960s were passed in conditions of uproarious squalor, lodging in one room in an Oxford slum.

Fortunately, I knew a good-natured Mr Chaundy, who ran a typewriter and typewriter-maintenance shop. When I bumped into him one day, I told him something of my troubles; he took me into his shop in the Turl and presented me with a used portable typewriter. It was an act of great kindness. That typewriter went everywhere with me, including to Jugoslavia for my six-month tour there, where I used its metal lid for a pillow.

But by then I had met up with a young lady by the name of Margaret Manson. I was literary editor on the local broadsheet, the *Oxford Mail*, in those days an excellent newspaper. I saw Miss Manson walking down the office corridor to take up the job of secretary to the editor. She had style. There was something in the way she held her head, perhaps just slightly to one side, that caused me to think that here was a lady who was shy but had courage. I fell in love on the proverbial spot.

Margaret, who was of Scots descent, had been secretary to Sir David Webster, then the director of Covent Garden Opera House. She was a brilliant secretary and, in 1965, she made me a brilliant bride.

For a successful marriage, one is probably well-advised to sacrifice something of oneself or one's habits. 'Let me not to the marriage of true minds,' says Shakespeare's sonnet, 'admit impediment.' To cling to all the liberties one enjoyed as a single person does admit impediments. After two bohemian years on my own, I felt this deeply. However, one great advantage informed my second marriage. I had been no one at the time of my first marriage, and felt myself to be no one; now, this time, Margaret took me on as an established writer. Why, one morning when she went to fetch in her bottle of milk from her doorstep, in the early days of our acquaintanceship, had she not found on that same doorstep a mysterious award – a Hugo, no less – for my "Hothouse" stories?!

It greatly assisted her understanding.

And her acceptance of my eccentric way of life.

Life, as it does now and again, had taken a turn for the better. We went to live in a thatched house near Wheatley, a short cycle ride from nowhere, yet only four miles from Oxford, where we were immensely happy – and where Margaret gave birth to our son Tim.

Margaret was a tall slender lady, with a face that frequently blossomed into the loveliest of smiles. She was elegant in every way, her hands were an artist's hands, and she never had *moods*. We lived rather an easy conjugal period together.

By this time, we possessed two typewriters. All my rough drafts were retyped and formatted by Margaret. She was a fast and accurate typist; nevertheless, mistakes occasionally cropped up. Then it was a case of getting out the Tipex and leafing through the top and four carbon copies of the manuscript, anointing each in turn. A laborious business it was.

It amazes me now to think how hard and continuously I worked in these years, striving to build a secure basis for our family life. Of course I had acquired a secretary by this time. Margaret and I always rejoiced when a large cheque came in. What luck!

Reading the memoirs of my old friend, Kingsley Amis, I see how easily he took life. But I was driven to write a novel per year, with several short stories to accompany it. Although we took long holidays, I seemed to be always at work, writing almost continuously from about 9.30 in the morning and knocking off only at six in the evening. Of course, some of this time was spent answering letters, as now I answer e-mails; my friends and fans were a communicative lot. One great advantage I enjoyed was that my wife took over the business aspects of our enterprise, which never exactly secured my interest. Year by year, the graph of our earnings increased steadily, all through the 'sixties and 'seventies; it was only in the 'eighties that the graph began to show jagged peaks.

It was in the 'eighties that we bought ourselves two new electronic typewriters. This was during the brief era of the golf ball. These machines were fast but noisy; my Helliconia trilogy was typed on them. In action, they sounded like machine-gun fire. When the 'phones rang, it was best to stop typing.

The advent of the computer saved us much work. Margaret was the first of the two of us to buy one. She bought an IBM, a poor blind thing which I could never use. The purchase came with a two-day tutorial in person by a member of the company's sales staff.

Immediately, Margaret's labours were reduced. With what rejoicing she threw out the shallow box of carbon papers! Now we could reproduce as many fresh copies of a manuscript as were required, simply by pressing a button.

I was fortunate in having a good literary agent, Hilary Rubenstein. With his foreign agent, Maggie Noach – who later became an agent in her own right – my sales increased and my books were published in translation all over the world. Margaret and I began to work less hard. Margaret took up pottery, at which she became expert. She was also a very green-fingered gardener, having the cool patience which that employment requires. Many a time I would wander out and talk to her as she worked her long lovely flower bed, while I took a break from my computer.

My computer... Yes, Apple Mac became a strong player in the field. We junked our IBM and both took to Apple Macs as waterproof ducks take to proverbial water. Apples had screens and colour and life and personalities. We loved them. Their little keys clicked as our parents' false teeth had done. They continue to click.

Margaret's Apple coaxed her into putting together an ambitious bibliography of my work. This proved her master-work, although later she compiled an elegant anthology of reminiscences of people who lived where we did, on Boars Hill, outside Oxford. I had always kept a file of 3 × 5 cards in a wooden file drawer, on which were recorded titles of stories, articles, poems and novels, with details of their publication. Working initially from these, Margaret embarked on an ambitious project of annotating everything I had ever written. It was a work of profound love and patience.

She found an American publisher almost as diligent as she, a man whom I had met called Rob Reginald, who lived in the hills of San Bernardino above the city of Los Angeles. There Rob ran the famous Borgo Press with his wife, Mary (oh, how vital are wives!).

After many years and much labour, Margaret's bibliography was published: *The Work of Brian W. Aldiss*, published in 1992. It is No. 9 of Rob's series of Bibliographies of Modern Authors (ISBN 0-89370-388-5), edited by Boden Clarke (Rob himself, in disguise).This considerable volume contains no less than 360 pages. It is no mere listing, but contains comments and reviews and illustrations and jokes and various snippets of information available nowhere else. I still marvel at it. *No one else in the world could have compiled this book: only Margaret Aldiss!* It still serves as a valued work of reference, long after her death...

Yes, my darling wife died. She developed heart trouble, which she took lightly; but increasingly, as time went by, the worry became a serious puzzle. Coronary experts were perplexed. And this heart question masked a more serious matter, a cancer, growing stealthily in the secret recesses of her body. We were both working on my autobiography, *The Twinkling of an Eye*, when the cancer was diagnosed. Margaret did not live to see the book published. Those who contract cancer in the pancreas have little chance of life. Another dear friend of mine, Sharon Baker, also died of the same malady.

Margaret remained courageous and uncomplaining to the end. She died at home, lying in my embrace, on the afternoon of 6 November 1997. All members of my family were assembled by her bedside. She was six years my junior; my feeling was that I should have died instead of Margaret – as I would have done, had I had any choice in the matter.

After her funeral, attended by crowds who knew and loved her, a desolating silence fell in our house, and in my psyche.

*

I found in Margaret's computer a file labelled, how characteristically, 'My Health', in which she detailed the progress of her illness.

As I began by saying, I kept a journal, although there had been little time for such refinements in her terminal months; I would scribble in it in the evenings, when my wife lay upstairs in bed, slowly turning into an old white-haired woman.

With the aid of these two sources, I began to write a record of Margaret's death and life, of our love and our family (by this time we had acquired four children, two boys, two girls). My grief, like the proverbial wolf at the door, woke me early every morning, scratching at my mind. Or I would start up in the dead of night. Oh, that winter of '97.... I had no thought but to hurry downstairs, grab a mug of tea, and return to my computer. When dawn sulked grey at my windows I would fall asleep on my chaise longue.

In this obsessive style I composed *When the Feast Is Finished* (a quote from Ernest Dowson's poem, 'Cynara'), the book of all my books of which I am most glad to have written: a memorial to Margaret's precious life. It does preserve something of our happiness and her spirit. I cannot look into it even now without weeping.

Margaret was my dear wife and companion for all but forty years.

Of my life since, when I have largely recovered myself, and made many new friends and new loves, I need not speak. But the wreaths remain fresh on Margaret's grave, which lies in Headington cemetery, not half a mile down the road from where I live.

14

Living with Julian

Kathleen Symons

It was in 1950 that Julian and I bought our first house. For the first years of our marriage we had lived in flats all over London, St John's Wood, Pimlico and lastly Blackheath where our daughter, Sarah, was born in 1948. The move to the country was not taken lightly – indeed Julian, the urban man, had serious misgivings but in the end agreed as long as it would not be forever. In fact we stayed there for five years to the day we moved in and Julian's first non-fiction book was published in 1950 almost as soon as we settled in. This was the biography of his brother A. J. A. Symons, author of *The Quest for Corvo*, the acclaimed 'experiment in biography' published in 1934 and who had tragically died at the age of forty-one.

The book's reception surprised Julian. I quote: 'It received long laudatory reviews almost everywhere. One or two friends of AJ said I had blackened his name, some enemies said that I had whitewashed a literary villain of the period, but the consensus was almost embarrassingly friendly.' I and several of our friends have always considered *A. J. A. Symons: His Life and Speculations*, the actual title of the book, among the best of Julian's work.

As I have said, we settled down in Kent and Julian could not have found it too irksome because another very good book, one of his best crime novels, *The 31st of February*, was published also in 1950.

To be sure most of the writing had been done before we moved, but the novel was finished in his study up a second staircase with a rope handrail and access to the roof. Sarah, by now twenty months old, delighted and amused herself by climbing on hands and knees up these stairs and knocking on the study door and being let in by her indulgent father who always said he was very happy to see her.

In 1947 George Orwell, who had been a friend of Julian's for some years, persuaded the *Manchester Guardian*, for whose paper the *Manchester Evening News* George wrote a weekly column called 'Life, People – and Books', to give Julian a trial, as with the success of *Animal Farm* he wished to give it up. They did rather reluctantly and Julian wrote the column for ten years.

During our five-year stay in Kent he worked very hard although we had lots of fun, too. Many friends came to visit and our son Marcus (known from an early age as Mark) was born in 1951 at the Kent and Canterbury Hospital. We had acquired a very old pre-war car and Julian drove the fifteen miles to the hospital in terrible weather to visit us both every evening, which lifted my spirits enormously. With great good fortune I had found a splendid girl, Sylvia, to look after Sarah and as soon as I got home she partly took over Mark as well.

In those years Julian published biographies of Charles Dickens and Thomas Carlyle and researched his biography of Horatio Bottomley as well as two crime novels: *The Broken Penny* and *The Narrowing Circle*.

We moved back to London in 1955 to a beautiful house in Blackheath near to our great friends Roy and Kate Fuller. The house faced the Heath and was very spacious with Julian's study in the semi-basement but with a big window. We had said goodbye to Sylvia some years before when she left us to get married and now we embarked on a successful series of au pairs. Sarah, now six, was at school all day, going and coming home on her beloved red buses, and very irritable if her father or I picked her up in a rather better car than our first one.

Happily he was not one of those writers who like to read the day's work each evening to their spouse or partner. My task was to read the completed manuscript and to make corrections. These consisted of noting that the names of the characters did not change during the course of the book, something that did occasionally happen, or that the colour of their eyes remained constant. I also checked relationships of characters, which sometimes baffled Julian not only in fiction but also in real life. Because I was concentrating so hard I did not read the book for enjoyment until the proofs arrived. He liked to discuss his latest book if he wanted advice on female clothes or names or locations but rarely on plots. We did this usually at dinner or over breakfast. It was around 1958 that Julian started to review for the (London) *Sunday Times* and he continued to do so up to his death.

I always enjoyed seeing the pile of new crime novels, as I was an avid reader of the genre. In 1962 from the current batch I selected one by an unknown author and with an intriguing title. This was *The Ipcress File*, the first novel by Len Deighton. I had to read it twice to grasp all the complications and then in great excitement told Julian he must read it at once and that it was a certain winner. I am glad to say I was quite right and happily Julian agreed with me and gave it a very enthusiastic review. This was the start of a long friendship with Len.

Around this time, with Sarah aged eleven and at boarding school and Mark aged eight also at boarding school, Julian started doing some tours for the British Council. In 1962 I went with him to Holland for a three-week trip. We travelled all over the country by train, always on time, clean and very comfortable. We were met at the station by one or possibly two members of the local literary society and taken to the house of our hosts for the night, who gave us a delicious dinner, then on to the place where the lecture was to be given. Always there was a very good audience, knowledgeable and appreciative. In fact one audience largely consisting of nuns was so intelligent and well read that Julian had to work hard to answer their questions to their satisfaction. On another occasion we were taken to the Arnhem Museum where there were some lovely Van Gogh paintings we had never seen before. It was a really enjoyable tour.

During the eight years we spent in Blackheath Julian published five crime novels including *The Colour of Murder*, which won the CWA award for the best crime novel of 1957. Also his history of *The General Strike* as well as *The Thirties: a Dream Revolved*. In 1961 he received the Edgar Allan Poe award from the Mystery Writers of America for *The Progress of a Crime*. In between writing the books he also wrote many short stories and reviews.

By 1963 we decided to move again. We had, with the help of a splendid master builder, converted the semi basement into a three-bedroom flat completely separate from the upper three stories of the house which we then sold. We had found a seventeenth-century house on the outskirts of the village of Brookland in Romney Marsh which we moved into in the terrible winter of 1963. There was no suitable study for Julian so we asked another local master builder if he could make a room on the flat roof of the detached garage. This he did quite beautifully and Julian had a spacious study with two windows and lots of bookshelves and a very efficient oil heater called Florence. The whole thing was greatly admired by the local people and by our visitors, but in spite of the study he was never really happy in the Marsh and after six years we sold both the house and the flat and bought a house just by Battersea Park which everyone liked.

Julian was always at his happiest when he was researching a book and it was going well, but financially it was a bit of a worry with both children at boarding school and I quote him: 'My crime stories have been used to finance the writing of other books. None of them could I have afforded to write if I had not been financially bolstered by the crime stories.'

So now we are at Battersea with Sarah living in Cornwall and Mark at London University. In 1972 Julian had his 60th birthday and we gave a big party to celebrate it. It was while we lived in Battersea that I worked part time in a very good bookshop called the Caravel Press in Marylebone High Street. This was owned and run by my very dear friend Mary Clark, always known as Topsy. She was an idiosyncratic bookseller who only stocked books with dust wrappers she approved and which she would like to read herself. However, I did persuade her to order a few copies of *Jaws* when it first appeared, as it was obviously a bestseller though that was not a particular recommendation to her. But she would always order a book that a customer requested and go to a lot of trouble to help those who needed advice. The patrons of the shop were often doctors and specialists from nearby Harley Street who were strong on Evelyn Waugh and P. D. James. But also Ralph Richardson was a regular and Harold Pinter quite often dropped by. I enjoyed my days there and in fact did another stint when we came back from America and stayed until Topsy sold the shop.

Three years later we went to Amherst College for a year where Julian was to be visiting writer. 'This had come about by Bill Pritchard – that is, Professor William H. Pritchard, chairman that year of the English Department and a fellow admirer of Wyndham Lewis – asking casually whether I would like to go out for a year as visiting writer. I said with a casualness equal to Bill's own that it sounds a splendid idea'.

Julian was undeterred by the fact that he had never taught and so we found ourselves in the summer of 1975 in the charming town of Amherst, temporarily living in Emily Dickinson's house where she was born and where she lived for her last thirty years. Like much else in Amherst this formidable red brick mansion, built in 1813, is owned by the college. Later we moved to a typical white-painted clapboard house and quickly tuned in to shopping for everything at the supermarket and the necessity of a car. We enjoyed our year in Amherst enormously and Julian succeeded in his teaching triumphantly. Sarah and her boyfriend visited us in the autumn and Mark, who had been married just before we left for America, came also with Christine, his delightful wife who had been a fellow student at university. In fact we had a great many visitors from England all the time we were there.

New England is such a beautiful part of America and Boston, our nearest big city, so delightful that if we had been younger we would have seriously thought of settling somewhere within reach of it.

Summing up our year Julian quotes the comment of a graduating student: 'When I go back into the world I realize that in a lot of ways this really is Camelot, and you just have to appreciate it for what it is', and Julian adds, 'That seems just about right. Camelot, given stability and severity by quite a bit of New England high-mindedness. After a year, that seemed a good recipe for a liberal education.'

Apart from going often to Boston and Cambridge we also went for a weekend, when my sister was staying with us, to Cape Cod. We drove up to Provincetown, staying the night at Chatham, and back down the other side. The following day we went over to Martha's Vineyard where we boarded a coach, which kept breaking down, but which had a disarming young guide who not only told us all we wanted to know about the island with wit and humour but was adept at doing the running repairs that kept the coach on the road. The whole trip was vastly enjoyable.

We left Amherst at the end of June. We gave a big party to say goodbye to all the friends we had made and flew to Denver where we picked up the huge car which was to transport us to Los Angeles.

We drove across Arizona, calling in at the Painted Desert and the Petrified Forest and last but certainly not least the Grand Canyon, which stunned us with its grandeur and beauty. It was fantastically hot but the big car with its air-conditioning was a godsend. We stayed each night at a Best Western motel, which we thought wonderful – very comfortable rooms with a good café and, best of all, a pool in which we plunged immediately on arrival. We negotiated the Los Angeles traffic without any trouble and arrived safely at Hilary and Sandy Mackendrick's house where we stayed for three days. They were old friends from England and it was a great pleasure to see them.

We then turned the car in at the airport and flew to Rome where we stayed for two weeks. Julian loved being in foreign cities and would walk for hours, not on the tourist route (though we saw most of the usual sights), but in the alleys and side streets and the less frequented squares. He always wanted to get 'the feel' of a place. In fact, in the early 'eighties while on a British Council tour, and while exploring Naples, he was mugged by two young Italians who took what little money Julian was carrying but who pushed him over and he fell heavily. However, quite undaunted he carried on with the evening schedule and suffered no ill effects. I was not there but was told about it by a fellow tourist with great admiration.

After Rome we made our way by train and boat to Elba, where Napoleon had been briefly exiled in 1814–15. We planned to have a good rest before returning to England. This we did, swimming every day and after a delicious lunch having a siesta before doing some exploring in our hired car. It was lovely weather and we both became very brown. We got home at the end of August to a very sun-baked London and we were so happy to see the children again after such a long time. But then tragedy struck us. Sarah died twelve days after we got home and a week after her 28th birthday. To lose a child is the worst thing that can happen to any parent and is something one never recovers from; though the pain diminishes over the years it never goes away.

In 1980 we made our last move together. We had lived for two and a half years in Balham but we never really liked the house and we found a charming one in Walmer near Deal, not far from Dover on the East Kent coast! It was neither country nor town really but a village by the sea. It suited Julian very well as he had a post office almost opposite, a small supermarket and a good butcher and baker, and best of all it was within ten minutes' walk of the station with trains straight to Charing Cross. He had a good study looking onto the lovely walled garden and we both settled in very happily. In the summer we had friends visit us nearly every weekend when we would all go down to the beach – the swimming was quite dangerous as the beach sloped very sharply to the water's edge so one was out of one's depth after two steps into the sea. Of all our homes I liked this one best.

In 1976 Julian succeeded Agatha Christie as President of the Detection Club and was given the Grand Master Award from the Mystery Writers of America in 1982, two of his many awards that he valued particularly. He also became a member of the Royal Society of Literature in 1975.

While we lived in Walmer, Julian wrote several crime novels and one of his best was *Death's Darkest Face* published in 1990, the same year that he was awarded the Cartier Diamond Dagger by the CWA for a lifetime's achievement in the crime genre. We made several trips to America during the 'eighties and also to Canada and Finland, with Julian giving lectures at Amherst and in Toronto and touring Finland for the British Council.

In 1992 he was eighty and his publisher, Macmillan, gave him a splendid birthday party which he greatly enjoyed. For all our forays to London we stayed with Mark and Christine and their three children. Julian had suffered for some years with angina, which now got rather worse though it did not stop him doing anything he wanted to do. But cancer of the pancreas was diagnosed and in 1993 he had to pull out of a British Council tour of Spain.

However, he got better and in October 1994 he went on another Spanish trip. He very much enjoyed himself but came home very tired and about three weeks later on 19 November he quietly died sitting at the kitchen table.

Living with Julian was wonderfully easy – he was emotionally stable and, provided he had his study and his books, quite happy. He was a creature of habit so that he came downstairs precisely at one o'clock for a simple lunch and again at about four-thirty for a cup of tea. As long as he was able to be alone for part of the day to do exactly what he wanted, there was no dissension. This suited me admirably and he never minded when I went off for a week to stay with my sister. But life was never dull. We saw lots of friends at weekends, and Mark and Christine and our three grandchildren visited us regularly. We were together for fifty-three years and looking back on them and remembering all the happy times I am sure that living with a writer was the best life for me. He always made me laugh, very important to me, and he was wise, witty and kind and a perfect companion, dealing with all crises on our travels and at home with great good humour.

*

I have come full circle. In 1996 I sold the house in Walmer and moved back to Blackheath. I am now only ten minutes by car from Mark and Christine and my grandchildren and I live in a very pleasant flat with a pretty garden and a garage. Blackheath Village has changed a lot but it is still a proper village and the Heath is still a constant joy, as is nearby Greenwich Park. The 2003 London Marathon starts from there tomorrow! I am not very mobile as I have a weak right leg, but I have my car and shop and visit friends and go to the cinema to which I have become addicted! But I still miss Julian more than I can say.

15

When Writing Entered My Mind

Frances H. Bachelder

More than twenty years ago, at the University of California, San Diego, my older son and I attended a lecture given by a distinguished author. She wore a long skirt, blouse, and loosely-fitting light coat. Her hair was short and unruly with straight, uneven bangs hanging haphazardly over her forehead.

As I recall, she spoke for about an hour, looking up from her handwritten notes only a few times. She seemed to be a serious person, while her husband, who was sitting next to my son, appeared more jovial. Just before she began, he had leaned forward and said to me, 'How do you do? I'm John Bayley.'

The admiration for his wife, Iris Murdoch, was evident as the entire audience listened attentively and applauded when she had finished speaking. It was also obvious that John Bayley realized that this was her show, and I could not help noticing how proud he was.

Compatibility is possible, but a writer married to a writer is not always a pleasant situation for some people without other shared interests as well. Perhaps it's sports, or music, or hiking. Within the shared interests is the added dimension of being together as companions and friends, while at the same time maintaining one's independence. 'Closer and closer apart' is how Bayley describes his relationship with Iris.

The writer who marries may soon discover limitations such as daily family responsibilities, and therefore less time for this particular profession. When my husband was a university administrator, we became close friends with a couple at the school. The husband was teaching and also had several books published in science. It became obvious to us that the many hours he devoted to research and writing were not conducive to a peaceful home atmosphere as he had little time for his wife and children. This led to many misunderstandings and petty quarrels, with each one defending his or her position on the matter.

Both my husband and I enjoy writing. He never complains when I interrupt him to criticize my work. In fact, he has said that he likes to help.

One day we were sitting in the living room. He was reading the sports page and I was scribbling notes on a pad of paper, when a solicitor's knock on the door interrupted me. After he left, I went into the kitchen to start dinner when I was startled by a loud outburst from my husband.

'Hey', he called out, 'you have a gold mine for your essay in these few sentences!' Evidently he had noticed my notes on the table beside him. Visibly elated, he continued, 'I could write an outline for you to follow.'

For some reason, I balked at that. Then I thought, here I've been offered assistance and I'm tempted to refuse. Realizing my good fortune in having such a willing helper, I quickly welcomed his ideas.

Every day, about mid-morning, I feel the urge to sit down at my typewriter, but too often time drifts away because of household chores. As Kingsley Amis once said, 'Unless I've done a certain amount of writing by lunchtime, I find it tremendously hard, impossible to start after lunch, and very hard to start in the evening.'

Even though I take pleasure in writing, it's slow work because I go over every word many times. In my dictionary, however, the synonym for *word* is *fun!*

I was working on this essay one morning, while trying to cope with the aches and pains of neuralgia that followed an attack of shingles, when the telephone rang. The caller informed me that my first novel, *The Iron Gate*, had been accepted by a London publisher. Seven years of hard work had come to fruition.

Dazed by the news, I was still holding the 'phone when my husband came in. As always, he asked how I was feeling. I didn't respond to his question, but instead blurted out, 'Guess what?'

I couldn't say any more as tears filled my eyes and I mumbled something senseless. Frightened by my behaviour, he asked, 'What's wrong? Are you okay?'

Still in shock, I said, 'Oh, everything's wonderful! My novel has been accepted; it's going to be published!'

'That's great!' he said. 'I'm *so* proud of you.'

For two days he talked of little else and insisted that we go out to dinner to celebrate. Now *that's* compatibility.

In his book *Indirections for Those Who Want to Write*, Sidney Cox has a section on whether or not 'writers ought to marry'. Despite complications, he is in favor of it. When two people are successful in marriage, he says, it is indeed commendable and also 'desirable', especially if there are children involved. He adds, 'The fun and joy in living comes when we make incompatibles unite.'

Erica Jong once said that marriage to a writer is both 'great and...terrible'. She explained that because she and her writer husband, Jonathan Fast, share 'child-rearing' responsibilities, they have more time to write. They cooperate by reading each other's work and then offering criticism. The terrible part is that 'you tend to get very stir-crazy and house-bound since you have your home and office in the same place'.

Roger Garis in *My Father Was Uncle Wiggily* (1966) tells about the relationship between his parents, Lily and Howard, who were both prolific writers. While Lily was a nervous woman with a dominant nature, Howard was usually calm, and this helped to eliminate some disagreements that otherwise might have occurred. Since both wrote 'the same sort of books' and both were paid 'about the same', there was what Roger referred to as a 'Balance of Power' in the household. At times, though, his father would be unusually successful, and then 'Mother would take to her bed' with a headache. Usually, however, she was satisfied if he didn't get too far ahead of her in the number of books he wrote. Sometimes he would complete a book she had started, or re-write one for her.

The Bobbsey Twins is an example. Roger admits that he does not know which of his parents wrote *The Bobbsey Twins at the Ice Carnival*, but that matters little as Lilian McNamara Garis (alias Laura Lee Hope) was well known as a successful author herself.

Jean Auel's husband supported her writing even though she 'researched and made notes all night and slept all day'. But when the husband is a writer, unless the wife has some knowledge of the art of writing, it is difficult for her to understand her spouse. Some days he seems interested in the affairs of the world and even helps with chores around the house. On other days, she finds him sitting at his desk, staring out the window, and she wonders if he is concentrating on his writing or just daydreaming. She also wonders how he can hope 'to make a name and a living by any such process as "stringing words together"'.

It's often said that writing is the loneliest of professions. Although I realize that solitude is vital to thought, I believe that loneliness depends upon individual circumstances.

My husband, now retired, was away from the house for only three hours as I was busy typing. Suddenly, I lost interest. At that moment, the door opened and he walked in. After a brief conversation, he went up to his study and I hurried back to the typewriter. Spurred on with renewed enthusiasm, I wrote for an hour.

Writers' creative habits differ in that some prefer total isolation, while others need to balance solitude and solidarity. The creative process, however, is unexplainable. Although there are numerous possibilities, nobody understands what factors are responsible.

A writer friend once told me that whenever he had lunch in a certain cafeteria he chose a table next to a quiet wall. Although he was alone at the table, he was not lonely. Richard J. Foster wrote, 'Loneliness is inner emptiness. Solitude is inner fulfillment.' Evidently, this was one of the times my friend needed both solitude and solidarity, and he was able to find this by being alone and yet with people, which for some reason gave him a feeling of solitude. Later he said that ideas for a story were racing through his mind, but where they came from he didn't know.

At times, an inner vision of a story or character may come to us on a subtle level. But we must wait until the muse finds us 'sufficiently humbled to this process', as Wally Lamb says. In other words, we cannot force the creative process.

One of the most illuminating anecdotes that I have come across is in Jimmy Carter's book, *Living Faith*. He is remarkably frank about the problems he and his wife, Rosalynn, had in working together on *Everything to Gain*. I admire him for admitting how difficult their co-authoring became. 'It was only the last minute refereeing of our editor that saved the book,' he says, 'and, as we said only somewhat jokingly, perhaps our marriage.'

I wish I could say that I've always wanted to be a writer, but music has always been my first love. I vaguely remember as a child thinking that some day I would write a book, but that was the extent of it. As I grew older and my love for reading increased, I still had no inkling that some day I would want to write.

My family were musicians, not writers. My father played cornet in an orchestra, and when that disbanded, some of the former members used to come to our house to play. I remember lying in bed and enjoying the pleasant sounds. Eventually the pianist left the group, and I was invited to take his place. This was a tremendous boost for me and music became uppermost in my mind. Then for four years as pianist in the high school orchestra, I developed an even greater interest in music.

I loved school. Every morning when I entered the classroom, I was aware of a special aroma – probably from pencils, papers, and books. I could hardly wait for our lesson to begin. Latin fascinated me because I learned about the derivation of words in the English language. Translating Homer's *Iliad* and *Odyssey* from the Greek was challenging but exciting.

My favorite English teacher guided us through Shakespeare. This was 'classical music' to my ears and possibly the beginning of a real interest in words. As Henry Purcell wrote, 'Musick and Poetry have ever been acknowledg'd Sisters, which walking hand in hand, support each other....'

As I now recall, other instances also involved writing. As secretary of my senior class, I had the privilege of writing our class history. Perhaps the closest I came to writing was as a staff member for the high school paper. The editor asked if I would write articles and

I agreed. However, it was a short-lived assignment because the subjects were of little interest to me.

One last possibility was the time I set up a 'lending library'. This I also discontinued after a short time as business was poor. Another small step, but as far as I can remember, nobody encouraged me to write. Evidently, the drive or desire would have to come from somewhere deep within. Perhaps even the authors I was reading might offer further encouragement.

At a later stage in my life my husband, our two sons, and I lived in Amherst, Massachusetts, near Howard and Lily Garis. One of Howard's friends, Robert Frost, also lived in Amherst, and he often gave talks at the University of Massachusetts and Amherst College. What opportunities I missed to visit them and discuss how and why they wrote as they did!

Responsibilities as wife and mother took precedence during the mid-years. This, coupled with my devotion to music, which included taking and giving piano lessons, took much of my time. Committee work on behalf of the town of Amherst and the University also added to my schedule.

I didn't begin to take an active interest in writing until 1985 at the age of sixty-three. One day my older son gave me a copy of Barbara Pym's first published novel, *Some Tame Gazelle*. I was fascinated by it. For some reason I made notes in the back of the book. I do recall that the novel gave me a comfortable and contented feeling. The characters reminded me of many people I have known – good folks, helpful folks – not perfect, but always good friends. It's possible that the humorous incidents and funny remarks caught my eye, as when Pym wrote, 'Belinda gave a contented sigh. It had been such a lovely evening. Just one evening like that every thirty years or so. It might not seem much to other people, but it was really all one needed to be happy.'

My son, a successful author, noticed my notes and asked, 'Why don't you write an essay on Barbara Pym?' Astonished, I replied, 'Oh, I couldn't do that!'

But the seed had been planted in my mind and I became more enthused each time I thought about it.

So that was the beginning. He kept encouraging me, and finally, after a year or two, I completed the essay and sent it to him. One night

I dreamed that he called and said it was very good. The next day the 'phone rang. It was my son, and he said, 'It's perfect!' I was amazed. Since then, I've had additional essays published along with a bio-critical study and a novel. As much as I enjoy writing, however, music remains my number one interest.

One day when I was working on a book about Mary Roberts Rinehart, a strange thing happened. As I started to type, I became more and more interested in a certain section. After typing six pages, I stopped, glanced at the clock, and was surprised to see that two hours had slipped by. I was tired, but exhilarated, as I slowly awakened from my 'literary trance'. Did I write those six pages, or was it the will of another entity?

I have learned a lot from writing. It has taught me to appreciate other writers' works. It has shown me that authors and musicians use rhythms that are strictly their own. Writing gives me a peaceful feeling. Nothing bothers me when I'm writing, as if I'm on an island of my own making. When I've had a successful time with words, my work is both enjoyable and productive. I now know the true source of a certain contentment I feel when writing.

A few years ago my husband did a lot of writing for a rough draft of his 500-page book. Due to illness, he hasn't been able to do much since. But his desire is still focused on it. I'm now going to devote much of my time helping him to re-work it. I know he needs the stimulus to resume work. My goal is to see that his book is published.

16

Pen and Ink: The Life and Work of Christopher Isherwood and Don Bachardy

James J. Berg

> What shall I write about Don, after seven years? Only this – and I've written it often before – that he has mattered more and does matter more than any of the others. Because he imposes himself more, demands more, cares more—about everything he does and encounters. He is so desperately alive.
>
> Christopher Isherwood, 14 February 1960

When the writer Christopher Isherwood met Don Bachardy in early 1953, both of them looked younger than their actual ages. In truth, Isherwood was 48 and Bachardy was 18. They met on the beach in Santa Monica, California, where Isherwood had lived for nearly fifteen years and where he had recently had a brief affair with Bachardy's older brother, Ted. The story of Isherwood and Bachardy is the story of two artists, one rejuvenating his career and the other just beginning. Isherwood was the famous author of *Mr Norris Changes Trains* (1935) and *Goodbye to Berlin* (1939). Bachardy was a typical southern California teenager, looking for experience and direction in life. Over the years, Isherwood became increasingly public about his sexual orientation and included gay-themed material more explicitly in his fiction, switching to outright autobiography for his final works. Bachardy developed into a successful portrait artist, whose subjects include Hollywood celebrities, noted authors and composers, and Jerry Brown, the former Governor of California, whose official portrait Bachardy painted in 1984. What began as a beach fling grew into a thirty-year relationship that had long-lasting consequences for the life and work of both men. Together they became the 'First Couple' of the nascent gay rights movement.

As a young man, Christopher Isherwood's sexual preference was for men who were, in one way or another, 'other' than he was. Living in Germany in the 1930s, he found sexual relationships more satisfying with the often younger, working-class Germans who did not speak his language. One of these, Heinz Neddermeyer, was the model for Waldemar in the 'Ambrose' section of *Down There on a Visit* (1962). A teenager when he met Isherwood at a villa outside Berlin, Heinz is identified by name in *Christopher and His Kind* (1976), Isherwood's memoir of the 'thirties. After Isherwood's emigration to the United States in 1939, he had both short-term and long-term relationships with younger men, most significantly Bill Caskey and the man he calls Vernon Old, both of whom are treated extensively in Isherwood's diaries.

Isherwood settled in California, where he had gone to visit Aldous Huxley and Gerald Heard, two fellow British writers who were prominent pacifists. Isherwood had realized that he himself was a pacifist and sought Heard's and Huxley's guidance. They, in turn, introduced him to Swami Prabhavananda, a Hindu monk who founded the Vedanta Society of Southern California. Isherwood became a devotee and briefly considered becoming a monk. The call of the outside world was strong, however, and after the war Isherwood needed to remind himself of the right way to live. A prolific diary-keeper, he wrote on 11 December 1950: 'Calm, meditation, work, regular habits, study, discipline, proper exercise; the absolutely necessary regime for middle life.' Having been heavily influenced by Prabhavananda and Vedanta, Isherwood claimed that people don't change unless and until they are ready to: 'which comes first, the influence or the predisposition to be influenced in a certain way?' he asked in a 1960 lecture ('A Writer and His World'). Isherwood's religious conviction did not completely settle him. In fact, the years from 1945 to 1951 have been described as Isherwood's 'Lost Years'. According to Katherine Bucknell, editor of Isherwood's diaries, his life was 'out of control' and reached a 'new-low of dissipation' in this period due to 'excessive' drinking and sexual activity. Yet a longing for domesticity permeates many of Isherwood's post-war diaries.

In the early fifties, as his relationship with Bill Caskey was falling apart, Isherwood contemplated living either on his own, at a Hindu monastery south of Los Angeles, or with some other man. On May 6, 1951 he wrote: 'I must confess, I want to be looked after. I want the background of a home.... What I really want is solitude in the midst of snugness. Well, you won't get it, Mac'. When the break-up with Caskey was final, Isherwood felt himself to be going through a change of life, a male menopause. At the same time, he had also reached a new financial security due to, in part, *I Am a Camera*, John van Druten's stage adaptation of *Goodbye to Berlin*. The play opened in 1951 and became a hit. (*I Am a Camera* was filmed in 1955 with Julie Harris as Sally Bowles.) In 1952, seeking companionship as well as domestic tranquility, Isherwood went to Bermuda with a young man and restarted the novel he'd begun in 1949, *The World in the Evening*.

Isherwood completed the penultimate draft of *The World in the Evening* in January 1953, and, in a remarkable sense of the 'readiness being all', he met Don Bachardy the following month. The first mention of Bachardy in Isherwood's diary is on 6 March 1953, written in the aftermath of Ted's nervous breakdown. By the time he wrote this account, Isherwood and Bachardy had begun their affair:

> Ted was dragged away, screaming and fighting, in handcuffs. And his little brother Don cried in my car afterwards: 'Chris, he's really *insane*.' I feel a special kind of love for Don. I suppose I'm just another frustrated father. But this feeling exists at a very deep level, beneath names for things or their appearances. We're just back from a trip to Palm Springs together, which was one of those rare experiences of nearly pure joy.

This initial entry portends much for their relationship, particularly in the early years. Ted Bachardy's mental illness would prove a preoccupation for his brother, and both Isherwood and Bachardy would fear that Don's own youthful instability might transform into full-blown psychosis. In addition, the couple would battle the 'names for things or their appearances' for years. When they met, Isherwood was living in Evelyn Hooker's garden house. Hooker was the pioneering psychologist whose studies of homosexual men in the 1950s laid the groundwork that led the American Psychiatric Association to declassify homosexuality as a mental illness. (Her paper, 'The Adjustment of the Male Overt Homosexual', argued that male homosexuals were at least as well adjusted as their heterosexual counterparts. She first presented her findings at a conference in 1956.) As was true of Isherwood's other friends, Hooker and her husband, Edward, were scandalized by Isherwood's relationship with Bachardy. When the two decided to live together in late 1953, the Hookers were concerned about the legality of the arrangement. Isherwood and Bachardy had to find another place to live.

Not surprisingly, Isherwood continued to view his relationship with Bachardy as a parental one as well as a romantic and sexual one. A mere six months after their first meeting, Isherwood wrote on September 22, 1953: 'I'm very happy in my father relationship with Don, except that he makes me feel so terribly responsible. It's nearly as bad as Heinz all over again. Nearly, but not quite, because Don is a lot brighter, and really much more able to look out for himself.' Bachardy himself knew the way many of Isherwood's friends and associates viewed him, and he determined to be of help to Isherwood and to make something of his own life. His first act as a help-mate was typing the final, polished draft of *The World in the Evening* from Isherwood's dictation. The novel had the most difficult gestation of any of Isherwood's fictional works. Once it was completed, however, Isherwood was back in form. In the following years, he resumed more regular diary-keeping, completed an anthology of English short stories, worked on a number of screenplays, started *Down There on a Visit*, and began his career as a college lecturer.

As their relationship progressed, Isherwood and Bachardy adapted and changed their ways of interacting with each other. Isherwood gradually saw himself less as a parental figure and began to see their relationship as fraternal as well as romantic. He said to

Winston Leyland in a 1973 interview, collected in *Conversations with Christopher Isherwood*, 'All the relationships I've had have been with younger people than myself. I say "brother" rather than "son" because I don't like to think of the person I love as being a reproduction of myself. The idea of a brother suggests a greater polarity between us.' This sense of magnetic attraction did not extend to Isherwood's own brother, Richard, who was also gay and continued to live in England with his mother until her death. For Isherwood, leaving England was also leaving his family and its firm hold on its own history. So on a visit in February 1956, Isherwood reacted strongly against Richard's protestation of love, 'which only embarrassed me, because I don't love him – most certainly not as a brother. I have had a hundred brothers already and a thousand sons – and all this talk about blood relationships nauseates me.' Isherwood's sense of family changed to include Bachardy (and others before him) and exclude his biological relations. With Isherwood's encouragement, Bachardy's role as help-mate/typist changed over the years as well. Isherwood recognized Bachardy's intelligence and encouraged him to keep his own diary, parts of which have been published in *The Isherwood Century*. The two became writing partners for the first time on a stage adaptation of *The World in the Evening* in 1958–59.

A few overriding characteristics of the young Bachardy come through in Isherwood's published diaries: his emotional volatility, his search for a vocation and development as a visual artist, and his charm. The Bachardy temperament was of much concern to both men in the early years. Under Don Bachardy's name in the index for Isherwood's *Diaries, Volume One, 1939–60*, the subheading for 'depressions' has seventeen citations and the one for 'outbursts and resentfulness' has twenty-nine. Bachardy's own concern is evident in his agreeing to consult a professional psychologist. On 19 April 1956 Isherwood recorded:

> Don also went to see Evelyn Hooker about his state of mind and problems. Evelyn seems to have reassured him, insofar as the state of his mind is concerned. She didn't think it neurotic of him to be upset, under the circumstances. In other words, she thinks that our life together constitutes a genuinely big problem. Now of course I quite see this. And yet I can't, in my weakness, help feeling hurt

when I'm treated as a sort of classic monster – a standard monster, almost – out of a textbook, like a dragon in a fairy tale. Don, on his side, cannot understand that I mind. I ought to accept my monsterhood humbly, he thinks.

Bachardy's challenge was to grow as a person himself while continuing in a relationship that was as complex as it was satisfying. Isherwood's description of Bachardy's 'state of mind' corresponds closely to Bachardy's own feelings. In May 1956, some weeks after seeing Dr Hooker, Bachardy wrote in his diary: 'Another sudden and inexplicable scene with Chris yesterday. I don't really know why I make these scenes – the least little thing seems to set me off.' He recounts the situation and then continues:

> This incident started me smoldering. By the time Chris joined me on the beach I was full of resentment and rebellion and made a scene. First accusing him of possessiveness and a lack of genuine interest in me, I then said that I felt bored, lethargic and useless and wanted to go to New York by myself. I blamed him for everything that was wrong with me and, by exaggerating my unhappiness, made him feel I hate him without really saying so. When I get carried away in my despair and confusion, I want to wreck everything for no good reason. Then I cry, and make Chris cry. Afterward I feel guilty, and so silly, and just as unsatisfied as usual.

There were several reasons for Bachardy to be agitated on that particular day, including a recent bout of hepatitis that put him in the hospital and would soon do the same for Isherwood. But the 'resentment and rebellion' he felt also relate to the way Bachardy felt he was treated by Isherwood's friends.

On a visit to Somerset Maugham and Alan Searle the previous winter, Bachardy wrote: '[T]he friends, familiars, companions, guardians, all in fact who take the trouble to have an intimate relationship with any famous artist, almost always find themselves universally suspected, bitched, even hated, and finally, ignored. Frank Merlo, Walter Starcke, Chester Kallman, Robert Craft – they all suffer this treatment and in their turn put off those who try to be their friends – even those in similar situations.' In his early twenties, Bachardy was feeling an extraordinary need to assert himself and, in effect, to *become* himself. He enrolled at the University of California, Los Angeles that spring to study theater and at the Chouinard Art School (now California Institute of the Arts) in the summer. Isherwood's reaction to the incident above was to recognize in July 1956 that 'Don is going through a phase which is very important in his development... I think that the art school may really be an answer to his vocational problem.' It *was* the answer. With Isherwood's encouragement, Bachardy studied the visual arts and pursued a career as a commercial artist and designer.

Their relationship continued to have tensions, and one of them was about monogamy. As a gay man in his twenties, Bachardy demanded, and Isherwood conceded, a certain amount of sexual freedom. In Isherwood's diaries, Bachardy's trysts are recorded in light of his 'freedom' or nights that he spends in town. On 11 July 1958 Isherwood wrote, 'Don apologetically announced this morning that he'd quite forgotten but he had a dinner date tonight. Well – so what? It really is better, I guess, since his "freedom" has been officially recognized. Anyhow I know it's the right thing and I'm in favor of it unshakably – in principle.' Isherwood suggests here that the couple had had frank negotiations about monogamy and its alternatives, and that the difference between the principle and the reality was recognized by both parties. Bachardy's attitude toward his sexual activity outside of their relationship 'was that I had a certain priority to have experience because Chris had had all of his before I knew him, and he owed me that freedom. However unfair it may have seemed to Chris, that was my attitude'.

After twenty years with Bachardy, Isherwood elucidated a philosophy about long-term relationships to Winston Leyland:

> Love is tension. What I value in a relationship is constant tension, in the sense of never being under the illusion that one understands the other person... you know you can never understand him, never take him for granted. He's eternally unpredictable – and so are you to him, if he loves you. And that's the tension. That's what you hope will never end.

Those tensions were vividly present in the first decade of the Isherwood–Bachardy relationship, and at least once they threatened to end the union permanently.

As an artist, Bachardy was developing his own style of portraiture, using primarily pen and ink to draw from live models. His renderings of Isherwood, his most frequent model, began to grace the covers of Isherwood's books in 1962 with *Down There on a Visit*. Bachardy was determined to be a professional rather than a commercial artist, and he decided to continue his studies at the Slade School of Art in London. He left Los Angeles in January 1961. Isherwood joined him in April and spent nearly half of the year in England, returning to Los Angeles in October. Bachardy remained in London through the end of the year and had his first art show there. Then he traveled to New York for his first US exhibition and returned to Los Angeles in February 1962. In a summary of the as-yet unpublished portion of Isherwood's diaries, Katherine Bucknell described their relationship as 'strained and a crisis air enters... during the winter and early spring [of 1963], Bachardy decides he wants to live alone'. Bachardy described 1962–63 as his 'ten-year itch' and 'the bumpiest time for us'. Perhaps in response, the novel Isherwood was working on, *The English Woman*, became less about an expatriate woman and more about an Englishman living in Los Angeles and coping with the loss of his lover.

A Single Man, published in 1964, can be seen as a variation on Isherwood's own life with key elements changed or missing. In a matter-of-fact portrayal of a gay Englishman, the protagonist, George, is a professor at a state college. He is very much alone, and, unlike Isherwood, he has no basis of philosophical or spiritual support. He also has no circle of gay friends, and no partner to come home to. George's lover, Jim, has died in a car accident while in Ohio visiting his parents. George has led a very discreet life, and the price of that discretion is that he cannot grieve openly. He does not share his widowhood with his neighbors, colleagues, or students. George resents his situation as well as the basic inequality of gay relationships. (Isherwood's first gay-identified characters appear in *The World in the Evening*, although characters in his early novels are also often read as homosexual or bisexual.)

Bachardy told Armistead Maupin in a 1983 interview that he felt that Isherwood 'was imagining what it would be like if we split up because I remember that period was a very rough time for us'. In the novel, he evokes quite well the feelings of the one left behind in the house the couple used to share:

> The doorway into the kitchen has been built too narrow. Two people in a hurry... are apt to keep colliding here. And it is here, nearly every morning, that George, having reached the bottom of the stairs, has this sensation of suddenly finding himself on an abrupt, brutally broken off, jagged edge – as though the track had disappeared down a landslide. It is here that he stops short and knows, with a sick newness, almost as though it were for the first time: Jim is dead. Is dead.

Although Isherwood does not name his protagonist after himself, as he did in several earlier works, his own life is very much in evidence in this novel of middle age. In as much as George lacks the comfort of Isherwood's Vedanta philosophy and his relationship with Don Bachardy, these missing elements are what help to define him as a *single* man.

The inequality of gay relationships was not only an issue for fiction. It was an issue that Isherwood and Bachardy faced together as a gay couple. Isherwood had always been open about his sexuality to his friends and associates, and he remained so when he moved to Los Angeles. At a time when gay men such as Rock Hudson, Anthony Perkins, and Montgomery Clift kept their sexuality secret, there was an active gay community in Hollywood, mostly made up of behind-the-scenes professionals: directors, set designers, make-up artists, and writers. Yet Isherwood and Bachardy were often the only openly gay couple at Hollywood parties in the 1950s. Their age difference compounded whatever homophobic reaction they might have gotten. As Bachardy described the situation to Maupin, 'I was just regarded as a sort of child prostitute.... Joseph Cotten once said within earshot that he deplored the company of these "half-men".' The longevity of their relationship helped put to rest the scandal of the their age difference. The longer they remained together, however, the more important it became to put their relationship on a more solid legal and financial footing.

As a young man, Bachardy had been supported monetarily as well as emotionally by Isherwood: 'If he hadn't encouraged me,

I would never have been an artist,' Bachardy told Niladri Chatterjee in 1997. Isherwood's financial stability fluctuated until the success of I Am a Camera and its musical adaptation, Cabaret, brought a measure of comfort to their lives. (Cabaret opened on Broadway in 1966. The film, with Liza Minelli as Sally Bowles, was released in 1972.) As gay men, Isherwood and Bachardy enjoyed none of the legal protections of married, heterosexual couples. Although they bought their house together, the deed was not held jointly, and there was no guarantee that Isherwood's will, in which he left his estate to Bachardy, would not be contested. Isherwood was in fairly good health until the early 1980s, although his nearly hypochondriac diary entries show that he was increasingly concerned about it as he grew older. Bachardy explained that by the late 1970s, 'Chris was getting to be an age when he could quite likely get sick at any moment. We had heard horror stories from friends of ours, queer friends, one of whom wasn't allowed to be in the hospital room because he wasn't a relative and wasn't a spouse.' Eventually, around 1980, the two decided that Isherwood should actually adopt Bachardy. 'We had a very good friend at that time who was a lawyer who made it very easy.' In this way they created a legal relationship where California and United States law did not recognize one.

Between 1963 and 1980, that is, after the bumpy years and before the adoption, Isherwood and Bachardy spent several weeks of every year living apart – on opposite coasts or in separate countries even. Isherwood remained mostly in Los Angeles, and Bachardy alternated between New York and London. This had more to do with Bachardy's profession than any difficulties in their relationship. As a portrait artist, he earned more income in London than he did in the United States. One US commission, with the New York City Ballet, kept him traveling frequently between New York and Los Angeles. After the difficulties of 1962–63, however, Bachardy maintains there was never a time when the two did not consider themselves partnered. In 1968, David Hockney painted a portrait of the couple sitting in matching wicker armchairs in their Santa Monica living room. This portrait solidified their status as a gay couple. Throughout the decade that followed, in fact, Isherwood and Bachardy became icons of the gay rights movement on the west coast. Personal friends with dozens of photographers and visual artists and living in the epicenter of American culture in Los Angeles, they were more photographed than Gertrude Stein and Alice B. Toklas. Until Ellen Degeneres met Anne Heche, they were probably the most photographed same-sex couple in the world. It was Armistead Maupin, author of *Tales of the City* and a close friend, who dubbed them 'The First Couple' in 1983.

At the time of the Hockney portrait, the two began another collaborative project, one that would keep them working together for several years. Their stage adaptation of *A Meeting by the River* was produced at the Mark Taper Forum in 1972, directed by James Bridges, director of the films *Urban Cowboy* and *The China Syndrome* and part of their extensive network of gay friends. According to Bachardy, 'The collaboration was designed by Chris and me, consciously or unconsciously, as a means to keep us together. We just thought it would be nicer if we could be together more of the time. Instinctively we both hit on this idea of collaboration.' This renewal of their professional collaboration also produced the teleplay for an NBC production called *Frankenstein: the True Story*. They began work on the project in 1971, and the adaptation was broadcast in 1973. The literary collaborations put a stop to their frequent separations and contributed significantly to the durability of the relationship.

Isherwood was practiced in artistic collaboration: he co-authored three plays with W. H. Auden in the 1930s and worked with many other writers, such as Aldous Huxley and Terry Southern, on numerous screenplays. The Isherwood–Bachardy works, all but *October* (1981), seem to have followed the method of many artistic collaborations. Bachardy described the process to Chatterjee:

> We discussed the story in detail for days, weeks. We worked out the construction together. We each had ideas, made suggestions, and developed from each other's suggestions until we had a general direction, a general sense of our characters and how they were going to interact. And then at that very decisive moment when the first serious words of the script were to be written, I took my place at the typewriter and Chris dictated to me.... We had a very symbiotic relationship. And that's always how our collaborations worked.

While Bachardy describes the classic Hollywood creative sessions — long discussions, followed by outlines and treatments, culminating in a typed script — he suggests that his role was secondary. 'My great skill was as a typist: it's one of my great claims to being a writer.' Bachardy felt that the 'real writing' was in Isherwood's dictation, and this is consistent with Bachardy's image of himself as a visual artist.

Despite his modesty, when Bachardy collaborated on a screen play or stage adaptation with Isherwood, he brought a 'deep appreciation and knowledge of film's technical side', as Robert and Katharine Morsberger have shown. Growing up in the Atwater neighborhood of Los Angeles, Bachardy was a lifelong fan of the movies. Like many teenagers in the later 1940s and 1950s, he collected movie memorabilia and magazines. He used to sneak into movie premiers with his brother by pretending to be with their 'parents', adults who, in reality, were unrelated to them and unaware that Don and Ted were following them into the theater. To this day he keeps on his kitchen wall a photograph of himself with Marilyn Monroe, taken at just such an occasion. Bachardy's visual acuity was developing throughout his twenties as he variously studied drama, set design, and visual arts at UCLA and Chouinard.

Two of the final Isherwood–Bachardy collaborations were in print form. *October* is a collection of thirty-one diary entries written by Isherwood in October 1979, and thirty-two portraits drawn, mostly in pen and ink, by Bachardy during the same month. As an artist who only draws from live models, and one who continues to work nearly every day, Bachardy's drawings are a visual diary complementing Isherwood's written one in *October*. (Bachardy's written diary often details his sessions and the models who sit for him. For an example, see *Stars in My Eyes* [2000]). Several of Bachardy's models, including Gore Vidal and David Hockney, are mentioned in Isherwood's entries as well. A portrait of Isherwood is the first drawing in the book. Isherwood comments on that sitting:

> Don often describes his work as a confrontation. He himself, with a pen gripped in his mouth ready for use when it is needed instead of a brush,

> reminds me of a pirate carrying a dagger between his teeth while boarding the enemy. He seems to be attacking the sitter. So now I counter-attacked. Summoning up all my latent hostility, I glared at him unwaveringly, with accusing eyes. While he was working, he didn't seem to be noticing this. Yet he recorded it. The finished drawing is scary; my old face is horrible with illwill. Most satisfactory.

Later in the month, Isherwood described their respective art forms:

> Don's single-session drawings or paintings which he never retouches; my gradual production, by much trial and error through many months, of longish proseworks – seem closely related to our characters. Don is all impatience, energy, aggression. I'm patient, lazy but persistent.

Another Isherwood entry was written after watching Bachardy in a public demonstration of his work at an art center. Here Isherwood reports Bachardy's manner of talking to an audience, which mirrors Isherwood's own manner of talking about his writing to interviewers and audiences: 'he answers in a matter of fact tone, never resorting to philosophical-aesthetic statements'. But he makes a further comment that, while true in general, will be quite untrue in the final Isherwood–Bachardy collaboration: 'What he requires from the sitter is live motionlessness – "live" being the operative word. He wouldn't take the smallest interest in a corpse, even a quite fresh one.' In fact, the one corpse Bachardy did take an interest in was Isherwood's own.

In his book *Christopher Isherwood: Last Drawings* (1990), Don Bachardy did what few artists, even portraitists, have done: he chronicled a life in decline. As Isherwood battled cancer from 1983 until his death in January 1986, Bachardy drew Isherwood in all stages of illness and consciousness. He continued drawing, in fact, for several hours after Isherwood's death. In the text accompanying the drawings, Bachardy comments on the images and the process. He quotes Isherwood's lifelong friend, Stephen Spender, who called the drawings 'both merciless and loving'. Bachardy countered, 'since *real* love is merciless, one might just say my work is loving – merciless is redundant'. The process was symbiotic, according to Bachardy: 'It is the most intense way I know of to be with Chris. It

is the only situation now in which we are both truly engaged.'
The symbiosis reached its height with Isherwood's death: 'While
Chris was dying, I focused on him intensely hour after hour. I was
able to identify with him to such an extent that I felt I was sharing
his dying just as I'd shared so many other experiences with him. It
began to seem that dying was something which we were doing
together.'

For over thirty years, with few models to go by, Christopher
Isherwood and Don Bachardy created their relationship as they
lived it. What might have begun as filial became fraternal then
companionate and collaborative. If Isherwood the writer acted as
a father or older brother in his support of Bachardy's becoming an
artist and a man, so too the artist Bachardy is supporting Isherwood's
literary legacy after his passing. He has transferred Isherwood's
papers to the Huntington Library in California and established the
Christopher Isherwood Foundation to support Isherwood scholarship. Bachardy has also included the Foundation in his will: the
house in Santa Monica where he and Isherwood lived, and where
he still lives, will go to the Foundation on his death to provide
a haven for writers and scholars.

Part II

The Problems

17

Forget She (or He) Is a Writer, and All May Be Well

John Bayley

Who, of all writers, would have been most difficult to live with? Tolstoy would be my premier choice for tiresomeness, although his partner would also have been subjected to sudden fits of almost overwhelming charm. Dostoevsky, perhaps surprisingly, would surely be much easier. He and his second wife, Anna Snetkina, who was also his secretary and typist, lived together in great harmony and affection. His partner wouldn't see much of Shakespeare, which would perhaps have suited them both, but their relations would have been perfectly amicable. And the same goes for Dr Johnson.

Writers can be lived with easily if each party takes the other for granted, as in any more or less agreeable domestic relation. The fatal thing, domestically, would be to dramatise the relation or – still worse – to exploit it in the way that Zelda and Scott Fitzgerald did, or as the Byrons did, or, in his own prim secretive way, T. S. Eliot. But Vivienne was the cross he needed, as well as a heaven-sent inspiration for *The Waste Land*. How many writers, one may wonder, have got profitable and powerful results in their art from exploiting the horrors of their domestic situation?

To lapse now into pedestrian autobiography, and to my own situation, married for more than forty years to a novelist and philosopher of world-wide distinction. T. S. Eliot in the *Four Quartets* remarks with determined humility, and not very convincingly, that 'the poetry does not matter'. I could say, however, and with conviction, that for me and my wife, in our married relation, the novels, and the philosophy, *really* did not matter. As a writer and thinker she was 'Iris Murdoch': to me, and to her in our life together, we were simply the pet names we used to call each other. No relation could have been more separate than that between her 'professional' being, which in her own private and unpretentious way she took very seriously indeed, and our muted existence, as of a pair of equally private animals, to which indeed we sometimes compared it. Animal existence was not serious at all – far from it; it was just the way we lived, and the way we liked to live.

I suppose we talked a bit about what Iris was writing, and about the novel, as well as about literature in general, but this seemed to happen so casually, and in a sense so unmeaningfully that neither of us paid much attention to it. I always enjoyed moments together when Iris suddenly wrote something down, or asked me for a scrap of paper so that she could scribble something on it. That was the nearest I came to seeing the brain of a great writer operating, so to speak, in its own undercover way. But she never lost herself in what used to be called 'a brown study', or seemed to need silence while she thought something out. Nor did she tell me what it was she wrote down, and I never asked her.

When she wrote her last novel, *Jackson's Dilemma*, Iris was already beginning to suffer from Alzheimer's disease, although it was still some time before the condition was diagnosed. It was heartbreaking to see her puzzling over what she was doing, and, for the first time, seeking help from me, as well as reassurance. I was very happy to reassure her, because I felt sure that the novel, as it developed, and because she – again for the first time – wanted me to read while she wrote it, was going to be as moving and as fascinating as any she had yet written. Nor was I wrong. *Jackson's Dilemma* is a haunting and enigmatic work, and Jackson himself a mysterious and memorable figure. His mystery takes hold of the reader's imagination, and the ending of the novel is, at least to me, quite specially sad and beautiful, touching and moving. Jackson feels that he has done what he can and what he came for; and now, the work over, he has 'come to a place where there is no road'. He is not ill, or in despair, but he feels there is no further work for him to do. In a diary entry of the time Iris noted: 'How much I should like now to talk to Jackson'.

Less than a year after completing the novel Iris was writing again in her diary. She was beginning, she felt, 'to sail away into the darkness'. It was in a sense the magician and artist speaking, and bidding farewell to her art. It was the writer speaking. To me, her fellow-animal, she said nothing, knowing that I understood.

Jackson's predicament had become her own, with the added poignancy that Jackson, however memorable, is only a character in the last novel, while Iris, his creator, was a very real person, and even the nightmare of Alzheimer's could never change her. Her sweetness of character remained to the end. She could no longer write, and I grieved for her and with her about that: but our relations were just the same, since, where the pair of us together was concerned, she had never really been a 'writer' at all.

18

Getting Along with Myself

Nadine Gordimer

There seems to be some confusion, here: I *am* the writer. So I can only conclude that I shall be relating what it is like to be living with myself. Not that there isn't a situation cited: everyone is faced with the basic problem of the self. A secret intimacy which, it is said, influences all others. First Know Thyself. Perhaps the most difficult relationship of all?

I've had to live with myself through a long life as a writer and as a woman. It wouldn't have been much different existentially had that life been between the writer and a man. Whatever the gender, we writers have to make, no matter how, clear distinction between what life-space is reserved for the writer and what must be that of the – what shall I term it? – socio-biological life. Sounds grandiose, that term, but I can't settle for 'emotional life' because there are strong emotions involved in the product of the writing life.

The apportionment of time and attention means self-discipline of a very strict kind. A journalist has a deadline to meet. The poet, novelist is her/his own boss. The publisher may specify, in a contract, when the manuscript shall be delivered, but this is on the writer's estimate, as task-master, of when it shall be fulfilled by the workings of an imagination which keeps no clock or calendar. If the advance payment runs out before the work is achieved, that's the nature of the gap between creativity and commerce.

It goes without saying that no writer waits for what people who are not writers call inspiration. Not that it doesn't come; but usually not in the hours set down for the writing-table, the typewriter, word-processor (or whatever the tool may be). Those hours are for the transformation of something already occurred, themes that take hold, beneath some other activity or situation. Waking up in the middle of the night. Ceasing to hear what the battle in a bar or a meeting is about. A displacement to a level of another irresistible, intense concentration elsewhere. I think I began to write, relating narratives, conversations, impressions silently to myself as a child sitting in the back of my parents' car on drives long or short. Now I often have this same sort of experience on long-distance flights; between a *here* and a *there*, the demands of exchange with other people, I'm living with myself: the self of the individual imagination. (The collective imagination is what you and I enter through literature, the theatre, films.)

I believe writers, artists in general, have something of the monster in their personality. If selfishness *is* monstrous. Like most writers – I'll guarantee – I've had to accept in myself that I would have to without compunction put the demands of my writing generally before human obligations – except, perhaps, while falling in love. On the principle that every businessman or woman executive is protected from random visitors and telephone calls by a guard of receptionist and secretary, I long ago made it clear to everyone, even those closest and dearest to me, that during my working hours no-one must walk in on me. Since the house where I live with others is also my workplace, I've made as an exception only an interruption to tell me the house is on fire. When my children were too young for boarding school my writing hours were those when they were absent at day school, and during the holidays the monster-writer decreed that they keep out of sight and sound during those same hours. But I got what I no doubt deserved one day, when my small son transgressed, playing outside near my window, and I heard him reply to a friend's question 'What's your mother's job?' – 'She's a typist.' His response to living with a writer.

I've found myself to be a secretive person to live with. I don't know if this is general, for writers. I have been unable to share with anyone the exigencies, the euphoria at having arrived at what I wanted in my work or the frustration at finding it lacking. I cannot understand how the great Thomas Mann could bring himself to read the day's stint of writing aloud to his assembled family each evening. I've always been convinced no-one could reach what I really was saying in a piece of writing until I had satisfied myself finally that it was the best I could possibly do with it.

My man, Reinhold Cassirer, with whom I lived for forty-eight years, sharing everything else in our lives, never saw a story or novel of mine in the making, although he was always the first to read it when it was done. He completely respected and protected this, my privacy.

A novel might take as long as three or more years. He should have been the one to respond to what it must have been like, living with a writer.

19

The Pantomime Horse

Amanda Craig

My husband was once rung up by a newspaper, the (London) *Daily Telegraph*, and asked what it was like to live with a novelist.

'Like being the back end of a pantomime horse', he said. I have always thought this a perfect metaphor for the absurdity of living with a writer. Your partner is invisible, apart from maintaining that illusion of that strange, cavorting parody of a horse having a pair of hind legs – while you, the public face, are actually wearing a mask. Yet unlike the back end, you can at least see where you're going. Your partner, your back end, can push blindly but receives neither applause nor credit.

Living with a writer must be so horrible that it is a wonder anyone chooses to do it. For a start, I have yet to meet even the nicest of us who is not, at heart, a kind of monster. How but through utter selfishness, arrogance, single-mindedness and bloody-mindedness would a novel ever be written? Graham Greene claimed that every writer must have a chip of ice in his heart, and this is uncomfortably close to the truth. No matter how warm, how engaged as a human being, there is this necessary detachment that does not sit easily with a happy love-life or a well-balanced family. If, in addition, you happen to be the kind of novelist intensely interested in people, and in producing an imaginary history from certain observed psychological traits, you are going to be far less tolerant of any flaws in a partner. To a novelist, mild indolence speeds towards tragedy brought about by sloth; attention to personal appearance is magnified and distorted into grotesque vanity; and every motive or action is fraught with ominous possibility. We tend, I suspect, to see the world both more vividly, and more garishly. This makes us prone to the very flaws we attack (for nobody attacks a moral flaw more vigorously than those who suffer from it).

Vain, self-dramatising, self-pitying, arrogant, callous, foolish, censorious and just plain selfish – why does anyone put up with us? I suppose because we also have to contain and express the opposite qualities, too. Someone entirely made up of faults would be hopeless at creating characters for readers to engage and sympathise with. So novelists are also more selfless, brave, loving, humble, wise and generous than might be normal, too. Dr Johnson observed that the best part of a writer is found in his books, but it is not as simple as that. It is my belief that anyone who writes a novel, no matter how bad, becomes a richer human being simply by being forced to fully inhabit the bad in themselves, and to become more aware of their own potential for good. What they then do with this awareness is another matter. Some of the greatest rogues and liars of recent history have, like Sir Lawrence Van der Post, been very different from the saintly person projected by their writing; whereas those who write acidulously and seemingly without charity can, like the late Auberon Waugh, be the kindest of people in private.

Certainly, when I first met the man who became my husband, one of the things that interested him in me was my being a (then unpublished) novelist. He is an economist who had read philosophy and politics at Oxford, but he could also have won a scholarship to read English, having been an outstanding scholar at school. His oldest friend has always believed that he subsumed his own creativity into mine, which is not the case, but it's certainly true that our passionate love of reading is one of the great bonds between us. There are fewer people around than you might think who share the same love of children's books, which over time I have found to be a key ingredient in many deep friendships. The value children's literature places on courage, fidelity, imagination and adventure tends to be lasting ones. My husband was a merchant banker when I first met him, but within a week of our going out together had given it up to do a PhD. Far from having found myself a rich boyfriend, we had years of poverty together. Although this was hard, it focused each of us wonderfully on what it was we really wanted to do with our lives, at a time in the 1980s when most of our contemporaries were intent on getting rich. Being poor meant that our entertainment was mostly books, books and more books. My error, in writing my first novel, was to assume that all readers would be as well-read and alert to irony as he was....

In stories and films about writers, you always get told their debut was an instant success and that the worst a couple has to face is the temptation of the successful writer by the world, the flesh and the devil. You don't hear of the opposite happening, which is much, much more common and far harder on a relationship. The anguish of a writer's partner at a bad review is as bad as that of the writer (though as for the writer, time and experience modifies this). It is failure, not success, that tempts a young writer to go off with someone who could (possibly) change their fortune. Those who live with a writer have the additional difficulty of trying to conceal their own sadness and being a source of comfort and courage, where the author can, if so inclined, indulge in prolonged breast-beating.

The parallels between what is required from a new father, and from a new writer's partner are, I think, peculiarly strong. For fathers, too, the birth of a child is a huge and traumatic event, and one that takes their lover away from them into a world from which they are largely excluded. Yet they have to be strong, and sane, the fixed compass-foot to which the other foot, in Donne's metaphor, must return. They have to not interfere, to stay at home, to trust.

Occasionally, at literary parties, I've come across the spouses of writers, lonely figures desperately trying to mingle with writers. The reaction of the authors present is invariably resentment and boredom, for such events are not social events, or an opportunity to meet famous people. A literary party may be a forum for flirtation and friendship, but it is predominantly a seething world of professional networking, manipulation and scrutiny in which the writer's partner has no business to be. It does sometimes happen that a newly successful young author is seduced by someone who offers an instant entrée into the new world they've just discovered. I've seen it happen for both heterosexual and homosexual authors; it's very cruel, because inevitably the seducer moves on to the next promising young thing, and the discarded one is left with a broken-hearted partner and a tarnished relationship. The literary world can be smiling and kind, but it can also be a jungle, and a wise partner is one who stays discrete from it. They can just about attend their own writer's launch-party, but they shouldn't expect to be given any attention by the other invitees. This is a different world, with its own codes, snobberies, gossip, scandals and loyalties. It takes years to learn your way round it, and a partner can inadvertently cause huge offence – or worse still, bore.

Yet neither should they be locked out. I've also seen marriages in which the writer excludes their partner from their professional social life, which is rude and unkind. Why should they put up with all the mood-swings, demands and financial instability of living with us, and never meet any of our colleagues? Although a writer's life is usually no more exciting than that of an accountant, many non-writers perceive a curious glamour attached to writing books. Often, the result is disappointment. My husband has come to a number of literary dinner-parties at which the level of spiteful gossip has horrified him. Fortunately, my own friends aren't like that. I think he finds us all amusing, faintly absurd, and interesting; some have become friends of his, too. He has learnt that the quickest way of getting on with other novelists is to read one of their books, and ask them about their work. As writers are used to other writers never bothering to read them, he tends to be recognised as exceptionally intelligent and charming.

What you need in a writer's partner is a combination of rock-solid faith, a sense of the absurd and deep sensitivity. You need someone who can accept, at the end of their own day's work, the fact that they can come home to find one or other of the following: a delicious dinner and a happy writer, or someone sobbing onto the unpeeled potatoes because their new book isn't working. As with a manic depressive, the highs are very high and the lows are very low. It's only with time, experience and great determination that a writer learns to approximate normality. In one sense, a partnership between two writers is doomed for this reason, for how can you know that you won't both be down at the same time, or madly competitive, like Plath and Hughes? On the other hand, who else is likely to be so helpful, so understanding? There are authors like Margaret Drabble and Michael Holroyd, or Maggie O'Farrell and William Sutcliffe, who appear to be mutually supportive to the highest degree. Almost all the authors I know who are happily married, however, have partners who aren't writers, and who work in solid, professional jobs of the kind writers neither understand nor (often) respect. The ones whose marriages have ended in acrimony are those who inspire their partner to try their luck as writers too. Invariably, what they produce is a pale parody of their partner's writing, which embitters them and fills them with resentment and incomprehension as to why they, too, aren't published. No writer should ever sleep with, live with or God forbid marry an aspiring writer – not without reading what happened to J. D. Salinger. After all, who wants to see a pantomime horse with two heads?

20

Can This Collaboration Be Saved?

Anne Bernays and Justin Kaplan

Several years ago, when we decided to collaborate on *The Language of Names*, the biographer A. Scott Berg urged each of us to keep a journal. Writing a book together was sure to make an interesting story, he said. We found his enthusiasm ominous, suspecting that he had in mind a kind of meta-narrative featuring two viewpoints on a four-decade-old marriage as it followed a declining arc toward self-destruction.

For several reasons, laziness being the least of them, we never followed his suggestion. Each of us was afraid such a journal would act like a negative sundial, telling only the cloudy hours – disappointments, false starts, disagreements, even rage – and serve as a durable reminder of trials that might otherwise evanesce. Why go out of your way to rack up woes that might incriminate the other party? Didn't we have enough worries without committing them to paper? We'd heard tales of horror about couples who broke up in the middle of a project or vowed never to try it again.

If we had had enough grit to keep journals, however, here's how some of the entries would read:

> J. K.: Talk about imp of the perverse! Left a great job in book publishing so I could work by myself. Now I'm in a nonstop editorial meeting, with me accountable to A. and A. accountable to me. Like Ambrose Bierce's

version of marriage – 'a community consisting of a master, a mistress and two slaves, making in all, two'.

A. B.: J. testing me again: knows only thing that will get me into a library is to see last time someone checked out one of my novels. Sent me to Harvard to Tozzer anthropology library. After giving me rapid-fire directions, dragon at front desk followed me to stacks and, seeing I was in wrong place – actually feeling faint, with numbers and letters swimming sickeningly together – said, 'Don't you know your alphabet?' Took much too long locating and plundering obscure journal. J. could have done same in 10 minutes.

J. K.: Maybe this will pass, but right now I don't think it's going to work out. Different rhythms, standards, exactions. A. needs first-draft feedback right away. Those typos of hers are driving me bananas! Maybe we should have stuck to travel pieces – quick in, quick out. Egypt was a breeze compared to this daily slog.

A. B.: J. and I disagree whether or not it's interesting that Thurgood Marshall's grandfather changed his first name from Thoroughgood. I want it in text; J. wants to leave it out – 'Who cares?' Compromise effected: we stick it in footnote.

J. K.: Another lunch-hour manuscript consult coming up. Suppose I don't like what she's going to show. Gotta be diplomatic – say the 'positive' things first, but then – what about the rest of the day?

A. B.: Distraught. Thinking of laying down my tools. Cracked my brain over 'Literary Names' for weeks; finally get a draft I like; give it to J., who says, 'What is this? Why did you pick this chapter?' Unable to answer. 'We both agreed I should do it, don't you remember?' J. points out shortcomings, mainly things omitted or out of sequence. I'm so ignorant I don't even know what it is I don't know. Remind him I don't have his background – or his trick memory. J. thinks I'm lazy. Worse than being stupid?

A. B.: Back on horse. J. has found patience to coach me. Needs more, here and here and here. I tell him, 'You do Toni Morrison. You've read it. I haven't.' He agrees. Hug briefly. Forgiveness on both sides.

By now – that is, three years after we began – we've learned to anticipate an automatic response whenever we say we've written a book together (the word 'actually' always hangs in the air). There's a pause, a quizzical smile, and then a nerveless witticism to the effect that it's nice to see you two are still talking to each other. Responses like that suggest an even darker view of the hazards of collaboration than the one we had when we started out. Still, given the tensions and abrasions that exist in the most ideal solitary writing circumstances, it's reasonable to wonder why we were willing to put domestic tranquility on the line.

There have been successful collaborations, of course: Beaumont and Fletcher wrote a dozen or so plays together; Frederic Dannay and Manfred Lee wrote nearly a hundred detective novels as Ellery Queen. And we knew of others who chose to work together because it gave them confidence, imposed discipline, doubled their literary capital and widened their range. But we were convinced that writing in tandem is a little like two people walking a tightrope while holding hands. So risky does this balancing act seem – especially in retrospect – that it's not surprising relatively few writers attempt it. Collaboration involves the kind of full-scale homogenization that goes against most writers' grain: above all, a writer wants to sound *sui generis*. Writing is a solo enterprise. By its very nature collaboration is perverse, a partial surrender of both personal style and narcissistic gratification for the sake of the whole. Some of us become writers simply because we like to be alone, our own bosses. There was even an inherent perversity in the subject we chose to write about, since nobody seems to agree on what a name is to begin with.

When collaborators happen to be husband and wife the difficulties are compounded, for now there are emotional as well as literary bullets to be dodged. What happens, for instance, when the partners don't agree on attack or structure? Who decides? More perilous, what happens when one fails to live up to the expectations of the other? Can this kind of disappointment be kept from spilling over into 'real life'? Can you allow yourself to be as brutally demanding about your partner's work as you think you are about your own?

Style, or 'voice', is an elusive but pervasive characteristic of written prose and hangs on vocabulary, sentence structure and variation, idiom, pace, purpose, mood – and more. Some years ago John Updike complained in an interview that no matter what he wrote it always ended up sounding like John Updike. Why was he complaining? Most of us spend years trying to develop a distinctive and recognizable voice. Yet in writing our book we made a concerted attempt to meld our separate voices, each trying to take on the rhythms and idioms of the other, in the hope that the final product would be seamless and still have a voice of its own. The biographer relaxed, became less literary, more conversational and unbuttoned. The novelist became more muscular, more cadenced and conceptual. We met in the middle.

What brought us to The Language of Names was a confluence of interests and a shared belief that names are much more than merely nominal: they have a profound, almost magical, but mostly unacknowledged role in daily discourse and social choreography. At first, it was comforting to think of our subject as circumscribed, self-limiting, but the more we read, the wider and deeper the subject seemed to grow. By the time the research phase of the operation was over – assuming that it's at all possible to separate research from writing – we had about three yards of file folders full of drafts, notes, clippings and photocopies and a couple of shelves of related books and journals. We had agreed to divide up and assign this material according to what we considered our particular strengths and interests. Disagreement had not yet entered the picture, since research is a nut-gathering enterprise, although there's always a working hypothesis in charge. It was the selection of which nuts to use and which to throw away that led to conflict. But as we went about transforming our ideas and raw materials into a book, we saw that two heads, undeniably different and often stubborn, could sometimes be better than one. Each of us applied to the other for editorial suggestions, 90 percent of which were gratefully acted upon.

The temptation to make a metaphor out of a work partnership and apply it to marriage is irresistible. Like marriage, collaboration is not to be entered into unadvisedly or lightly. Still, most men and women in longtime, stable marriages wouldn't dream of trying to create something together, other than a child, because they realize that under the tightrope there's not only no net but a vat of boiling oil. As in a marriage, the success of a collaborative relationship depends largely on patience, tact, negotiation and respect, not to mention the capacity to be amused when the urge to throttle may seem overwhelming.

21

Maugham's Marriage

Jeffrey Meyers

I

Maugham was a homosexual and spent most of his life living with men. But in the decade between 1905 and 1915 he had love affairs with four attractive and professionally accomplished women, and portrayed them in his work. Violet Hunt appeared as Rose Waterford in *The Moon and Sixpence*, the revolutionary Alexandra Kropotkin became Anastasia Leonidov in *Ashenden*, the actress Ethelwyn Sylvia (Sue) Jones inspired Rosie Driffield in *Cakes and Ale* and Gwendolyn Syrie Barnardo Wellcome was the model for Mrs Tower in 'Jane' and Lady Grayston in *Our Betters*. Maugham's marriage, unlike those that sustained and inspired other writers, was utterly miserable. He married Syrie in 1916, divorced in 1928 and hated her for the rest of his long life. She intensified his misogyny and provoked some of his most vitriolic portraits of women.*

---

* See Jeffrey Meyers, *Married to Genius* (London: London Magazine Editions and New York: Barnes & Noble, 1977). This book, one of my slighter efforts, received very little attention. An editor at Harper & Row, which owned Barnes & Noble, was pleased to inform me that the book was not publishable. 'Yes, it is,' I replied. 'Why do you say that?' he asked. 'Because you published it.' But as the first book on this subject, it was influential, both for the way it determined the direction of my own work and for the impact it had on other writers. It contained chapters on Tolstoy, Shaw, Joyce, Woolf, Conrad, Mansfield, Lawrence, Hemingway and Fitzgerald, and I went on to write biographies of the last five. It was also a model, most notably, for Phyllis Rose's *Parallel Lives: Five Victorian Marriages* (New York, 1983) and Brenda Maddox's *Nora: a Biography of Nora Joyce* (Boston, 1988). Maddox interviewed me about Nora, praised my pioneering work — and then left me out of her acknowledgements and bibliography.

Syrie's father was the great Victorian philanthropist Dr Thomas John Barnardo. Tiny, frail and almost totally deaf, Barnardo was born in Hamburg in 1845. His Jewish family left Germany, after a wave of anti-Semitic riots, when Barnardo was still a small child. They settled in Dublin, where he later converted to Evangelical Christianity and preached fervently in the slums. After briefly studying medicine in London (he never actually became a doctor), he planned to become a missionary and convert the heathen in the wilds of China. But he decided instead to rescue homeless children in his own country, and with typically demonic energy founded more than forty orphanages in London and throughout England.

Syrie (short for Sarah Louise) was born in 1879, one of seven children (of whom four survived), including a mentally retarded dwarf. Brought up in a strict and pious household amidst a horde of waifs and orphans, Syrie (nicknamed 'Queenie') spent her Sundays reading the Bible and singing hymns. She played the organ while her father raised money in London churches, and never smoked or drank. Syrie first met Henry Wellcome, a Wisconsin-born chemist and pharmaceutical tycoon, at her parents' house in Surbiton, on the Thames, in 1899. They became engaged on a cruise up the Nile in 1901. Though Wellcome was twenty-six years older than she, his religious background, commitment to medical research and impressive wealth (which might be channeled into Barnardo's orphanages) made him seem the ideal husband. They married in 1901, and two years later had a mentally retarded son, whom they farmed out to a foster family. The marriage ended acrimoniously in Quito, Ecuador, in 1909 when Wellcome accused Syrie of adultery with an American financier. Like Maugham, he believed she was a 'deeply immoral' woman. After their separation Syrie, who had a hot temper and sharp tongue, told a friend: 'Ever since our marriage, the greater part of our time has been spent, as he well knows, in places I detested, collecting curios... sacrificing myself in a way I hated, both to please him and to gather curios.'

Reacting against her pious background, Syrie had many lovers. The leader of the pack was Gordon Selfridge, another Wisconsin tycoon, who had made his fortune in England by founding the huge Oxford Street department store that still bears his name. Like

Syrie, the flamboyant Selfridge came from a puritanical family, but knew how to spend money. He took long holidays in Monte Carlo, gambled and owned racehorses, and was seen about town with glamorous and socially prominent women. A contemporary gossip columnist wrote that 'Selfridge is as much one of the sights of London as Big Ben. With his black morning jacket, grey-striped trousers, white vest slip, pearl tie-pin and orchid buttonhole, he is a mobile landmark of the metropolis.'

Maugham first met Syrie in late 1913, when he was still in love with Sue Jones, and she was married to Wellcome and involved with Selfridge. In February 1914, soon after Sue had rejected his proposal and married her Irish nobleman, Syrie and Maugham became lovers. The thin-lipped, large-nosed Syrie was more attractive than beautiful. She had fine brown eyes and lovely skin, was fashionably and expensively dressed, and wore large – but fake – emerald rings. Her biographer wrote that Syrie was independent-minded, unreflective and brassy, qualities which must have once appealed to her [future] husband but gradually stood out more and more harshly against his own reticence.

Maugham dined frequently at her house and was delighted to go to bed with her. Syrie – a divorcée, adulteress and kept woman – flattered him by declaring she was madly in love and surprised him by suggesting they have a baby. He gallantly (if rather passively) went along with her wishes, but she miscarried their first child. It's surprising that Maugham, a medical doctor with a knowledge of genetics, would risk a second pregnancy with the thirty-five-year-old Syrie, whose brother and only child were both physically impaired and mentally retarded, and who had just had a miscarriage. Nevertheless, when she became pregnant again in late November 1914 he took her to Rome (Italy had not yet entered the war and it was close to his favorite bolt-hole in Capri) where she could have their baby in secret. Though not cut out to be a father, he wanted to have a child.

Wellcome had settled only £2,400 a year on Syrie and Selfridge had been paying for her luxurious house in Regent's Park. In 1915, when Syrie nobly refused Selfridge's offer to settle £5,000 a year on her (more than double Wellcome's sum), Maugham wrote a rather cryptic letter to the painter Gerald Kelly, his closest friend and confidant, suggesting that Syrie was pregnant and had broken with Selfridge. The sordid situation shocked Maugham and made him extremely uneasy. He couldn't bring himself to praise or defend Syrie's behavior, though he saw that her impulse to be honest had finally destroyed the edifice of secrecy and lies on which her life was built. Unwilling to lie about his own feelings, Maugham hoped to be kind, firm and just. If that led to a break with Syrie, he would have no regrets.

The affair reached its crisis when Wellcome hired private detectives to follow Syrie. When he found proof of her adultery, Syrie tried to kill herself by swallowing a whole bottle of Veronal pills. She had deceived Maugham by telling him that Wellcome had given her freedom to do as she pleased. But, Wellcome's biographer stated, "there is certainly no evidence for this...highly improbable [assertion]...in Wellcome's correspondence with his lawyers'. When his detectives got wind of Syrie's pregnancy, which Maugham was particularly eager to keep out of the courts, Wellcome sued for divorce and named the conveniently well-off and unmarried Maugham, rather than Selfridge, as co-respondent.

Sir George Lewis, a reliable old friend and noted lawyer, told Maugham that Selfridge, to avoid becoming involved in the scandal, had broken with her and that Syrie, living well above her means, was heavily in debt. 'You're to be the mug to save her,' Sir George warned. 'You're cruelly trapped and you'd be a fool to marry her.' Maugham certainly did not want to marry her but, remembering that he had been orphaned as a small child, replied: 'if I don't I shall regret it all my life....I could not bear to think what [the child's] future would be if I didn't marry its mother.'

Maugham had often tried to solve his problems by a change of locale. After Syrie's first and second pregnancies he had fled to his old refuge in Capri. The aesthete Ellingham Brooks, aware that Maugham was being trapped, feared that an unholy woman would invade their sanctuary and disrupt their homosexual life. The novelist Compton Mackenzie, who also lived on Capri, remembered Brooks in the summer of 1914 'coming along one day in a great flutter to say that Maugham had got himself involved with a married woman and that he was going to have to marry her. "I don't know what

I shall do if Maugham brings a wife to the [Villa] Cercola. I don't think [E. F.] Benson will like it at all either."'

In a fascinating letter to Syrie, written in the 1920s and not published until 1962, Maugham frankly stated that he married her out of a strange mixture of compassion, guilt and self-sacrifice. But, he said, she knew quite well the true state of his feelings:

> I married you because I thought you loved me and I could not bear to think that in a life in which I did not find much to praise you should suffer for something which was innocent. I married you because I was prepared to pay for my folly and selfishness, and I married you because I thought it the best thing for your happiness and for Elizabeth's welfare, but I did not marry you because I loved you, and you were only too well aware of that.

After the painful experience of his own marriage, his comments on matrimony were savage. In 'The Escape' he insisted that nothing but immediate flight could save a man once a woman had decided to trap him. He told his friend Ann Fleming that the institution of marriage had completely lost its point and was appropriate only for communicants in the Anglican Church. In *The Summing Up* he regretted that he had sacrificed himself to unworthy women (like Syrie) because he did not want to hurt them.

The awkward situation – emotional, moral, legal and financial – hastened to its climax. Maugham's only child Elizabeth (always called Liza, after the heroine of his first novel) was born illegitimately in Rome on 1 September 1915. The birth by Caesarean section was difficult and dangerous, and Syrie wept when told she would be unable to have any more children. Wellcome divorced her in February 1916. Considering Maugham's frequent condemnation of marriage in his early novels and Syrie's all-too-obvious faults, it must have been very difficult indeed for him to marry her. But he did so, incongruously enough, in a sleazy ceremony in Jersey City, New Jersey, on 26 May 1917. He remembered 'standing with my bride-to-be before a justice of the peace – who first sentenced the drunk in front of us, then married us, then sentenced the drunk behind us'. The happy couple went on their Jersey shore honeymoon with their twenty-month-old baby and her nursemaid.

Compton Mackenzie, on the scene at Capri, ironically observed that the usually egoistic Maugham, moved by Liza's plight, had acted out of character: 'It was the only time in his life that Willie behaved like a gentleman; the result was fatal.' Trapped by Syrie's pregnancy, Maugham incurred the wrath that Wellcome had originally felt for Gordon Selfridge. Selfridge, in turn, managed to pass her on to the unfortunate Willie, and escaped without paying a penny. Though Syrie loved Maugham, she made him intensely miserable, and marrying her was the greatest mistake of his life. Living with her confirmed his misogyny and deepened his already cynical attitude to life, and he resolved in the future to be wary of altruistic acts.

II

Maugham's ten years with Syrie were as arduous and exhausting as his decade of struggle for literary success. He was a sophisticated man of the world who had known Syrie for three years before he married her, yet he did not learn what she was really like until, after their wedding, the fur began to fly. He lived with her on and off – mainly off – for a decade, saw that their characters and interests clashed, and soon came to hate her. He knew she was poorly educated, and found she was also ignorant and superficial, vain, materialistic and philistine. He called her 'a foolish woman who has never been interested in anything really except social position. She is, and always has been, a snob' – though Maugham himself liked nothing better than entertaining royalty. When they lived in Switzerland after Liza's birth, Syrie, on her own for most of the time while he was absorbed in his writing, became irritable and quarrelsome. He would repeatedly tell her, 'don't make me scenes', and was greatly relieved when she decided to return to England. In March 1916 he told his brother Frederick that 'the future cannot have in store any worse harassment than I have undergone in the last eight months'.

Syrie drove Maugham mad with her pleas for attention and hysterical outbursts. She complained that he compelled her to remain on the staircase and put her in mortal danger as bombs fell on London during the Great War. Though a bomb would have saved him the trouble of strangling her, Maugham would not have remained at her side if the danger had been great. In his bitter letter to Syrie he complained of how bored he was by her constant nagging, her obsession with the trivia of furniture and frocks, her intellectual limitations that left him starved for conversation. When Maugham and his friends discussed books, Syrie, feigning interest and in several tones of voice, would merely declare: 'How extraordinary!' All she wanted to do, he lamented, was to buy expensive clothes and be fashionably dressed. Writing in January 1920, Maugham explained how he, like many others trapped in marriage, gradually adjusted and came to accept his miserable state: 'In married life there are times when one feels things are so hateful that it is worthwhile doing anything to get out of it, but one goes on — for one reason or another — and somehow they settle down more or less, and one becomes resigned or makes allowances or what not, and time goes on and eventually things seem not so bad as they might have been.'

Their conflicts focused on four aspects of domestic life: their sexual relations, their houses, her decorating business, and the way she brought up Liza. Maugham, of course, was familiar with Syrie's sordid past and she knew all about his homosexuality. He thought she understood that he could not and they would not have a normal sexual life. But her love grew as his hatred intensified, and he felt she had betrayed their tacit agreement by making intolerable sexual demands. Thinking, no doubt, of Syrie, he wrote in *Of Human Bondage* (1915): 'She was the sort of woman who was unable to realise that a man might not have her own obsession with sex.' In *The Hour Before the Dawn* (1942) he observed: 'I don't think sexual relations are very satisfactory unless they spring from mutual desire; unless they do that there's something rather humiliating about them for both parties.' In this case, however, he felt more humiliated than Syrie. Maugham, who really loved men but tried to love women, found it difficult to accept, and even fought against, his deepest sexual feelings. In one of his most frequently quoted comments, Maugham, explaining his bisexuality and the failure of his marriage, exclaimed: 'I was a quarter normal and three-quarters queer, but I tried to persuade myself it was the other way round. That was my greatest mistake.'

Maugham and Syrie moved frequently. They lived in four different and increasingly grand houses as both became more and more successful in their professions. They began by displacing his old roommate Walter Payne, and lived in Maugham's modest but fashionable Georgian house at 6 Chesterfield Street, off Curzon Street, in Mayfair. After the war, in the spring of 1919, they shifted to a larger, four-story house at 2 Wyndham Place, off the Marylebone Road. Four years later they moved slightly south to a more impressive five-story house at 43 Bryanston Square. And in 1927 they transferred to even grander premises at 213 King's Road, near Oakley Street and the Albert Bridge, in Chelsea.

Syrie, a wonderful hostess, knew how to entertain. The cosmopolitan Osbert Sitwell recalled that the most interesting guests came from Maugham's world rather than hers: 'Mrs Maugham and her brilliant husband...were always particularly kind to the young and gifted. There in Wyndham Place, in the large beige-painted, barrel-vaulted drawing-room of this eighteenth-century mansion, their friends were privileged to meet all the most interesting figures connected with the world of art, literature, and the theatre in both England and America.'

The great trouble, from Maugham's point of view, was that Syrie enjoyed all the benefits of living in these houses while he suffered all the inconveniences. He complained to the young writer Godfrey Winn that Syrie's friends, all strangers to him, had (like Penelope's suitors) occupied his home and depleted his stores: 'I used to write all day in my house in Chesterfield Street, and come down to dinner dead tired and not knowing one of the guests in my own house, eating my expensive food. They had all been invited by my wife.' On other occasions he had, with some embarrassment, to cancel invitations to his own friends when he belatedly discovered Syrie was giving yet another party.

Worse still, he sometimes found when returning from abroad that he no longer had a place to write. In the spring of 1919 Syrie appropriated his quiet study in Chesterfield Street and forced him to work in a small room overlooking the street. In March 1920 she rented their house on Wyndham Place, and cut him off from his study as well as from his essential books and papers. She offered him a small bed-sitter in a cheaper rented house, where he felt he was 'too old to pig it' and was unable to write. On the King's Road, Syrie – with no conception of an author's needs, despite all her years with Maugham – once again interfered with instead of assisting his work. Maugham paid all the bills, but often got shut out of his own house: 'The Glebe Place annex [to the King's Road house] was intended for Maugham, so that he could have his own entrance and a private suite. He used it from time to time, but said that he found it less than satisfactory to have his workroom converted to the gents' cloak room whenever his wife entertained.' When Syrie gave a party, his orderly papers, if not put away, were disturbed, even stolen. She cared nothing about his work – except for the prestige it brought and the money it earned.

Syrie's interest in furniture and houses soon blossomed into a thriving enterprise. In 1923 she opened a fashionable interior decorating business which, with all her social contacts, became an immediate success. Cecil Beaton, a mutual friend, caustically described how her innovative ideas had taken hold: 'Syrie caught the "no color" virus and spread the disease around the world.... [She] bleached, pickled or scraped every piece of furniture in sight. White sheepskin rugs were strewn on the eggshell-surfaced floors, huge white sofas were flanked with white crackled-paint tables, white peacock feathers were put in white vases against a white wall.... Mayfair drawing rooms looked like albino stage sets.' Another precious client, swept away by her designs, noted the destructive aspect of her business: ' "Syrie's", on Duke Street, already a Mecca for the fashionable, was full of her plaster-cast palm tree décor, limed and whitened Louis Quinze pieces (mostly nineteenth-century reproductions, which didn't stop the outcry that Mrs. Maugham was ruining antique furniture).' Syrie's white-on-white décor suddenly became the rage on both sides of the Atlantic, but the craze came to an end when her clients realized that white soon became soiled and needed constant cleaning. Nevertheless, she was instrumental in changing the way people furnished and decorated their homes. Dark, heavy, ornate Victorian and Edwardian interiors gradually gave way to the bright, open look of modern houses.

Maugham, watching from the sidelines, never missed a chance – in his stories, letters, conversations, or memoirs – to put the knife into Syrie. In 'Jane' (1923), he satirized Syrie as Mrs Tower, who was 'seized with the prevailing passion for decoration.... Everything that could be pickled was pickled and what couldn't be pickled was painted'. Mocking the current cant, he added: 'Nothing matched, but everything harmonized.' He told a close woman friend, Barbara Back, who disliked Syrie almost as much as he did, that Syrie, after exhausting all her good taste in trade, had nothing left for life. Beverley Nichols, a disciple who later turned against Maugham, recalled him mocking, through his stammer, her sycophancy and greed. 'She is almost certainly on her knees to an American m-m-millionairess', he told Nichols, 'trying to sell her a chamber p-p-pot.' And at one of their dinner parties Maugham felt obliged to warn his guests 'to hold tight to your chairs. They are almost certainly for s-s-sale'.

In his memoir 'Looking Back' he accused her of dealing unscrupulously, even illegally, with her clients, forcing them at times to take legal action to recover payment for a fake she had fobbed off as an antique. She was almost sent to prison when her insurance company discovered she had sold a valuable jade necklace, claimed it was stolen and put in for the loss. When Maugham warned or reproved her, she would 'make me scenes', accompanied by bountiful tears, till three in the morning. No matter how often she wore him out, he still had to get up early and write sparkling dialogue. Syrie *was* reckless and irresponsible. In October 1922, while driving a car, she killed a woman on a bicycle; then used all her wealth and influence to bring in a verdict of accidental death.

Nichols, in his partisan defense of Syrie, conceded that Maugham was 'terribly proud of being a father... and had a father's tenderness for [Liza]'. In his travel book on China, Maugham dropped his impersonal mask and, in a rare display of affection, described Liza, at the age of five or six, 'very smart in the white squirrel I brought her from China, coming in to say good-bye to me.... I play trains with her while her pram is being got ready'. He told her 'a little story before she [went] to sleep' and fondly observed that 'she looks really very nice in her pyjamas with her hair done up in two plaits'.

After Maugham moved permanently to France and wanted to preserve his tax-free status, he could spend only a limited amount of time in England. As the pretty little girl grew up into a teenager – she looked rather like the actress Geraldine Chaplin – his personal relations with her were confined to formal annual luncheons at Claridge's hotel. 'You can imagine what an ordeal it was for me,' he told a friend, 'and must have been for her, poor darling.' Maugham took no part in bringing up Liza, who was mainly cared for by nannies. But he felt she had absorbed her mother's snobbery, superficiality and materialism, and could not refrain from criticizing both Syrie's maternal possessiveness and Liza's immature dependence. Other people noticed the suffocating intimacy of mother and daughter. One of Syrie's friends remarked that Liza 'and Syrie were *very very* close. In fact, at the time I thought far too much so. And I said to Liza, "Really, you should try to detach yourself a little bit from your mother's apron-strings." I told her I thought it was just a little bit ludicrous at her age. I mean, even after she married Vincent [at the age of twenty-one] she was absolutely in her mother's pocket.'

Syrie had many staunch defenders, including Osbert Sitwell and Noël Coward, both in her lifetime and, after Maugham's attack in 'Looking Back', after her death. The intensely intellectual Rebecca West called Syrie 'an extremely talented and original and entertaining person with a curious driving industry'. She noted, though Maugham had insisted that Syrie took no interest in books, that she 'was oddly well read'. The condescending Lytton Strachey, who dined with the Maughams in the mid-1920s, sensed the strained atmosphere, the incongruity of their marriage and Maugham's manifest misery. He called Maugham 'a hang-dog personage... with a wife. Perhaps it was because I've eschewed such things for so long that I was amused – the odd mixture of restraint and laisser-aller struck me freshly – but eventually it's just that that becomes such a bore.'

Bruce Lockhart, an astute spy who knew both Syrie and Maugham, took a very different view from Rebecca West. In his diary he noted: 'Somerset Maugham is a peculiar man – has terrific inferiority complex, hates people, yet is a snob and cannot refuse a luncheon where he is to meet a countess. Life ruined by a wife who is coarse and irritating. Once he was having tea in his own house with a friend, when his wife came in. Her voice downstairs irritated him so much that he hid behind the sofa and stayed there until his wife had left again!' Lockhart is doubtless exaggerating, but there is no question Maugham found his wife intensely annoying. Lockhart went off the rails, however, in retailing some gossip he probably picked up second-hand from Maugham's lover Godfrey Winn. Lockhart maintained that an unnamed woman (Barbara Back) was intimately involved with Maugham's strange sexual habits and had a stranglehold on him: 'because of his homosexual nervosity he could not perform alone. The liaison was à trois. The third was Godfrey Winn! Maugham... is a man who has tried everything: drugs, etc., but he has an iron self-discipline and is now master of himself.' This tale collapses under close examination. His affairs with Violet Hunt, Sasha Kropotkin, Sue Jones and Syrie Wellcome proved that Maugham was perfectly capable of heterosexual relations. Sue would not have continued their affair for eight years, nor would Syrie have married him and continued to make sexual demands if he were not. In any case, he valued self-mastery and would never expose himself to the repeated humiliation of sexual impotence. If there is any truth to this story, Winn may have been alluding to a homosexual ménage à trois with Maugham and his lover, Gerald Haxton.

A professionally posed photo of Maugham and Syrie, taken about 1925, vividly exposed the unhappy relations observed by Strachey and Lockhart. The couple are in their sitting room, with a painting and flowers in the background and a Persian carpet (slightly rucked up) on the floor. Maugham, staring severely at the camera and leaning casually on Syrie's padded armchair, looks rather dashing in his full dark mustache, knotted polka-dot tie, waistcoat with looping gold watch chain and gray spats on highly polished shoes. Syrie, seated below him, is stylishly attired in black (with a fluffy white blouse and white stockings). She wears a turban-like hat, with a jeweled pin, pulled down to her eyes, fox fur draped around her shoulders, satiny dress and shoes with a strap. Heavily made up, her dark hair cut short, she also has a severe expression, and gazes into the distance as if to emphasize their separation. The effect is chilling.

Our Betters (1915), one of Maugham's best plays, is a scorching satire that exposes shameful secrets beneath society's brilliant surface. Arthur Fenwick, an American war profiteer who has made a fortune in England and pays Lady Grayston's bills in return for sexual favors, is clearly based on Syrie's lover Gordon Selfridge. As one character remarks: 'This is a strange house in which the husband is never seen and Arthur Fenwick, a vulgar sensualist, acts as host.' Syrie, sharing Maugham's life when he wrote the play, is drawn and quartered as the hypocritical and rapacious Lady Grayston. One close friend condemns her behavior: 'there's something very like heroism in the callousness with which you've dropped people when they've served your turn.... What makes it more complete is that what you've aimed at is trivial, transitory and worthless.' Another friend writes her off by stating: 'I know her through and through, and I tell you that she hasn't got a single redeeming quality.'

Maugham, fascinated by the 'pattern' of his life in both *Of Human Bondage* and *The Summing Up*, must have been struck by the cruel irony in his relations with Ethelwyn Sylvia Jones and Gwendolyn Syrie Wellcome. Sue's pregnancy (followed by a miscarriage) prevented her from committing herself to Maugham, who loved her deeply, and she married another man. Syrie's second pregnancy (following a miscarriage) while she was married to another man, forced Maugham to marry her. His caustic portrait of Syrie in *Our Betters* hammered the final nail into their matrimonial coffin.

III

The acquisition of the Villa Mauresque and move to France in 1926 represented not only a commitment to Gerald, but a rejection of Syrie. It was clear well before Maugham bought the Villa, and even before he dutifully married Syrie, that his attempt to share a life with her, however irregular, was doomed. When Willie Ashenden, in *Cakes and Ale*, remarks that authors' wives are odious, he is surely speaking for Maugham. In 1925 he mentioned Syrie's all-too-frequent complaints and his offer to let her divorce him – though he would not, despite his extreme unhappiness, initiate the suit: 'I hope during my absence she will cease her complaining about me to all her friends (which must be tedious for them).... She has only to say the word and I am willing to let myself be divorced.

I cannot change and she must either live with me as I am, or take her courage in both hands and make the break.'

In *Home and Beauty* (1919) the lawyer Raham condemns the humiliating need to expose one's adultery in public to obtain a divorce (a practice also satirized in Evelyn Waugh's *A Handful of Dust*, 1934), and gives Maugham's views on how the hypocritical law should be reformed. He believed that 'when two married persons agreed to separate it was nobody's business but their own. I think if they announced their determination before a justice of the peace, and were given six months to think the matter over, so that they might be certain they knew their minds, the marriage might then be dissolved without further trouble. Many lies would never be told, much dirty linen would never be washed in public.'

When their divorce, initiated in 1928, was finally granted by a court in Nice the following May, the long-suffering (but perhaps still guilt-ridden) Maugham accepted a greatly disadvantageous settlement. Though both had been unfaithful and Syrie had built up an extremely lucrative decorating business, he 'agreed to a lump sum payment of £12,000, £2,400 a year in alimony until Syrie remarried [which she never did], and £600 annual support payments for Liza. As well, Syrie was given the house in the King's Road, fully furnished, and a Rolls Royce'. Glad to be rid of her at last, Maugham threw in the chauffeur with the Rolls. Wellcome had settled £2,400 a year on her in 1910; Maugham, with much less money, maintained her market value and paid the same price. In April 1929, a month before the divorce became final, he heard that Syrie was still spreading the vindictive rumors about his sexual life with Gerald Haxton that she had first used to blackmail him into marriage in 1917. Though he pretended to be indifferent to the slander and told his niece that 'no one attaches the smallest importance to anything said by that abandoned liar', he was deeply hurt.

Like many divorced couples, their battles continued until death. In the early 1930s Maugham exposed Syrie's fraudulent attempt to force him to pay her income tax. She had told Inland Revenue officials that between 1926 and 1930, when Maugham was living in France, that they were actually living together in England and that he was responsible for £2,000 of her tax. After a French lover had jilted her, she made a second suicide attempt, jumped out of a mezzanine window in Cannes and broke both wrists. In December 1940, when Maugham, Syrie and Liza were all living in America, Maugham said that Syrie, who had always tried to dominate Liza, had become completely hysterical and had a disastrous effect on their grown daughter: 'Syrie has been making a terrible nuisance of herself and leading Liza a hell of a life. She has been making dreadful scenes and threatening to commit suicide: in fact the whole bag of tricks. Liza has only stood firm on one thing and that is a refusal to live with her.' Before sailing for America during World War II, Syrie had panicked about the thought of being torpedoed and asked Maugham what she should do if the ship went down. 'Swallow, just swallow', he advised her. 'I am assured that when you find yourself in the water, if you open your m-m-mouth wide, it's all over much more quickly.'

IV

In the spring of 1955 Syrie, whom he had scarcely seen for thirty years, became ill and took to her bed. But she was very tough, Maugham thought, and didn't seem to get any worse. On July 28 a telegram from Liza announced that her mother had died at the age of 76. Still bitter about the £2,400 alimony he had been paying every year since 1929 and anticipating the title ('Looking Back') of his last attack on Syrie, he wrote: 'It would be hypocrisy on my part to pretend that I am deeply grieved at Syrie's death. She had me every which way from the beginning and never ceased to give me hell. Her hope, for some years, I have been told, was that she would survive me. I wonder, when she looked back, if she ever did, whether it occurred to her what a mess she had made of her life.' Syrie's dishonesty and lies, he felt, had led to her lonely and miserable death.

In 1962 – when Liza's lawsuit to regain the paintings Maugham had given her revived his bitter memories of her birth, his unfortunate marriage and his costly divorce – he retaliated by publicly exposing Liza's illegitimacy and attacking Syrie in a three-part autobiographical essay, 'Looking Back'. Though Maugham 'cut all the best—or worst—bits out of it', the fascinating second part was the real bombshell. Maugham described meeting Syrie; her Jewish origins; her first marriage and child with Wellcome (not mentioning that the boy was mentally retarded); Selfridge's liaison with and financial support of Syrie; her love for Maugham; their adulterous sexual relations; his involvement in her scandalous divorce; his high-minded reasons for marrying her; their bizarre plan to give away their own child as soon as it was born; Liza's illegitimacy; his work as a secret agent in Russia; his convalescence in a Scottish sanatorium; his friendship with Haxton; his insistence on freedom to live and travel with Gerald; her slanderous accusations about his private life; her tedious 'scenes'; her snobbery; her intellectual shallowness; her bitchy character; her unscrupulous business dealings; her constant interference with his work; her suicide attempts; and, finally, their divorce.

Maugham's editor Alexander Frere, 'shocked at what seemed to him the ramblings of a madman', felt that 'Looking Back' would wound Liza and damage his reputation. When both Heinemann and Doubleday refused to publish it as a book, Maugham was furious and dismissed Frere as his literary executor. Graham Greene, in a letter to the *Daily Telegraph*, called it 'the sick Maugham's senile and scandalous work'. And the politician Robert Boothby (offering an amateur medical diagnosis) agreed that 'the brain went gradually, slowly, gradually, but the last two years, when he wrote that final dreadful book, the brain had gone'.

Maugham's friends had frequently remarked that 'he hated anything to be known about him, and was very, very cagey, and we never discussed certain subjects at all.... He is so restrained and so well disciplined that we may find ourselves wishing that he would sometimes let himself go'. In *The Summing Up* he had put a limit to intimacy and refused to lay bare his heart. But in 'Looking Back' the impulse to express his most personal feelings overcame his notorious caution and reticence. He boldly and bravely dropped his mask, spoke out against hypocritical social conventions and finally told the truth. His critics and Syrie's friends, who never had to live with her, questioned the propriety and condemned the caddishness of the attacks on his dead wife and living daughter. But they could not refute Maugham's charges.

'Looking Back' may have violated the rules of decorum, but it is far from being the ramblings of a senile, brain-damaged madman. The memoir contained many poignant and penetrating revelations and showed Maugham in full command of his formidable satiric powers. Deeply wounded by Syrie, who he felt had ruined his life, he fought back with his pen. 'It cost him great pain,' Kenneth Clark observed, 'but it was something he had to get off his chest.' Maugham's late masterpiece, which deserves to be published as a book, belongs with fiercely honest retrospective works like Hemingway's *A Moveable Feast* (1961); Anthony West's *Heritage* (1984) about the parents who had rejected him, Rebecca West and H. G. Wells; and Paul Theroux's *Sir Vidia's Shadow* (1998).

Maugham was an unwilling bridegroom, but he had social as well as literary ambitions, wanted to conform to the prevailing mores and thought a 'good' marriage would enhance his career. In his autobiographical *The Summing Up*, he gave a naïve but poignant account of what he expected in marriage. He hoped it would bring peace from the disturbance of chaotic and troublesome love affairs, provide a tranquil and settled existence, allow him all the time he needed to write, and enable him to live a free yet dignified life. In fact, none of these hopes was ever realized. His love affair with Haxton, whom he met before Syrie became pregnant, inevitably caused tumultuous complications with his wife. She constantly interfered with, even prevented, his writing, and his life became more turbulent than ever. Seeking freedom, he found only bondage. His relations with Syrie left a residue of permanent hatred and, at the very end of his life, a legacy of scandal and recrimination. Maugham would pay dearly for his generous impulse and façade of marital respectability.

22

Being Two of Us

Mary Ann Caws

What is it like, teaching and writing alongside someone you love? Particularly when you are driven, as I am, it can be like living on the verge: perhaps not of a nervous breakdown, but on the verge of something. In my case, it was divorce. This is the way it came about; I shall write it as fiction. Although it is not really entirely that, its clear exaggerations and exasperations can be attributed – perhaps – to that form of seeing and transcribing events and feelings.

It was all a very long time ago as I speak from here, now, in New York where I teach and write and live. And remember, rightly or wrongly, or most probably both.

We both had degrees from Yale, mine a simple MA, Ralph's a PhD (I have changed both names, in accord with fictionalizing the matter and the memory, although it little matters). When we married, in 1962, in Yale's Dwight Chapel, we left New Haven. Ralph suggested I return and finish my degree there, but, stubbornly, I did not.

I looked up to him, understandably: Ralph was, and remains, intensely smart, sensitive, attractive: I have not seen him for over fifteen years, as I write, or rather rewrite, this narrative about part of our marriage.

The narrative begins as we find two jobs at the State University in Michigan. Ralph was hired as an instructor, and me as a faculty wife. That is to say, I was given the post of assistant reference librarian for interlibrary loans. Forget my training, forget my longings, this job meant wrapping books for mailing, and answering a question or two. The intellectual life was not what you would call ideal, nor was the practical one very comfortable.

We lived all winter in a summer cottage by a lake. The chill was intense, and lasting. The bathtub was green canvas, purchased from a Sears catalog, exactly what we could afford. We had to fill it under the faucet, and bring it downstairs after each use, to dump the water out upon the lawn. The fish insisted on dying in the lake and floating to the top. This was not the way I had imagined the setting of our marriage. Ralph found much to correct in my behavior and house-keeping – again, this is as I think of it now, let me cover my imprudences – and I would lose my temper at him. So he always won.

I think it was the tub that got to me most. Not the cold, not the way the damp made everything feel moldy, but the tub and its care.

'Serena, it is definitely your turn to empty the tub. The *canvas* tub.'

This was his way of reminding me that he was not brought up to take his baths in a canvas tub. Actually, I was not either, even if I am *Amurrican*. The scene, which repeated itself frequently, is still vivid in my mind. I would rush to empty out the tub: it would be heavy coming down the stairs, and occasionally I would spill a good bit on the way.

'Serena dear, I do think it is advisable to contain the liquid within the container.'

When it was Ralph's turn, I tried to keep the same bantering tone: 'Ralph, the tub. Green thing. Upstairs.'

Unperturbed – he would remain always unperturbed – Ralph would move with great precision towards the tub. Having first finished the chapter he was reading or writing, he would undertake this dull chore himself, with a small smile and total equanimity. That he always had, and I, rarely. I had ups and downs of enthusiasm, but equanimity I was not graced with. My over-reactions were exhausting.

'Not bad,' he would say of some piece of writing or cooking. That was as high as the compliments went. As for the derogatory remarks, they were similarly muted. Ralph could be a very muted man.

I would try to enthuse less over small things. Enthusiasm is definitely in my nature, and I would have a struggle against it here, as I did when I was little. In Michigan, however, by the frozen lake, my ongoing struggle was generally satisfactory, as it was at my job.

My boss, Mary, sniffled all the time in the Reference section of the library, and left little wads of used Kleenex around; I continued to mail out books on Interlibrary Loan. At lunch, I would read. The rest of the time, I would staple things together and pack books; I would sometimes be allowed to look things up, if Mary could not figure out where to do this, which occurred with a certain frequency. So much I never learned: like about the relation between chlorophyll and why leaves turn brown – is there one? I could never understand the science part of newspapers, let alone the games. A user had only to ask something like: 'In what year did the Cardinals... or the Dodgers... or Billie Jean King...,' and my mind would go completely blank.

As for the teaching I had thought I had been preparing myself to do at Yale, it was pointed out to me that I had only a Master's degree and, on top of that, from an Eastern Institution. In those places, said the head of the Foreign Language Department, 'they teach differently.' They also learn differently, he said. There was, he continued, 'a different clientele' here in the Midwest, so how could I have expected a teaching job? I had, though. Stanley, one of Ralph's colleagues pointed out helpfully that perhaps I could serve as an assistant to Ralph for his research.

'You seem to have a brain,' said Stanley with a little smile. I was about to say how greatly relieved I was that he should think so, but took a breath, as Mother had taught me to, and said nothing. How could I? Fuming inside, I thanked Ralph's colleague, who had his hand on my arm.

*

In the university library, the books frequently disappeared. There was no one to check on this at the door. Nor did anyone seem to find it humorous that the chapter on Ethics was razored out of *Hastings' Encylopedia.*

I read avidly at lunch, and began to hatch the scheme of writing for myself someday. A novel about Southern living, that is what I would most like to do, and 'I seemed to have a brain,' after all. I presumed that, even married to an Englishman, I would still count as Southern, although upon occasion, I was finding it hard to count as anything at all.

Our views differed greatly on things. I would prepare a menu for friends: not perfect, as Ralph was quick to point out: 'Well, darling, you know, I should rather prefer, let's see, sorrel soup, perhaps a *vitello tonnato* with asparagus to follow, and – maybe a Grand Marnier soufflé. Would that be possible? Thank you so very much.'

It was like the three-minute egg: 'Thank you, dear. I will read,' and 'Thank you dear for preparing things.'

I looked up *soupe à l'oseille* in Elizabeth David – that great writer on French food, unputtable down for many of us. Where do you get sorrel around here? Does our veal have any taste? Do I want to add something from Jane Grigson's *Mushroom Feast?* Do I cook the main course and then the soufflé, or can I prepare the basic part of the soufflé while I am going along? Do we have any Grand Marnier? I am using Bee Nilson's *Desserts.* I am feeling used.

My mind is not on *vitello tonnato.* It is on a lecture I am supposed to give so the people at the university can see I know how to teach, say, a course on modern French writers if there just happened to be a need. Ralph could of course do it all, but then, he *is* Ralph. I look in at him. He has both feet up in his Cordovan loafers from Clark's (my father's style, but with tassels), darkish brown socks (knee-high), beige whipcord trousers, and an open-necked olive green shirt with a Liberty foulard. His horn-rimmed glasses are sitting slightly forward on his nose. My jeans are torn at the knee, my hair is hanging limp with my mind likewise.

Now it has happened. My index cards have just spilled all over the floor, for my upcoming lecture, which is supposed to be witty and light. 'Surrealism and the Shakes', I have called it. They said, 'Don't go to any lengths. We just have to appeal to the audience.'

'Oh fine,' I could say. 'I thought of something that will appeal to the audience. How about "Fearing Foucault"'? Don't trust anyone's sense of humor, though, and besides, it has no zip, just a bit of irony. Irony doesn't go over.

The hundreds of index cards I have just spilled unnumbered (of course) are scattered every which way. I look down, I look up, and there is a stunned silence across the room. Then:

'Serena, dear, I don't believe it. You've dropped your index cards once more?'

Once more into the breach: sounds like *Henry V*, Lawrence Olivier style. I think of Ralph standing handsomely before his men, discoursing simply but with eloquence. He has a....

'Serena, I believe I asked you a question?'

'Sorry, Ralph. My mind must have been wandering.' What was he asking? I have already forgotten. I am crouching on the floor picking up the index cards.

'Do you terribly much mind my asking, Serena? Did you number the cards in the way I suggested?'

God, I did not. No. Whoops. And he was kind to think of telling me to do it. What a good idea. 'Ralph, you are absolutely right. I shall do that immediately.'

'Yes, I think it will help. Especially for someone who has your tendencies.'

I feel my cheeks burning. My stomach is knotting up. I should bite my tongue. I do not. 'My tendencies?'

'Why, you are just a trifle irregular in your habits, wouldn't you say? A bit chaotic, perhaps? You surely see what I mean without my having to spell it out.'

I am annoyed. He has succeeded in Getting my Goat. My mother would say: 'Oh, don't let this get your goat.' Whatever it used to mean then, I see what it does now.

'No, Ralph, I think you should spell it out.'

Silence.

'We Americans, you know, we are not altogether quite as bright' as you might hope to have found us. To have found me, especially. Zingo. Got him.

'Excuse me, darling? No, I certainly was not impugning your brightness. Ah no.'

'Ah no?' Bite your tongue, Serena, breathe slower, Father always said. 'Slow down.'

This would go on for minutes, like hours. When would I ever learn to leave well enough alone?, I continued to wonder, sitting now on the floor.

'Serena, have you decided on the menu? Would you care for me to give you a hand?'

Learn to accept. Think of grandmother. Honey attracts more flies than vinegar, and all that.

'Of course, Ralph. Thank you so much.'

So it would proceed, with results always predictable. Ralph would prepare a superb dinner, cast it off lightly or give me all the credit, never drop his cards on the floor, and would be always charming.

'Serena, heavens, how very lucky you are!'

'Serena, what a treat your husband is! How he spoils you.'

I did not feel spoiled, just tired. Very tired indeed. How could I possibly live up to Ralph?

One cold day in the unheated cottage by the Michigan lake, in a fit of jealousy, I grab the scissors from the desk. I slash my favorite picture of Ralph as a teenager, with that mop of hair I love, right across the middle. Another day – or is it the same one? – my rage clouds every such picture, even in retrospect. I see myself chasing him with a knife around the yard beside the lake with the dying and redolent fish, out of a jealous temper. Ridiculous there in full daylight, panicked at the possibility of really hurting this man I adore. I am clearly crazy at ten in the morning in my nightgown with a kitchen knife, like some comic movie.

*

When we moved to the University of Kansas – 'Flat lands make flat minds,' said our friends at Michigan – we found a congenial atmosphere. I was allowed to work at the university press while getting my doctorate in Romance Languages and teaching. At the press, however, my dreams of editorial acumen remained unfulfilled. Each stylistic alteration I dared had to be checked with the authors. Many of them were given to flowery phrasing, the sort of Fresh-Winds-Blowing-In-From-England style. I was in fact employed for what was thought to be my skill with commas.

I was never sure of any skill. Taking my comprehensive exams, I must have responded badly. In front of an office-full of my colleagues, my adviser came with his wide smile. He proceeded to tell me, carefully enunciating every syllable with utmost clarity, precise as he always was, his very white teeth showing to their limit, how disappointed they all were in me. Unable to stop shaking all over, tears pouring down my face, I conferred with Ralph.

'I have let them down.'

'Oh, goodness, I am so sorry.' He really seemed to be. 'How did you do that?'

I explained, and Ralph held me gently. 'Well, perhaps you should consult with your chairman tomorrow. Go in first thing, why don't you? Surely you'll feel better.'

So I went to the chairman the next day and expressed, between sobs, my dismay that I had 'let them down'. This was what you least wanted to do in the South, 'let someone down'.

Dr Carman was startled by the expression and protested: 'Not at all', he said. 'You have it wrong.'

Whichever way, I had it wrong: I often felt that. Either I was stubbornly persuaded I was right, or afraid I was not up to what was expected. This pattern continued, familiar to many faculty wives: I always felt at fault.

I had really hated that time in Michigan, and blamed perhaps too much upon it. How could I not have hated the sight and smell of those fish dying in the lake, and the imbalance in our jobs? I had felt unvalued and underused, as well as unappreciated by others, and began to take their opinion for my own. Maybe after all, I *should* just be doing someone else's research, incapable of doing anything on my own. And maybe that would never change. Did Ralph value my potential work, as my father had not? What could I write that wouldn't be desultory, vacuous? That would be more like philosophy? I had after all begun as a philosophy major, but who would know it now? Whereas on his side, Ralph taught both philosophy and science, the latter about real facts. We in literature felt less sure of facts and were supposed to spend our time questioning texts.

They, at least, were neither true nor false, so they had to be interpreted. You got judged either on some theory you interpreted by, and how convincing it was, or in your acute analysis. More given to analogy than acuteness or theory, I could see trouble ahead.

*

Ralph had to teach courses in science and the History of Thought seventeen hours a week. In one class, he was fond of showing the freshman girls how to prick their fingers to find their blood type, and in the other, of teaching them how to 'put their own thoughts in the light of Thought Itself' or something that sounded like that. They seemed to find his help on such projects enormously enlightening, and so he enjoyed it all. That was natural; it was all natural, and it certainly took a lot of time. I never somehow felt in the mood to do a lot of helpful research about that. Or in fact about anything else. A rough year.

'I have designs on your husband,' a dishy blonde in Ralph's freshman science class said to me one day, at some reception, and indeed I believed it: who wouldn't? I did too, after all. Surely no one could fail to be struck by his brilliance.

One day the phone rang. For Ralph, so I called him:

'Fine, Serena, I'll take it in my study.' And then: 'Serena, I must leave for a few minutes.'

Ralph pointed out, gravely and rapidly, with his coat on, that the student was actually threatening to commit suicide unless he arrived instantly. Was I right, or insanely on the wrong track? 'Jealousy only hurts the jealous,' did I hear someone say, or did I just make it up? Now, in any case, I heard myself protesting:

'Ralph, don't you understand? They just want to get you out there.'

'Darling, professors have duties to their successors in the field, which I have to take seriously. I will be back before long.' and then, tenderly: 'You look a bit frazzled: why not have a tiny nap?'

He was tender, yes, and yes, I was frazzled. Even frenzied, with wondering continually about what was going on 'historically', from initiator to successor in 'the field'. Frenzied. Perhaps crazy.

We are in a shopping mall in Kansas City. At some remark of Ralph's that sounds utterly heartless to me, I rip off my blouse in fury. This pent-up anger recurring from childhood. It feels like slapping my grandmother so long ago, like pouring the coffee over the food for Ralph's colleagues: why? Why did I have all this anger in me, and why couldn't I, knowing it, help it? Ralph was not to forget any of these scenes easily. I had my own jealousy-provoking tendencies, after all, and it was like a double fault. These were, off and on, difficult years.

We moved, shortly thereafter, to New York, Ralph for a job at a funding corporation, me for a part-time job at Barnard, where at least I could teach literature, as I had always longed to. Perhaps things would work out.

I am being offered the Barnard job. My father says he assumes I am not taking money for it. I am also having my first article published, based on my thesis. Excited, I phone my parents. My mother suggests I write the publishers a thank you note. 'It is so good of them.' My father wants to know how much I am being paid. Nothing, I say, and hear an aggrieved silence. I do not say I have to pay for offprints.

My colleagues are all elegantly dressed, and at ease. They never seem to make mistakes in appearance, in pronunciation, or in anything else. I feel I am there on sufferance.

At a small dinner with a few officials from Ralph's foundation, its vice-president offers to find me a job in New York. 'Nothing', he says, 'is too good for his employees' wives.' I manage to stammer out that I have one, but thank him as best I can. He is vaguely surprised, and expresses his delight with my good fortune.

'Gracious me,' he says. 'Aren't you the lucky one, though?'

I am delighted with my good fortune, too, but concerned that it may not last. I may be found out, in my shaky sense of French grammar: it is the literature I am passionate about. But I have an extraordinary forgetfulness about which nouns are feminine and which masculine. This forces me to use a great many circumlocutions, like 'une espèce de' – that way, the noun's gender doesn't matter. Yet I was beginning to feel, even at women's colleges, that my own gender does very much matter.

*

Time went on: we returned for a semester to Kansas, where Ralph was offered a prestigious teaching post and a large house with a piano. The foundation let him go. I gave up my job at

Barnard with regret, for the chairman told me I would have been kept on. Our timing, he said, was bad. That was not all, but I said how sorry I was. I was more than sorry, for I would have liked to stay.

When we returned to New York, I was pregnant. I lost my job at Hunter College over this, because you were not supposed to be a bad influence on the students, I suppose. My mother pointed out how right was this decision, and suggested I would not want my students to see me with a big tummy.

When the baby had come, I got my job back, but in reduced form and salary, for evening classes. Through my friend Richard Rorty, whose aunt was the President of Sarah Lawrence, I was offered a job there in the day, replacing someone whose hip had broken, and remained teaching at Hunter College at night. Always afraid of missing the train, I found the commute out to Bronxville mentally as well as physically tiring. I continued nursing my baby daughter, of course, and only substituted the formula for the times I absolutely could not be there.

Then the night course consisted of fifty beginning students who had worked all day, like me. Their heads would droop on their shoulders, but they all kept on. I was impressed, if exhausted.

At Sarah Lawrence, my students were asked, by other students, 'why they had chosen to study with a woman'. It was bad enough not to speak classically perfect French, and not to have classically perfect features; it was worse, I felt, not to be a tall and elegant male. Having to nurse the baby, wanting to write, and trying to overcome the feeling that I had, somehow, lost Ralph's love, I almost succumbed to despair. My optimism and even my habitual enthusiasm ebbed in a hurry. Things grew harder. I would teach, I would write, I would nurse my daughter, and I would spend the middle of every night studying. But I would not let on how hard I found it. Stubborn, and probably stupid.

For the Bryn Mawr alumnae magazine, I was asked to write up my experience of career and marriage. I tried to focus on what had really been going on in Michigan with the strain and the bathtub; then in Kansas, with my getting things wrong and Ralph always getting them right; and finally in New York, where I kept hoping it would feel different. Whereas it had seemed to me in our preceding situations that life would be like that as long as it lasted, here it had a chance to change.

I wanted to write a piece that would convince me, and others, that it would work. That you could commute, combine careers and family, and remain yourselves, together. I thought it sounded truthful and optimistic; later, a few perceptive readers told me how it sounded just the opposite. It was called, in a tone of hope: 'A Double Allegiance', and some of it read like this:

> In New York, I first taught at Barnard and then, when I lost my job by returning to Kansas, I returned to teach at Hunter College, a job which might have been on a tenure track, except that I found myself pregnant, and the system forbade continuation under those circumstances. I remember weeping in the chairman's office; Professor Gonzalez had not stood up when I came in, had stared at his blotter when I announced my problem, and did not look up when I left.
>
> When after my daughter's birth, I at last retrieved a position at Hunter, it was still a matter of teaching only beginning grammar classes instead of the literature classes I so much wanted to try. My list of publications, by now relatively long, did not help in the slightest. The rate of pay had been lowered to an hourly stipend for what was called an 'assistant tutor', $2.50, clearly less than the hourly $3.00 I had to pay the babysitter. My husband had the good grace not to mind; he thought it was fine I should be teaching, so long as the baby was cared for. Care was expensive, and I would have preferred my salary to cover it. On the other hand, I was glad to be useful somewhere, and felt I was.
>
> Doubt was repeatedly expressed, by every chairman in the City University system whom I went to see about a possible real job, about my continuing to want to teach or to publish now that I was saddled with an infant; I did want to, intended to, and did; but the two chairmen who had received my request favorably both 'phoned, by some unerring sense, when the baby was throwing a temper fit, or heading on all fours towards a bag of carpet tacks. Perhaps indeed I would not be able to write, read, or think any longer. I was not managing things well, Ralph would have suggested, never saying it outright.
>
> We had waited many years to have children, perhaps too long. Though I was exhausted, I took to writing in the middle of the night, the only time I was sure of peace. I was hired to teach at Sarah Lawrence in the suburbs of New York, where the French teacher had just broken her hip. I made a lousy role model, though, and that is what I had been explicitly hired to be. Moved by poetry, I would choke up in class, emotion coming out in all the wrong places. When personal life proved difficult, as it often did, I hardly retained my cool exterior. Involved in conversation with someone, realizing suddenly I had to get back

on time to nurse the baby, I would be too shy to explain why I had to rush. I would awkwardly cut off the chat, and still sometimes miss the train. I remember leaving a barefoot, blue-jeaned, charming student wondering aloud why I seemed always to have less time than X or Y, those leisurely gentlemen professing at their leisure before they were picked up by their smiling wives. I prefer not to drive, compounding problems further, for I tend to fall asleep at the wheel: as a driving instructor with whom I had just shown that tendency for the third time explained to Ralph: 'The road just doesn't keep her interest.'

Ralph with grace and ease, professed and chaired on the local scene and arranged international historical meetings; by terrible contrast, when I was pregnant with our second child and he drove me up in the evening to teach an extra course in the Bronx, I threw up with a great lack of elegance, all over the students' papers I was frenetically grading in the car.

'Serena, really!'

This is the way it would be always: I would have babies, throw up, and not recognize things, and he would elegantly teach and be.

Yet it was other ways too: I was proud of becoming a British subject because of Ralph's birth, glad to give him a fellow foreigner to live with. I had the privilege of a double allegiance, to two countries and two ways of being. We had for ourselves another dual allegiance: both of us doing the same thing, writing or doing research, speaking and traveling, together and apart. All the problems of competition and cooperation, of time-sharing and friend-sharing we feel we can manage. We are different, to be sure, but it works:

'Which one?' the children always ask the callers for 'the professor', while I instinctively answer: 'He's not here,' or 'Just a minute.'

Yet we balanced. I figure as an example in some of his historical musings, in a different guise. The last time, it was in a green coat, I remember. Not that I ever wear green, but it fit the piece well, as it did some poem he wrote about me and my chaos. Ralph has all the talents, I think.

We live together, teach and translate and write together, argue and make up: our allegiance makes our bond indissoluble. This marriage is worth what it takes for what it gives.

*

That is what I wrote. 'I call happiness this marriage of wit and love,' I had ended. Could I make my fictions truth? I could not, and we are now divorced. I choose to think that we have, however, remained friends.

In any case, my Bryn Mawr piece must have touched a chord in my fellow alumnae: mail poured in from wives who had done just that, combined careers and sometimes commuting, and I began to feel I should never write anything academic again.

I do, though, of course. In fact now, with no compunction whatsoever, I write what I like. I have a close friend, no longer feel used, and love teaching my seminars in literature and art.

Acknowledgement

This essay is adapted from *To the Boathouse: a Memoir*, by Mary Ann Caws (Tuscaloosa, Alabama: University of Alabama Press, 2004).

23

The Mystery of the Vanishing Wife

Laurel Young

Had Agatha Christie married well, she might never have begun to write detective fiction. The world's most famous mystery novelist, creator of amateur detectives Hercule Poirot and Miss Marple, recalls in her autobiography how she loved to read mysteries as a child, especially Sir Arthur Conan Doyle's Sherlock Holmes stories. One day the young Agatha Miller told her older sister, Madge, that she would like to write such a story herself. Madge replied that she had also considered it, but that 'they are very difficult to do', and she doubted that either she or Agatha could manage it. 'It didn't go further than that,' Agatha recalls, although at the back of her mind remained the wistful thought, 'some day I would write a detective story'.

'Some day' seemed unlikely ever to come. The Millers were an affluent family who expected their daughters to marry within their own class and to manage a household of servants rather than to work outside the home. Agatha speaks of her sister as 'the talented member of our family'; Madge published several stories in *Vanity Fair*, 'quite a literary achievement in those days'. Following a lavish coming-out season in New York, however, she married the eldest son of a wealthy manufacturer and, Agatha recalls, 'did not write any more short stories after she married'.

Agatha had less ambition than Madge. 'How much more interesting it would be if I could say that I always longed to be a writer,' she admits, 'but, honestly, such an idea never came into my head.' She continues, 'I only contemplated one thing – a happy marriage' to a man her mother told her would be 'Your Fate'. Agatha decided that her 'Fate' lay not with any of her wealthy suitors but rather with her only impoverished one, Lieutenant Archie Christie. To the Millers' horror, Agatha eloped with Archie on Christmas Eve, 1914. Two days later, Archie's regiment went to France. At loose ends during the War, Agatha went to work in a hospital dispensary in Torquay, thus gaining a working knowledge of pharmacology. The job was not a demanding one and Agatha began to write, just to fill the time. Surrounded as she was by poisons, she was inspired to begin the long-delayed mystery story. It would eventually be published as her first detective novel, *The Mysterious Affair at Styles* (1920), in which Hercule Poirot solves a poisoning case.

That might have been the end of Agatha's writing career, but when Archie returned from France the couple were in dire need of money. Jobs were scarce in post-war England, and by now the pair had a young daughter to support. Looking back from the 1970s, Agatha remarks, 'Nowadays I suppose I could have said, "I'll get a job," but it was not a thing one even thought of saying in 1923' – at least, not a thing a woman in her position thought of saying. The dispensary job had been a show of patriotism, a means of supporting the war effort, but the job ended with the war. And so, Agatha says, 'I tried to settle down to do some writing, since I felt that that was the only thing I could do that might bring in a little money. I still had no idea of writing as a profession.' Nevertheless, her novels and stories sold well, and in 1925 she attained true fame when the (London) *Evening News* published *Who Killed Ackroyd?* as a serial. Released in book form in 1926, *The Murder of Roger Ackroyd* remains one of her most acclaimed works, with its famous (or, for some readers, infamous) surprise ending.

After *Ackroyd*, Agatha struggled to complete *The Mystery of the Blue Train*, while physically and mentally exhausted from her rigorous, self-imposed writing schedule. In a span of six years she had produced not only six novels but also over seventy short stories. Her output was rewarded with financial success, and so she and Archie were able to leave their cramped flat in London and purchased a large country house at Sunningdale in Berkshire. Archie christened the new home 'Styles' in honor of the titular house in Agatha's first published novel. Agatha herself had a superstitious aversion to the name, however, since her fictional Styles is the scene of murder and familial strife. Her foreboding was prescient. 'Styles proved what it had been in the [fictional] past to others. It was an unlucky house,' she recalls. By the end of the year there would be a real-life mysterious affair at Styles, one rooted in great personal misery.

Agatha says of 1926 that this 'year of my life is one I hate recalling'. Already under professional stress with her latest novel, she suffered the loss of her greatest supporter – her mother, Clarissa Miller. Agatha recounts at length her extremely close relationship with her mother, and how she turned to Clarissa to meet the emotional needs Archie could not, or would not, fulfill. Agatha's grief at her mother's unexpected death from bronchitis was extreme, but she would not have succumbed to melancholia had she been able to share her pain with her husband. Painting Archie as selfish and immature, Agatha says that he 'had a violent dislike of illness, death and trouble of any kind', and was useless to his wife in her time of need. Agatha recalls, '[Archie] hated the feeling of sorrow in the house, and it left him open to other influences.' The 'influences' in question were those of a family friend, Nancy Neele. When Archie informed the still-grieving Agatha that he was having an affair with Neele and wanted a divorce, the strain became too great. Agatha left Styles on a cold December night, ostensibly to go for a drive and clear her head – and vanished.

Agatha's car was found the next day, abandoned beside the ominously named Silent Pool, a locale she had featured in one of her novels. The police dragged the pool for her body, and detectives and fans alike turned out in droves to search for the missing author. It took ten days for the police to trace Agatha to a spa in Yorkshire, the Harrogate Hydro, where she was registered under her rival's surname, 'Mrs Neele'. A number of conflicting accounts of the disappearance arose immediately upon her discovery. From Patricia D. Maida and Nicholas B. Spornick's *Murder She Wrote: a Study of Agatha Christie's Detective Fiction*, we know that Agatha's neurologist, Dr Donald Core, asserted that she had had 'an unquestionably genuine loss of memory'. Janet Morgan, in the authorized biography, concurs, adding that Agatha's dreamy nature might have made her more vulnerable to such an attack. 'Under unreasonable strain, deeply unhappy with herself, she might have induced a loss of memory,' Morgan suggests. Archie insisted to the press that Agatha was 'suffering from a nervous breakdown owing to "literary overwork"', thus shifting the blame from himself onto the career he had never supported.

There is some ground for the idea that Agatha staged the disappearance to get revenge on Archie, whom the police for a time suspected of murdering her. While at the spa Agatha wrote to Harrods' department store to inquire about a diamond ring she had lost there the previous week. She asked that when the ring was found it should be forwarded to Mrs Neele at the Harrogate Hydro. Since she knew she was Agatha Christie when she lost the ring, presumably she would not have remembered it had she suffered from stress-induced amnesia. In *The Life and Crimes of Agatha Christie*, Charles Osborne offers a compromise, theorizing that Agatha was 'close to nervous collapse' but lucid enough to have 'staged her disappearance in such a way as to cause the maximum distress' to Archie. But as Maida and Spornick point out, 'Whether brought on by amnesia, hysteria, or rational intent the disappearance produced the *same effect* – to focus on Colonel Christie and the woman with whom he was involved.' Archie had hoped to keep Nancy Neele's name away from the press. Thanks to Agatha's choice of pseudonym, it was on the front page of almost every newspaper in England.

Although in her autobiography Agatha makes no mention whatsoever of her disappearance, everyone from relatives to critics and biographers has hastened to fill in her silence. There was some fear of suicide at the time. In *Agatha Christie and the Eleven Missing Days*, Jared Cade explains that Agatha

> had recently visited her chemist, Charles Gilling, to have a sleeping draught made up for her and during their conversation methods of committing suicide had been mentioned. The authoress had allegedly said, 'I should never commit suicide by violent means when there is such a drug as hyoscine available.'

(According to Michael C. Gerald in *The Poisonous Pen of Agatha Christie*, hyoscine, an alkaloid, produces dreamless sleep and was once commonly used for anesthesia during surgery.)

Along the same lines, Archie, in an interview with the (London) *Daily Mail*, said: 'She never threatened suicide, but if she did contemplate that, I am sure her mind would turn to poison,' because 'she used poison largely in her stories.' In this same interview, he added: 'Some time ago she told her sister, "I could disappear if I wished and set about it properly." They were discussing what appeared in the papers, I think. That shows that the possibility of engineering a disappearance had been running through her mind, probably for the purpose of her work.' Archie could offer no suggestion as to why Agatha would suddenly feel the need to research her latest novel by enacting a mystery herself. (For that matter, staged disappearances do not figure in *The Mystery of the Blue Train* [1928], the novel on which Agatha was working at this time.) He set a precedent, however, with his assumption that Agatha's choice of genre must necessarily influence her behavior. It is a highly selective assumption: Agatha also wrote romantic fiction, yet no one expected this to make her real-life relationship successful. Why, then, should her fictional mysteries manifest themselves in her life?

In the same curious conflation of life and art, the press cited detective novelists as authorities on real-life crime. The (London) *Daily News* interviewed Dorothy L. Sayers, who discussed four possible solutions to the mystery of Agatha, adding 'a voluntary disappearance, also, may be so cleverly staged as to be exceedingly puzzling – especially if, as here, we are concerned with a skilful writer of detective stories, whose mind has been trained in the study of ways and means to perplex.' The (London) *Daily Mail* interviewed Edgar Wallace, who said: 'That she did not contemplate suicide seems evident from the fact that she deliberately created an atmosphere of suicide by the picturesque abandonment of her car.' This seems a curiously backwards logic, unless Wallace is working from the idea that in good detective fiction the obvious solution is never the correct one and that Agatha's authorial pride would not allow her to live out such a shoddy mystery. Both writers in turn used elements of Agatha's disappearance to produce further mystery fiction – Sayers in her detective novel *Unnatural Death* and Wallace in a short story called 'The Sunningdale Murder', both published the following year (1927). If Agatha did stage the disappearance, it was her fellow mystery writers, rather than herself, who profited from it in print.

In the almost eighty years since Agatha's disappearance, many of the facts have been irretrievably lost. In *Agatha Christie: the Woman and Her Mysteries*, Gillian Gill admits, 'The kind of investigation in retrospect that Hercule Poirot and Miss Marple engage in with such success ... was impossible in reality.' This, however, has not stopped critics from trying. Although few literary studies of Agatha's writing exist, there is an ever-growing body of criticism about her life, and especially her disappearance. The most recent and exhaustive study is Jared Cade's *Agatha Christie and the Eleven Missing Days* (1998). Other book-length studies include *The Agatha Christie Mystery* (1976), by Derrick Murdoch, and Gwen Robyns' *The Mystery of Agatha Christie* (1978). A number of critical works include at least one chapter devoted to attempts to provide a definitive solution. There is also a novel, *Agatha* (1976), by Kathleen Tynan which was turned into a film of the same name in 1979, starring Vanessa Redgrave as Agatha. In the contest among biographical sleuths, the line between Agatha Christie's work and her life becomes more blurred than ever, to the point of becoming indistinguishable.

Even more than Sayers or Wallace, contemporary critics consistently read Agatha's life as though it were one of her novels. Agatha was shy and seldom gave interviews, leaving herself open to Patricia Maida and Nicholas Spornick's suggestion that she deliberately 'created an aura of mystery about her own person'. Cade, who believes that Agatha staged her disappearance to spite Archie, insists: 'Unable to cope with the loss of her husband, she had sought to punish him in the only way she knew how: through intrigue, mystery and revenge.' He does not explain why Agatha's successful fictional model would be 'the only way she knew how', assuming instead that her knowledge was confined to what she chose to include in her books. Robert Barnard in *A Talent to Deceive: an Appreciation of Agatha Christie* says, 'Like Dickens, Agatha Christie left behind her one last unsolved and unsolvable mystery,' although Dickens left the ending of *The Mystery of Edwin Drood* unwritten due to his death. Agatha, on the other hand, lived and wrote for many more years, never intending to solve her private mystery for the public. Barnard also notes that Agatha had written of moments of memory loss and mental unbalance prior to the disappearance, but that 'the account of her mental state earlier in the year is Agatha's alone, and she is, after all, mistress of the misleading clue'. That is, he feels that readers should have learned from *The Murder of Roger Ackroyd* not to trust Agatha's narrators, even when the narrator is Agatha herself and she is writing nonfiction. Gill is perhaps the most candid of the critics: 'We need a Hercule Poirot on this case, discovering and analyzing documents that he lays before the reader, just as he did in *Styles!*' No such great detective is forthcoming, although many seek to fill the position.

When all else fails, critics read between the lines of Agatha's fiction itself. Cade sees a solution in a short story entitled 'The Edge', where, he claims, she 'duly vented the intense jealousy she felt towards her younger rival', Nancy Neele. The story does involve jealousy and adultery, although other parallels are few. Many others claim that the solution lies in *Unfinished Portrait* (1934), one of several romances which Agatha published under the name Mary Westmacott. Osborne calls *Unfinished Portrait* a 'crypto-autobiographical novel' with 'clues to the mystery of her behaviour' [...] 'inextricably embedded' in it. Maida and Spornick say that 'although the *Autobiography* is useful, the work that reflects the real Christie is still her *Unfinished Portrait*'. There are indeed many parallels between the *Portrait* and the *Autobiography*; perhaps Agatha found it easier to write about her trauma while hidden behind a nom de plume.

What would Agatha think of the continued interest in her personal mystery? A reserved woman, she might well have preferred that her private misfortunes should remain private. However, Agatha's fame as an author made publicity inevitable both at the time and ever since, and in the aftermath of her tragedy she began to come to terms with that fame. Even before their marriage came to its dramatic conclusion, Archie was 'more of a hindrance than a help to his wife's career as a novelist', as Gill says. He was uninterested in Agatha's work and jealous of her success. It is ironic, therefore, that his final act of marital cruelty, his insistence on a divorce she did not want, led Agatha to accept her identity as a writer. Post-divorce, she struggled to complete *The Mystery of the Blue Train* in order to support herself and her daughter Rosalind. She recalls,

> I was driven desperately on by the desire, indeed the necessity, to write another book and make some money. That was the moment when I changed from an amateur to a professional. I assumed the burden of a profession, which is to write even when you don't want to, don't much like what you are writing, and aren't writing particularly well.

Agatha admitted to herself what her fans already knew – that she was not a dabbler but a skilled detective writer, albeit a reluctant one.

In time Agatha would come to revel in her authorial identity. Following her divorce in 1928, however, her main impulse was to travel, to get away from her painful memories. Her first thought was to visit the West Indies and Jamaica, but she changed her mind and went instead to the Near East, going from Calais to Istanbul on the Orient Express. On this trip she befriended Leonard Woolley, an English archaeologist. Two years later she returned to visit Woolley, this time meeting his assistant, Max Mallowan. The meeting proved fortuitous, both personally and professionally. Agatha married Max in 1930, and the marriage endured. Unlike Archie, Max supported and encouraged Agatha in her writing. He also inspired some of her finest work: traveling with him on his archaeological expeditions, Agatha found exciting new settings for her novels. *Murder in Mesopotamia* (1936), *Death on the Nile* (1937), and, most famous of all, *Murder on the Orient Express* (1934) appeared within a few years of her remarriage. Although Agatha provided her fans with no more real-life mysteries, they were more than compensated by her prolific output of fiction. If Agatha Christie's disastrous first marriage caused her to begin a career as detective novelist, her peaceful second one ensured that she continued, eventually achieving the sobriquet of the Queen of Crime.

24

Room for One

Betty Fussell

There was room for only one writer in our house, our lives, our marital continent. It would have been the same if I'd said lawyer, doctor, professor, but writer had a different sound. Writing was serious stuff; it dealt with the verities of life and death and sex and sorrow. Writing was not about money, and those who confused the two were sellouts to crass commercialism, like Norman Mailer who, after a promising beginning, was headed straight for the primrose path that had swallowed so many golden boys, like Scotty Fitzgerald or, God help us, old man Hemingway. Or so we thought, in our callow youth, when we met at a small Southern California college and fell in love, or rather I fell in love, with a writer born.

I married this college sweetheart partly because he *was* a writer. His talent was evident. He'd come out of the War with a lot to say and his talent would give him the means to say it. In those days he tried everything, short stories, poetry, fictional bits and pieces. But he wasn't going to get trapped by the Romance of the Novel. No way. The Great American Novel was a contradiction in terms, except for Huckleberry Finn. His heroes were not novelists but satirists like H. L. Mencken or S. J. Perelman. He read Twain's great work, not without reason, as a satire on the follies of American culture north and south. He came out of the War an angry young man at war with his culture. He'd been physically and emotionally wounded, and that wound would fuel his writing life – the two were synonymous – for the next fifty years in essays and longer works of nonfiction that ranged in subject matter from pastoral images of World War I in England to matters of class in America. But the matrix of whatever he wrote was what had happened to him and fellow infantry soldiers in the trenches, in World War II.

As a high school and college girl, I was excluded from the War, which meant that I was excluded from everything that mattered – to him. I was excluded from writing, because he was the writer. I had written little poems, playlets, sketches, booklets from the time I could hold a pencil or a pen, but they didn't count. They weren't serious. I'd earned pocket money in college, for beer and cigs, by writing other people's term papers. But these weren't serious. They weren't professional. It was just school work and I'd long ago discovered how to get maximum results from minimum efforts in that racket. The fact is I didn't profess to be a writer. The fact is I didn't dream of any profession. To have a profession, that's what men did. I wasn't at all clear what women did except to help their men in their chosen profession. And what wonderful luck to find a man who chose the profession of writing because writing was about Art, and Art was what mattered most in a world trembling on the brink of blowing itself up first with an atom and then with a hydrogen bomb. Life was short, Art was long.

Like many other women in the post-War 'fifties, I defined myself in relation to my man, and since he was a writer and a teacher, a combination that guaranteed a minimum income of $3,000 a year, I was to be his help-mate in all things. In my view, his job was to become a really good writer, although that process was made much more difficult by the strictures of the academy in its determination to outdo the Germans in the rictus of Germanic scholarship, in order to excrete the humanities in as scientific a way as possible. Many writers whom I knew at that time lost their voices during the laryngitis-inducing exercises of graduate school, some recovering later with no residue but a slight hoarseness, some lost for good.

In my view, my job was to be his secretarial assistant as needed, as well as his social secretary, his nourisher, his bed-mate, and eventually his breeder. My job was to not be anything not related to him. I did not understand that at the time, but I had lots of company in that misperception. So, like many another faculty wife, I typed his thesis – the three carbons with zero mistakes – on the loyal Royal, proof-read book manuscripts out loud word by word – zero tolerance for error – and made editorial suggestions only when asked. When the children came, my job was to keep them out of his hair, out of his office, out of his hearing because Daddy was at work. Daddy was the only one doing Real Work. Daddy was writing.

This is not to blame the man or the writer he was then. His priorities were a given of the time and place, or at least of the academic place which was a part of that time. It was not the writer's fault that he had married an incipient writer who didn't know how to create, and for a long while didn't have the courage to create, a writing life of her own. It was so much safer to let someone else take the risks and suffer the hazards involved in any writing. Self-involvement, self-absorption went with the territory of the writer. So why should his help-mate complain if she felt that she and the children were alike excluded from the interior rooms of the writer consumed by the demands of his craft? In the summertime I would take the children off to Cape Cod while the writer sweated over his books at home, in a house without air conditioning. He might commute on the weekends, but the books came first, outweighing comfort, pleasure, or family. And I had to agree. Not by compulsion, but by unspoken – and sometimes spoken – agreement, the work came first.

His work. And after a while the imbalance got to me. I was no longer happy in my job. Tending the husband, the house, the kitchen, the children, the cats was not enough for me. For a long while I thought I just needed to find something I was good at on my own, something I could take credit for, gain recognition for, have my name attached to as if I were a person in my own right and not just a name on a dedication page. Cooking did it in the 'sixties. With the help of Julia Child and others who were transforming cooking into a culinary art, I got really good at cooking and my husband and I created a super kitchen for our evening performances. But even elevated to art, cooking was still as ephemeral as housework in that there was nothing to show for it once the dinner was done. Cooking is the one art that produces works which must literally be consumed to be valued. The better the art the more total the consummation.

But I wanted work with a longer shelf life. I wanted a beginning, a middle, and an end, represented in the corporeality of a copper pot, a glazed platter, an oil painting, a book in hard covers. I wanted to create an object, not just be part of a process. I'd been writing all along, on the side, between meals, between courses of another kind when I went back to graduate school to pursue a degree that turned out to be barely worth the paper it was printed on. Part-time teaching, like cooking, was a process with even less tangible results. The ritual of writing, on the other hand, was like the ritual of eating: you could taste each word in itself, then combine and recombine each with the flavors and textures of other words, other sentences. But the great difference was that at the end of the ritual you had something to hold in your hand, something that resisted gravity, something other than a stomach with bulk and weight. So I let the simmering pot come to the boil and set out to write a book.

This was not a good thing to do in relation to the writer in the house. This change was not part of the agreement. While I had no pretensions to being the big serious writer that he indeed had proved to be and had gotten recognition for, I did want to use words to shape what I had seen and felt and tasted in the smaller rooms of my experience and imagination. I wanted to give voice to the domestic, as opposed to the epic, scene. I wanted to write my own kind of book in my own kind of way. I wanted to occupy a very small corner in the sacred room reserved for writing. Finally, I violated the closed door and the sign, 'KEEP OUT. WRITER AT WORK.'

Such a willful violation meant that our attempts to negotiate a new agreement were doomed from the start. I see now that it was only a matter of time. The fierceness of my needs conflicted almost totally with the fierceness of his. The betrayal was that I now put mine first. He couldn't understand why I wanted to take up something that I was not good at, could never be good at. I was good at cooking, he was good at writing. My place was the kitchen, his was the writing room. Looking back, I'm surprised that we lasted as long as we did, trying out various strategies to keep together while swiftly careening apart.

To subvert the fact that our house was symbolically divided forever in just this way, I took to subletting a room a couple of days a week in New York to create a room of my own, a place in which to write. It's understandable why my husband couldn't understand and resented this move. He couldn't understand that I was not trying to escape my husband; I was trying to escape my husband the writer. And six degrees of separation worked. Alone, I was freed from his disapproving scowl. Alone, I could work out the problems of academic jargon that afflicted my prose and of the pretentious overreaching that afflicted my concepts. Alone, I could sit down in front of my IBM Selectric – so much had times changed – and wrestle with the demons inside.

The marriage could not hold, no matter what specific event would serve as catalyst, which I wrote about in my last book, My Kitchen Wars. That was my tenth book in the twenty years since we split, so some kind of proof was in the pudding that demonstrated there was only room for one pudding at a time in our particular mold. I would have to break the mold if I wanted to continue to write and so I did and am sorry, then and now, that this was so. At the same time, as even non-cooks know, there's no omelet without breaking eggs. I've paid for the breakage in many ways, but I've also had the pleasure and sensual satisfaction of all those omelets, which for me has taken the form of a row of books, some small and inconsequential booklets of recipes, others large tomes on the history of American food, and one that has nothing to do with the kitchen at all.

Now, instead of spending all my time at the stove, I spend it hunched over the keyboard of my faithful Dell. Or sometimes faithful, sometimes treacherous Dell. I chew over words like the fibers of a tough hanger steak. I spit out the occasional expletive like a seed. I roll a phrase around in my mouth like a mouthful of Pinot Noir to test its fruitiness and acidity. I like this job better than my old one because at last I am responsible for every word that is caught and held between those hard covers, which will of course erode in time, but last a whole lot longer than any omelet.

25

Peter Levi: A Corresponding Friendship

Rob Rollison

Peter Levi's poetry first drew my eye in 1961 as I thumbed through an anthology of contemporary poetry edited by Elizabeth Jennings:

> Over the roof, high in among the gloom
> you come to a remote, airy room,
> a hexagon resting on pure light
> where mind can shoot to any height
> or in a ripe curve down the leaded dome
> dissolve in mere formality
> of that grave, simple century
> that here for a mind at peace hung this home

This fusion of ethereal delicacy with sharp, geometrical angularity would have attracted the most jaded poetry reader. But the moment was logged in my mind by the letters after the author's name: Peter Levi SJ. Here was a contemporary poet writing poetry which was not only compelling in itself, but was from within the religious order which had, however uncomfortably, housed Hopkins. It was also the order which had taught me for twelve of my then twenty-one years. I had even aspired to join them, but their clear-sighted discrimination considered me unsuitable.

I quickly searched the university library, and found that Peter Levi was a young poet – thirty years old – with three titles to his name. The first, from which the anthology piece came, was titled *The Gravel Ponds* (1961); the second, a co-translation of the exciting Russian poet of the moment, Yevgeny Yevtushenko's *Selected Poems* (1961); and the third, a history of the London Jesuit college, Beaumont. Further research in a dictionary of contemporary authors gave me an outline of his background, and I later filled in more detail.

I found that he was born in Ruislip, in 1931, then an outer semi-rural suburb of London. His father was a well-to-do carpet merchant born in Constantinople. He was sent to a Christian Brothers school in Bath. In an autobiographical slice of his TV series *Art, Faith and Vision* he revisited that school, and recalled spending many hours there 'praying for death'. His final school years were spent more happily at the Jesuit college, Beaumont, in Windsor Great Park; later as a novice Jesuit he was commissioned to write a history of that school. Anecdotes from it and his semi-autobiographical work *The Flutes of Autumn* (1983) record an affection for his Jesuit teachers, especially the more aged and eccentric. But unlike me, on leaving school Levi went directly into the Jesuits.

He had some trouble adjusting to the demands of training. At Roehampton, in their first two years, the trainee priests were sent to teach religion in Sunday schools. Levi's class was in the Harrow Road, 'as rough a parish in as rough an area as you could well hope to find'. His Sunday school sessions were held 'in a sub-divided, unheated cellar, darker and far grimier than the catacombs'. 'The children were poor and distinctly ragged...the truth is that I at least was terrified of my pupils; they lived in a world I had never known'. In 1954, after the two years' initial training and a further two years reading mediaeval philosophy, Levi went to Campion Hall, Oxford, to read Classics. He then read theology at Heythrop College at Chipping Norton, and was studying there when *The Gravel Ponds* was published. During the years of his training Levi was allowed considerable personal freedom to travel overseas, principally to Greece, where he began his first archaeological research. He also rattled around various archaeological sites in Britain on an unreliable, gear-slipping motor bike, visiting Hadrian's Wall, the

Chanctonbury Rings and the Rollright Stones, references to which can be found in his early poetry.

Greatly daring, I immediately dashed off a letter to him – the first I had ever written to a recognised poet. To my astonishment and delight a reply came quickly, clearly appreciating my interest and responding directly to my importunate questions about 'literary influences'. From Chipping Norton, Oxfordshire, to Adelaide, South Australia, where I lived, seemed a huge literary adventure in itself. The letter was warm, specific in detailing influences and our mutual admirations: Robert Frost, Edith Sitwell, Thomas Hardy, Yeats and Pasternak, with the bonus of a name then magical to me and other young readers of American poetry – the 'beat' poet, Gregory Corso, whom Levi knew personally. But there were more mysterious names which were quickly to become familiar and accustomed reading to me: Seferis, Eluard, Ernst Fischer, the Austrian Marxist critic, as well as names which ought to have been more familiar, such as Horace, Aeschylus and Callimachus. In theory, the Jesuits had taught me the last group, but my attention must have wandered. A particular passage from that first letter made conscious reference to Horace's *Ars Poetica* and introduced a dominant theme in Levi's life (it appeared again in the title of his Oxford Lectures on Poetry): 'what one studies is the art of poetry itself, no matter in whose hands'. Altogether, his letter reinforced existing poetic attachments, opened exciting new horizons – and completely enchanted me.

I eagerly sought out *The Gravel Ponds* (1960) and I will always value it as one often does a first book by a much loved poet, for the power of its initial personal impact, as much as for its intrinsic quality. But in this case, I still estimate it to be his best book, carefully crafted and teeming with human feeling. The childhood and youth recorded in the poems glitters with a young poet's fascination with water, architecture and pottery. The title poem grieves over a 'tightening net' which 'traps all creatures/ even the wildest'. A noose (imposed values, external demands, social restraints) closes on human beings. The young, who might be swans in freedom, are actually 'doomed stage characters,/ pursued murderers or slum lovers'. This sharp humanism, altogether without religious warrant, struck me forcefully at a crucial time in my life; a time when my religious faith was being severely tested and found wanting. Yet here was a Jesuit poet who actually knew Gregory Corso and within a poem dedicated to him wrote simultaneously of the religious light of eighteenth-century chapels alongside the 'electric night' shuddering, 'the sun stinking of gin/ and she asking him in'.

I naturally bought his second book of poems, *Water Rock and Sand* (1962), which I found showed a different and more intimate Levi. Poems personally, knowingly, dedicated to a series of mainly young Oxford friends, yet remote, in that such closely dedicated poems hoarded clusters of references excluding the public reader. The third, *Fresh Water Sea Water* (1966), was private in a different sense again. Edward Lucie-Smith talks of this new poetry as 'veering sharply towards surrealism'. This movement towards surrealism, with its convolutedly private references and associations, combined to keep me, and other readers and reviewers, at arm's length. But I persisted in reading everything he published.

Peter had by this time been ordained as a priest and returned to Campion Hall as a tutor in Classics. I had completed my history degree, and was beginning my working life as a high school teacher. We began an irregular correspondence. After my second letter to him, and his reply, we seem to have made an unspoken commitment to keep track of each other. His letters and postcards to me bore increasingly exotic postmarks: not just Oxford, but Athens, and a range of Balkan cities that were the stuff of legend to me.

In my letters I asked him about his poetry, and other writing. He said little about his own work, but his replies to questions about 'the art of poetry' in relation to other poets were helpfully direct. For example, he discussed the importance of writers he admired such as John Clare and Robert Lowell. He also discussed poetic techniques, such as Tennyson's use of English alcaeics. He emphasised how much Horace meant to him. I see now that this tendency to talk about other people's work rather than his own was characteristic of him; his lectures as Oxford Professor of Poetry displayed the same tendency.

The prevailing note in my letters, however, increasingly became an insistent request that Peter spell out some connection between his poetry and his religion. Looking back I see that in many, perhaps too many of my letters, I was urging him to help me survive in that no-man's land on the frontier between poetry and religion. When I announced, no doubt with youthful solemnity, that I could no longer believe in the Catholic faith, he replied: 'leaving the Church is a big move into the cold and dark, but I do see that in someone's personal life-history it can seem a necessary and humanly decent thing. I suppose you don't leave it if you believe what I believe'. The next lines of that letter, posted in Athens, ought to have deterred me from any further forensic probing into what was apparently for him a perfectly healthy body of belief:

> I think God will gather the just, who are made just by their believing and good lives, from the four corners of the sky, and that this process is already going on, and that it is the Church. There are a lot of visible things one would like to change. Christianity is apparently a sort of chameleon of industrial societies – but not quite, it is also a salamander I think. It can live in the fire and simply we must do that. Do you find all these metaphors confusing? But I can only say I actually believe in the Church (since this is the truth about me). What else could I say to you? Nothing that you don't know I dare say.

This letter, with its genuineness and concessions to separateness ought to have satisfied whatever indefinable craving I had for certainty.

I thought of Levi as a Catholic poet, but he wrote relatively few overtly religious poems, and most of these were cast as verse sermons. I greeted them with special joy, though *Death is a Pulpit* (1971), a volume of sermons in verse, was elusive and often densely obscure. Peter was aware of the possibly crude expectation religiously-minded readers such as myself would place on his being a 'Catholic poet'. In responding to the *Poetry Book Society Bulletin* announcing his receipt of their prize for the best new book of poems for 1960, he wrote:

> one might expect a Catholic poet to imitate more than I do the immense ghost of Hopkins, but his *negative virtues* (my italics) are what one most envies; his not being subject to Catholic delusions of grandeur, or the ecstatic violence of phrase and shoddy poverty of conception, or the mere linguistic vices that hang like an aura around so many Catholic reputations.

Levi was clearly referring here to the lush spiritual undergrowth inhabited by the hounds of heaven haunting minor poets like

Francis Thompson, whose poems were still being quoted in Church sermons in the 1950s, though he was long dead. Peter was emphatically not going to proceed down the decadent path where Thompson or Ernest Dowson cast their wild orchids. Nor did he aspire to be the kind of poet, like R. S. Thomas, who tested his religious beliefs through poetry's struggle with the agon of modern unbelief. Levi never wrote religious poetry of Thomas' directness:

> after long on my knees
> in a cold chancel, a stone has rolled
> from my mind, I have looked
> in and seen the old questions lie
> folded and in a place
> by themselves, like the piled
> graveclothes of love's risen body.
>
> ['The Answer', 1978]

He pursued 'the truth' about which he had written to me: 'A Catholic poet needs begin as Hopkins did and as Baudelaire did from the truth of his own mind, a truth not easily attained to,' he wrote. In the same *Bulletin* he was clear that 'the only poet from whom I have consistently tried to learn... is Horace'.

The 'negative virtues' of Hopkins which Peter envied remain tantalising unspecified. It is relatively easy to say what they were in Hopkins' life: the poetic celebration of Nature richly infused with the grandeur of God, but which could not be given full expression. Hopkins' duties as priest and teacher were constantly in opposition to the aesthetic luxury which a life devoted solely to poetry would have permitted. Hopkins chose and endured a regimen which not only shunted him from one dreary task to another as he lived the full discipline of Jesuit life but even imposed a cruel restraint on his publication of poetry. The near despair of the 'terrible sonnets' bears witness to the negative virtue (restraint of individual liberty in giving wholly to the greater glory of God). The course of Peter's life ran much more smoothly for the most part. He joked once that having fouled up the personal life of one poet, the Jesuits compensated by letting him explore his own liberty. In fact, he said in an interview with Karen Armstrong in a Channel 4 programme *Tongues of*

Fire (1987) that the discipline of Jesuit life taught him liberty. This may indeed have been his own 'negative virtue'.

As a result of his visits to Greece, Peter made a new translation of Pausanias's *Guide to Greece* (1971). In 1971–72, he extended his interest in the classics and archaeology a step further, when he travelled through Afghanistan in the company of the late Bruce Chatwin, the well-known travel writer, and his wife Elizabeth. From this experience emerged one of Levi's finest books – and in fact his first full-length prose work – *The Light Garden of the Angel King: Journeys in Afghanistan* (1972). The overall research objective in this expedition was to determine how far east Alexander the Great's armies had penetrated. But it is one of the finest travel books written in the twentieth century and compares favourably with Robert Byron's *Road to Oxiana* and Eric Newby's *A Short Walk in the Hindu Kush*. This is a book which is sensitive to the history, religion and customs of the Afghans, both in their Buddhist past and Moslem present. It received high acclaim from reviewers, and is still worth reading, not least because it describes an Afghanistan now lost. Encouraged by the success of this travel book, Levi wrote another in 1980, *The Hill of Kronos*, but this is a lesser work. It adds little to the world of Greek travel writing, and but for the record of a quaint incident when the military establishment mistook him for a spy, it has no political dimension whatsoever.

During this time, my own life continued in a much less spectacular way. I married, and moved from school teaching into the history department of a teachers' college that over the years grew into a university. I was also writing my own poems, which bore close resemblance to a variety of contemporary poets. A recent, painful, rereading of them shows almost no sign of Peter's prints. Lots of Lowell, scatterings of Larkin and Berryman by the tankard-full, almost as though my closeness to Peter's verse and thinking was being avoided in case he should ever read it. I never sent him a line of mine. He had shown me the way into so many poets I might otherwise have missed. But to me, his own poetry remained obdurately inimitable. He was close as a master, but never a model.

Perhaps, as the intensity of anti-Vietnam war activism involved me, I felt the need to write poems which directly reflected our street demonstrations and public meetings. Peter's poetry, while it referred sympathetically to past and present revolutionary writers, particularly in *Life is a Platform* (1971) with its epigraph from Cesar Vallejo, and *Death is a Pulpit* (1971) dedicated to the Spanish revolutionary Gustavo Duran, seemed to keep political activism at arm's length in these years. I knew that he'd been personally close to the influential Marxist, John Berger, and dedicated a long poem, *Canticum*, to him, but soon after, had some kind of falling out with him.

Given my interest in Peter as not just a Catholic but a Jesuit poet, I was stunned to read in a *Times Literary Supplement* note about halfway through 1977 that Peter had announced his resignation from the priesthood 'due to illness', and with the blessing of his superiors. The note emphasised that he remained a believing Roman Catholic. I didn't feel able to write to him about this, and he didn't write to me. But as my wife and I were planning a trip to England later that year, I hoped to meet my long-time correspondent, and ask him about it. I felt sure that I could track down his new address through the Jesuits.

We arrived in London in late 1977. From there, I rang Campion Hall, and was given Peter's new address and phone number. I rang him, and he answered warmly, telling me that he was now married – to Cyril Connolly's widow, as I later found out. When I proposed a meeting, he asked me to ring again 'early in the new year', as he was trying to finish a novel – a new departure in itself. His tone gave every indication that he would welcome a meeting. In the first week of 1978 I rang him again, eager to fix a time for my first meeting with someone who'd played a significant part in my reading, in fact in my life. This time, however, his tone of voice was cool, even brusque. He told me that he was far too busy with his novel to meet me 'even for a cup of coffee'. I urged upon him that we could meet just briefly, but he became exasperated and terse. He did not actually hang up on me, but the numbing effect was the same.

This interchange left me sad, rather than outraged. I was prepared to allow for the change in his lifestyle that would inevitably result from his leaving the priesthood, and his marriage. But part of me felt that I was being treated as an importunate colonial who had no place in this new world of his. Was I only good enough for the celibate and possibly lonely world of the priesthood? Within months of returning to Australia I rang him, inquiring about poetic work in progress, and whether he had finished the novel. I suppose I was testing the waters – and I found them tepid. Basic information was supplied but there was no real warmth. I also wrote him several letters asking about his work in progress, to which there was no reply.

I continued to read his work and follow his life in English literary journals. He published two more books of poetry, *Five Ages* (1978) and *Private Ground* (1981). These were, as the title of the second suggests, very focused on his local concerns: the natural history of North Oxfordshire, various aspects of classical studies, his family and friends. The poems were increasingly impenetrable to outsiders. The long awaited novel, *The Head in the Soup* (1979), was based on a Levi-like Oxford archaeologist, quaintly called Ben Jonson, who becomes involved in a complex search for treasure, climaxing in the Colonels' Greece. This was followed by two further novels, but they fell short of the first, lacking sustaining narrative or credibility.

Somehow I still felt I couldn't entirely give up a correspondence which had meant so much to me. So in 1982 I sent him a beautifully illustrated book of Australian art, hoping, no doubt, to win back his interest and regard. He wrote back – 'My dear Robert' – thanking me for it, but saying that at his age – about fifty – he 'had a thirst for privacy' in his life and in his religion, and was protecting both by writing fewer letters.

> I am sorry to pain you or to let you down. But there it is. I can't manage to go on writing. I feel great affection for you, but correspondences live rather on curiosity than affection, and I feel less and less curiosity about the post, or about anything else that comes into the house from outside. I like old music, old books, and a very few, very old friends once a year.

The clear message was that I was not an old friend, and that the correspondence was at an end. This was a far more final put-off than his refusal to meet me. Later, re-reading the semi-autobiographical *Flutes of Autumn*, I came across the following: 'It is no use loving people unless you like them and they amuse you; it is a presumption, an impertinence.' Perhaps I was not amusing enough.

In 1968, Peter had written a verse script for a BBC Viewpoint production about ruined abbeys, produced by Mischa Schorer. In the 1970s he scripted and presented two television documentaries: *Foxes Have Holes*, about derelicts and meths drinkers; and *Greece – the Black Years*, an overview of the years 1968–72 when the extreme right-wing Colonels enforced their dictatorship. I saw none of these, but did obtain videotapes of the four programmes *Faith, Art and Vision*, a Channel 4 television series produced in the late 1980s, in which he was both script writer and presenter. The series contained interviews with the writer Iris Murdoch, the sculptor Elisabeth Frink, the painter Cecil Collins and the composer John Tavener. It was an interesting series, though few of the interviews penetrated deeply. From my perspective, the most interesting part of the series was the first episode, which contained autobiographical material about his life at school in Bath, and a photograph of him as a schoolboy in uniform.

But I could not help noting that this very public exposure of Peter as a TV presenter sat strangely with the comments he had made to me in his letter ending our correspondence, in which he talked about deliberately choosing a quiet life 'without public duties or social duties or distractions'. Was this what he meant by being 'left undisturbed for about twenty years with his family'?

In 1984, Levi was elected Oxford Professor of Poetry, after an unsuccessful try at the previous election. I ignored the ban and sent him a congratulatory note, but got no reply. I sent no more letters, but continued to read any material he published. Aside from fairly regular book and television reviews, usually in the *Spectator*, this consisted mostly of literary biographies. He produced biographies of Shakespeare (1988), Pasternak (1990), Tennyson (1993), Edward Lear (1995), John Milton (1996), Horace (1997) and Virgil (1998). The output was prodigious, but only the Shakespeare and the Horace received really favourable critical comment. The common ground in most of the reviews was that the books added little to what was already known. Several months before the publication of the Shakespeare biography, he published *A Private Commission: New Verses by Shakespeare*, in which he claimed to have discovered new poems from the Huntington Library in California. These verses, which Levi was prepared positively to attribute to Shakespeare, received considerable attention in the popular literary press such as *The Times*, the *Guardian* etc. Shakespearean scholars were scornful of his claims, however, and some were uncharitable enough to suggest that Levi's 'find' was just a way of promoting his book. Little came of the claims.

In 1996, Levi wrote another Greek travel book, *A Bottle in the Shade*. In the introduction, he referred to his 'decay of eyesight', a phrase which I noticed immediately, because in January of that year, a detached retina had deprived me of sight in one eye. A year later, in his introduction to *Horace: a Life* (1997) he wrote 'now...my eyes, like his [Horace's] are deteriorating fast'. In that same year, news reached me through English friends that Peter was effectively blind, able to perceive light, but not objects. Any resentments or wounded feelings I might have harboured towards him vanished in a burst of empathy. I immediately wrote a letter of condolence, mentioning my own loss of one eye and difficulty with the remaining one. I quickly received a reply, obviously dictated. 'My dear Robert, I am so sorry about your eye, and hope you are getting on well with the other. You mustn't take this as an invitation to a further or deeper exchange of letters...'. This second sentence struck me then, and still does, as extraordinary. He was at this stage still contributing regular reviews of books on tape to the *Spectator* and presumably dictating those. And I had not even hinted at resuscitating a by-now thoroughly defunct correspondence. Furthermore, I had endured enough deprivation through my vision loss to be very economical with my own correspondence. But his – there is no other word for it – *egotistical* assumption that I was using this coincidence of circumstance as a lever to raise the coffin lid of our correspondence beyond an empathetic chink still amazes me.

So after being reader of his poetry for nearly forty years what drove me to persist in what, for at least half that time, could be called an unbalanced relationship? From my reading after the first book of poetry it was clear to me that my motivation in maintaining the relationship was not based on the intrinsic merit of his poetry. Peter Levi was no Eliot or Hopkins. Considered amongst even other poets who had strong religious affiliations – R. S. Thomas springs to mind as both clergyman and poet – Levi was not in the same league. The easy answer is the hardest, at least in the burden it places on my vanity: there was a spiritual hiatus in my religious development. Was my uncertainty looking for company? Or was I looking for solid fragments of belief to shore against my ruins? The sad fact is that I had invested a kind of nostalgic craving in Levi's poetry and prose, and in his status as a Jesuit. Indeed, I seem to have had less trouble severing myself from the beliefs and practices of the Roman Catholic faith than I did from the Jesuit order. After all, Peter was only the most glamorous and exotic Jesuit with whom I maintained a correspondence. Even today, 2004, I write regularly to several of my former Jesuit teachers.

Two things followed from such an unstable, needy correspondence. Firstly, a frustration on the part of the supplicant, and secondly, the placing of an abnormal strain on what ought to have been an equable exchange of views and feelings. I was asking for more than he could give.

But I do not regret our correspondence. Peter lived a life which embodied several things which were valued throughout my youth and middle age, marriage and parenthood. Firstly the spiritual resources of a deeply held religious faith; secondly the capacity to hold the world in a poetic balance with that faith; and thirdly, and here our worlds almost converged, he continued a critical intellectual relationship with the world based on humanism deriving at least as much from his Catholic origins as from the academic rigours of a teaching and writing life. In retrospect I can see and rejoice in the melange of qualities which make what a present-day Jesuit, Andrew Hamilton, defines as 'good conversation': 'the mixture of exploration, misunderstanding, mutual discovery and the shifts of mind and heart that form the climate in which truth can shine'. I would like that ample definition of good conversation to apply equally to my writer–reader relationship with Peter. For all that I have said of inequality, there was a time in the early correspondence when that definition applied squarely. It is sad to end with the obvious observation that in the post-Jesuit period of our letters the exploration was exclusively mine, the misunderstandings all-enveloping and the shifts of mind and heart too radical to sustain such a climate. In the end we were two men with radically impaired sight in different countries of the mind united on a negative affirmation of damage in the final dictated letter.

But in a correspondence which I sought to stretch across forty years, to say that it was half successful in duration is surely equivalent to saying that I have sight in one of my two eyes.

Peter Levi died on 1 February 2000.

26

Damned by Dollars: *Moby-Dick* and the Price of Genius

Hershel Parker

One of Melville's younger granddaughters told her children that the price of genius was too high for a family to pay. My topic is the price of genius, the price of beauty – what it cost Melville and his family for him to give us *Moby-Dick*.

In early May 1851, when he had finished almost all of *Moby-Dick* except the concluding chapters and late insertions, Melville wrote Hawthorne about 'the silent grass-growing mood in which a man *ought* always to compose', a mood that could seldom be his: 'Dollars damn me; and the malicious Devil is forever grinning in upon me, holding the door ajar.' Critics have tended to take these words as a playful commentary on the strains of authorship: the printer's devil, the boy who runs with copy from author to compositor, is peering into the writer's study, hands outstretched for new pages to carry to the print shop; the harassed author never has enough time quite to perfect his prose before surrendering it to the printer.

Melville went on to say that because dollars damned him, because he was so rushed, 'the product is a final hash,' and all his books were botches. We have not taken Melville's own judgment seriously, partly because for a long time, after the Melville revival in the decade after 1919, the centenary of his birth, we have seen him as a great writer and Moby-Dick as a great book, not a botch. Moby-Dick was seldom taught in colleges before 1950. Indeed, there were very few professors of American Literature until a few years after the War, when for the first time American Literature programs or departments became common. Before that, in the 1920s and 1930s, most teachers who loved Moby-Dick had to wait twenty or thirty years to teach it, as the late Robert Spiller told me ruefully. The wide teaching of Moby-Dick in colleges coincided with the triumph of a theory of literature, the New Criticism, which dictated a method of classroom teaching appropriate to a period when new colleges were being founded to accommodate the returning GIs, colleges that had to start their libraries from scratch, competing with many other new colleges doing the same thing. Old books and newspaper files were hard to buy (even as other libraries were simply trashing their bulky bound newspapers) and major manuscript collections for the nineteenth century were seldom on the market.

Being committed, by the current theory, to ignore biographical evidence as irrelevant to criticism and to see any poem or novel as a perfect work of art made the life of a teacher simple. Even works which any commonsensical reader would regard as obviously the product of disparate and unresolved impulses – such as Melville's Pierre – could be celebrated cleverly in articles entitled 'The Unity of Pierre'. Far more intensely did critics celebrate the unity of Moby-Dick. Decade after decade, critics resolutely ignored Melville's own words, and often ignored also even an obvious anomaly in the text such as the momentous introduction and sudden removal of Bulkington. Almost no one celebrated Moby-Dick as a great book which nevertheless contained elements that the harried author had not harmonized to his own satisfaction. The conspicuous exception, Harrison Hayford's 'Unnecessary Duplicates' (now available in the 2001 Norton Critical Edition of Moby-Dick) was published as late as 1978. Of course, critics proclaimed, Moby-Dick was a unified work of art, not a botch. Likewise, critics could not take seriously the possibility that dollars had really damned Melville. How could he say he was damned? Why, he had the rare satisfaction of knowing for the rest of his life that he had written a great book! Why, within three decades after his death he had ascended into the highest literary realms, compared not to J. Ross Browne the American whaler but to Sir Thomas Browne the Restoration physician and moralist, compared not to William Scoresby the whaling authority but to William Shakespeare! The 1940s literary approach which ignored biographical facts is still dominant in the study of American Literature, however disguised over the last decades as phenomenology, as structuralism, as deconstruction, as the New Historicism. Here I use long-forbidden evidence, biographical evidence, in looking at Melville's gamble that he could write a great book which would be immensely popular, and at the human consequences of that gamble.

After his return from the Pacific in 1844, Melville began the semi-autobiographical *Typee* in New York City and finished it in 1845 while living with his mother and four sisters in a rented house in Lansingburgh, New York, now part of Troy, across the river from Albany. In 1845 the Harpers rejected his story of living with South Sea natives in the Marquesas as impossible to be true. Delayed a year, Melville's career began with that book, *Typee* (London: John Murray; New York: Wiley & Putnam, 1846). Relying on George Putnam's judgment, Wiley had rushed *Typee* into print without reading it, then promptly made Melville expurgate sexual passages along with all the criticisms of Protestant missionaries. By late 1846 the newspapers and magazines published by the lower Protestant churches had united against him, and for the rest of his active career Melville was hounded by what we would classify as right-wing Christians. (Presbyterians, a notably missionary-minded denomination, were particularly hard on Melville; that was why he recklessly made Ishmael claim to be a good Presbyterian.) Melville's career was consolidated by *Omoo* (London: John Murray; New York: Harper & Brothers, 1847), a semi-autobiographical account of his experiences on his second whale ship and in the islands of Tahiti and Eimeo. The Harper brothers had been shrewd enough to snap up the successful author they had spurned, but Melville never got over his early resentment toward them. Once he found he could run up a tab at the Wiley & Putnam and then at the Harpers bookstore, he began buying books that he needed if he were to write books, eating up his profits in advance. On the strength of the popularity of *Omoo*, Elizabeth Shaw and her father, Lemuel Shaw, the chief justice of the Massachusetts Supreme Court, decided that her eleven-month engagement to Melville could be followed, in August 1847, by marriage.

Herman Melville did not have enough money to get married. His father-in-law set him up in New York City, advancing him $2,000, a thousand of which went as down payment on a twenty-one year indenture of lease on a house on Fourth Avenue priced at $6,000. That left a thousand dollars for Melville to use in moving himself, his bride, his mother, and his four sisters from Lansingburgh to Manhattan, setting up housekeeping there, and living on until it ran out. His lawyer brother Allan and his own bride, Sophia, from a wealthy Bond Street family, moved in at the same time, and by 1850 there were four live-in servants. Allan may have contributed to payments listed in the indenture as 'rent', or may have made mortgage payments, and may have contributed to household expenses in other ways. There were mortgage payments to make on the $5,000 as well as the 'rent', whatever that was. No one has done a good job with equivalents, not even the US government with its inflation charts, which would suggest that $2,000 in 1847 would equal some $50 thousand or more today. But in terms of comparable New York City property values, $2,000 in 1847 would buy something roughly like $2,000,000 now: you have to multiply not by twenty-five or thirty but by a thousand. Everyone acknowledges that a million dollars is not what it used to be, and $2,000 now certainly isn't anything like what it used to be. This was very serious money – two years' income for an average urban family, or more.

Melville had made a start on his third book, *Mardi*, before his marriage. After the move to New York he admitted that he was spending his profits in advance and began systematically borrowing books instead, whenever he could restrain himself from buying his own, but he gave himself permission to take more than a year and a half in writing that book, the first in which he dared to be ambitious of literary greatness. The Melvilles' first child, Malcolm, was born early in 1849, shortly before *Mardi* (London: Richard Bentley; New York: Harper, 1849), was published and widely attacked – having already lost Melville his first English publisher, who read it and rejected it. In April 1849, Melville paid Wiley about $40 for the plates of *Typee* so the Harpers could print from them, without having to buy them, and become Melville's sole United States publisher. Abandoning his hopes to turn at once to another ambitious book, Melville instead wrote a book designed to be popular, *Redburn* (London: Bentley; New York: Harper, 1849), and then immediately wrote another one, *White-Jacket* (again Bentley and the Harpers, 1850). Hurt by a new London ruling that held that Americans could not obtain copyright in Great Britain, Melville managed to sell *White-Jacket* in England only because he went there and charmed Bentley into taking a chance on it after several other publishers had rejected it outright. Melville did not get enough from Bentley for *White-Jacket* for him to fulfill his most intense desire. His heart was set on a *Wanderjahr*, a footloose exploration of Italy, the Holy Land – the Grand Tour, justified, for a thirty-year-old husband and father, by the fact that he would be gathering material for popular new books. On the especially long voyage home, in January 1850, frustrated, ambivalent, aspiring, he began planning a book that would be popular as well as ambitious – a book about whaling.

Melville worked hard on it, probably writing at first without much reference to source books. After three months, he described it to the younger Richard Henry Dana as half done – not unrealistic, because the previous summer he had written *Redburn* in two months then had written *White-Jacket* in the next two months. Melville's first break from work seems to have been a hurried excursion to West Point. At some point (about this time?), he came upon the passages on Tupai Cupa in George Lillie Craik's *The New Zealanders* (London, 1830) and, as Geoffrey Sanborn discovered, promptly introduced Queequeg into the manuscript, endowing him with aspects of Tupai Cupa's appearance and history. Melville needed some basic books about whales as well as books about whaling, but one important book was not easy to get: Putnam had to order Thomas Beale's *Natural History of the Sperm Whale* (1839) from England. By the time it arrived, on 10 July 1850, Melville needed more of a vacation. His visit to Pittsfield began merely as a vacation at his late uncle's farm, but he brought the whaling manuscript with him, and for at least a few days in the second half of August he worked on it there. The widow and children had sold the great old house, in need of repairs – moldering, but a mansion – and the land (250 acres) for $6,500; the purchasers, the Morewoods, would not take possession for several months. Melville had not known the farm was for sale. Once he found that he had just missed the chance to buy the farm (which one of his cousins in 1848 had called his 'first love'), he was filled with an absolutely unreasonable jealousy. Then once he had made friends with Nathaniel Hawthorne, who for several months had been living outside nearby Lenox, Melville knew that if he were to do justice to his book he had to live in the Berkshires, starting immediately. Melville's behavior makes some sense if you calculate the power the Berkshires held in his memory, from the times he had visited his uncle Thomas Melvill and later from the summer of 1837, when he had worked the farm before teaching at a rural school in the nearby mountains. His behavior makes some emotional sense if you take account of his disillusion at the way his friends among the New York literati were viciously sniping at each other, and particularly if you consider his exaltation at the possibility of finishing his book with Mount Greylock in view to the north and his new friend Nathaniel Hawthorne a few miles away to the south. If he remained in Manhattan, he could not make the book as good as it could be. Besides, he had been amazingly responsible several months before: he had cut short his stay in London just as he was meeting marvelous literary men and artists, and he had sacrificed the year-long Grand Tour that surely would have proved of such high economic benefit to his family, in the long run. Now the most important thing in his life was that he make the whole book as great as the part he had written.

 Melville was not being rational, but he was persuasive. His father-in-law, after already advancing him the $2,000 in 1847, advanced him $3,000 more toward the purchase of Dr John Brewster's farm adjoining the old Melvill property. For a total of $6,500 – exactly the price of the Melvill farm – he bought a much smaller farm (160 acres) and a decrepit old farmhouse – a house that had never been grand, as his uncle's had been and would be again. This might seem barely rational of Shaw. But for his money Shaw got the assurance that as long as he paid his annual September visit to hold court in Lenox he could see his daughter and her family in Pittsfield, and during the rest of the year she would be only a direct ride away on the new railroad that ran right across Massachusetts.

In mid-September 1850 Melville probably turned over to Brewster the $3,000 that Shaw had just advanced him. He arranged at the same time that Brewster would hold a mortgage of $1,500 on the property. That leaves a discrepancy of $2,000. The best I can figure it, Brewster agreed, verbally, to wait a while for the $2,000, say a month or two, until the indenture of lease on the highly desirable Fourth Avenue house could be sold at a tidy profit and Melville could turn over $2,000 of the proceeds to him. When Melville returned to New York, T. D. Stewart (a friend from Lansingburgh) offered to loan him whatever he needed to tide him over, but Melville refused: he would not need the loan. In October 1850 Melville and his wife along with his mother and three of his sisters moved to the farm, which he promptly named Arrowhead. Perhaps his brother Allan had already purchased his new house on Thirty-First Street, for he and his wife and two children, one a new baby, along with one Melville sister, were preparing to move out of the Fourth Avenue house within a few weeks. By Christmas the Fourth Avenue house was empty but unsold. In January 1851 Allan talked about buying it himself, because he and his wife were unhappy being so far uptown (that far uptown was out of town, remote from everything, they had found), but that proved to be just talk. Meantime, Melville had not gotten settled in a writing room until well into November, and then he had to be dispossessed for the family Thanksgiving (including the aunt and cousins) to be held there because there was no room on the first floor big enough for the tables. His wife had taken the baby and fled the chaos to Boston, the only place you could celebrate Thanksgiving properly, and did not return until New Year's Day 1851. The older sister also fled, hurt as she left by Herman's irritation at having to drive her to the station during his writing hours, and his mother and two remaining sisters spent December in frustration, imprisoned: he would not trust them to drive the horse, Charlie, and he hated taking time off from writing to drive them where they wanted to go and wait to bring them back, or drive home and return for them. In January, he was so desperate for concentrated writing time that he suddenly let them test-drive Charlie and thereafter trusted them to go where they wanted.

The discomforts and inadequacies of the farmhouse became more apparent all the time, and by the end of February 1851 it was clear that the cooking facilities were too primitive for the cook (they always had a cook or else were actively recruiting one), the outdoor well was inconvenient, they needed an inside kitchen pump, the parlor walls were soiled, some of the upholstered furniture looked worse after the move, certain rooms needed painting, and the barn in particular required painting. In the dead of winter, Melville hired men to start the renovations – maybe before the first of March. The first order of business was grotesquely impractical – digging foundations in the still-frozen ground, and not just for a kitchen and a wood house but also for a narrow piazza on the cold north side of the house. This piazza, too small for a whole family to use, would be Herman's vantage point for viewing Greylock from the first floor, just below his small window for viewing it in his writing room before starting his day's task.

In March the lease on the house in town was sold at last, the buyer paying $7,000, of which $5,000 went to the mortgage, which had remained at that figure. That left $2,000 for Melville, minus any rents or other fees that he may have owed. If he were behind in payments on the mortgage, then that amount would have come out of the $2,000. In any case, as he admitted five years later, the sum received had fallen 'short of the amount expected to have been realized'. Instead of having $2,000 to turn over to Dr Brewster, six months late, perhaps with no interest being charged on it, he had somewhat less than $2,000, and he had workmen to pay as well as Dr Brewster. He would need more money, just to pay Dr Brewster the remainder of the purchase money, not counting the $1,500 mortgage. In March Melville began thinking of taking Mr Stewart up on his generous offer to help a friend in need, but as a last resort. First, on 25 April, Melville wrote to Fletcher Harper asking for an advance on his whaling manuscript. A clerk at the Harpers brought Melville's account up to date on 29 April, and on 30 April the Harpers sent their refusal, citing their 'extensive and expensive addition' to their plant and pointing out that Melville was already in debt to them for 'nearly seven hundred dollars'. At once, on 1 May, Melville borrowed $2,050 from Stewart, for five years, at 9 per cent interest. Some of the money, maybe a good deal of it, went to make up the $2,000 Melville had to pay Dr Brewster, some of it went for the workmen at Arrowhead. Some of it was earmarked to pay a compositor in New York City, for in his anger at the Harpers Melville decided to pay for the setting and plating of the book himself in the hope of selling the plates to another publisher for a better deal than the Harpers would give him. In early May, not later, as we had thought, Melville carried the bulk of the manuscript to town, and left it with Robert Craighead, the man who had stereotyped *Typee* for Wiley & Putnam. *Moby-Dick* had to be a great financial success, and there was some hope that it would be. Richard Bentley, Melville's British publisher, gave Melville a note for £150 (about $700, after Melville took a penalty for cashing the note early). Melville had the money to make the $90 annual mortgage payment to Dr Brewster in September and to pay Stewart his semi-annual interest of $92.50 on 1 November 1851, more than a month after the three-volume *The Whale* was published in London, a week after the Melvilles' second child, Stanwix, was born, and two weeks before the publication of the Harper *Moby-Dick*. (The American title, a last minute substitution, reached London too late to be given to the book there.)

    Some of the London reviews were full of extravagant praise. On 24 October, 1851, the London *Morning Advertiser* concluded that the three volumes reflected more credit on America and were 'more honourable to American literature' than any other works it could name. On 25 October *John Bull* called this the most extraordinary of Melville's books: 'Who would have looked for philosophy in whales, or for poetry in blubber? Yet few books which professedly deal in metaphysics, or claim the parentage of the muses, contain as much true philosophy and as much genuine poetry as the tale of the *Pequod*'s whaling expedition.' The *Leader* on 8 November said that *The Whale* was 'a strange, wild, weird book, full of poetry and full of interest'. The *Morning Post* on 14 November said that 'despite its occasional extravagancies, it is a book of extraordinary merit, and one which will do great things for the literary reputation of the author'. The *Weekly News and Chronicle* on 29 November echoed the *Leader*: it was 'a wild, weird book, full of strange power and irresistible fascination for those who love to read of the wonders of the deep'.

Normally, many British reviews of Melville's books had been reprinted in the United States. This time, for crucial weeks, the only reviews of the three-volume *The Whale* known in the United States were two hostile ones published in London on the same day, 25 October, in the *Athenæum* and the *Spectator*. They were hostile largely because there was no epilogue in the English edition to explain just how Ishmael survived. Most likely, Bentley had told his compositors to shove all the etymology and extracts, all that distracting junk, into the back of the third volume, and in the process of shifting things around the single sheet containing the epilogue (half a page of type, scrunched, very likely from being on the bottom of the tall stack shipped across the Atlantic) had gotten lost. One of the rewards in carefully re-reading the book is the chance to see just how early and how deftly Melville began preparing for Ishmael's survival, but without the epilogue any first-time reader could be excused for assuming that Melville had violated the basic contract between writer and reader: if you create a first person narrator, you make sure he or she lives to record the story somehow. The loss of the epilogue tainted the whole British reception, freeing hostile reviewers to write scathingly of Melville, and forcing friendly reviewers to find ways of praising the book despite such an obvious flaw. The fact that only the *Athenæum* and the *Spectator* reviews were reprinted in the United States was worse than bad luck – it was disastrous for Melville.

On 20 November 1851, the reviewer in the Boston *Post* saved himself work by constructing his long review mainly from the *Athenæum*, which had declared that the style of Melville's tale was 'in places disfigured by mad (rather than bad) English; and its catastrophe is hastily, weakly, and obscurely managed'. As it happened, the *Athenæum* did not spell out just what was wrong with the 'catastrophe' it condemned. The reviewer in the *Post* confessed not to have read quite halfway through the book, and so had no notion of what the ending was like. Any Bostonian might have laid aside the *Post* knowing that the London paper had been contemptuous of *Moby-Dick* but having no idea why the reviewer thought the catastrophe was so bad. In case anyone in Boston had missed the review in the *Post*, the sister paper the *Statesman* reprinted it in full, long quotations from the *Athenæum* intact, two days later, on 22 November. The *Spectator* review was reprinted in the New York *International Magazine* for December, and not reprinted again, as far as is known. The *Spectator* gave a clearer indication what was wrong with the ending of the London edition, saying that the *Pequod* 'sinks with all on board into the depths of the illimitable ocean', narrator presumably included, but the complaint was muffled by the different charge that Melville continually violated another rule, 'by beginning in the autobiographical form and changing ad libitum into the narrative' – something that any reader halfway into the book might have agreed with.

Long before he saw a set of *The Whale*, Melville saw at least what the *Post* reprinted from the *Athenæum*, but unless he saw the *International Magazine* he did not know for sure that the epilogue had been omitted from *The Whale*. He made no protest to Bentley, it is clear, and no American reviewer read the *International Magazine* and seized the chance to challenge the Londoners: 'Aren't these Brits odd? They are saying Ishmael does not survive, but right here in my copy Ishmael is rescued by the *Rachel*.' Later Melville saw a handful of some of the short quotations from a few reviews besides those in the *Athenæum* and the *Spectator*, including the ones in *John Bull* and the *Leader*, but he never, in all the rest of his life, ever had any idea that despite the loss of the epilogue many British reviewers had showered honor on him as a great prose stylist.

In the United States Melville's friend Evert Duyckinck reviewed the book promptly in two successive weeks in the New York *Literary World* – an influential, tone-setting paper. The first installment was devoted to belaboring the coincidence that the book was published just as news was arriving of the sinking of the *Ann Alexander* by a whale off Chile. In the second, 22 November, Duyckinck complained about Melville's irreverence toward religion, the 'piratical running down of creeds and opinions.' He had warned Melville politely in his review of *White-Jacket* early in 1850 that he would not countenance irreverence. There was strong praise from some reviewers in the United States, but it did not last long, and it was submerged by the ferocious religious reviews, such as the one in the New York *Independent* on 20 November:

> The Judgment day will hold him [Melville] liable for not turning his talents to better account, when, too, both authors and publishers of injurious books will be conjointly answerable for the influence of those books upon the wide circle of immortal minds on which they have written their mark. The book-maker and the book-publisher had better do their work with a view to the trial it must undergo at the bar of God.

The low church religious press would have leapt on Melville anyhow, but Duyckinck lent intellectual and literary respectability to such pious denunciations.

In the first two weeks after publication the Harpers sold 1,535 copies of *Moby-Dick*, but in the next two months or so they sold only 471 more, and after that sales dwindled rapidly. Meanwhile, Melville was writing a new book, a psychological novel based on what he had learned about his own mind in the last years and in which he played off Dutch Calvinist Christianity against Bostonian – and British – feel-good Unitarianism. Self-analysis had began in earnest two and a half years earlier, after Melville had written *Redburn* as a fast, easy book because much of it was autobiographical. In late May 1849 his nineteen-year-old brother, Tom, was sailing out of Manhattan for China, the age Herman had sailed from Manhattan to Liverpool on his first voyage, in 1839, and going on board Tom's ship triggered memories of ten years earlier, when his brother Gansevoort (dead in London just after arranging the publication of *Typee*) had seen Melville off from those docks. In early June of 1849, as he wrote his story, he had done a reckless thing, to use his later words: he had dipped an angle into the well of childhood, gone fishing in his own memory, where who knew what monstrous creatures might be brought up. Melville had been psychologically naïve still in planning a fast and easy expedition into his childhood. The intense psychological unfolding that began in the act of writing *Redburn* (or the aftermath of having written it) had allowed Melville to write *Moby-Dick* and *Pierre* – the first version of *Pierre*.

What happened to *Pierre* I have told in the HarperCollins Kraken Edition (1995), illustrated by Maurice Sendak, and in Volume 2 of my *Herman Melville: A Biography, 1851–1891* (2002). Briefly, Melville took the manuscript to New York about the first day of 1852, just as some extremely hostile religious reviews of *Moby-Dick* were appearing. The Harpers read the manuscript and offered him an impossible contract: not the usual fifty cents on the dollar after costs but twenty cents on the dollar after costs. *Moby-Dick* was not going to be as popular as *Typee*, not even as popular as *Redburn*, sales figures already showed. What was he to do? What he did, after a few days, was reckless to the point of being suicidal. He began enlarging the manuscript with pages about Pierre as a juvenile author (a wholly new turn in an already completed manuscript), then with pages about Pierre's immaturely attempting a great book. In some of these pages he maligned Pierre's publishers. The Harpers honored their contract to publish *Pierre*, on such ruinous terms to the author, but by the next summer, after the ferocious reviews of *Pierre* began to appear, they quietly began letting literary people know that they thought Melville was crazy – 'a little crazy', to be exact – not too crazy to keep people from buying *Redburn* and *White-Jacket*. *Pierre* lost Melville his English publisher, who figured if he continued to sell copies of the books he had in print he would eventually lose only £350 ($1,650) or thereabouts by publishing Melville, somewhat short of $50,000 in present purchasing power. Bentley would have printed *Pierre*, expurgated (as he had silently expurgated *The Whale*, without consulting Melville at all), if Melville had taken his generous offer to publish it without an advance and to divide any profits it made. During most of 1851 Melville had felt little guilt about his secretly borrowing $2,050 from Stewart: after all, the whaling book was so good that it had to succeed, and he could pay Stewart back before his wife and father-in-law found out about the loan. After January 1852, when he knew the Harper contract was disastrous, he may have hoped against hope for three or four months that all would work out, that Bentley would like *Pierre* and offer a handsome advance, or even that against all odds *Pierre* might sell so well in the United States that he would make money – even at twenty cents for every dollar the Harpers took in (after recouping their expenses) rather than fifty cents. Melville may have denied in January 1852 and denied again in April and May 1852 that his career was over, but it was, however long he might try to postpone the death gasps. When *Pierre* was published in the summer of 1852 it was savaged as no significant American book had ever been savaged. 'Herman Melville Crazy', read a headline I discovered decades ago. Reviewers already had called Melville crazy for writing *Moby-Dick*, and accusations that he was insane recurred, still more strongly, in the reviews of *Pierre*, confirming in the minds of his mother-in-law and his wife's brother and two half-brothers that Melville was insane as well as a failure. That fall Melville tried to interest Hawthorne in writing a story he had heard that summer about a woman on the coast of Massachusetts who had nursed a shipwrecked sailor and married him, only to have him desert her. From mid-December 1852 or so, Melville wrote the story himself, finishing it on or around 22 May 1853, the day his first daughter, Elizabeth, was born. The fate of *Moby-Dick* and *Pierre*, and his new labors on the book about the abandoned woman, *The Isle of the Cross*, had taken their toll on his health. As a sailor, Melville had been an athlete, and late in 1849, on the voyage to England, could still climb 'up to the mast-head, by way of gymnastics'. In the summer of 1851 he fearlessly climbed high in a tree on an expedition to Greylock. That vigor disappeared. In a memorandum made after his death Melville's widow recalled: 'We all felt anxious about the strain on his health in Spring of 1853' – perhaps as early as April, when his mother was so concerned that she wrote her brother Peter Gansevoort hoping he could persuade his political friends to gain Herman a foreign consulship from the new president, Hawthorne's college friend Franklin Pierce: 'The constant in-door confinement with little intermission to which Hermans [sic] occupation as author compels him, does not agree with him. This constant working of the brain, & excitement of the imagination, is wearing Herman out.' The year before, on 1 May 1852, Melville had defaulted on the semi-annual interest payment of $92.50 that he owed his friend Stewart, and he had defaulted again that November. His mother's letter was written a week before he defaulted for the third time. Elizabeth Shaw Melville may have recalled this period in early spring as the time when the family was most concerned about Melville, but the worst came at the end of spring, in June, when he carried *The Isle of the Cross* to New York City only to have the Harpers refuse to publish it, just at the time when it was quite clear that he had no hope of gaining a foreign consulship.

Melville was thoroughly whipped, but bravely he started writing short stories within weeks or even days of returning home with the manuscript of *The Isle of the Cross*, which he retained for some months, at least, and probably some years, before presumably destroying it. When a single letter of his has sold for much more than $100,000, the value of that manuscript, if it emerged today, might rival that of the most expensive paintings in the world. But in September 1853, with the manuscript in his possession still, Melville defaulted on the payment of $90 due to Dr Brewster. The money went for preparations for the wedding of his sister Kate to John C. Hoadley. Several weeks later, he defaulted, as he did every six months now, on the interest he owed Stewart.

Melville wrote to the Harpers late in November 1853 that he had 'in hand, and pretty well towards completion', a book, 'partly of nautical adventure'; then he qualified himself: 'or rather, chiefly, of Tortoise Hunting Adventure'. At that time he promised it for 'some time in the coming January', and asked for and received the advance – a dollar for each of the three hundred estimated pages. He had specified that he was expecting 'the old basis – half profits' – not the punitive terms he had accepted for *Pierre*. Now he paid Dr Brewster the $90 he should have paid in September. This slight relief was followed by catastrophe. On 10 December 1853, much of the Harper stock of printed books and sheets was destroyed by fire, and the brothers charged Melville all over again for their costs before giving him royalties on his books – in effect, hanging on to the next $1,000 or so he earned. That is, to emphasize the unconscionable nature of their behavior, the Harpers recouped their losses in the fire by charging their expenses against him not once but twice.

If in mid-December Melville thought that after their disaster the Harpers could not possibly publish any book right away, then the straightforward thing would have been to write them and ask in so many words if they would be able to publish the book they had just given him the advance for. If they had replied that they could not be back in business for six months, he could not have returned their advance because he had already spent much or most of it, but he could have asked their permission to try to place the tortoise manuscript elsewhere and to turn over to them $300 if he got that sum from another source or, more reasonably, turn over to them $300 worth of articles for their magazines. Instead, he seems to have made an expedient, emotional decision that does not look wholly defensible. He decided to get more money from another publisher for the tortoise story, or for part of the tortoise material – or at least for material also dealing with tortoises. The batch of pages Melville sent to George Putnam on 6 February 1854, seems to be what was published in the March Putnam's as the first four sketches of The Encantadas, the second of which was 'Two Sides to a Tortoise'.

In mid-February 1854 Melville endured a 'horrid week' of pain in his eyes (words Allan Melville quoted back to their sister Augusta on 1 March). Melville had been crowding Augusta with pages to copy for him, overworking her and overworking himself. He was suffering from public shame brought on him by Pierre, private shame at having been late with a payment to Brewster, and shame at his continually defaulting on the interest he owed Stewart, compounded by shame at doing something with the tortoise material that looks less than honorable, no matter that the Harpers were themselves behaving abominably. No wonder he was sick.

In the next two years Melville wrote a full-length book, Israel Potter; several stories; and 'Benito Cereno', which proved long enough to be serialized in three installments at the end of 1855. Early that year, with 'Benito Cereno' far along, if not quite finished, he collapsed. In her memoir his widow recorded: 'In Feb 1855 he had his first attack of severe rheumatism in his back – so that he was helpless.' How long he was helpless is not clear. The timing of the attack suggests the possibility of couvade, because his wife gave birth to her fourth child, Frances, on 2 March 1855. This pregnancy had proceeded in pace with the monthly installments of Israel Potter, the last of which appeared in March, before book publication. Melville knew that his sister

Kate Hoadley was also pregnant (she bore her daughter on 30 May 1855). In 'Tartarus of Maids' Melville made the narrator say: 'But what made the thing I saw so specially terrible to me was the metallic necessity, the unbudging fatality which governed it.' The unbudging fatality of the gestation process was a reminder to him, during each of the last two of his wife's pregnancies, of the passing of months, including the Mays and Novembers in which he missed interest payments to Stewart and the September in which he had missed a payment to Brewster. (He missed the September 1855 payment, too.) The day of reckoning was approaching remorselessly – 1 May 1856 – and Melville was progressively less able even to hope to avert the disaster. Malcolm's life had begun in triumph; Stanwix's life had begun in distress – with Lizzie's horribly painful breast infection and the doctor-enforced early weaning of the baby, while Melville was reading reviews of *Moby-Dick* and writing *Pierre*. Melville's daughters' lives began when his state was even more miserable. After Bessie's birth Melville had failed to get *The Isle of the Cross* into print and had failed to obtain a consulship; before Frances's birth he had become helpless from rheumatism.

According to his widow, Melville's first attack of severe rheumatism in February 1855 was followed in June by an attack of sciatica, which lasted through August, according to some comments made in September 1855. Nevertheless, later that year Melville began a satire on American optimism, *The Confidence-Man*, and continued to work on it during the early months of 1856; during all this time, apparently, T. D. Stewart was threatening to seize the farm – the same property already mortgaged to Dr Brewster. Melville wrote his plight into the manuscript in the story of China Aster. In April 1856, just before the entire loan of $2,050 and back interest (and probably interest on the interest) became due, after living with the literally crippling secret of his debt since the first of May 1851, Melville had to confess his folly to his father-in-law and throw himself on Shaw's mercy. For once, luck favored Melville, and he managed to sell off half the farm swiftly. Yet the sale was not simple (as Lion G. Miles recently discovered): the buyer paid for the property in three annual installments, nothing up front in 1856. Shaw must have advanced the money himself to pay off Stewart then recouped it out of the buyer's 1857 and 1858 payments. Loving and magnanimous still, Shaw recognized how ill Herman was and advanced him still more money for a trip abroad in hopes of restoring his health. Before he sailed, Melville had completed *The Confidence-Man*, which on its publication in 1857 earned him not a penny, so he was out for the paper and ink in which he wrote it, and the paper and ink with which his sister Augusta copied it, and Augusta had copied it for nothing. At least she could see it in print, unlike *The Isle of the Cross*, which she had also copied.

After his return from his journey to the Holy Land and Europe in 1856–57, the next word of Melville's health is in 1858, as his widow recalled: 'A severe attack of what he called crick in the back laid him up at his mothers [sic] in Gansevoort in March 1858 – and he never regained his former vigor & strength.' The next year on 21 November 1859, his neighbor Sarah Morewood, mistress of his uncle's grand old house, wrote to a friend: 'Herman Melville is not well – do not call him moody, he is ill.' (The back pain recurred: Melville's mother at Christmas 1867 described Herman as then finally able to go out: 'his trouble was a "Kink in his back"'. In 1882 he suffered again what his wife described as 'one of the attacks of "crick in the back"'.)

In the late 1850s Melville may not have put enough food on the table. At least one year, his father-in-law sent money for winter provisions. Melville earned a little money from lecturing for three seasons, late 1857 to early 1860. In early 1860 he completed a book of poems that two publishers rejected and that was never published, though some of the surviving poems may have been in that volume. In 1861 Judge Shaw died and Elizabeth Melville inherited enough money to support herself, her four children, and her husband for a few years. Melville's old debt to the Harpers was finally erased by sales in 1865, and he published a poorly received book of Civil War poems, *Battle-Pieces*, in the summer of 1866. The Harpers did not pay Melville for the war poems they printed in *Harper's Monthly*, and they charged half of the expenses of printing *Battle-Pieces* against his account, so that he half-subsidized the edition. Melville did not have regular earnings until late in 1866, when he took a $4-a-day job as a custom officer in New York City, a job he held nineteen years. We know now that there was a terrible marital crisis in early 1867. Elizabeth's brothers encouraged her to believe Melville was insane and with her minister, Henry Bellows, explored the possibility that she might leave him. Her strength of character emerged in verses she wrote to commemorate her prayerful decision to stay with her husband. That fall the Melville's oldest child, Malcolm, shot himself to death at age eighteen. Melville's life contracted even more tightly after 1869, when he began secretly working on a new poem that grew to 18,000 lines. He paid to have *Clarel* printed in 1876, using money his uncle Peter Gansevoort had left for that purpose; it was contemptuously reviewed, and in 1879 the publisher made him authorize the destruction of the remaining bound copies and sheets, which were cluttering up the office.

In the next decades after its publication *Moby-Dick* was seldom mentioned in print. Melville's loyal friend Henry T. Tuckerman praised it in 1863 as having 'the rare fault of redundant power'. In 1884, the English sea-novelist W. Clark Russell said the sailors' talk in the forecastle scene in *Moby-Dick* 'might truly be thought to have come down to us from some giant mind of the Shakespearean era'. The family heard about this article and in March 1885 Melville's cousin, Catherine Gansevoort Lansing, with Lizzie Melville in tow, sallied out to Brentano's on Union Square to order the September 1884 *Contemporary Review*, the one containing Russell's article. Thereafter, some in the family began to understand that Herman Melville had been an important writer. Even before Melville's death in September 1891, and abundantly thereafter, Elizabeth Shaw knew that her husband was being recognized as one of the greatest American writers, and she proudly guarded his reputation as best she could. In this endeavor her older daughter, Bessie, born on or about the day *The Isle of the Cross* was completed, assisted. Mrs Melville died in 1906, Bessie in 1908 – late enough to have met with a would-be biographer, Frank Jewett Mather, whose plans fell through because Houghton Mifflin would not advance him $500 for the project. In the centennial of Melville's birth and in the next few years, first in England and then in the United States, Melville was at last saluted as belonging with Shakespeare and other great writers of the world.

None of this extraordinary fame impressed Melville's surviving daughter, Frances. Until her death in 1938 she blamed him for her sister Bessie's arthritis (caused by insufficient food, she thought), blamed him for her brother Malcolm's suicide in 1867, blamed him for innumerable acts, such as rousting her and her older sister out of bed at least one night early in 1876 to help him proofread *Clarel*, blamed him for her brother Stanwix's wasted life and early death (in 1886). She alone remembered that her father's in-laws (always excepting Judge Shaw) had believed every newspaper and magazine assertion that Melville was insane; she alone remembered that for some time in the 1860s her mother may also have thought him insane, on the basis of his behavior, presumably, as well as on the full authority of many unimpeachable writers in the press; and she alone knew that her Bostonian uncle and half-uncles had tried to devise a way her mother could separate from her father without creating a scandal. Frances Melville Thomas told her oldest daughter that she did not know 'H. M.' in the new light of world fame: her resentments were so strong that his new reputation was a disparagement of her own memories and her own feelings. Two of her daughters were old enough to remember Melville well and to have known Mrs Melville intimately, as young women, so they were able to correct Frances's views by their own memories, but the two younger daughters, born near the time of Melville's death, remembered Mrs Melville less clearly and were more dependent on Frances for information about their grandfather. At least one of them absorbed Frances's lesson that the price of genius was too high for any family to pay. Now, in the twenty-first century, the surviving great-grandchildren and the great-great-grandchildren (themselves middle-aged) feel entitled to whatever simple or complex pleasures they can find in being descended from Herman Melville. For them, the high price of genius has at last been paid, perhaps in full.

Acknowledgement

This essay is revised from its first printing in the Second Norton Critical Edition of *Moby-Dick* (New York: 2001), edited by

Hershel Parker and Harrison Hayford. It was written as the Samuel D. Rusitzky Lecture at the Old Dartmouth Historical Society New Bedford Whaling Museum on Johnny Cake Hill (across from the Seamen's Bethel), June 26, 1997.

Conclusion: A Perilous Art
Dale Salwak

I have been privileged to live among writers all my life, and I find that many of their experiences have carried over into my lessons in the classroom. Here, in an imagined letter to one of my students (now herself a writer and teacher), is an exploration of the power and the perils of the creative life.

Dear Kelley,

Set aside all distractions. Clear your mind. Be still, listen, and soon you might connect deep inside with a whisper, or a constant whirring, or perhaps an ache that pulses or even rages. It emanates from a painful reality all teachers are subconsciously aware of every moment of their professional lives: Teaching can be a perilous art.

I imagine you are as surprised to read these words as I was to hear them from a professor thirty-five years ago. After all, haven't my letters emphasized the positive aspects of our chosen profession? Haven't I celebrated the many ways that colleagues and students enrich our minds, our experience, our very souls? Isn't the most compelling aspect of our professional lives the fact that we are paid to do the work we love? What is so perilous about any of that?

Well, to use the word in this context is not an invitation to despair. I am not implying, as some might, that over the years our profession loses any of its luster or charm or sparkle, or that our work in and out of the classroom necessarily leads to burnout and depression. Nor am I connecting *perilous* with the gravity of some subjects we teach or the bleakness of some books or the failure of some students.

No, it goes deeper than any of that.

As a child living in Amherst, Massachusetts, I grew up hearing the poetry of Robert Frost. 'Birches', 'Apple-Picking', 'Stopping by Woods on a Snowy Evening', among others, spoke truthfully to me of a world that I knew and of a people that I was raised among.

On occasion Mr Frost would visit the college, and so my father, an administrator at the nearby university, invited me one evening to a fireside chat arranged for a select number of students and faculty. A black-and-white snapshot from the time shows me as a ten-year-old sitting cross-legged in my bathrobe, pajamas, and slippers. The expression on my face is confused. In the background sits the poet himself, with his big white head and hanging brows, smiling boyishly as he gazes at his audience.

I remember none of his spoken words, of course, but I do remember his tone and the feeling it left with me. Here was a good-humored, soft-spoken, larger-than-life figure in whom I sensed a peculiar sadness – a sadness, as I learned much later, that in an odd paradox grew more pronounced the more blessed he felt.

'Nothing gold can stay,' wrote Frost in a poem by the same name, a reality he faced every day in his work as indeed we must face in ours. To step into the classroom and connect meaningfully with our students is to suffer some ache of separation when the term is over. To experience breakthroughs in the laboratory and advance in our field of inquiry is to lament the day when someone takes over and carries our work farther than we ever could have. To attach our devotion to any classic of literature or music or art is to invite a kind of inevitable humiliation, for the classic itself will far outlive both ourselves and our attempts to understand and appreciate it. Like Frost, who knew so well the short-lived satisfaction of the creative instinct, we discover how quickly the seasons appear to pass if we are immersed in what we love to do. When we find our true vocation, when we have learned to recognize a compelling purpose to teach, then we do not want its challenges and considerable satisfaction to end.

In part this feeling is related of course to the passage of time – of which there is never enough for reading all the books or writing all the essays or teaching all the classes we would like. We grow older, but our students seem not to, and each year we see the image of our younger selves reflected in the faces of eighteen- and nineteen- and twenty-year-olds; and mixed with our delight in the work is a nostalgia for when we were in school – a less complicated, relatively free time, our lives filled with as-yet untapped potential. The classroom becomes a kind of memento mori, therefore, and Wordsworth's 'still, sad music of humanity' becomes our music, subtle yet insistent, as a week becomes a month becomes another year, and we indulge in the sensations of every possible moment lest that be the last opportunity to do so. And at commencement, as we watch the students walk by with their diplomas, we realize that most of these good folks we'll never see again. Probably they were not yet alive when we were born, but a more poignant truth is that they will likely be here long after we are gone.

As you progress, Kelley, it's important that you remain vigilant (as did Frost all his life) for any telltale signs of a dwindling of your own youthful fire. When William Dean Howells, filled with regret that his best years were gone, was about to leave Paris to care for his dying father in the United States, he said something to his friend Jonathan Sturges that ought to be emblazoned upon the office wall of every teacher: 'Oh, you are young, you are young – be glad of it: be glad of it and live. Live all you can: it's a mistake not to.... I haven't done so – and now I'm old. It's too late. It has gone past me – I've lost it. You have time. You are young. Live!'

Example is probably better than explanation at this point. I discovered the above passage bracketed in one of my professor's texts. Soon after he'd died at age seventy-seven, his son invited me to peruse his library of over 9,000 books for some I might like to acquire. In volume after volume the penciled marginalia, all in his own hand, testified to an unquenchable vitality, to a mind deeply engaged in what he was reading at the time, to a man fully alive to the text and, by implication, to the world. I remembered that same vitality and good sense infusing his classroom as he raced along and we tried to keep up with our notes. It was a privilege just to watch the man at work. Each day I came away feeling my *self* enlarged, alert, and refreshed.

I had every reason, therefore, to assume of my professor that with age and experience came confidence and personal security. But as the son revealed to me that afternoon at his home, behind his father's moral earnestness and vibrant spirit an ominous sense of unease had been working away toward the end of his professional life. Some mornings he awoke, sweating with fear that whatever had made him able to work the day before had vanished, and that he'd go to his classroom and find himself paralyzed. Or he would toss and turn at night, wondering if he had perpetuated through his lectures as much misunderstanding as understanding, as much error as truth. Students reported that his lectures became less sonorous, more jagged, more on edge; photos from the time showed that his face had grown wax-pale and drained. Consumed with self-doubt and a conviction that something dreadful but indefinable had gone wrong, he developed an impregnable carapace around his inner self, refusing to share his deep personal feelings and thoughts with his wife or close friends. 'I don't know why', his son told me, 'but he went stale and lost interest in everything – and as he sank, I saw the effects of that on him, and on mom, and on his students.'

This sense of almost intolerable strain is familiar to innumerable creative people – not just teachers – reminding me of what Thoreau wrote a century and a half ago: 'the mass of men lead lives of quiet desperation.' In my thirty-one years as a college professor I've witnessed or heard of three nervous breakdowns, one suicide, and seven firings, as well as numerous infidelities, habitual backbiting, and a handful of student-filed grievances for alleged sexual harassment, or worse. And each time, I've wondered how and why so many maladies could bedevil such a seemingly noble, stimulating profession that offers so much to its practitioners, its students, its community, and the world at large.

Teaching (like writing) is not a job – it is a state of mind with a unique set of assumptions. One commentator has likened the teacher's life to 'one long, arduous journey of self-analysis' – sometimes painful, sometimes 'joyous, victorious and beautiful' – that requires not only a stripping away of our illusions, poses, and pretenses of all kinds but also both the vision to see beyond our faults, no matter how dismaying, and the tenacity to keep working toward our potential through all manner of discouragements. Periods of anxiety and dissatisfaction are not uncommon even among seasoned teachers. You say that you feel neither as well-read nor as confident and mature as you had hoped? Your mastery of a particular novel is somewhat unsure? Your grasp of a particular genre is not without contradictions? I'm not surprised. I would be much more concerned if a caring, competent instructor did not go through such periods, for the alternatives are overblown self-confidence or callous indifference. Don't imagine teaching is easy, and don't give up when you find that it is hard. 'Tussle with the difficult things', said Robertson Davies, 'and in the end they will reveal their meaning to you, and that meaning may help you over many a difficult place.' Even for the most accomplished men and women, it is never easy bridging the gap between where we are and where we want to be, between what we are and what we would like to become. As an undergraduate, the distance between the lectern of my English literature professor and the front row of desks where I sat was a mere eight feet, but I knew it would take many years and much effort to cross that divide and earn the inestimable privilege of standing where he then stood.

But as Frost knew well as both a writer and a teacher, so we too learn: art extorts a high price from its creators. If he were here today, Kelley, he'd say to you or to any ambitious creative artist – write all the books you care to write, teach all the classes you want to teach, give of yourself to your students and to your institution, but try not to let your busy professional life irreparably skew your sense of proportion and balance. There's a lot to lose if we fail to fulfill our dreams of professional success, but even more to lose if in pursuing those dreams we end up neglecting the one person who is, beyond all others, our deepest concern: our innermost Self, or Soul. 'It is the fundamental, animating element in your intellectual and emotional life', said Robertson Davies, 'and you must be very careful of it.'

What I believe overwhelmed my professor can entrap any of us, if we ignore the Self: without our realizing it, intellectual and spiritual torpor, indifference, and lethargy can take root; our sensibilities wither; our relationships with people, including students, become stunted; and we end up emotionally shriveled, no longer able to draw sustenance from the life we've chosen. To this diminution of potential medievalists appended the term *acedia*, or in modern parlance, *sloth*. A chronic lack of enthusiasm, a refusal to take risks, a lost capacity to feel – all these are symptoms of this phenomenon. Frost battled against this every day, and so must we.

But this is not the only peril inherent in teaching. In Jacques Barzun's analysis of the profession, he says that 'the regard for it is a lost tradition'. Indeed, there is no shortage of critics waiting to embrace our discomforts. Complain to the general public and you'll witness a dozen 'knowing' nods among those who harbor contempt for the hard work of achieving academic mastery. If ever you feel you're not taken seriously by society, and if that pains you, do not let the critical voices embitter or discourage you. Many times you are going to have to walk against the cultural current. We live in a society in which there is at most only a partial comprehension of that slow, deliberate, exhaustive search for truth that is the quest of every serious student and teacher and writer. We live in a culture that tends to denigrate reason and applaud feeling. Many individuals outside the profession haven't the slightest idea of the energy, expertise, and effort that go into making the classroom a crucible of ideas and learning. No matter what blind spots the surrounding culture suffers from, teach the best you can in the circumstances in which you find yourself. Wealth, status, or power are not the only standards by which quality of life is measured. Be careful not to let such ignorance of or apathy about the nature of your work awaken in you any spite. You do not teach to earn the world's approval or support; if you adopt that attitude, the inevitable disappointment will grate upon you, honing a hardened edge, and you'll compromise the reasons you're in the classroom to begin with: a love of learning, a love for students, and a desire to master your field. To paraphrase Aldous Huxley, experience is not what happens to us; it is what we do with what happens to us.

Kelley, please don't confuse my cautionary observations with negativity or pessimism about what we do. My purpose here (as in all of my letters) is not to undermine teaching but to uncover as much about the profession as I possibly can, and that includes explaining some of its inherent perils. Idealism by itself can be a fragile foundation; tempered with an honest, open realism, it can foster vitality, enthusiasm, even passion for the marvelous, sometimes magical, sometimes maddening job we perform.

If talent for the art of teaching is within you, it will assert itself early in life. If it does not, it's best to move on to another profession. Students can always sense if their teacher is not genuine. No gestures or pronouncements can prevail over that deep instinctual knowledge. At eighty, when asked for the secret of happiness, the English sculptor Henry Moore said: 'The secret of life is to have a task, something you devote your entire life to, something you bring everything to, every minute of the day for your whole life. And the most important thing is – it must be something you cannot possibly do.' Hold onto that challenge and it will inspire you daily. What will endure is the imprint we leave upon our students, and their appreciation, whether expressed or not, of the impact we have made on them. Today, for example, I dropped off my fifteen-year-old son on his first day of high school and discovered that his Health-Science teacher was a former student of mine. I suppose that should have made me feel old, but instead I felt gratified and not a little thankful. When she was in my class I couldn't possibly have known that she would be instructing my son a decade later. But now here she is, shaping his life – and the lives of all her students – in still unseen ways. What I passed along to her, she will pass to others, a legacy that few occupations can claim.

Continue to give thanks for the extraordinary opportunity you have every day. To each of us is given a unique identity and a realm of responsibility. If we are at all attentive, wrote C. S. Lewis in 'Love Thy Neighbor', it soon dawns on us that it is 'a serious thing' to live in a world where there are no 'ordinary' people. 'It is immortals with whom we joke, work, marry, snub and exploit' – and I would add, *study* and *teach* and *write*. What we say and do in the classroom makes a difference for years to come.

Adopt a methodical, unhurried approach to your work. Use humor: it reassures people and helps them to relax. Take your work seriously, but always keep in your heart the words of G. K. Chesterton: 'Angels can fly because they can take themselves lightly.'

And above all, never lose touch with your Inner Self.

Index

Adams, Henry, 32
Aeschylus, 191
Albaret, Celeste, 66, 71
Aldiss, Brian, 92–8: *The Brightfount Diaries*, 93; *Shouting Down a Cliff*, 93; *The Twinkling of an Eye*, 97; *When the Feast Is Finished*, 98
Aldiss, Margaret, 94–8: 'My Health', 97–8; *The Work of Brian W. Aldiss*, 97; *see also* Manson, Margaret
Alexander the Great, 195
Alighieri, Dante, 27
Amis, Kingsley, 95, 108
Archimedes, 89
Armstrong, Karen, 194–5
Armstrong, Neil, 30
Arnold, Matthew, 'Dover Beach', 23
Auden, W. H., 124; *Poets of the English Language*, 27
Auel, Jean, 110
Austen, Jane, *Persuasion*, 23

Bach, Johann Sebastian, 70
Bachardy, Don, 114–27: *Christopher Isherwood: Last Drawings*, 126; *Stars in My Eyes*, 125; *see also* Isherwood, Christopher
Bachardy, Ted, 114, 116
Bachelder, Frances H., *The Iron Gate*, 109
Back, Barbara, 155, 157
Bainbridge, Beryl, 38
Baker, Florence, 30
Baker, Sharon, 97
Barnard, Robert, *A Talent to Deceive: an Appreciation of Agatha Christie*, 181–2

Barnardo, Dr Thomas John, 147
Barzun, Jacques, 228
Baudelaire, Charles, 194
Bayley, John, 107
Beale, Thomas, *Natural History of the Sperm Whale*, 206
Beatles, The, 70
Beaton, Cecil, 154
Beattie, Ann, 79
Beaumont, Frances, 144
Beebe, William, 30
Bell, Quentin, x
Bellows, Henry, 220
Benson, E. F., 150
Bentley, Richard, 210, 211, 212, 214
Berg, A. Scott, 142
Berg, James L. ed.: *Conversations with Christopher Isherwood*, 118; *The Isherwood Century: Essays on the Life and Work of Christopher Isherwood* (with Chris Freeman), 118
Bergen, Candice, 28
Berger, John, 196
Bernays, Anne, *The Language of Names*, 142, 145
Berryman, John, 195
Bierce, Ambrose, 142–3
Bonaparte, Napoleon, 31, 104
Boothby, Robert, 161
Boswell, James, *Life of Johnson*, 27
Bottomley, Horatio, 100
Bradbury, Malcolm, 3–12
Brazzi, Rossano, 28
Brewster, Dr John, 207, 208, 209, 210, 216, 218

Bridges, James: *Urban Cowboy*, 124; *The China Syndrome*, 124
Brookfield, Ernest William, 46–7, 53
Brookfield, Norman, 47, 53
Brooks, Ellingham, 149
Brotherton, Mary, 21
Brown, Jerry, 115
Browne, J. Ross, 204
Browne, Sir Thomas, 204
Bucknell, Katherine, 116, 121
Burke and Wills, 30
Burnett, Frances Hodgson, 16, 17
Burton, Richard, 31
Burton, Sir Richard, 31
Byron, Lord (George Gordon), 131
Byron, Robert, *Road to Oxiana*, 195

Cade, Jared, *Agatha Christie and the Eleven Missing Days*, 179, 181
Callimachus, 191
Camelot, 103
Carlyle, Thomas, 71, 86, 100
Carow, Edith Kermit (Mrs Theodore Roosevelt), 32, 33, 35
Carter, Jimmy: *Everything to Gain*, 111; *Living Faith*, 111
Carter, Rosalynn, *Everything to Gain*, 111
Caskey, Bill, 115, 116
Cassirer, Reinhold, 136
Caws, Mary Ann, 'A Double Allegiance', 173–4
Chaplin, Geraldine, 156
Chatterjee, Niladri, 123, 124
Chatwin, Bruce and Elizabeth, 195
Chesterton, G. K., 229
Child, Julia, 186
Christie, Agatha, 105, 176–83: *Death on the Nile*, 183; 'The Edge', 182; *Murder in Mesopotamia*, 183; *The Murder of Roger Ackroyd*, 177, 182; *Murder on the Orient Express*, 183; *The Mysterious Affair at Styles*, 177; *The Mystery of the Blue Train*, 177, 180, 183; *Unfinished Portrait*, 182; *Who Killed Ackroyd?* (serial), 177; see also Westmacott, Mary
Christie, Archie, 177, 178, 179, 180, 181, 182–3
Christie, Rosalind, 183
Clare, John, 192

Clark, Kenneth, 162
Clark, Mary (Topsy), 102, 103
Clift, Montgomery, 122
Collins, Cecil, 198
Colt, Susannah, 71, 72, 75–6
Connolly, Mrs Cyril, 196
Core, Dr Donald, 179
Corso, Gregory, 191–2
Cotton, Joseph, 122
Coventry, F. H., 14
Coward, Noël, 156: *Blithe Spirit*, 50
Cox, Sidney, *Those Who Want to Write*, 109
Craft, Robert, 119
Craighead, Robert, 210
Craik, George Lillie, *The New Zealanders*, 206

Dana, Richard Henry, Jr, 206
Dannay, Frederick, 144
David, Elizabeth, 166
Davies, Robertson, 227
Degeneres, Ellen, 124
Deighton, Len, *The Ipcress File*, 101
Dickens, Charles, 61, 66, 100, 181–2: *The Mystery of Edwin Drood*, 182
Dickinson, Emily, 103
Donne, John, 86, 87, 88, 139: 'I am two fools, I know', 86–7
Dostoevsky, Fyodor, 131
Dowson, Ernest, 194: 'Cynara', 98
Doyle, Sir Arthur Conan, 176
Drabble, Margaret, 37–9, 141: *The Oxford Companion to English Literature*, 38; *A Summer Bird-Cage*, 40
Duran, Gustavo, 196
Durbin, Deanna, 14
Durrell, Laurence, *The Alexandria Quartet*, 33
Duyckinck, Evert, 212–13

Edel, Leon, 28
Eliot, George (Mary Ann Evans), 4, 28, 31: *Middlemarch*, 22
Eliot, T. S., 131, 199: *The Waste Land*, 131; *Four Quartets*, 132
Eliot, Vivienne, 131
Eluard, 191

Fadiman, Anne, 67–76
Falter, John, 78

Farmiloe, Tim, 56
Fast, Jonathan, 109
Faulkner, Estelle, x
Faulkner, William, x
Fenwick, Arthur, 158
Fischer, Ernst, 191
Fitzgerald, Edward, 21
Fitzgerald, F. Scott, 8, 10, 11, 31, 66, 131, 184: *Tender Is the Night*, 8
Fitzgerald, Zelda, 8, 10, 66, 131: *Save Me the Waltz*, 8
Fleming, Ann, 150
Fletcher, John, 144
Foster, Richard J., 110
Foucault, Michel, 167
Fowles, Elizabeth, xi
Fowles, John, xi
Fraser, Antonia, 42
Frayn, Michael, 42
Frere, Alexander, 161
Freud, Sigmund, 8
Frink, Elisabeth, 198
Frost, Robert, 112, 191, 224–5, 227: 'Apple-Picking', 224; 'Birches', 224; 'Nothing Gold Can Stay', 224; 'Stopping by Woods on a Snowy Evening', 224
Fuller, Roy and Kate, 100
Fussell, Betty, *My Kitchen Wars*, 188

Gama, Vasco da, 30
Gansevoort, Peter, 215, 220
Garis, Lilian and Howard, 109, 112: *see also* Hope, Laure Lee
Garis, Roger, *My Father Was Uncle Wiggily*, 109
Gerald, Michael C., *The Poisonous Pen of Agatha Christie*, 180
Gifford, Emma Lavinia (Mrs Thomas Hardy), x–xi, 64
Gill, Gillian, *Agatha Christie: the Woman and Her Mysteries*, 181, 182
Gissing, George, 57
Gladstone, William, 22
Godwin, William, 38
Golding, Alec and Mildred, 48, 49
Golding, Ann, 44–55; 'Life in a large family', 50
Golding, David, 49, 50

Golding, Eileen, 49
Golding, Judy, 50
Golding, William, 44–55; *Darkness Visible*, 52; 'Fable', 51; *Free Fall*, 48; *The Inheritors*, 52; *Lord of the Flies*, 50, 51, 52; *The Pyramid*, 54
Gosse, Edmund, 17
Gosse, Philip Henry, 17
Greene, Graham, 137, 161
Grigson, Jane, *Mushroom Feast*, 166
Grimm, The Brothers, 70

Hall, Donald, x
Halperin, John, *Trollope and Politics*, 56
Hamilton, Andrew, 200
Hardy, G. H., 57
Hardy, Thomas, x–xi, 17, 41, 64, 191: *Jude the Obscure*, x, 41; *Tess of the D'Urbervilles*, x
Harper, Fletcher, 209, 210
Harris, Julie, 116
Harrop, A. J., 13, 14, 15, 16, 17: *The Amazing Career of Edward Gibbon Wakefield*, 16; *New Zealand after Five Wars*, 14; *Touring in New Zealand*, 13
Harrop, Ann Barbara, 14: 'Meet you at the station', 14; *see also* Thwaite, Ann
Hastings' Encyclopedia, 166
Hawthorne, Nathaniel, 11, 202, 207, 215
Hawthorne, Mrs Nathaniel, 11
Haxton, Gerald, 157–9, 161
Hayford, Harrison, 'Unnecessary Duplicates', 203
Heard, Gerald, 115
Heche, Anne, 124
Hemingway, Ernest, 11, 184: *The Garden of Eden*, 11; *A Moveable Feast*, 162
Hemingway, Mary, 11
Henry the Navigator, Prince, 30
Hoadley, John C., 216
Hoadley, Kate, 216, 218
Hockney, David, 123, 125
Hogarth, Catherine, 66
Hogarth, William, 'The Distressed Poet', 65–6, 73, 75
Holmes, Richard, 42
Holroyd, Michael, 42–3, 141: *Lytton Strachey*, 37; *George Bernard Shaw*, 38

Holt, Henry, 72
Holt, Susannah, 71–2, 75–6
Homer, Iliad, 111; Odyssey, 111
Hooker, Edward, 117, 119
Hooker, Evelyn, 118–19; 'The Adjustment of the Male Overt Homosexual', 117
Hope, Laure Lee (Lilian McNamara Garis), The Bobbsey Twins, 110
Hopkins, Gerard Manley, 189, 193, 194, 199
Horace, 191, 194, 198, 199: Ars Poetica, 191
Howells, William Dean, 225
Hoyer, Linda Grace, 77–8, 81–3: Enchantment, 78, 81; The Predator, 78n, 81
Hudson, Rock, 122
Hughes, Ted, 66, 141
Hunt, Violet, 146, 157
Hutchinson, Mary, 66
Huxley, Aldous, 115, 124, 228

Isherwood, Christopher, 114–27: Christopher and His Kind, 115; Conversations with Christopher Isherwood, 118; Diaries, Volume One, 1939–60, 118; Down There on a Visit, 115, 117, 121; The English Woman, 121; Frankenstein: the True Story (teleplay with Don Bachardy), 124; Goodbye to Berlin, 114, 116 (stage adaptation: I Am A Camera, 116, 123; musical adaptation, Cabaret, 123); A Meeting by the River (stage adaptation with Don Bachardy), 124; Mr Norris Changes Trains, 114; October (with Don Bachardy), 124; A Single Man, 121; The World in the Evening (with Don Bachardy), 116, 117, 118, 121; 'A Writer and His World', 115
Isherwood, Richard, 118

James, Henry, 19, 32: The Ambassadors, 27, 28
James, P. D., 103
Jaws (Peter Biskind), 102
Jennings, Elizabeth, 189
Jesse, Matilda, 19
Johnson, Pamela Hansford (Mrs C. P. Snow), 56–64; A Bonfire, 60; The Humbler Creation, 59; An Impossible Marriage, 59; The Last Resort, 59; The Unspeakable Skipton, 59
Johnson, Samuel, 27, 131, 138
Jones, Ethelwyn Sylvia (Sue), 146, 148, 157–8
Jong, Erica, 109
Jowett, Benjamin, 20

Kafka, Franz, 89–90
Kallman, Chester, 119
Kaplan, Justin, The Language of Names, 142, 145
Kelly, Gerald, 149
Kennedy, Ted, 72
Kenyon, Jane (Mrs Donald Hall), x
King, Billie Jean, 165
Kingsmill, Hugh, Made on Earth, 38
Kipling, Mrs Rudyard, 86
Kott, Jan, 27
Kropotkin, Alexandra (Sasha), 146, 157

Lansing, Catherine Gansevoort, 220
Larkin, Philip, 15, 195
Lawrence, D. H., 31
Lear, Edward, 18, 19, 20–1, 198
Leavis, F. R., 60–1: The Significance of C. P. Snow, 60
Lee, Alice, 32
Levi, Peter, 189–201: Art, Faith and Vision (TV series), 190, 198; A Bottle in The Shade, 199; Canticum, 196; Death is a Pulpit, 193, 196; Five Ages, 197; The Flutes of Autumn, 190, 197; Foxes Have Holes (TV), 198; Fresh Water Sea Water, 192; The Gravel Ponds, 189–91; Greece – the Black Years (TV), 198; Guide to Greece by Pausanias (trans.), 195; The Head in the Soup, 197; The Hill of Kronos, 195; Horace: a Life, 199; The Light Garden of the Angel King: Journeys in Afghanistan, 195; Life is a Platform, 196; A Private Commission: New Verses by Shakespeare, 198–9; Private Ground, 197; Selected Poems by Yevgeny Yevtushenko (co-trans.), 190; Water Rock and Sand, 192
Lewis, C. S., 229
Lewis, Sir George, 149
Lewis, R. W. B., 33

Lewis, Wyndham, 103
Leyland, Winston, 118, 120
Lincoln, Abraham, 32
Lockhart, Bruce, 156–7
Lodge, Mary, 9
Lost Weekend, The (movie), 70
Lowell, Robert, 192, 195
Luce, Clare Booth, 33, 34, 35
Lucie-Smith, Edward, 192

MacCarthy, Desmond, 58
Mackendrick, Hilary and Sandy, 104
Mackenzie, Compton, 149, 151
Maclean, Alan, 56
Maclean, Donald, 56
Maida, Patricia D. and Nicholas B. Spornick, *Murder She Wrote: a Study of Agatha Christie's Detective Fiction*, 178–9, 181, 182
Mailer, Norman, 68, 184
Mallowan, Max, 183
Mann, Thomas, 136
Manson, Margaret (Mrs Brian Aldiss), 94–8
Marshall, Thurgood, 143
Mather, Frank Jewett, 220
Maugham, Elizabeth (Liza), 150–3, 155–6, 159–61
Maugham, W. Somerset, 119, 146–62; *Ashenden*, 146; *Cakes and Ale*, 146, 158; 'The Escape'. 150; *Home and Beauty*, 159; *The Hour Before the Dawn*, 152; 'Jane', 146, 155; 'Looking Back', 155–6, 160–2 passim; *The Moon and Sixpence*, 146; *Our Betters*, 146, 157–8; *Of Human Bondage*, 152, 158; *The Summing Up*, 150, 158, 161–2
Maupassant, Guy de, 90
Maupin, Armistead, 121–2; *Tales of the City*, 124
McCarthy, Mary (Mrs Edmund Wilson), 27, 66
McPhee, John, 69
Melvill [sic], Thomas, 206, 207
Melville, Allan, 205, 208, 217
Melville, Augusta, 217, 219
Melville, Elizabeth (Bessie), 215, 218, 220–1

Melville, Elizabeth Shaw, 205, 215, 218, 219, 220, 221
Melville (Thomas), Frances, 217, 218, 221
Melville, Gansevoort, 213
Melville, Herman, 202–21; *Battle-Pieces*, 219; 'Benito Cereno', 217; *Clarel*, 220, 221; *The Confidence-Man*, 218, 219; *The Encantadas*, 217; *The Isle of the Cross*, 215–16, 218, 219, 220; *Israel Potter*, 217; *Mardi*, 205; *Moby-Dick*, 202–3, 210–12, 213, 214, 215, 218, 220; *Omoo*, 204–5; *Pierre*, 203, 213–15, 218; 'Tartarus of Maids', 218; 'Two Sides to a Tortoise', 217; *Typee*, 204, 206, 210, 213–14; *The Whale*, 210–11, 212, 214; *White-Jacket*, 206, 212, 214
Melville, Malcolm, 205, 218, 220, 221
Melville, Sophia, 205
Melville, Stanwix, 210, 218, 221
Melville, Tom, 213
Mencken, H. L., 184
Merlo, Frank, 119
Miles, Lion G., 218
Milland, Ray, 70
Miller, Clarissa, 177–8
Miller, Madge, 176–7
Milne, A. A., 17
Milton, John, 6, 38, 198
Minelli, Liza, 123
Monroe, Marilyn, 125
Moore, Henry, 229
Morewood, Sarah, 219
Morgan, Janet, 179
Morris, Edmund: *The Dude from New York*, 31–2; *Dutch: a Memoir of Ronald Reagan*, 33; *Great Adventures That Changed Our World*, 30–1; *The Rise of Theodore Roosevelt*, 33; *Theodore Rex*, 33
Morris, Sylvia Jukes, 27–36: *Edith Kermit Roosevelt: Portrait of A First Lady*, 32–3, 34, 35; *Great Adventures That Changed Our World*, 30–1; *Price of Fame*, 33, 36; *Rage For Fame: the Ascent of Clare Booth Luce*, 33, 34, 35
Morrison, Toni, 143
Morsberger, Robert and Katharine, 125
Murdoch, Derrick, *The Agatha Christie Mystery*, 181
Murdoch, Iris, 107, 132–3, 198; *Jackson's Dilemma*, 133–4

Naddermeyer, Heinz, 115
Naipaul, Pat, 25–6
Naipaul, V. S., 25–6; *An Area of Darkness*, 25; *The Killings in Trinidad*, 26; *The Loss of El Dorado*, 26; *The Mimic Men*, 25–6
Neele, Nancy, 178–9
Newby, Eric, *A Short Walk in the Hindu Kush*, 195
Nichols, Beverley, 155
Nilson, Bee, *Desserts*, 166
Nixon, Richard, 16
Noach, Maggie, 96

O'Farrell, Maggie, 141
Oates, Stephen B., x
Old Vernon, 115
Olivier, Lawrence, 167
Orwell, George, 100; *Animal Farm*, 100; 'Life, People – and Books', 100
Osborne, Charles, *The Life and Crimes of Agatha Christie*, 179, 182

Pasternak, Boris, 191, 198
Pausanias, *Guide to Greece*, 195
Payne, Walter, 153
Penelope, 153
Perelman, S. J., 184
Perkins, Anthony, 122
Pierce, Franklin, 215
Pinter, Harold, 42, 103
Plath, Sylvia, 66, 141
Ponce de Leon, Juan, 82
Pritchard, William H., 103
Proust, Marcel, 66, 71
Purcell, Henry, 111
Putnam, George, 204, 206, 217
Pym, Barbara, *Some Tame Gazelle*, 112

Queen, Ellery (Frederic Dannay and Mandred Lee), 144

Redgrave, Vanessa, 181
Reginald, Robert and Mary, 97
Richardson, Marion, 34
Richardson, Mary, 34
Richardson, Ralph, 103
Rinehart, Mary Roberts, 113
Robyns, Gwen, *The Mystery of Agatha Christie*, 181

Rockwell, Norman, 78
Roosevelt, Edith Kermit, 32, 33, 35
Roosevelt, Theodore, 30, 31, 32
Rorty, Richard, 172
Routledge, George, 22
Rubenstein, Hilary, 96
Russell, W. Clark, 220

Saint-Gaudens, Augustus, 32
Salinger, J. D., 141
Sanborn, Geoffrey, 206
Sartre, Jean Paul, *Huis Clos*, 50
Sayers, Dorothy L., 27, 180–1: *Whose Body?*, 87; *Unnatural Death*, 181; *The Unpleasantness at the Bellona Club*, 87
Schorer, Mischa, 198
Scoresby, William, 204
Searle, Alan, 119
Seferis, George, 191
Selfridge, Gordon, 147–9, 151, 158, 161
Sendak, Maurice, 214
Shakespeare, William, 27, 32, 94, 111, 131, 198, 204, 220; 'Let me not to the marriage of true minds admit impediment', 94; *Love's Labour's Lost*, 87; *Twelfth Night*, 50; *The Winter's Tale*, 50
Shaw, George Bernard, 38
Shaw, Lemuel, 205, 207–8, 218–19, 221
Sheehan, Neil and Susan, 71
Shields, Carol, 86
Simeon, John, 22
Simpson, Wallis Warfield, 31
Sitwell, Edith, 191
Sitwell, Osbert, 153, 156
Snetkina, Anna (Mrs Fyodor Dostoevsky), 131
Snow, C. P., 56–64: *A Coat of Varnish*, 60, 62; *Death under Sail*, 62; *In Their Wisdom*, 62; *The Malcontents*, 62; *The Realists*, 62; *Science and Government*, 62; *The Search*, 62; *Strangers and Brothers*, 56–9, 61–3 (*The Affair*, 59, 61–2; *The Conscience of the Rich*, 59, 61; *Corridors of Power*, 59, 61; *George Passant*, 58, 61; *Homecomings*, 61; *Last Things*, 61, 64; *The Light and the Dark*, 61; *The Masters*, 57, 61–2; *The New Men*, 61; *The Sleep of Reason*, 61; *Time of Hope*,

Snow, C. P., – continued
58, 61); *Trollope*, 56, 62; *The Two Cultures*, 60–1; *Variety of Men*, 62
Southern, Terry, 124
Spender, Stephen, 126
Spiller, Robert, 203
Spornick, Nicholas B., 181
Spurgeon, Caroline, 27
Stanley and Livingstone, 30
Starcke, Walter, 119
Stein, Gertrude, 66, 124
Stendahl (Henri-Marie Beyle), *Le rouge et le noir*, 58
Stevenson, Robert Louis, *Dr Jekyll and Mr Hyde*, 68
Stewart, T. D., 208, 209, 210, 214, 215, 217, 218–19
Stokowski, Leopold, 60
Strachey, Lytton, 37, 60, 156–7
Streisand, Barbra, 72
Strunk, William and E. B. White, 73
Sturges, Jonathan, 225
Sutcliffe, William, 141
Swami Prabhavananda, 115
Swift, Clive, 38, 40
Symons, A. J. A., *The Quest for Corvo*, 99
Symons, Christine, 103, 105, 106
Symons, Julian, 99–106: *The 31ˢᵗ of February*, 99; *A. J. A. Symons: His Life and Speculations*, 99; *The Broken Penny*, 100; *The Colour of Murder*, 101; *Death's Darkest Face*, 105; *The General Strike*, 101; *The Narrowing Circle*, 100; *The Progress of a Crime*, 101; *The Thirties: a Dream Revolved*, 101
Symons, Marcus (Mark), 100, 101, 102, 103, 195, 106
Symons, Sarah, 100, 101, 102, 103, 105

Tavener, John, 198
Tennyson, Alfred Lord, 17–23, 192, 198: 'Enoch Arden', 20
Tennyson, Charles, 18
Tennyson, Emily, 17–23
Tennyson, Frederick, 21
Tennyson, Hallam, 17, 18, 20
Tennyson, Lionel, 20
Theroux, Paul, 25–6: *Sir Vidia's Shadow*, 162

Thomas, Dylan, 60, 61
Thomas, Frances Melville, 217, 221
Thomas, R. S., 194, 199: 'The Answer', 194
Thompson, Francis, 194
Thoreau, Henry David, 226
Thurber, James, 78
Thwaite, Ann: *Emily Tennyson: the Poet's Wife*, 22; *The Young Traveller in Japan*, 15; *Waiting for the Party*, 16; *see also* Ann Barbara Harrop
Thwaite, Anthony, 15–16, 22–3: 'Together, Apart', 23–4
Tillett, Michael, 46
Toklas, Alice B., 66, 124
Tolkien, J. R. R., *Lord of the Rings*, 13
Tolstoy, Leo, 131
Tolstoy, Sonya, 31
Tomalin, Claire, 42
Tongues of Fire (TV), 194–5
Tremain, Rose, 42
Trollope, Anthony, 56, 57, 62
Truman, Harry, 32
Tuckerman, Henry T., 220
Tupper, Martin, 22
Twain, Mark (Samuel Langhorne Clemens), 11, 184
Tynan, Kathleen, *Agatha*, 181

Updike, David, 78–9
Updike, John, 80–4, 144: *The Centaur*, 81
Updike, Wesley Russell, 81–2, 83–4

Vallejo, Cesar, 196
Van der Post, Sir Lawrence, 138
van Druten, John, 88, 116
Van Gogh, Vincent, 101
Vidal, Gore, 27, 33, 125
Virgil, 198

'Walking with Dinosaurs' (TV), 13
Wallace, Edgar, 180–1: 'The Sunningdale Murder', 181
Waugh, Auberon, 138
Waugh, Evelyn, 103: *A Handful of Dust*, 159
Webster, Sir Daniel, 94
Webster, John, *The White Devil*, 40

Wellcome, Henry, 147, 148, 149, 150, 151, 159
Wellcome, Gwendolyn Syrie (Sarah Louise) Barnardo ('Queenie'), 146–62
Wells, H. G., 162
West, Anthony, *Heritage*, 162
West, Rebecca, 156, 162
Westmacott, Mary (alias Agatha Christie), *Unfinished Portrait*, 182
Whiting, John, *Marching Song*, 50
Whitman, Walt, 21
Wilson, Edmund, 66
Wilson, Harold, 28
Winn, Godfrey, 153, 157
Wolfe, Thomas, 56
Wollstonecraft, Mary, 38
Woolf, Leonard, x
Woolf, Virginia, x, 17, 31: *Freshwater*, 17
Woolley, Leonard, 183
Woolner, Thomas, 18, 19, 20
Wordsworth, William, 66, 225: *The Prelude*, 43
Wyeth, Andrew, 72

Yeats, William Butler, 191
Yevtushenko, Yevgeny, *Selected Poems*, 190

The manufacturer's authorised representative in the EU is Springer Nature Customer Service Centre GmbH, Europaplatz 3, 69115 Heidelberg, Germany. If you have any concerns regarding our products, please contact ProductSafety@springernature.com

Printed and bound by CPI Group (UK) Ltd, Croydon, CR0 4YY
23/03/2026
02076673-0013